three skeins
of caledonia blue

three skeins
of caledonia blue

Elizabeth Duvivier

SOLIDEN

Providence
2024

elizabethduvivier.com

Cover art by Elizabeth Duvivier
ISBN 978-1-7330324-1-4

Book design by Elizabeth Leeper
Typeset in Brandon Grotesque and Sabon

This is a work of fiction. Names, characters, places, and incidents are
the products of the author's imagination or are used fictitiously.
Any resemblance to actual events, locales, or persons, living or dead,
is entirely coincidental.

Printed in the U.S.A.

SOLIDEN

Providence
2024

for Autumn Coe Song
best, bestie, bestest

I like the novelist who confessed that the only thing to have stayed with him after reading Anna Karenina was a detail of a picnic basket holding a jar of honey.

—Sigrid Nunez, *The Vulnerables*

SKEIN I

On the third day Mathilde has to get up. There is only so much of her depressed ass Anjanette will tolerate. Plus, tonight is the circle.

Mathilde stares at the ceiling. She waits for a spark, a sign, something. How do people get up every day, she wonders. Her head lolls to the left and she sees Anjanette has left a bag of candies from Cardullos on the nightstand. They are the ones she loved as a kid, the ones she and Anjanette would ride their bikes for miles in the rain to go and get. Mathilde stares at the bright packaging, then rolls away.

Get up, get up, get up, she chants. The tips of her fingers flip the edge of the curtain back and forth. She is a grown woman with two adult children. Her behavior is unacceptable.

Get up, now.

She kicks at the sheets and tugs on the shade. It snaps up to reveal a cloudless blue sky and the roof of the house next door, 64 Clement. God, does she love that house. With the back of her thumb, Mathilde scrapes sleep crust out from the corners of her mouth as she tries to see it from a better angle.

For all the years she lived there with her parents, the house was painted pale gray with white trim. Now the exterior is a blue so dark it borders on charcoal. The front door and mullions of the bay window are an acid, antifreeze green. A mid-century modern cube has replaced the original Victorian porch ceiling light fixture.

Hipsters from Brooklyn, Anjanette had said.

I'd never have guessed, Mathilde had replied, then shrugged in an effort to offset the sarcasm. She had no right to be bitter. It wasn't her house anymore. They could do what they liked. Why should she care?

Mathilde pulls away from the window and flops back onto the bed.

She remembers walking home from school and pausing on the sidewalk to look up at the houses; the contrast was clear. Not the shape, particularly. Both Victorian style built around 1900 with clapboard siding, shingle roof, a side porch, and wide, wooden steps up to the front door. But her parents' house on the right, indistinct—without so much as a maple tree to offer shade—was fronted by a flat expanse of grass. No flower beds. One lone juniper bush, kept trimmed short, squatted by the bay window.

On the left, number 62 looked like a live painting. A massive tangle of yellow roses, purple wisteria and honeysuckle covered half the house and clambered up to walk along the second-floor eaves before draping down in a luxury of vines and leaves on either side of the front portico. No grass to be seen, only a bit of moss around the pavers. Blooming shrubs—spirea, lilac and forsythia—and a happy mix of perennials were cut neatly in half by a brick walkway that lead down to the street.

Her parents didn't choose 64 Clement. Maybe that's why they never loved it. It was Mathilde's namesake—her father's Auntie Mae—who gave it as a wedding gift when the rest of her father's Boston Brahmin family had cut him off for marrying Rosie, the Irish girl from Hull.

But Auntie Mae is dead, long dead.

And Mike is dead. Not long dead. Nineteen months and—how many days? She's not sure.

It's September. Today is Thursday. Tonight is Anjanette's circle. That's all she's got.

Mathilde sits up. Something is going on downstairs. She can hear voices shouting and the yippy sound of Mojo barking. She gives a last look out the window, down into the backyard where yellow leaves have dropped to form a soft halo around the base of the old oak.

Summer is done.

Mathilde pushes herself up out of bed and walks over to stand in front of the small mirror that hangs over the bureau. It isn't a pretty sight. Her hair has never looked worse. A patch of sunburn that runs from one side of her forehead across her nose is a reminder of what happens when she forgets sun screen; it also makes the rest of her skin look especially pale and sickly. Maybe she is sickly? She runs a finger across one cheek where even a swath of freckles can't hide the pallor. *Curls and freckles*, she remembers overhearing her father's mother comment. *Such an unfortunate combination.*

Who cares, she tells herself as she pulls on the gray joggers that are in a pile at the foot of the bed, *makes no difference at all.*

She heads downstairs to see what is happening. A few steps up from the first-floor landing, she stops and sits quickly, knees buckled to her chest as if she could make herself invisible now that she is in the center of all the activity.

Two men are grunting the fern in from the back porch where it lives every summer to place it back on its wooden pedestal in the foyer. The fern is massive with leaves so long that even up on its roost they fold into themselves on the parquet floor. Dirt dribbles a path behind the workers despite their effort to keep the plant upright as they move it to the front hall.

Normally, Lonny would be closely supervising this activity but her attention is with her daughter. She and Anjanette are facing off about the circle meeting tonight while Mojo skitters back and forth yapping as if his two cents will settle the argument.

"That dog is getting on my last nerve," says Lonny. Anjanette scoops Mojo up with one arm using the other to emphasize her point of view. She gestures to the living room.

"We'll be in there. We'll stay out of the dining room and the kitchen. Anyway," Anjanette gives a nod up to where Mathilde sits, pretending to be invisible. "Mattie will help me clean up. You won't even know we were here."

Lonny doesn't turn her head to look up the stairs. She takes a step closer to her daughter, hands on hips, voice fierce with heat and annoyance. "Girl, I told you weeks ago I was hosting my knitting group's anniversary dinner here tomorrow night. You knew this and you didn't change your plans."

Mathilde sees that Lonny is in shoes with a good heel, Anjanette is barefoot and yet, Lonny is forced to look up at her daughter who is a clear head taller.

Lonny doesn't suggest having the circle upstairs. She knows that no one ever goes up into Anjanette's space. Mathilde feels again the gift to have been taken into Anjanette's sanctuary, she knows it is not something Anjanette would ordinarily offer to anyone. Of course if Lonny saw the rooms stuffed with Anjanette's hoarding as Mathilde has now been privy to, she would also know that there isn't room for a group of people to sit down anywhere. Still—

"We always meet on the third Thursday of every month," says Anjanette. "Why you getting all up at me? Your ladies don't come until tomorrow. We'll be long gone. No problem."

"Oh, good night!" Lonny booms. She has been trying to keep her voice contained because she is keenly aware of the workers by the fern and does not want to lose her cool in front of them, but Anjanette is pushing her right to the edge. "I'll problem you right up those stairs. I don't want your stinky incense and candle drippings and lounge lizards making a mess of my living room. Jesus take me now."

Anjanette calmly switches Mojo to the other arm. Her voice is soothing. She knows she will win this argument simply because Lonny has too much else to do this morning. "Momma, it's gonna be fine. You'll never know we were there."

Lonny cuffs Anjanette on the shoulder. Twice. "Listen to me. I am done with you. Get out of my sight and take that smooth talking mouth of yours with you."

Lonny walks with a measured step over to the fern that is now settled on the pedestal and begins adjusting the leaves. Lonny's back is straight under the crisp poplin dress; its fitted belt and sophisticated lines make Mathilde even more conscious of being in pajamas at this hour of the day.

"There's a vacuum in the kitchen pantry closet," Lonny tells the workers, a subtle directive for them to go and hoover up that trail of dirt.

Anjanette gives Mathilde a victory smile. She sets Mojo back on the floor and walks up the stairs with him close on her heels. She presses a hand on Mathilde's head as she passes her friend. "Go get some food before we're all banned from the kitchen."

"Oh, that's okay. I can wait," says Mathilde.

"You better than me," says Anjanette as she continues up the stairs.

When Lonny walks out to hang a wreath on the front door, Mathilde slips down into the kitchen. The caterers are in a focused assembly line producing trays of hors d'oeuvres. Mathilde maneuvers around them to get a plate, knife, bread, peanut butter, and coffee. She carries her breakfast into the dining room thinking it will be the best place to stay out of the way, but as she is about to sit down, she catches sight of Lonny on the front walk giving a hug to Gerri who has just arrived. Lonny and Gerri are now in their seventies but have been close friends since they got their masters degree in accounting at Northeastern.

Mathilde grabs her mug and plate and rushes up the two flights of stairs as quickly as she can without spilling her coffee. She has known Gerri since she was a teenager. There would be no small talk. Gerri would naturally ask Mathilde how she's doing and Mathilde can't bear to have that conversation right now.

Back in the attic bedroom, Mathilde settles her breakfast on the nightstand and surveys the room as she sits to catch her breath. Pretty much every square foot is filled with some kind of houseplant except for where the narrow bed is pushed into the corner. If some people have a green thumb, Anjanette was dipped in a green river; her way with growing things is full body magic.

A child's old wooden school desk is covered with succulents and the occasional cactus. The three side drawers of the desk have been pulled open to create space for still more pots. One large kalanchoe sits in the bottom drawer; its late season, glorious orange second bloom a testament to Anjanette's prowess. The bookcase holds families of ivy, ferns, jade, and plants Mathilde doesn't know the names for. A trio of eucalyptus arc grouped on the floor with a giant plant Mathilde thinks might be a fig tree. There is a spider plant, babies spilling from all sides, that hangs from a big ceiling hook. And, in the center of the room, on its own small but tall table painted hot pink, sits a spectacular maidenhair fern, empress of the kingdom.

Mathilde scootches back in the bed so that she can eat. Her initial sip of coffee—hot and, to her surprise, flavored with hazelnut—brings the first moment of ease since she woke up. Directly below her, there is a comforting beat coming from Anjanette's studio, a steady rhythm under whatever music she is listening to that seems to say everything is okay.

And everything is okay. Look at where she is.

Mathilde presses back against the pillow and balls her hands to her throat. The littlest bit of excitement flutters in her chest. She is on the third floor of 62 Clement, Lonny and Anjanette's house. Anjanette has been her closest friend since they were both nine years old, but Mathilde has never slept over. Well, wait, that's not entirely true. There was that one time when Lonny set her up to sleep on the living room sofa because she needed Mathilde to come and stay with Anjanette who had gone to New York City.

Dedham, Massachusetts
October 1994

Mathilde stands in the kitchen of the house in Dedham. She presses the phone to her ear and spins away from the sink full of breakfast dishes as if Lonny could see what she is looking at. Mathilde is twenty-nine years old but Lonny's voice always makes her feel like a little girl.

With one foot, Mathilde pushes the basket of unsorted laundry out of view. The chaos seems to be getting worse now that Toby is sixteen months old and Susannah, who is nearly eight, leaves a ticker tape parade of crayons, paper, glue and glitter in her wake. Sometimes Mathilde wants to scream in exhaustion, in frustration, in some nameless outrage—at the inane, endless cycle of cleaning.

But in this moment, Mathilde realizes she is smiling. It's a rare treat to get a call from Lonny. Mathilde listens expectantly. Perhaps there is a lecture at the college Lonny is calling to suggest, or maybe it's time to bring donations up for the annual Clement Street yard sale—her beloved Clement Street. Where she grew up in number 64. Where Lonny and Anjanette still live in number 62.

"I need you to come up here and deal with that girl—" says Lonny.

Mathilde is confused. Lonny never asks for help. Something is going on with Anjanette? Lonny only calls her daughter 'that girl' when she is annoyed.

"I would," says Mathilde. She flounders to find the right words. She would never say no to Lonny, but—her stomach clenches as the thought of seeing Anjanette. "Anjanette and I haven't been talking much lately."

Much lately is a lie. They haven't spoken since June when Anjanette left Toby's first birthday party. Mathilde looks across the kitchen to the junk drawer where she knows there are a handful of half-written letters to Anjanette that she hasn't sent.

"Well Anjanette isn't talking to anybody right now, including me," says Lonny.

"What happened?" Mathilde asks

"She went to New York—"

"She went to New York!" Mathilde interrupts. "New York, CITY?" Anjanette never goes anywhere. "Who'd she go with?"

"Listen," Lonny's voice tightens. "I don't have time for this. Gerri's just pulled in the drive."

Every October, Lonny and her friend Gerri go some place in upstate New York to buy yarn or something like that.

"It's my knitting weekend," Lonny continues, "and that girl upstairs is not spoiling it. All I know is she got it in her head to take the bus to New York for some art show. When she got back, she went upstairs and hasn't come out of her room except to sneak down like a damn raccoon in the middle of the night to eat my food. And now it's Friday and I'm— hang on."

Mathilde can hear Lonny open the back door and call out to Gerri that she needs another minute. The sharp zip of a bag or a purse being closed and Lonny is back on the line.

Mathilde's doesn't know what to say. How can she go to Lonny and Anjanette's house right now? The drive to Cambridge takes at least twenty-five minutes. Susannah is at school, but what is she gonna do with Toby? Mike left for work hours ago. Plus, her mouth keeps going dry every time she thinks of seeing Anjanette after that horrible birthday party fight.

I don't know who this is, Anjanette said, flinging an arm toward the Dedham house where the birthday party was in full swing, *but it isn't you.* The wind whipped at Mathilde's blouse. She looked down to see she was gripping an ice cream scoop in one hand.

She watched as Anjanette climbed into the cab and it drove away.

Lonny takes her silence as a yes.

"I've made up a bed for you on the living room sofa," says Lonny. "I'll put the key under—"

"Did you try making her a baked ziti?' Mathilde interrupts. "Anjanette would climb a mountain for—"

"Child, I don't have time for this. You know it has to be you. Anybody else is gonna get scared off by her growl. Now you coming?" Lonny's voice isn't just frustrated. Mathilde can hear a tiny bit of fear in it, too. Lonny clearly feels this is more than one of Anjanette's moods.

Immediately, Mathilde's whole body floods with connection. Mother. Both Mathilde and Lonny are mothers. Lonny is worried about her baby. Something is wrong with her child and she can't make it feel better. Lonny is scared for Anjanette.

"Lonny, go on with Gerri. I'll take care of it." Mathilde marvels at the deep calm in her voice. How is she so calm? "I'll be there in a couple of hours."

"You can bring the baby," says Lonny.

"Nope," replies Mathilde. "I'm calling Mike. I'll tell him to come home now. He'll manage just fine without me."

Lonny makes some kind of affirmative sound and tells Mathilde where to find the key.

The line goes dead.

On the way north from Dedham, Mathilde stops at Star Market to pick up three jars of Gerber's vanilla pudding and then, as she winds her way through Inman Square, she leaves the car running—double parked—so she can race into Tomarelli's to grab a tomato pie. This is the bait she needs to lure Anjanette out of her den.

Mathilde flicks on the lights and sets down her packages in Lonny's kitchen. Immaculate. It smells exactly as it did the first time she ever came through the back door. Mathilde releases a happy sigh into the quiet. Mike is home with the kids. She can't remember a time when she's been away from them both for more than a few hours, and here she is on a Friday night at Anjanette's. It's like a party except, of course, it isn't.

First she has to find out what is going on.

The summer they became friends—the summer of Anjanette's broken leg—Mathilde learned the well-guarded secret: Anjanette likes baby food. And of course, it wasn't long before Mathilde's shameful secret was also discovered: she belonged to the Danielle Steel fan club and received a monthly newsletter that she grabbed from the mail before her mother could ever see it.

Is this what friendship is predicated on, Mathilde wonders as she climbs the stairs to the second floor. Shared secrets?

"Hey ya," Mathilde raps on Anjanette's door with the spoon. "Open the door."

Mathilde listens for a sound. "Hey," she raps again. "I know you are in there."

Mathilde puts on her best mad voice, "Anjanette Jubilee. Do not make me come in there. I will smack you up. I will smack you up good."

She hears something crash. Then steps. The pocket door slides open. Anjanette is wearing a sweatshirt over shortie pajamas. She is doubled over laughing.

"Girl," Anjanette can hardly get the words out. "The idea of you trying to smack me up." The laughing gets harder, almost choking.

"I could totally smack you up," says Mathilde. Anjanette's laughter causes all the tension Mathilde has been holding in her chest since the call with Lonny that morning to break like a dam. The last time they'd seen each other was so bad she worried Anjanette would never talk to her again. And here she is, wheezy with laughter.

Mathilde is also laughing, but her laughter is a lot closer to crying. They slide their backs down the wall landing to sit on the hardwood floor. Anjanette's legs out straight; Mathilde's legs, crossed in, like a yogi.

Mathilde cracks the vacuum sealed lid of the baby food jar and hands it over to Anjanette. Then the spoon. Anjanette scoops a mouthful of the custard onto her tongue all the while trying to stop laughing.

"Oh my god," Anjanette says, resting the spoon on her thigh. "I might never recover. You are goddamn hilarious."

Vanilla custard gets the door open, but it isn't until hours later as they sit on the old, beat-up, orange velvet sofa in Anjanette's studio eating Tomarelli's tomato pie that the conversation really starts.

Mr. Tomarelli was Anjanette's eighth grade art teacher. His brother and uncle owned the pizza shop that was only a few blocks down the street from school. Sometimes on Saturdays when most of the girls they knew were off watching the boys play soccer or football, Anjanette and a couple other kids would show up at Mr. Tomarelli's art room to keep working on projects. Mr. Tomarelli's art room was only for art majors and he kept it that way by scaring everyone else away. He had lots of black curly hair down to his shoulders, a big, bushy mustache, and a loud voice. His eyeglasses had a thick strip of masking tape on the bridge where they had broken. Mathilde wanted to ask him why he didn't just buy new glasses, but he was so grouchy and she was only allowed to tag along because he adored Anjanette, so she did all she could to stay out of his way.

When it was time for the kids to go home, Mr. Tomarelli would bring in a large rectangle box and send each of them off with a square of tomato pie wrapped in waxed paper. Mathilde and Anjanette would eat it as they walked home.

"It's too bad the pizza is cold," Mathilde said.

"It's not pizza," Anjanette corrected her.

"Yes, it is," insisted Mathilde. "Just without cheese."

"Exactly. Not pizza." Anjanette won the argument as she always did. "Tomato pie."

After Mathilde has gotten Anjanette to take a hot shower, put on clean clothes and they have played gin rummy for hours, Mathilde goes down to the kitchen and brings up the tomato pie. They settle onto the orange velvet sofa that lives on the far wall of Anjanette's studio and often doubles as her bed.

"Why is the tradition to eat pizza hot and tomato pie cold?" Mathilde asks.

"I don't know," Anjanette replies. "Why don't you go do your research thing—then tell me all about it later?"

"How about you tell me what happened in New York City?" Anjanette looks surprised by the turn. Mathilde has caught her unexpectedly.

"You went to an art show—" Mathilde leaves the sentence hanging for Anjanette to finish. And slowly, between bites of tomato pie, wiping her mouth on her sleeve and her fingers on her cargo pants, Anjanette explains what happened.

She went to New York for one reason: to see the group exhibition at the Drawing Center that everyone was talking about. There is a young, Black artist named Kara Walker whose work has generated such hot and fierce debate that Anjanette figures the only way to know what it is really about would be to see it for herself. Plus, there is another undeniable magnetic pull; Kara is close to Anjanette's age. A Black female artist who has done it—gone to the best art school in the country, gotten an MFA and is now showing in New York City.

Not only has Anjanette not gone to college, she didn't finish high school—an impassable breach between her and Lonny who built her entire career in the bursar's office at Radcliffe College. Because of her mom's job, Anjanette could have had college tuition covered at a number of Boston colleges just like her brothers did.

But Anjanette refused, saying going to school would never help her become an artist and now here is Kara Walker proving her wrong. She had to see for herself.

"You didn't like her show?" Mathilde prompts when Anjanette's story winds down into an extended silence.

"It's not about liking it," says Anjanette. "It was fucking brilliant."

"So that's good."

Anjanette lies down on her side and reaches for the blanket. She pushes her feet against Mathilde's hip.

"Can you go now? I'm tired."

Mathilde lifts one of Anjanette's bare feet and tickles the sole lightly.

"Quit it," Anjanette says, kicking her foot free.

"I'm going downstairs, but I'll be here in the morning. I'm spending the night."

"Don't you have some babies you need to take care of?" Anjanette's voice is muffled by the blanket she has pulled over her head. "And a husband? Why don't you go back to them? I don't need you here."

"Good thing I'm not here for you then," says Mathilde as she hits off the light. "Nighty night."

In the morning, Mathilde stands in the doorway of Anjanette's studio eating pancakes fresh from the griddle. She lets the scent of their edges crispy with butter reach Anjanette. Mathilde dips each bite into a small cup of warm maple syrup before humming with pleasure when it hits her mouth. When Anjanette commands that she bring her some, Mathilde says, "Nope. You gotta come downstairs and eat at the table like grown-ups do."

Anjanette doesn't move.

"I also made whipped cream," says Mathilde.

"I hate you," says Anjanette. She groans as she stands up and begins walking toward Mathilde, arms out. "Gimme. Lemme taste."

"Nope." Mathilde dances away and carries her plate down the stairs. "Gotta come to the kitchen."

At the table, after pancakes. Coffee in their mugs is no longer hot.

"So the show was brilliant," Mathilde begins.

Anjanette knows Mathilde is not going to let this go. She sighs heavily. "It was brilliant. Kara Walker is brilliant. And I am not. There, you happy now?"

"There can only be one brilliant, female, Black artist?"

"Don't be stupid."

"Then what is it?"

"I'm just not that good. Okay? You happy now? In fact, I'm not good at all and now I have to figure out what I should be doing with my life.

And it's probably gonna take me a while so why don't you go home and when your kids are all grown up, come on back and check in on me. Bring the grandkids."

"Well that sounds like a plan," says Mathilde. She goes over to the junk drawer and digs around for a yellow legal pad and a pen. She sets the paper and pen down in front of Anjanette.

"Let's get this in writing, shall we?" says Mathilde. "I, Anjanette Jubilee Colson, born the eleventh day of August 1965—" Mathilde puts her hands on Anjanette's shoulders. "Start writing," she intones.

"You're being a jerk and this isn't gonna work—" says Anjanette.

"Hey, look who's a poet and doesn't know it."

"Oh my god," Anjanette groans. "Stop. Go home."

"History decrees that we need written records of momentous decisions and this is one: the day you ended your life as an artist. Now let's go." Mathilde begins walking around the kitchen dictating to Anjanette who props her chin with the palm of her right hand, elbow on the table, while she writes with the left.

Mathilde digs out every single story and myth she can remember about artists, warriors, and spiritual seekers. How they transcend the dark night of the soul. She weaves them into an epic recantation that she makes Anjanette write down.

Anjanette finally puts down the pen. "Okay, I get it." She rubs at the back of her neck with both hands and presses her forehead toward the table. She sits back up. She is slumped and looking defeated in a way that Mathilde has never seen her.

"I wasn't feeling good before I got there," Anjanette begins. "That was the longest bus ride I've ever been on and I was scared of getting lost and I'd eaten a tuna fish sandwich for lunch and drank too many cokes which was definitely not a good idea. So things were feeling really off before I went in and then, I was standing there, feeling rocked." says Anjanette. "Just blown away. And then, the more I looked at Kara Walker's work, the more I thought about the use of silhouette, how the silhouette naturally avoids the subject—it doesn't let you look at it directly—yet there it is, all the time, staring you in the face. And it was just so powerful. And horrifying. And brilliant. And obviously came from that place where you can't put things into words. And I felt so small. Powerless. Like everything I ever made didn't matter. Wasn't smart like that. Wasn't about big historic important things. Things that will change the world. My stuff isn't like that. You know. My stuff is just, you know, me."

Mathilde doesn't respond.

Finally, Anjanette breaks the silence. "Now you got nothing to say? You don't even look worried that I've completely messed up my life. You could at least pretend to understand."

Mathilde doesn't laugh but she can't bury the smile that rides a rush of relief pouring up out of her chest. She had imagined such worse things had happened to her friend traveling alone to New York City, but this—this was almost comical given how resolutely sure of herself Anjanette has always been.

"Only an artist goes into their studio and gets weird for ten days thinking they are not an artist," says Mathilde. "So if you think I'm not worried about the crisis you're in, well, yeah, what exactly am I supposed to be concerned about? You are an artist. You've always been an artist. So you went to New York and it was scary and gave you diarrhea. Big whoop. Instead of getting inspired, you got intimidated. So what. Maybe if you got out more, that would happen more. Maybe if you had gone to art school that would have been part of your daily life. I don't know. I just think it doesn't matter. Just because Kara Walker is young, Black, female, and fabulous with her way of making art doesn't mean you don't get to also be young, Black, female, and fabulous with your way of making art. C'mon. Life or history, or whatever you want to call it, isn't one person's story. It's a pantheon. Be part of the pantheon. Then all the stories get told. All of them. Hundreds and thousands and hundreds of thousands and then, those can all add up into one big, shared thing. We get her silhouettes, we get your stuff, we get everybody's stuff and then we get to see the whole picture. Or not. I don't know. You know I'm not the expert here but think about Mr. Tomarelli, he would—"

Anjanette interrupts. "I don't want to be an art teacher."

"Well that's clearly not a worry since nobody'd ever hire you anyway," says Mathilde. "But you're missing the point. Keep making your stuff your way and don't worry what anyone else is thinking. You *know* you're good at that. You *know* it's your superpower."

"That I don't care what other people do?"

"No, that you don't care what other people *think*. If you got out more, you would see that's a superpower." Mathilde gets up and begins loading the dishes into the dishwasher.

"So, you went into the big bad city and got lost," she continues. "But now you're home. So be home. Have you been to Berlin? No. London? No. Montreal? No. You haven't been to any of those places but they all have an art scene. They all have artists you've never heard of and it didn't bother you before. Maybe those artists are happy, or maybe not, maybe they're miserable, maybe they are way more successful than you will ever be, maybe they're all making millions of dollars—"

"That seems unlikely."

"Who cares," continues Mathilde. "You're an artist. Deal with it." Mathilde folds the dishtowel into thirds and tucks it over the stove handle the way Lonny likes it done.

Mathilde takes the sheet of paper Anjanette has written on and flips it over. She scribbles a few words then hands the pen to Anjanette.

"This is your pact," says Mathilde. "Sign it." Anjanette looks like she might put up a protest, but clearly, the morning has taken it out of her. Or maybe, she likes what Mathilde has written. Either way, she scrawls her signature and pushes the paper away.

"Excellent." Mathilde rolls the paper into a scroll and lightly bops Anjanette on the head. "Get dressed and let's go to Cardullo's. I promised Mike I'd bring him back a couple bags of cheese straws and I need to get on the road before traffic gets crazy."

Mathilde watches Lonny who stands by the front door waiting for Gerri's car. The knitting club's anniversary dinner is tomorrow night and Gerri has no doubt heard about the morning's stand-off with Anjanette, so she is coming to take Lonny out to dinner.

Of course, it's possible that Gerri always comes to spirit Lonny away on the Thursday nights that Anjanette hosts a circle. Mathilde can't be sure.

Lonny has put on lipstick and is wearing a pretty pink scarf.

Mathilde feels the deep burning in her chest begin to throb. It should be Timo taking Lonny out for a special dinner, thinks Mathilde. Lonny is a widow, too. Mathilde hates that word: widow.

Mike was so young when he died, fifty-seven. Timo was even younger than that when he died because she and Anjanette were teenagers so he must've been like forty-one. God. Mathilde lets out a sigh and looks around quickly to make sure no one heard her.

When you say those words, until death do us part, you really do not imagine it could happen in the middle of an ordinary morning when you have plans to go to the hardware store and get a new rake and a couple packages of lawn + leaf bags. You really think it means that someday, when you are both all shriveled up and toothless, someone's gonna come along and tip you out of a rocker into a big hole in the ground and throw dirt on your head and you won't really care because by that time you're so old anyway.

The headlights of Gerri's green sedan flash into the front hall as the car turns into the drive and idles, waiting for Lonny.

Anjanette walks out of the living room eating tortilla chips from her open palm.

"What time you coming back?" Anjanette asks Lonny.

"Put a plate under that," Lonny says, exasperated. She walks out the door and pulls it shut tight behind her without answering Anjanette.

Once Lonny is out of the house, Anjanette moves about the living room, lighting candles, getting some music going, burning incense. Mathilde brings in more nibbles—another bowl of chips, veggies and dip, a plate of apple slices spritzed with lemon juice to keep them from turning brown.

"What is this rabbit food?" says Anjanette. "Where's the good stuff?"

Mathilde ignores the question. "I haven't told you how much I like your hair like that," she says. "It's very cool."

Anjanette has her annual October art show in two weeks and always does some kind of big style transformation for opening night. Right now, she is wearing her hair cut close to the scalp with the tips of the curls bleached white.

"Listen," says Anjanette, she drags the word out as she licks the salt from her fingers. "This is the most goddamn easy hair. I may never grow it out again." She wears big earrings and a stunning marigold halterneck jumpsuit in some silky material that drapes beautifully and is twisted to create an artful, wrap-effect silhouette. It has an open back and falls to fluid, wide legs.

"You look amazing," says Mathilde. "But how do you go to the bathroom? Don't you have to take the whole thing off?"

"There you go," says Anjanette. "Always looking for the silver lining."

Mojo rushes the door to announce people that have begun to arrive for the circle.

Years ago, when Anjanette told Mathilde about her plan to create a monthly gathering for women that she was going to call simply "the circle," Mathilde was delighted. And, she refrained from responding that a woman's circle is an ancient, sacred practice in many cultures. Anajnette would have only shrugged. It wasn't that Anjanette ever got annoyed by Mathilde's need to share historical perspective, it was more that Anjanette didn't seem to need it. It didn't fuel her life the way it did for Mathilde.

For Mathilde, there is a vibration, a connection to something bigger whether or not the other women are aware that they are carrying on a tradition of female ancestors by coming together to form a community that supports and celebrates the feminine experience.

But tonight, Mathilde isn't feeling so good about joining in. She hasn't been to a circle since before Mike died. She makes a point to sit at the far end of the room on one of the window seats that flank the fireplace. The group probably has as many as thirty or forty people in it, but only about fifteen or twenty ever show. Sort of like the bookclubs Mathilde has been part of now and again although Anjanette's circle is not like any parties Mathilde has attended in Dedham where meetings move from house to house but always look the same.

If there is one thing the women walking through Lonny's front door have in common is that they do not look the same; there is a complete range of age and clothing style. The mixed bag of appearance is reflected in the offerings they bring. Bottles of wine yes, but also flavored seltzer, a tray of pot brownies, Kimbap, vegan bliss balls, spicy cashews, and honeyed almonds, Briouats, a bouquet of sunflowers, crystals and dahlias to make a mandala on the coffee table and always, an excess of chocolate.

Teddy, Lonny's cat, surprises Mathilde by suddenly jumping into her lap. He kneads her legs a bit before settling. Mathilde is grateful for the companionship. People are finding their spots.

She watches the female greeting rituals: squeal, connect, kiss, touch each other's earrings, compliment outfit or shoes, compliment hair— Annika comes in with Senegalese twists and Anjanette is all over her.

"Did you go to Delphine's like I told you?" asks Anjanette.

"Girl!" says Annika, "You know I did." She does a couple of quick poses, showing off her long locs, a few in the front have a super thin cord of gold twisted through them.

Teddy startles and jumps from her lap. Mathilde looks up to see someone standing next to her.

"Okay if I join you?" It's Rosni. The window seat is more than big enough for two besides, Rosni is petite. She could fit even if it was meant for one.

"Sure, hi—" Mathilde scooches over a bit even though she doesn't have to.

"Don't move, I'm good," says Rosni. She drops her Fendi bag to the floor and slips off the strappy heels to tuck her feet into a cross-legged position. Rosni is a psychologist and yoga teacher.

"Did you come here straight from work?" says Mathilde, knowing the answer but trying to buy time. She should have known she would see Rosni tonight but somehow it had not occurred to her and she is feeling embarrassed and exposed. It was Rosni that Anjanette enlisted to get Mathilde released from McLean, the psych hospital.

That was Monday, or was it Tuesday? Because it's circle night, she knows today is Thursday, but the rest is kind of a blur.

The day Anjanette and Rosni brought Mathilde from McLean up to the third floor, Rosni looked around the quasi greenhouse with misgiving. "This is a lot of green," she had joked, trying to make light of the situation. "Not a lot of room to move around up here."

"Can't have too much green," said Anjanette, nudging a few plants out of the way so she would have floor space to set down Mathilde's bags. "And anything is better than being at that place." Anjanette was adamant Mathilde did not belong in a psychiatric hospital.

Mathilde looks away from Rosni. She watches as the cat steps carefully out of the living room and heads back to the kitchen. A memory of her last conversation with Rosni flashes. The words a jumble—something about how she always feels like a bystander, her life a ball being kicked down the street and she doesn't want to do that anymore but doesn't know how to do it right. Mathilde is hot with embarrassment.

She must've sounded like an idiot.

Rosni reaches over and touches Mathilde on the arm, a firm squeeze that carries all the warmth of a good hug, then turns her attention to Anjanette who stands in the center of the room. Mathilde pushes down the tears that want to surge up behind her eyes.

Anjanette settles the group and leads them through the rituals that have been created over the years. First, they go around and each person shares a word or color or feeling that best sums up where they are in this moment. Next, Anjanette carries an oracle deck around the room so that everyone has a chance to pull a card.

Mathilde loves this part. It allows her to look around the room and observe each of the people who are here tonight, some of whom she has never met before.

Over the course of the night, the conversation widens. Topics pinball from the superficial to the serious, from national news to personal updates. The brownies have started to take effect and laughter begins to roll through the room. Someone announces that she recently learned laughter is a vibrational orgasm and people begin sharing other odd facts. Mathilde is feeling light and happy and floats one out to the group.

"In Tibet," she Mathilde says, "the word for art is the same word for God."

"What the hell, Lady Anthropologist," says Anjanette, a bit delighted. "Why have you never told me that before? What else are you holding out on me?"

The flash of Gerri's car lights lets everyone know Lonny has returned. The front door opens. Lonny walks in. She is in high spirits. She might also have a bit of the buzz on. Everyone calls out greetings. Those who know Lonny best get up and go over to give her a kiss and hug. Lonny perches on the edge of a sofa arm. She seems not to mind the state of her living room with people sprawled, candles burning low, food platters mostly crumbs and rinds.

When Lonny smiles wide, as she is doing right now, there is a deep dimple on her right cheek. Her hair is full snow white. She wears it combed into a soft bun at the back of her neck as she always has. Unlike her daughter whose hairstyles change more often than the weather, Lonny has worn her hair exactly like this for as long as Mathilde has known her.

"What are you all getting on about?" Lonny asks. The conversation is directed to her for the few minutes that she stays, but then, when she is offered some chocolate, she waves her hand.

"Not for me, I have my knitting club's anniversary party tomorrow night. Time for this old girl to get some sleep." She says goodnight and walks to her room which is on the other side of the dining room.

The women understand that is their cue to head out. Anjanette puts on a song to end the circle which, over the years, provides a kind of ritualistic closure that feels almost ceremonial. Tonight, she has chosen one that had been a favorite of her and Mathilde's so many years ago. As Chaka Khan belts out "I'm Every Woman" people dance, groove, shake and spin with arms to the ceiling.

Mathilde carries glasses into the kitchen and finds Lonny there in her bonnet and wrapper heating up some milk. This is the first time she and Lonny have been alone together since Anjanette brought her up to the third floor.

"How are you, girl?" Lonny pulls Mathilde in for a good hug. She steps back leaving her hands on Mathilde's shoulders to look over Mathilde as if inspecting her. "Now what is going on with your hair?"

Mathilde recoils and breaks free. "Oh yeah," Mathilde says as she presses a hand up to her head. She pats and smooths at what she knows is some crazy-ass-looking hair. She realizes no one else in the circle had mentioned it. She stares down at the floor as if she can find an answer there.

"Yeah, I need to—" Mathilde says. "I've been meaning to—"

Lonny changes the subject. "Everything okay up there?"

Mathilde relaxes. Clearly, Lonny is questioning the state of house-keeping as the second and third floors are Anjanette's domain.

"Aside from feeling like I am in a terrarium—" says Mathilde. "It's perfect. Comfy and quiet."

"Well, don't get too used to the quiet. That girl plays a lot of loud music when she's working, but I'm glad to know she's got you comfortable." Lonny gestures to the broom closet. "You know where to find the cleaning if you need it."

"It's so good to be here," says Mathilde.

"Want some?" Lonny lifts the pot of warm milk up for a moment before pouring it into her teacup. Never a mug for Lonny, always a teacup.

Mathilde shakes her head. "No, thank you."

People come in with more glasses and empty bottles. Mathilde goes back to gather up the bowls and platters. When she comes back into kitchen, Lonny is gone. Mathilde loads the dishwasher, washes the platters, wipes down the counters, folds a dishtowel to hang from the oven's wide handle and flicks the light off when she's done.

Lying in bed later on, Mathilde wonders how she could have done it differently. How is it that she is the one who has fallen off the track? Didn't she always secretly believe she was so much smarter than all her neighbors back in Dedham? Apparently not—they have no trouble following the prescribed path. They probably always knew she was the loser—the one who couldn't make it work. All that striving and driving, all those endless mornings of packing lunches, stupid hours wasted on plastic bins and labels to keep the garage clear of clutter so if the doors were open and neighbors drove by they would see, she had her shit together.

But if she always knew she was barely hanging on, wouldn't everyone else know, too?

A burst of laughter, muffled by the floorboards, reaches her. Anjanette has someone in her studio. Now they are going down the hallway. A trail of small laughs and bits of conversation float up the stairwell before the door to Anjanette's bedroom shuts.

The next morning, Mathilde sits at the kitchen table prepping jelly jars with ferns and ribbons for Lonny who is making posies from a sink full of cosmos, dahlias and hydrangea.

They both hear murmuring at the front door before it opens and closes. Someone has just left the house. The heavy slap of Anjanette's bare feet can be heard coming down the hall.

"Annie," sings Anjanette, dancing into the kitchen, "don't wear no panties."

Anjanette wears a kimono printed with tropical birds over sexy, shortie pajamas. Her hips sway, shoulders shift as she moves toward the coffeepot. "Annie don't wear no panties," she croons.

"You can tell Annie that she better have her damn pants on in this kitchen," says Lonny.

Anjanette comes up behind her mother and burrows her face into Lonny's neck for a kiss, then puts her hands on Lonny's hips and presses her belly against her mother's back while she continues swaying. "Annie don't wear no panties," Anjanette sings.

Lonny turns to face her. She is laughing. They dance a little bit together. This is the kind of teasing Timo would do. Lonny's dimple is in full view.

"Go on and get," says Lonny after a few minutes. She shakes her daughter off and turns back to the flowers.

"Is that cinnamon toast?" Anjanette asks. Mathilde nods. Anjanette lifts a piece to her mouth and eats it as she heads out.

"There better be a plate under that," says Lonny without turning around. Mathilde hands her plate up to Anjanette who takes it in one hand, the toast in the other as she leaves the room.

Mathilde holds the paper plate with both hands. She moves stiffly and can't reach up to itch her neck which is sweaty. The cookies teeter and threaten to spill off the plate and onto the grass as she steps through the hedge that divides her backyard from the house next door. Mathilde hates doing new things. Tears push into the corners of her eyes. She swallows hard repeatedly to keep them down. She is nine years old and this is the worst day of her life.

She steps slowly up the creaky wooden treads onto the back porch of Anjanette's house, but hesitates before tapping on the screen door. This is all her mom's fault. Her mom's terrible, stupid idea.

A few days ago, Anjanette broke her leg skateboarding with her brothers.

"You have no idea what it's like to be sick and confined to a bed," Mathilde's mother said as she piled the cookies onto the plate. "How you can't do anything. How frustrating and lonely it is."

Anjanette is her same age and in her class, but she doesn't know Mathilde exists. At least Mathilde doesn't think Anjanette has ever noticed her.

Her mother lifted Mathilde's chin up so that they were connected eye-to eye. The voice grew even more sharp. "You are going to bring these cookies to that little girl and you are going to sit with her or there will be no getting your ears pierced on Saturday."

Mathilde wriggled out from the grip under her chin.

This is so unfair. Mathilde spent months wheedling her mother for pierced ears. All the cool girls have pierced ears. She doesn't want to start fourth grade like a loser. She has to have pierced ears if she is going to survive.

Her mother doesn't understand. She's always pushing Mathilde to make friends, but Mathilde can't tell her how it is—girls are mean. And they don't like her. Mathilde remembers how they made fun of her on report card day. *We know what you got—all Fs—fat, freckled and frizzy.*

Anjanette is never mean, not by design anyway. She simply moves through the world in her own orbit and lets others be magnetized to her. When she wears bright pink nail polish everybody copies her. Anjanette is the first girl in school to have pierced ears. Her hair is puffy and soft; it bobs gently like cotton candy when she wears it loose. Sometimes she pins it back from her face with brightly colored plastic barrettes that have butterflies or daises on them. Anjanette's barrettes are nothing like the flat metal barrettes Mathilde's mother buys in packages of ten from the drugstore.

Mathilde taps on the door, hoping no one answers.

Anjanette's mother doesn't yell to Anjanette that she has a visitor. She leads Mathilde through the kitchen and into the living room where Anjanette is propped up on the sofa looking anything but bored, sad, or suffering.

Half a dozen flower arrangements with get-well cards sticking out are set about the room. Brand-new stuffed animals—a bunny, kitten, and two teddy bears sit along the top edge of the sofa. The coffee table is loaded with paper, crayons, markers, stickers, and a cardboard cylinder filled with pencils. Anjanette looks up from the big sketchbook on her lap when Lonny comes in with Mathilde.

"Momma," says Anjanette. "Can I have my watercolors?"

"May I please," responds Lonny.

"May I please," intones Anjanette, annoyed.

"For the last time, not in my living room. Ask me again you're gonna have two broken legs."

Lonny raises her eyebrows at Mathilde as if to say, *she's all yours* and walks back to the kitchen.

Mathilde stands for a few minutes. "I brought you some cookies," she says finally.

Anjanette looks up. "I'm not hungry. Will you turn the fan off?"

Mathilde puts the cookies onto the table where a fan blows cool air at Anjanette's face and shuts it off. She edges over to look at the stack of books sitting on the coffee table. *The Last of the Mohicans*. Looks like a boy book.

"Is that a good book?" asks Mathilde

Anjanette shrugs. "I haven't read it. I only look at the paintings."

"You mean the pictures?"

"Before they are pictures they are paintings."

"Oh," says Mathilde looking more closely at the cover to see what she means.

Anjanette isn't welcoming or unwelcoming. It's as if Mathilde is a bird that flew in through the window and is bumping about, looking for a place to land.

When Anjanette gets hot again, Mathilde turns the fan on. In a little while, Anjanette asks her to turn it off. This continues a few more times until Lonny marches into the room, lifts the fan from where it points straight at Anjanette's face and repositions it so the stream of air is directed at her torso and leg. Lonny leaves the room without saying a word. She doesn't do it crossly like Mathilde's mother would—sharp and irritated. Her gesture is straightforward, direct, and swift with a gentle edge like Mathilde's father when he sweeps a spider into a kleenex before taking it outside.

After that small adjustment, Anjanette seems to relax and stops asking for the fan to be changed. Mathilde settles into the plush chair next to the sofa.

"Does it hurt?" Mathilde asks. The cast on Anjanette's right leg is enormous. It reaches from her foot where only her toes poke out and goes all the way up to the top of her thigh.

"It did," answers Anjanette emphatically. Her head tilts from side to side as she rubs the pencil back and forth quickly to fill in a part of her drawing. She looks up at Mathilde and yawns. "Now it's the itching that's the worst. Do you want to sign it?"

"Can I?" Mathilde is thrilled to be asked.

"May I—" drawls Anjanette and they both laugh. "Here," Anjanette reaches over and hands a red marker to Mathilde. "Or do you want to use a blue one? The green is all dried up. My stupid brother left the cap off."

"What should I write?" asks Mathilde, a bit intimidated by the graffiti of drawings and words that already cover most of the white plaster.

"Can you draw a squirrel?" asks Anjanette.

Mathilde shakes her head no. "I can't draw anything."

"Then write something nice about me."

When Mathilde gets up to leave, Anjanette tells her to come back the next day.

For the rest of the summer, Mathilde comes over every day and settles in across from where Anjanette is installed on the sofa. Sometimes Anjanette's brothers come charging down the stairs pausing only for a moment before heading out the front door.

"Don't touch my albums," Joseph threatens his sister.

"I won't," Anjanette replies. Not a lie because it's Mathilde who changes the records on the record player.

"You can listen to mine," Daniel calls back over his shoulder as he drops gracefully down the front steps, "just not the Al Green." Daniel is in junior high, which seems so much older than Joseph and Ten who are still in the same school with her and Anjanette.

Ten pauses to check in on his little sister.

"You good, AJ?" he asks, pumping a fist into his baseball mitt. His given name is Isaiah, but everyone calls him Tender, or Ten.

"Bring me back some licorice?" Anjanette says. And he always does. Swedish fish if the concession stand is all out of the ropes of penny-a-piece red licorice.

The house is often empty during the day. Anjanette's parents are at work. Her brothers are in little league or shooting hoops at Lorentz Park or at the movies. Never home until dinnertime, which is when Mathilde is always gone.

On those long afternoons, Mathilde sits in the plush chair next to the sofa and reads to Anjanette who likes to listen to stories as she makes drawings. Or she has Mathilde put albums on the stereo, changing them out, returning them to their paper sleeve before slipping them into their cardboard cover and slotting them back onto the shelf where they live.

"Be careful," Anjanette warns. Joseph isn't the only one angry if any records get scratched.

A few times Anjanette asks Mathilde to pose for her while she draws which means sitting super still and not talking at all. Mathilde doesn't mind posing for Anjanette because it allows her to look at Anjanette in a way she normally can't or it would be rude. Bright green cotton shorts and a white tank top are what Anjanette wears most days—that or stretchy terrycloth gym shorts. This means her one long healthy leg is exposed.

Anjanette's thigh is dark with a sheen like the mahogany mantel that gleams above the fireplace, her bare shoulders smooth and perfect, her face a mystery. Mathilde hates that she can never hide her emotions; if she gets embarrassed or angry, a rash flames up her neck to set her earlobes on fire for all the world to see. Mathilde looks down at her thigh. She is also wearing shorts, but hers are tan plaid; they cut a tight line into her thighs so that her skin bulges out pink and jiggly like a hunk of uncooked chicken.

"Don't put your head down," commands Anjanette from where she sits on the living room sofa with cushions propped behind her back. Her cast stretches the length of the sofa, stiff and long. There is a small red pillow under the heel. "Keep it where it was."

In August, just before school is about to start up again, Anjanette and her family return from the Vineyard where they vacation every summer. Mathilde rushes over to knock on the back door. It has been so boring while Anjanette was away.

The screen door creaks open and Anjanette steps out. She preens a bit as Mathilde stands in awe; the front of Anjanette's hair has been artificially lightened.

"Did your mom let you do that?" asks Mathilde.

"Do what?"

"Put the *Sun-In* in your hair?" says Mathilde.

"It's my hair, I can do what I want." Anjanette reaches up to touch it as if to underscore her ownership.

"She didn't get mad?"

"Oh," says Anjanette, her hand drops down to her side and she winces a tiny bit at the memory. She glances behind her into the kitchen to make sure her mother is not there before she whispers, "She got *wicked* mad."

"What happened?"

"Nothing," replies Anjanette. "My daddy was there. He said it looked fine."

Timo is a big man with an easygoing energy. When things go wrong, he laughs softly and says, *well that's alright then, that's alright then* even though Mathilde can feel a sadness under his understanding ways. Maybe it's because his family is in Louisiana and he misses them.

Anjanette is his baby girl who can do no wrong. Her drawings and paintings make him proud. "That comes from my side of the family," he says. "Cane River magic." They also look alike. Where Lonny is small-boned with a complexion that has the smooth perfection of a pecan, Anjanette and her daddy have skin dark as a late summer night sky when you can see the moon but still, there's a shimmer of blue. They are both tall, with strong shoulders and wide, exuberant smiles.

Plus they both love making stuff. Timo has a woodshop in the basement with a corner for Anjanette's paints and easel. Once her cast is replaced with one that comes up to her knee, Anjanette is able to navigate the steps to the basement so they can hang out there.

"So let's paint them," says Anjanette.

They are talking about what they are gonna wear on the first day of school. Mathilde has been complaining about her boring, flat metal barrettes.

"We can do that?" Mathilde asks.

Anjanette makes a dismissive sound. "You can paint anything."

And so, on the first day of fourth grade, Mathilde wears pale blue barrettes with white polka dots as she walks behind Anjanette—who still needs to use crutches—carrying all of their books and lunchboxes.

It's morning, again.

Get up you goddamned lazy cow. Mathilde's eyes stay shut, comforter held tight under her chin. Last night, when she went to bed, she was so sure tomorrow would be the day she gets back on track. It will be a clean start, fresh slate.

And then, thud. Tomorrow is today and the engine will not turn over.

Why should it? No one needs her. No dinners to make. No appointments to remember. Mathilde rubs at her head. God, her hair is a disaster. She pulls the palms of her hands down over her ears in an effort to flatten it.

Below the floorboards, Anjanette's music is loud and strong. The beats shout that she is revving up her firepower: Alicia Keys, Mary J. Blige, and now Missy Eliot. She can hear Anjanette singing. Her annual art show is happening next week. This year it will be at The Cooper Gallery on Mount Auburn Street.

Anjanette's activity only serves to emphasize the weight of sludge Mathilde feels buried under. It's as if aliens came in the night and extracted all the marrow from her bones. She has no volition. She can't remember the last time she was eager to wake up and she hates herself for feeling this way.

She looks over at the Belgian chocolates from Cardullo's that Anjanette has left on the nightstand. Mathilde reaches over and unwraps one from the package, milk chocolate rice crisp with raspberry nougat, her absolute favorite.

Years ago, as a young married woman looking to impress, Mathilde would make the trip from Dedham knowing full well the hassle of juggling toddlers and trying to find a place to park in Harvard Square, just so she could go to Cardullo's for artisanal cheese and the perfect crackers for a gift basket. But also, maybe—she was trying to connect with a time when she didn't know life could become a string of poor decisions.

Anjanette pops the door open and Mathilde bolts upright.

"Momma wants you to help her in the garden for ten minutes," Anjanette announces. She props the door wide open, then thumps back down the stairs.

Mathilde rubs at her face and throws back the coverlet. So much for lying in bed all day. Not when Lonny raised four kids while working full time and still managed to knit them each a matching set of hat and mittens. Lonny, who made her sit down and eat soup with them when Mathilde's parents weren't home and the house was dark. Lonny, who is seventy-four years old and still baking bread, putting up tomatoes and volunteering at her church each Sunday morning.

Get up you goddamned lazy cow.

Outside, Mathilde wears one of Anjanette's graphic t-shirts and the gray joggers she has been living/sleeping in for days on end. Lonny hands her a rake to pull the leaves into a pile and a large trash bag to pick up anything she finds from the party Friday night.

The knitting group's anniversary party was a gala event. Mathilde got to see how beautiful everything looked before people began arriving, but when Anjanette headed out on a date, Mathilde went back upstairs. She would have loved to sit, out of view, on the second floor landing so that she could listen to the conversations below, but that would be super weird. Rude. Instead, Mathilde tucked herself back into her nest on the third floor where she watched the festivities from above. Women's voices lifted up to the open window. And, as the sky grew dark, the garden seemed a fairyland of tiny white lights and sparks of laughter.

While Mathilde rakes, Lonny undoes the ties that hold the huge garlands of fat white hydrangeas that had been strung with twinkle lights along the side fence. The flower heads drop heavily to the grass. Lonny moves steadily, systematically. She doesn't talk to Mathilde. Once in a while she will gesture with a wrist or elbow what she wants Mathilde to do next, but mostly Lonny is in her own world, humming scraps of music, some Ella Fitzgerald bubbles in.

Amid the balled up napkins and the odd paper plate folded in half and tucked under a chair, Mathilde discovers a few stitch markers someone lost. She brings them to Lonny who looks at them in her palm and then laughs before pocketing them. "I know whose those are," says Lonny.

What, thinks Mathilde. You can know a person by what stitch markers they use? Knitters are crazy. But she doesn't say anything to Lonny.

There, says Lonny, not seeming the least bit winded or tired. On the contrary she seems radiant, energized. "I'm going to harvest the last of the lavender," she says.

She doesn't ask for help, but Mathilde stays alongside. Together they sort through the mound of stalks that still have their purple tips and wrap them into small bundles tied with twine. The smell is everywhere, rich, sweet, healing. Mathilde uses the neck of her t-shirt to wipe sweat from her face and neck. The day is glorious and she wishes she had shorts to change into.

"Oh my," says Lonny as the last of the flowers are set into a basket and Mathilde sweeps the debris from the workbench. "I could eat the side of a house. Let's heat up some casserole."

The fridge is stacked high with leftovers from the anniversary dinner: a gourmet salad of fingerling potatoes and green beans, a bowl of roasted golden beets with crushed walnuts and crumbled Roquefort. Lonny lifts a pan of baked mac and cheese topped with buttery breadcrumbs out from the oven, bubbling from its time under the broiler. The smell must have carried all the way up to the second floor because in a few minutes, the sound of Anjanette pounding down the stairs is heard.

"Oh, yes please," says Anjanette, sticking her face close to the pan and breathing in the smell. She looks over at Mathilde. "You got a workout." It isn't a compliment.

"And like you're a vision," replies Mathilde with a gesture to the paint splattered cut-offs that are rolled up over Anjanette's knees.

Lonny sits and gives herself a moment of quiet before she lifts her fork and begins to eat.

There is no small talk. Maybe Lonny is tired; that was a lot of work they just did. Anjanette is eating quickly. Her fork hits the plate sharply. She is wound up about the show, Mathilde can tell.

"Don't get wiggy," Mathilde says. "It's gonna be great. It always is."

Anjanette is not in the mood to be comforted. Her irritation at Mathilde's words is barely stifled. She takes her plate and heads upstairs to finish eating there. Lonny gives Mathilde a small shrug to say, let it go. Anjanette's temperament is nothing new.

Lonny finishes her lunch and puts on the podcast she likes to listen to. Mathilde cleans up, returning the pans to the fridge before she sits back at the table with a cup of coffee. She knows she should go upstairs and take a shower, but she doesn't want to.

"Here." Lonny sets a grater and a bowl of ginger to peel and grate in front of Mathilde. "My church group meets tonight."

Grateful for the task, Mathilde settles in and continues to help Lonny in the kitchen until it is nearly dark outside.

Lonny comes out of her room wearing a long, thin sweater and a scarf tied at her neck. She picks up the platter of warm gingerbread cakes that are covered in tinfoil, her purse on one wrist, knitting bag on the other and asks Mathilde to get the door for her.

"Tell that girl there's baked sweet potatoes and chili in the fridge. For you, too if you want."

Mathilde reaches over for another candy but there are only wrappers; she has eaten them all. In a rush of shame, she gathers up the wrappers and stuffs them under the mattress. She'll deal with them later, she thinks with a shaky exhale as she lies back.

I'm exhausted, Rosie would say, when Mathilde came home from school to find her lying on the sofa with a plaid blanket pulled tight around her and asked what was wrong.

Mathilde would walk toward the stereo where the record albums were in stacks on the floor. *I could put on Carole King and we could sing with her like you like.* Mathilde let her backpack drop to the floor and began holding up albums toward her mother. *Mom? How about Anne Murray? Or we could sing—*

Honey, can you just let me rest a little bit? her mother would reply, not looking at all like her mother. No lipstick. Her hair wasn't brushed. What she wanted was for Mathilde to be gone.

Okay, Mathilde would say and pull her knapsack up by its strap, half dragging it behind her as she headed to her room. But it wasn't okay. It didn't feel anything like okay. She hated her mother. Or at least, that's what she thought she was feeling.

The memory jolts Mathilde into acute awareness of this very moment. It must be at least nine or ten in the morning. She checks her phone. 10:45. Oh my god. She is still lying in bed. She has just stuffed empty candy wrappers under the mattress. She checks her phone again, but there are no new texts from her kids. She starts to type *good morning Chicken* to Toby, her son, then stops. If he writes back she will have to answer. He'll ask Mathilde if she's talked with Susannah.

The last time she talked to her daughter Susannah was in August. Avoiding conflict with Susannah is never easy but that day, Mathilde lost it it. Something Susannah said triggered Mathilde to scream a stream of terrible things before throwing the phone out the window. Thank god the window was open and the phone landed on the grass, unhurt. Mathilde isn't so sure about the relationship with her daughter. Mathilde shoves the phone under the mattress and rolls onto her back with an arm across her face.

Her children don't know what she's doing right now, do they? Do her kids feel about her the way she felt about her mother? The thought burns. Her chest and throat prickle with hot frustration. How is that possible? She was so careful not to make the mistakes her mother made.

Mathilde followed every recipe to the letter. Their house was beautiful, warm and friendly—everyone said so. Susannah and Toby's friends loved to hang out at their house. She made blueberry pancakes for twelve after a sleepover that had kept her up all night. The family room mutated into a video game hideout for everyone but her since she couldn't even watch her shows in there because of how they had rigged up the tv. There were Halloween decorations in the yard in October, fresh balsam wreaths on the door in December and windows full of red paper hearts in February. She and Mike were married for nearly thirty years and rarely squabbled, never fought in the way people do with yelling and screaming. How can your life fall apart when you did everything right?

It's not fair. Mathilde's parents are the Bickersons. To this day they still duke it out in endless, petty arguments. And look at them. Living their best life on a beach in South Carolina. Not that Mathilde wants anything like that. Riding around in golf carts, cocktail hour with their neighbors around the condo's concrete swimming pool where they talk about nothing for hours—zombieland.

And like she's one to judge. She's the zombie. But when did it happen? Was there a turning point? What if Uncle Wesley hadn't died? Would she have married Mike if she wasn't in such a world of confusion and pain?

64 Clement
Fall 1985

When she returns from her summer on Block Island—the summer between Sophomore and Junior year—Mathilde goes down to the basement of the dorm at Boston University where she had stored her stuff last Spring and loads it into the back of Mike's truck.

Mike helps her carry the boxes and suitcases up to the porch of 64 Clement, but then she waves him off. She lugs everything up to her bedroom on the second floor by herself, shuts the door and crawls into bed.

Her mother does not bother to knock a second time but walks in when Mathilde refuses to answer. Rosie sits on the edge of the bed, her hip pressed into Mathilde's back, and tries to find out what has happened, what is going on.

"Stop this right now. You have to go back to college." When the commanding approach doesn't work, her mother switches to guilt. "We've already paid for the semester." But Mathilde is not going to be sucked in by anyone, for any reason, ever again. She sits up and shouts at them both—by this time her father is standing in the doorframe, not quite in her room, but trying to help.

"I am grieving! This is called grief," Mathilde says. "You didn't let me go to Uncle Wesley's funeral. You didn't tell me he was sick. That he was dying. Leave me alone!"

Unaccustomed to such an emotional outburst from their usually shy and compliant child, her parents don't know what to do.

They leave her alone.

What gets her out of bed is Mike. Weeknights, he pulls up in front of the house in his slate blue Ford pickup truck. His construction job starts early and ends around four each afternoon, but by the time he gets back to his place, showers, puts on clean clothes and drives the forty minutes up I-95 from Pawtucket to Inman Square—the part of Cambridge where Mathilde lives—it is usually close to six o'clock. The Mike she met on Block Island—self-assured and full of stories—is different from the guy showing up to her parents' house. He seems intimidated by the way Mathilde's family lives; he thinks they are rich.

Mike is tall and strong, sunburned, and freckled, his muscles tight against the sleeves of the shirt and yet, she sees so clearly the little kid in him. His efforts to be liked by her parents from the fresh shave to the white button-down tucked neatly into his jeans make him seem so vulnerable to Mathilde; she watches how he tries not to walk too heavily on the Turkish carpet runner that leads from the foyer to the kitchen, the hallway they travel each night to sit on the back porch where September temperatures lull them into thinking it's still summer.

Her parents act like birds—fussy and distraught by a blue jay in their nest—and interrupt the young couple at random intervals. Mike is the first boy Mathilde has brought home so although her mother is secretly relieved (since she had begun to question the nature of the relationship between Mathilde and Anjanette) there is so much about Mike that upsets her. First, Mike is not a boy. He is nearly twenty-six and Mathilde has only just turned twenty. Second, he's been working construction since high school. Third, (and the biggest block if her mother were honest with herself which she will never be) Rosie cannot stand his accent.

Whenever Rosie makes some kind of remark that causes Mike to feel embarrassed about being from Pawtucket, Mathilde digs in. Her parents' chary attitude toward Mike deepens her growing loyalty to this sweetest guy.

"Next time she makes a comment like that," Mathilde reassures him, "just remind her that Rhode Island was the first colony to have religious freedom, the first state to declare independence from the British and the last state to sign the US Constitution. Massachusetts had witch trials."

Mike gazes at Mathilde with wonder before pulling her into big hug.

"My little encyclopedia," is what he calls her. Mathilde loves that he thinks she is smart. It is only years later when the gap between what holds their interest becomes a dead end like the cul-de-sac they eventually live on, but she can't see that now. All she knows is that Mike feels safe and true. She revels in how stress free it is to be in his world. He keeps things simple.

Anjanette is lukewarm. It isn't that she doesn't like Mike—she is glad he is coming round and taking care of Mathilde—it's just that Anjanette never sees it as a romance.

"All you guys do is eat pizza and then you sit around and watch as he fixes stuff up," says Anjanette.

It's true. Their dates do revolve around a shared love of pizza which began when Mathilde, as a kind of competition, took him to Tomarellis to prove he'd never had the best pizza. And then he took her to Federal Hill, the Italian section of Providence, where she had thick Sicilian pizza that was so good she had to admit defeat. Rosie rolls her eyes when she asks where they went on their date as nearly every time Mathilde replies, *we got pizza*. And, because Mike's toolbox is always in the back of his truck, doing little repairs for her parents also becomes part of his visit.

64 Clement wasn't in the best of shape back in the day when Tom and Rosie first moved in and since neither of them are the type to roll up their sleeves, they never get ahead of the upkeep that is constant and expensive. Over the years they can barely tackle the major fixes like a new roof, new furnace. An old house requires that you are handy or that you have the money to hire plumbers, electricians, roofers, and carpenters to fix the problem for you. Tom and Rosie have neither the money nor the DIY DNA.

Rosie finds it hard to resist Mike's offer to fix the back door handle that is always falling off. She lets him repaint the pantry that has water damage from some missing shingles, missing shingles that Mike replaces. Mike installs a new screen door. He repairs the back steps and handrails.

Mathilde finds Mike's effort to win over her parents kind of fascinating, like watching an ancient courtship ritual, but her mother's behavior puzzles Mathilde. Here is a great guy—Irish, friendly, hardworking—who obviously likes her daughter. You would think Rosie would be open arms, but Rosie withholds the chatty warmth she normally gives to guests. When Rosie comes out onto the back porch to inspect the work, Mike stands—a bit flushed with sweat, looking up from the bottom of the steps. Instead of a few words of appreciation, she offers him a bottle of cold beer.

"Mom," says Mathilde, "Get him a glass."

"Oh, I don't need a glass," Mike says before taking a sip from the mouth of the bottle.

Rosie turns with a smile for Mathilde. "He doesn't use a glass, darling." She steps back into the house. The screen door slaps shut behind her.

Tom likes Mike well enough, he just doesn't want his daughter dating a handyman—something he can never say out loud without feeling like he is behaving exactly as his father did. So, Rosie and Tom keep their distance. They extend the necessary pleasantries and trust the relationship will run its course quickly. They never invite Mike to join them for dinner which angers Mathilde. The more she knows of Mike's story, the more she admires him.

"Admire?" Anjanette is not impressed. "Not feeling the heat in that."

If Anjanette comes by, it is always late in the morning—nearly noon. For a few weeks in a row, she comes through the back yard lugging a basket filled with rattan, seagrass, raffia—it looks to Mathilde like the dead throwaway stuff you might find in the dumpster of a florist (she wouldn't be surprised if that is exactly where Anjanette collects her goods). Anjanette is deep in a phase of weaving objects out of natural fibers—she adds in crazy bits to the final pieces that became lampshades or odd sculptures. The dried grasses make a mess so Anjanette sits on the steps while Mathilde sits on the chaise lounge trying to knit a scarf. It's a lace pattern and not nearly as easy as Lonny had said it would be. Either that, or Mathilde is a hopeless knitter. Mathilde is pretty sure it's the latter.

Rosie comes out to offer coffee and buttered toast. When Anjanette declines, Rosie stands around for a few minutes. She makes some kind of commentary on what Anjanette is making, but seeing that Mathilde has someone to keep her company, Rosie slips away.

The sound of her mother's car leaving the driveway gives the girls space to continue their conversation.

"At least he's getting you off this back porch," says Anjanette. "I'll give him that."

"And out of bed," Mathilde says, in an effort to add points to Mike's scorecard.

"Uh, I'm thinking he's supposed to be getting you into bed," replies Anjanette, as she gives the fibers a hard tug to hold them in place. "Feels a little cold tomato pie, if you ask me."

"You've never been in love," Mathilde hits back. "What do you know?"

Mathilde doesn't tell Anjanette about the Sunday drives down to Gooseberry Island or out along the beaches of Newport where she and Mike sing along to the cassettes he plays on repeat: *America*, *Bread* and *The Carpenters*. Anjanette would have mocked her to death. And it is cheesy. Mathilde knows it is cheesy. She has also never felt so exhilarated as when she is fluttering her fingers out the open window while they cruise down the highway singing loud over the sound of traffic. Her hair is not golden but Mike makes sure she knows he is singing to her:

Will you meet me in the middle? Will you meet me in the air?
Will you love me just a little? Just enough to show you care
Well, I tried to fake it, I don't mind sayin', I just can't make it
Well, I keep on thinkin' 'bout you Sister golden hair surprise
And I just can't live without you can't you see it in my eyes?

On days when the windows are rolled up, Mike doesn't sing because he wants to listen to her voice. Mathilde knows if Rosie could see this side of Mike, she would love him. Music, singing, theater—these are the things that make Rosie come alive, but Mathilde never tells her mom about singing with Mike. She never tells Rosie that Mike knows all the lyrics to *Rainy Days and Mondays*.

On a Saturday in early October, Mike takes her to meet his grandmother which is followed by a tour of Pawtucket, the place he's lived his whole life. As they drive back, Mike shares his vision, his dreams. He is a planner. He believes all Mathilde's problems would be solved if she would just make a plan for her life.

A few weeks later, on a Wednesday evening in November, Mathilde and Mike are sitting on the porch swing under a gray wool blanket. Mathilde is curled into Mike's side. His arm is around her waist. They have just come back to 64 Clement after spending the afternoon down in Pawtucket helping Mike's grandmother make oatmeal cookies for the bake sale that happens each week after mass. The sky is dark but the temperature is not yet November bitter.

"That's new," Mike points to the large woven object that hangs from the corner of the porch ceiling. The rattan has been woven into somewhat of an acorn shape. Gold tassels and a few tiny brass bells hung from the central point at the bottom. It is illuminated from within by a mass of tiny twinkle lights.

"Anjanette made that," Mathilde says. Anjanette had instructed Mathilde to go into the garage and come back with a string of white Christmas lights that she had then stuffed into the belly of the shape. It was daylight when they first plugged it in, so it didn't seem as magical as it does now that the the moon is nearly full and the sky three shades of blue. Mathilde relaxes her cheek against the soft flannel of Mike's shirt. She realizes that these past weeks when she has been 'sick' are actually some of the sweetest days she can remember. There isn't so much confusion in her head. It feels like she doesn't need to do anything but this.

The only time she feels the acid in her stomach begin to swirl is when her mother reminds Mathilde it is time to get her things ready for the second semester that starts in January. When she tells Mike how she is feeling—that she doesn't want to go back to school, she wants to stay just like this cozied up forever—he gives her a small squeeze and says, "Let's get married."

"Okay," she says. "But what about school?"

"You can always go back and finish," says Mike, a bit shocked that she has agreed so readily.

But it isn't that simple. The wedding becomes a battle in all directions though, as per usual, Tom never gets into the fray. Mathilde knows her father doesn't think she should get married so young or put off finishing college or choose Mike—she senses all of that from him, but her dad says nothing (because he wasn't going to do what his father did). Her dad only has her pause in the stairwell as he is heading up and she is heading down. He touches her elbow and says, "you know there's no rush. Take your time."

The biggest battle is that Mathilde does not want to get married in a Catholic church. She hates the history of the Catholic church and does not want to be associated with it. And yet, Annie, Mike's grandmother, goes to mass every day. This is the most important thing for Annie and she is the most important person in Mike's world.

In the endless, unpredictable surprise that is her mother, Rosie does not create the mountain of resistance Mathilde expects. It turns out, Rosie has all kinds of dreams and visions for her daughter's wedding since she and Tom had such an unglamorous City Hall ceremony. Plus, ever since Princess Diana, poofy weddings are popping up everywhere like mushrooms after a rain.

"If you are going to get married in a church," says Rosie "for God's sakes, at least let's choose a good one. Do it here in Cambridge, or

Boston—I think Saint Cecilia's or Saint Paul's—those are both beautiful."

"Uh, first of all," says Mathilde, reveling in her new power to orchestrate how things are going to go. "You don't get to just walk into some church. You have to belong to it. And, I'm not saying we're gonna get married in a church. I don't want to get married in a church. The only reason I'm even considering it is for Mike's grandmother so if we do, it has to be her church."

Rosie fights hard to get the reception to be somewhere swanky on Beacon Hill or, at the very least, at a prestigious golf club. When fighting doesn't work, she pleads with Mathilde.

The simple decision Mathilde has made because of its promise of ease and no stress, has become a hot, emotional mess.

"Why can't we just elope?" Mathilde asks Mike.

Mike looks at her as if he doesn't understand the question. "That would break my grandmother's heart," he replies.

A decision has to be made. Mathilde has to choose whose heart is not going to get broken: her mother's, Mike's, or her own.

In the end, Mathilde chooses Mike's grandmother's heart.

They are married in February. There is snow on the ground and—because his grandmother insists—hot chocolate at the reception. The smell of incense hits Mathilde as she and her father begin walking down the aisle. The space feels cavernous and seems to swallow the bodies huddled at the front—most of them on the groom's side.

Rosie's best friend, Mrs. Silberman, is there dressed to the nines. Both she and Rosie wear dark glasses as if they are at a funeral. Mrs. Silberman keeps squeezing Rosie's hand as if to say, she is there for her. Lonny and Anjanette sit behind her parents. Lonny wears a velvet hat and a beautiful green wool suit. At the reception, Anjanette eats three slices of wedding cake (four if you count the slice she takes for the ride home) each time exclaiming, *oh my god this frosting!*—before grabbing Mathilde's hand and pulling her onto the dance floor when the music starts up.

Then it is over. She and Mike are newlyweds living in his grand-mother's two-bedroom house on Brown Street.

"I want you to have this," Mike's grandmother, says to Mathilde. There is no point in trying to decline; Annie is made of granite. So Mathilde does her best to smile politely as she takes the folded lace tablecloth, the framed photo of Mike as an altar boy, the set of four red bowls that had belonged to Annie's mother—or whatever it is that Annie has now decided belongs with Mathilde—before she stuffs it up onto the shelf of the tiny closet in the back bedroom that she shares with Mike.

And now, the question Annie asks every single morning without fail.

"Would you like to come to mass with me, dear?"

Mathilde grips the mug of coffee with both hands as if it could keep her attached to the kitchen table. She forces a smile before shaking her head in a way she hopes is not rude.

"Not today," she replies.

Not joining Annie for church on weekdays is less of a struggle than the weekly battle that happens each Sunday morning as Mike gets dressed to go with Annie to mass.

"Why can't you just come?" Mike asks as he knots the tie at his throat. "You're just sitting here. You could sit there just as easily. You don't have to do any of the prayers. It would mean so much to her. Besides," he says crawling onto the bed to put his face into her chest and work a row of kisses up her neck. "It's all the stuff you love—rituals, architecture, history, and stories."

Annie calls for Mike. He bounces off the bed, pulls on his navy blazer, then turns. He gives Mathilde a sad look, as if she were the one aban-doning him.

These first months of being married are odd. From the outside, she understands why her mother is too busy to visit—it is a decidedly unglamorous, newlywed life. But Mathilde doesn't care that she has to live in a house with old lady smells that's always drafty and cold. She doesn't care that all three of them use the one bathroom or that Annie—who lived through the Depression—is militant and restrictive around food. Meals are what Annie offers and they soon become as predictable as the days of the week: leftovers on Monday; boiled potatoes, cabbage and pork shoulder on Tuesday; fish chowder on Friday; pot roast on Sunday. It's boring, sure, but the freedom!

Hours when Annie is at church then doing the stuff she does after church, Mathilde luxuriates in bed reading without interruption—reading anything she wants. She sets an alarm so that she doesn't lose track of time and is gone before Annie gets back.

Mathilde scurries straight to the Deborah Sayles Library which is not even a mile away. When she crosses over the highway that cuts through the heart of the city, she walks with palms pressed against her ears, head down in the whippy wind. 18-wheelers scream past below, part of the piercing wall of sound created by a steady torrent of cars and trucks. But it is always worth it.

The moment she steps into the rich stillness of the library, the world drops away. It is a sanctuary—an absolute jewel in this otherwise dreary, broken streets and empty storefronts kind of city. Established when Pawtucket was a thriving mill town, the library is physically lovely with an elegant Greek revival exterior built from stone. Mathilde especially treasures discovering the fact that it was one of the first libraries in the country to remain open on Sundays so the Pawtucket mill workers—who worked six days a week—could have access to books—children too.

Each night at dinner, Annie asks her what she did all day. Mathilde quickly learns to give only the briefest recap. Mike and his grandmother have lived their whole lives in Pawtucket but have never stopped to wonder where the name Pawtucket comes from.

"It's Algonquin for river falls," says Mathilde as Annie hands her a plate with a scoop of baked beans and a pan-fried wiener on it. "And it's because of the falls, that had salmon and all kinds of fish, that this whole area had maybe the most people living here before—"

"Fall River," Annie interrupts her.

"I'm sorry?" Mathilde says.

"We call it Fall River. And Fall River is a different town. This is Pawtucket," continues Annie. Her knees crack loudly as she sits. Annie gestures for Mathilde to be quiet.

"Let us say grace," says Annie.

Mathilde gives Mike a look. He knows that she wasn't talking about Fall River. He slips a hand down to squeeze her knee as if to say, *let it go. Don't argue with Annie.*

Annie is the de facto matriarch of the sea of cousins that live in and around Pawtucket. However, Mike's parents are never part of the constant stream of people Mathilde has to meet. His dad lives in Warwick, only twenty minutes away, but Mike has long ago given up having a relationship with him. His dad did a tour in Vietnam and was pretty messed up when he came back. Mike's mom, Annie's youngest daughter, lives in Arizona or maybe California, Mike isn't sure. His mom got heavily into drugs and followed the whole hippie scene. She left him with Annie when Mike was a baby.

They are living with Annie until summer because Mike has saved enough money for a down payment on a house and the market starts up in May. This is the plan—Mike's plan. He has been taking money out of every paycheck since he first opened a bank account at fifteen. When Mathilde realizes how long he has been working on this plan, she begins to look at things differently. Up until then, she saw Mike as an unexpected turn of events in her life. But now she wonders, what if he had been trying to settle down with a wife for some time when he walked into the laundromat that rainy Sunday and she was simply the component that best fit the plan? So much looks different to her from this vantage point. Not simply the view over the city from the library's great arched window where she sits staring off into the distance. Everything.

Living in Pawtucket, she sees what she couldn't see before. Mathilde grew up in a college town. When she was in it, it was just her normal. Fish, water—like that. Now she lives in a mill town. The mix of people is different. What people talk about is different.

As a kid, college students were part of Mathilde's everyday life. Young women with long hair who wore boots with their skirts, or bell-bottom jeans with wide belts slung low on their hips. Women—the wives of graduate students—in saris who wore white socks and sandals, or who wore their baby strapped to their back with colorful fabric.

In particular, Mathilde remembers the two volunteers at her Girl Scout meetings. The ones who used the words 'feminist' and 'asshole' a lot. The volunteers—one favored a long, fringed vest and flouncy skirt, the other hip-huggers and a head wrap—only came a couple of times but she learned the most from them. Until the day of the mice ended it all.

The idea was for the girls to make cute little mice out of radishes for Thanksgiving centerpieces—the radish's thin white root hair was supposed to be the tail. This was not what the two college volunteers wanted to have the girls learn. More than likely, the mothers heard about the meeting where the volunteers burned incense and read poetry while the girls lay on the cold basement floor and decided more supervision was needed.

As always, Anjanette's mice drew a circle of admirers. By the time Mathilde gets home, her mice had lost their eyes.

"Three blind mice!" Her mother was not happy. "That's what I spent ten dollars on for your membership?"

The next year, her mother didn't sign Mathilde up for Girl Scouts. Either because her mother gave up trying to get Mathilde to have more friends, or she didn't want Mathilde around the volunteers who wore big earrings, didn't shave their legs, and talked about things like food co-ops and the pill. Or both.

Mathilde tried to fight back. "But Anjanette's mom lets her be in Girl Scouts. She doesn't care if the leaders don't wear bras."

"Speak to me like that again and you won't be seeing Anjanette for a week."

There was no worse threat. Anjanette was her best friend. More precisely, Anjanette is her only friend.

Mathilde feels that truth acutely as she sits in the Pawtucket library looking out over church spires and rooftops, feeling very alone in this unfamiliar city.

Boston
Fall 1984

Mathilde watches Uncle Wesley gesture to the waiter for more coffee. They are finishing an early dinner at Locke-Ober, the restaurant Uncle Wesley loves to mock but somehow can't shake free from. This is where his dad took him for lunch when Uncle Wesley was in college and—just like whatever drives turtles to travel hundreds of miles to lay their eggs on the same beach where they were born—the stuffy, overpriced ode to ruling class masculinity is always the place Uncle Wesley brings Mathilde on those surprise occasions he comes to dig her out of her dorm room at Boston University.

Uncle Wesley makes Boston feel comfortable and familiar. This is where he was born and raised. He makes Mathilde feel like she belongs here, too.

He isn't her real uncle, of course. Her parents, Rosie and Tom, have siblings but Mathilde barely knows them. The family they have is Wesley Morgan, Tom's roommate from Andover and Harvard and, one of the few people who didn't abandon Tom after he married Rosie.

Once, when they were walking to school, Mathilde told Anjanette how lucky she was to have an older brother like Daniel who was so kind and smart and listened to what you said. Anjanette replied, "but you have your Uncle Wesley." And it was true. Uncle Wesley was like a sweet big brother, but as she grew up, he became her friend.

The waiter refills their cups from a silver coffeepot that has a long, curved spout then steps away. Uncle Wesley drops three sugar cubes into his coffee and stirs it slowly. He listens as Mathilde finally opens up. It's so embarrassing. A few months into her sophomore year of college and she is lost, again. Last year, it felt like she had finally figured out what she should be doing when she discovered the world of anthropology and switched majors, but now, she is so confused. Uncle Wesley is the first person—the only person—she shares this with.

More than how problematic the field of anthropology is, Mathilde has a growing awareness that the entire, overarching academic structure itself is the problem. She keeps seeing the whole path of undergraduate, graduate, doctorate, post-doctorate as a spiral into quicksand, like the giant brain that sucked the soul out of Charles Wallace in *A Wrinkle in Time*. Maybe college isn't for her. Why can't she just make it work? Why can't she be normal? What is wrong with her?

Uncle Wesley doesn't laugh at her. He doesn't talk down to her or tell her to stop overthinking everything.

"I get it," he says. "Being outside the norm feels scary but being inside the norm feels like death." He rubs at one side of his neck. "I didn't know about the anthropology stuff, though. Last time we were together, you were all about it. But I know what you mean." He leans back in his chair and tips his head to one side.

"I guess you're gonna hate this then," Uncle Wesley says as he slides a copy of Franz Boas' *Handbook of American Indian Languages*, across the table to Mathilde. "Guess you see me now as one of those rapacious colonists going around landing my white ass on other people's countries."

Mathilde grips her hands in her lap. She doesn't want to say anything he might take wrong and hurt his feelings. She looks down at the gift of the Boas book. Uncle Wesley presents are always incredibly thoughtful and make her feel special. She wants to tell him how much she loves him, but everything is balled up in her throat.

"Look, kid," he says, "If you're thinking things are gonna make sense, or be fair, you can let that go. They won't. They never will." Uncle Wesley takes a long drag of his coffee. There are deep shadows under his eyes.

It's the first time Mathilde can remember seeing him heavy, as if there is a problem that booking a flight to another country can't solve.

"Just don't lose connection with the stuff that makes you happy, okay? You've always loved learning about people and different ways of doing things. Ever since you were little. Remember that time I took you to Shaker Village in Canterbury and on the ride home you were memorizing all those plants from that book by that lady—"

"186 watercolor drawings of native plants by Sister Cora Helena Sarle," says Mathilde.

"See? That's what I mean." Uncle Wesley reaches across the table for her hand. She puts her palm out and he wraps both of his hands around hers before giving a light kiss to the inside of her wrist. "Look at that memory of yours. How do you do that? You always notice all the little things."

64 Clement
Spring 1976

Every year, Uncle Wesley hosts a big New Year's Eve party at his brown-stone on Acorn Street in Beacon Hill before heading off for 'warmer parts,' as he puts it. When he returns in the spring, he arrives at 64 Clement bearing gifts. He brings Mathilde flamenco dolls from Madrid that have layers of fluffy skirts, brightly colored paper garlands from Mexico and this year, the year she turns eleven, a fabulous thick, wooly white poncho with hot pink tassels from Peru.

When Uncle Wesley shows up in the front hall booming hellos, Rosie rushes down the stairs in a brume of perfume wearing one of her best dresses. Tom wanders casually out of the den as if he is mildly surprised to see his old friend, but Mathilde knows her father always makes sure the grass is cut and the milk bottles are off the front porch when Uncle Wesley comes to visit.

Tom and Rosie are extra sweet to each other as if to show Uncle Wesley what a fun life they have, too. Rosie carries in a tray of cheese, cold cuts, specialty nuts, olives, and crackers from Cardullos—stuff they never normally eat because it is too expensive, but her parents pretend like it's a normal night of appetizers. They try hard to make Mathilde sparkle and shine. When she resists being put into the spot-light, Rosie laments that her daughter is less Shirley Temple and more Wednesday Addams. It becomes Rosie's story to tell Uncle Wesley about how Mathilde has won the library award for most books read: it's Rosie who runs upstairs and brings down the diorama of Cayuga longhouses Mathilde constructed while Mathilde burrows back into the wing chair in an effort to hide her cheeks that are flaming with embarrassment.

But Mathilde and her parents have few stories to offer that are anywhere near as entertaining as what Uncle Wesley has to share, so the focus quickly returns to the world traveler who flips cashews into his mouth from one hand and introduces her parents to things like Campari and soda, and how to make a caipirinha.

Uncle Wesley is the best, brightest part of their family unit.

It was Uncle Wesley who helped Mathilde's father get the job as a copy editor at Beacon Press.

Uncle Wesley was also best man at her parents' city hall wedding and pretty much the only guest since Rosie's family was appalled and ashamed that she was not getting married in a church. Of course, Tom's parents were more than ashamed and appalled—they were outraged—at what felt to them, a sudden, disastrous turn of events.

Mathilde's parents met on a Friday afternoon in July. Tom was a newly hired junior copywriter straight out of Harvard. Rosie was a secretary. They were coming out from the offices of Beacon Press, a publishing firm housed in the back of a narrow red brick building that sat at the top of Boston Commons. Tom was alone. Rosie was with two other women from the office and together the four of them headed down the grassy hill of the Commons to the luncheonette in downtown crossing which on Fridays, had the world's best fish chowder.

Rosie was older. Confident. Lively. Quick with words. Though as Tom discovered later, Rosie was not literary. It was happenstance that the secretarial school placed her in a publishing house; she didn't care where she worked as long as the job gave her money enough for theater tickets, shoes, nail polish and her favorite pursuit: shopping like a hawk in Filene's basement.

Their romance was fast. Rosie was twenty-five and unmarried. Tom was the first guy she'd dated who could actually give her the life she fantasized: big house, lots of kids, no money worries.

Tom's family is *rich*, Rosie squealed the word and dragged it out long, as she recounted their most recent date to her roommates. Rosie shared a two-bedroom apartment in Quincy with four other girls who commuted each day up to Boston.

Tom was twenty-two, a bit bookish and no match for the magnetic pull of the wild Irish lass, as he called her. She believed him when he confided that he wanted to be a writer someday. She convinced him to skinny dip with her in Hathaway's kettle pond on one of their picnic weekends out in Barnstable and, she was a fearless body surfer. Everything about Rosie seemed to fulfill his longing for a life that was less predictable and more poetic adventure.

"Wes," Mathilde's mother says Uncle Wesley's name like a caress. She crosses the living room to drop fresh ice into his drink. "Tell us the one about the discotheque in Ibiza." Rosie settles back next to Tom on the sofa. "The one where you all went swimming in the ocean after."

"Oh Rosie," says Tom, giving her a squeeze and leaving his arm to rest heavily across her shoulders. "Don't make the poor guy repeat himself. He's gonna think you're a big bore."

"You're the old bore," Rosie pokes Tom in the side. Mathilde watches her mother toss her hair and laugh off her father's comment, but Rosie's body has gone rigid.

Boston / Block Island
Spring / Summer 1985

Over the winter, Mathilde is so busy with school she doesn't think much about the news that Uncle Wesley didn't host a New Year's Eve party because he's selling the brownstone and moving to Miami. That was just his way. Always coming and going. Doing exciting, unexpected things. She didn't stop to wonder about any of it. Until that Tuesday in May when Mathilde opened her dorm room door to find her mother standing in the hallway, her mouth opening and closing.

"It's Wes," her mother crumples onto Mathilde's narrow bed, wheezing and trying to speak clearly but all she can say, over and over, "it's Wes." Mathilde stands by the bed, not understanding until the understanding hits her between the eyes and the room begins to shake and moan.

Her father follows Uncle Wesley's explicit instructions and submits an obituary to all the papers that says Wesley Cabot Morgan, III died in a parasailing accident. There is no service or burial in Boston. His ashes will be spread by friends at one of his favorite beaches in Brazil.

No one told Mathilde that Uncle Wesley was sick, Not just sick. Dying. When she saw him in November, why didn't he tell her? Why didn't she notice? Why was she so goddamn stupid focused on her own stupid bullshit nothingness that she didn't notice he was sick. Dying.

Was he trying to protect her from seeing first-hand the devastation of AIDS? But her parents! She cannot forgive them. They knew. How could they not have told her? They've always been open with her about his lifestyle. How could they keep this from her?

There is no closure for Mathilde, only turmoil. She isn't allowed to attend the ceremony in Key West because she has three final exams that week. In the obituary (which Mathilde clips and carefully tapes to the inside cover of the Boas book), it mentions Uncle Wesley is survived by his mother and two brothers. Mathilde hates that there is a whole part of his life she knows nothing about. All the questions she never asked him sink to the bottom of her heart, tangling into knots.

Once the semester ends, she shocks her parents when she refuses to go home to 64 Clement.

Instead, she climbs into the backseat of a VW bug with a broken taillight that is painted with sunflowers. She tags along with two other students from her dorm who are driving to Point Judith to catch the ferry to Block Island where they will make money waitressing all summer. Mathilde does not get hired as a waitress. The only job she can get is cleaning hotel rooms, but she doesn't mind. She works six days a week and goes to the laundromat on the seventh because she dreads the emptiness of the seventh day and takes other girls' shifts whenever she can. That is, until she meets Mike.

Some of the people she works with have access to a washing machine in the place they rent, but not Mathilde. Her housing arrangement is one shared room with three mattresses on the floor and a bathroom across the hall. That's it. They don't even have kitchen privileges.

There's a big, modern laundromat on the new harbor side of the island, but Mathilde's room is on the old harbor side of the island. She doesn't have a car and isn't about to spend her earnings to rent a bike, so she has no option but to use the laundromat that has only four washers, two dryers and inevitably, a machine out of service.

To beat the crowd of vacationing mothers who bring in baskets of towels that take forever to dry, Mathilde learns to get there first thing in the morning when the laundromat opens and often has her knitting with her. Mathilde's roommates mock her relentlessly for such an old-fashioned hobby so the only time she can knit in peace is late at night when they are all out partying and she has the room to herself or, Sunday mornings at the laundromat.

It doesn't matter that she is making a plain pullover, knitting always makes Mathilde feel hopeful—the promise of what is being formed between her hands, stitch by stitch, feels full of possibility—like maybe this time, it will look as good as the one on the model. Plus knitting is something she gets to talk about with Lonny.

It's raining the morning Mike comes in with a green duffle bag on one shoulder. Mathilde sits barefoot on top of the dryer trying to stay warm while her sneakers—which got drenched on the way over—bang around with her clothes. She looks down at her knitting, grateful to hide behind the activity of it, but also wondering if this guy is gonna make some kind of stupid comment about how only old women knit. If she could leave, she would. Mathilde doesn't want to stay in the small, cramped space with a guy whose head nearly touches the ceiling, but the rain is coming down so hard water pops up off the sidewalk.

Mike points to the sign. *Do not put sneakers in the dryer.*

Mathilde jumps off the machine. "I can take them out," she says.

"Don't," says Mike. He smiles. "I was joking."

Mathilde climbs back up on the dryer hoping that her body weight muffles the pounding. She pulls her bare feet in to sit cross-legged and watches Mike as he loads the washing machine. She has never seen a guy run laundry before; he knows exactly what to do. He separates his darks and whites. He puts the detergent in first.

When he glances over to see her watching him, she looks back down at her knitting, but for the next forty-five minutes there is nowhere to go because the rain has them pinned inside.

It feels easy and familiar to talk with Mike. It's almost like she has met him before. He's Irish Catholic like her mom's family and even reminds her a little bit of her uncles with his straight sandy hair and super pale, thickly freckled skin. He has a funny accent sort of like Southie, but different.

"Pawtucket," he says when she asks. "Rhode Island."

Mathilde knows all about Rhode Island. She tells Mike about the books Uncle Wesley gave her. Books about Roger Williams and the Wampanoag and the Narragansett.

And then, the most terrible thing happens. In that stinky laundromat with stained yellow walls and missing panels in the ceiling. Mathilde begins to cry. While the dryer underneath her shakes back and forth and the swish of the washing machine goes one direction, pauses, and then goes the other direction, she sobs, hard. Snotty. Choking.

Mike hands her a red bandanna. "It's not that dirty," he says. "You can blow your nose in it. I'll throw it in the next load when you're done."

But she doesn't give it back. The rain stops. They carry their clean laundry next door to the ice cream shop that is open on Sunday mornings because it also sells coffee and muffins. Mike buys two blueberry muffins, two orange juices and carries them over to where Mathilde sits in the corner booth. Mike explains all the anger and confusion she is feeling has a name—it's called grief.

For the rest of the summer, Mathilde does not take any extra shifts on Sundays. Mike has a truck. They explore Mohegan Bluffs and walk for hours on the beach during low tide collecting shells, stones, and bits of sea glass. A week before she is due to climb back into the VW bug and return to BU, Mike talks her into bundling up with blankets and pillows in the back of his pickup so they can stay up all night and watch the sun rise.

Anjanette pulls a shimmery black linen and silk piece from her closet and tosses it to Mathilde. "Put that on. Trust me. You can't tell how good it is until it's on."

The dress is really more of a tunic. It has a jewel neckline, no sleeves, a somewhat boxy shape but somehow it lands everywhere right. Chic, short and loose. Mathilde keeps turning in the mirror to get another look.

"Oh my god," she says, "It can't be this good. This is like the greatest dress on the planet."

"Right?" says Anjanette. She digs some leggings out from a bureau drawer stuffed with hosiery.

"Purple tights?" Mathilde cringes. "I can't pull that off."

"Aubergine," says Anjanette. "One, nobody is looking at you. Two, when have I ever not made you look fabulous?"

It's true. In eighth grade, when Mathilde began crumbling at the thought of the all-school presentation she had to do, Anjanette didn't only draw posters of the five tribes of the Iroquois Confederacy, she also helped Mathilde put together an outfit that made her feel strong and beautiful. Mathilde wouldn't have even known what Doc Martens were if it weren't for Anjanette.

The Cooper Gallery is sparking with the energy and voices of people dressed to the nines when Mathilde arrives. The turnout is sensational.

Mathilde sees Anjanette talking to Paul and walks over to join them. Paul grew up with Mathilde and Anjanette. It's like running into a cousin, completely familiar as if she had seen him a few weeks ago when, in fact, Mathilde only ever sees Paul at Anjanette's October show.

"You cut your hair," says Paul.

"Herself," Anjanette says with a drawl. Mathilde makes a face at both of them. Nothing like being fifteen all over again.

"It's very punk," offers Paul.

"Don't encourage her," says Anjanette. "She's gotta deal with that shit."

Anjanette leaves them to walk over to another group.

Mathilde finds herself standing next to a couple Paul seems to know.

"Mathilde lives in Dedham," Paul says. The couple looks to Mathilde to pick up the lead and offer more.

She feels the weight of what it would take to explain that she lived in Dedham for thirty-two years. How she and Mike raised their children there. Should she tell them that her husband is dead? That the house she never liked was sold last May? Maybe she should do a full-on TMI and mention that before checking herself into McLean a month ago, she gave herself a haircut with a pair of garden shears. Instead, she simply nods, yes—so much easier.

Paul and Mathilde don't talk as they move from image to image. He eats pistachios, slowly, depositing the empty shell into the pocket of his blazer until Mathilde gives him a look to quit it.

Mathilde has never missed an opening. Even the year she was nine months pregnant with Susannah, she was there, waddling about with Mike nervously accompanying her back and forth to the bathroom as if she was going to suddenly have the baby when all that was happening is that she would have to dribble a few droplets of pee every five minutes. Mathilde kept every poster from every single show—even the xeroxed 8" x 11" paper signs from the very early days that she and Anjanette stapled to telephone poles and thumbtacked to grocery store bulletin boards.

Mathilde gazes around the beautiful gallery space. It's only been the past few years that Anjanette has been showing her work in such upscale, traditional spaces. Thirty years to get the recognition she deserves, but damn if she didn't do it on her own terms.

Anjanette turns and sees Mathilde gazing at her. If she could, Mathilde would do one of their big celebration shimmies, but tonight's too fancy for that. Instead, Mathilde pumps her fist against her heart and points at Anjanette who gives a smile in return before turning back to the conversation she is in.

Whatever she thinks she knows of Anjanette's journey, Mathilde knows that she doesn't know the half of it. When they were thirteen, Anjanette was going to the Museum of Fine Arts so often that she was given a membership for her birthday. On many Friday afternoons and lots of Saturday mornings, Mathilde would trail along. One Saturday there was a new docent at the entry to the Textile and Fashion Arts, one of the collections they liked to frequent. He was a paunchy old white guy who wasn't that much taller than they were. Maybe a retired professor? He clasped his hands behind his back and leaned forward as if to impart great knowledge.

"Is this your first visit to a museum, dear?" he asked, directing the question to Anjanette.

She bristled at the implication and shook him off like a stupid bug that had landed on her shoulder.

"No," replied Anjanette. "But it's obviously *your* first day on the job." She walked past not waiting to see his reaction.

"What a dick," Mathilde whispered, pressing against Anjanette's shoulder. Anjanette didn't respond. They didn't talk about it, but the afternoon soured. It was a long time before Anjanette suggested they visit the textile displays.

Someone bumps into Mathilde. Her drink sloshes. "Sorry," Mathilde says to the guy's back as he walks away.

"He bumped into you," says Paul. "Why are you saying sorry?"

"I wasn't paying attention." Mathilde checks to make sure she hasn't spilled any wine on Anjanette's dress. Mathilde feels her lack of chatting with Paul must be rude. She wants to explain. "I get so nostalgic. So many memories always flood in. I get a bit lost in my head."

"You're good," says Paul. Mathilde smiles. What a pleasure to be released from the obligation of making conversation. They wait for the group ahead of them to move along. Mathilde gives Paul another smile. She likes that they can drift along together, each in their own world.

Anjanette was nineteen when the Guerrilla Girls launched on MoMA. She told Mathilde that nobody in the traditional gallery world was gonna be interested in the work of a young Black woman who had never finished high school. Her focus was to display her work where it would be understood and appreciated, so she put all her efforts to developing relationships with the NCAAA, as well as the art communities in Roxbury and Dorchester. She had shows in cafes and diners, in school gyms, in the lobbies of apartment buildings and once, in a barbershop.

Over the years she developed a fierce, local following and a couple of solid connections to gallerists in Chicago and Atlanta thanks to Morton Ainsley, a painter and professor at MassArt who was her self-appointed mentor. Morton, or Dr. M, as Anjanette called him, ensured she got the feedback and critiques she needed to develop. But outside of the occasional participation in a group show where she might agree to ship out a couple of pieces, Anjanette only releases new work once a year, in October.

This year, Anjanette has titled her show, CROWNS.

Images of cow parsnip and poppies are everywhere in pencil drawings and oil paintings. The plants are used to tell a story of transformation beginning with a cluster of cow parsnip, the circlet of tiny white flowers at the top of its tight orbs before it opens, is likened to a bevy of young girls. The tale moves through different iterations, plants together and alone, until it ends with a series of young warriors with the smooth heads and sculptural tufts of dried poppies.

Mathilde and Paul wind their way over to read Anjanette's version of the artist's statement. When she was just starting out, Anjanette resisted this traditional requirement but, eventually, she found a way to do it in her own unique way. For Mathilde, it is one of her favorite parts of the show—she loves getting a glimpse into Anjanette's process and learning more about what might have inspired the show—it's like finding the cherry at the bottom of a sundae.

This year's statement is a piece of paper ripped from a sketchpad with an old polaroid taped to the center. The word CROWNS is scrawled across the top in black magic marker. In the photo, which is faded and slightly out of focus, Anjanette's oldest brother Daniel is laughing as he sits in a chair with one leg draped over the arm, strings of purple and green beads across his chest, a crown on his head. In the thick white space at the bottom of the polaroid, a faint pen scribble: *1980, Mardi Gras king.*

The room begins to crush in on Mathilde. Daniel had a laugh like no one she's ever known. He was always so gentle and so kind—he had lent her his copy of Emerson's essay "Self-Reliance"—she still has it; she never got the chance to return it. They all thought he'd come back. An adolescent outburst. He'd be back.

Beautiful, beautiful Daniel. Where is he? Is he safe? Is he okay? Is he alive? Mathilde can barely stand. She feels Paul's hand on her elbow leading her to sit on a bench where she drops her purse to the floor, head to her knees.

The morning after the show, Lonny's car is not in the driveway.

Mathilde would have been down earlier but she got caught up in texts with Susannah. The last time they had spoken was before Mathilde checked herself into McLean. That call had ended badly with Mathilde shouting awful things at Susannah. When she got home from the show last night, she texted Susannah to say how sorry she was, how wrong she was. To tell her she loved her. Her daughter texted back this morning to say, *no worries. I probably said some things, too. I am between* *paychecks can you spot me $800? I can pay you back on the 15th.*

Mathilde carries her mug of coffee into the dining room where Anjanette sits at the table filing last night's sales into the ledger book. The ledger is old style. Every single painting or piece of art Anjanette has ever sold is recorded here. The pages stack up thickly because of the way Anjanette documents the piece with a photograph, and notes taped into place about who it went to and for how much. Mathilde knows better than to ask if Anjanette is keeping a digital record. Anjanette does not even have a cell phone.

"You should keep that in a safe deposit box," Mathilde says. "What if something happened to it?"

"You wanna be my husband or my momma?" Anjanette does not like to be told what to do.

Mathilde sits, heavily. "I'm just saying—" The coffee sloshes slightly as she sets it down.

"Well, don't." Anjanette cuts her off. Usually, Anjanette has a post-show buoyancy, a high she can ride for weeks, but not today. Anjanette scoops Mojo up off the floor. The dog licks at Anjanette's ear then settles onto her lap as she strokes his head.

What must it be like, Mathilde wonders, to be an artist in a family. It's a no win. Bring up what everyone wants to keep buried—knowing you are going to hurt, shock or somehow upset the people you love. What if they get mad and don't love you anymore?

Without Anjanette's music playing upstairs or Lonny's podcast running on bluetooth in the kitchen, the house has a deep stillness. It's the first time since she got here that Mathilde actually feels the space.

"Your mom's lucky you never left," says Mathilde.

Anjanette makes a face and gestures to the ledger. "You think I'd be doing this if I had to hustle?"

"No, I get that," says Mathilde. "I'm just saying—you don't know what it's like to have a house go empty. It sucks. You've buffered her from that."

"Yeah well," says Anjanette. She releases a long exhale of air and looks over at Mathilde the way she did when they were kids, about to share a secret.

"I saw Daniel. Last spring. He was driving a lawn mower at Mount Auburn cemetery."

Mathilde's heart picks up its pace after Anjanette mentions her brother.

"Did you talk to him?" Mathilde asks.

"I was so shocked to see him. I didn't know what to say. And then he rode away cause there were people arriving for a funeral. I've gone back again and again, but I haven't seen him."

Mathilde gets up and walks around the table to stand next to Anjanette. She bends down and wraps her arms around Anjanette's body. Anjanette buries her face into Mathilde's shoulder.

"I'm sorry I told you not to get wiggy. I'm an idiot." Mathilde hates that her words are so lame. "And, you're gonna see Daniel again. Somehow. I don't know how, but I know that I love you. I love you so much. I'm so proud of you. That was such a beautiful show. So beautiful. And, I really, really hope I don't have wicked B.O."

Anjanette snorts a laugh into Mathilde's armpit. She lifts her head up. Her eyes are wet. She wipes her nose on her sleeve. "I'm so tired," says Anjanette.

Mathilde releases the hug and sits in the chair next to her. She holds Anjanette's hand, gently circling the callouses in her friend's palm with her thumb.

"Fucking life," says Anjanette.

"I fucking hate it," says Mathilde.

Rhinebeck
October 2017

Lonny and her friend Gerri are bringing Mathilde with them on their yearly knitting weekend at a yarn fair somewhere in upstate New York.

"It's not a yarn fair," Lonny corrects her. "It's Rhinebeck." She says it as if they were headed to Coachella or Burning Man. Whatever, thinks Mathilde.

Mathilde gazes at the back of their heads. Lonny has tied a polka dot scarf around the soft bun of pure white hair at the nape of her neck. Gerri's hair is salt and pepper at the roots, but the top curls are bright magenta; she wears big orange earrings that swing as she talks. Their chatter is punctuated with gusts of high-pitched, lips together giggling as if they will always be young when they get together. Mathilde tries to follow along, but they are speaking a language utterly unto themselves. She doesn't understand any of the references to people or events, so she lets go and sinks back to burrow under the blanket of color rippling past.

Mathilde doesn't believe in angels or karma or anything that could be called magic, but this moment right here? She wishes this moment could last forever. Her head tilts to gaze out the car window at blue sky flocked with trees of gold, orange, red, and yellow rushing past. Riding in the back seat, she feels like a little kid. This bubble of nothingness—not responsible for driving, not expected to contribute to the conversation going on in the front seats—she can be lost in no time, no space, bathed in all this glory of color and sunlight.

What's disorienting is that she didn't say yes. This trip wasn't Mathilde's choice, but it wasn't as if there was an invitation to refuse—no soft suggestion, *you should come with us,* for her to decline. It was a directive. "You'll come with us," Lonny had said. And so here she is, in the backseat of Gerri's emerald green Toyota Avalon as it merges onto Mass Pike and heads west through the spectacle of October's foliage.

"We're here." Gerri reaches around to tap Mathilde's knee, then hits the lever under the steering wheel to pop the trunk. Mathilde sits up. No idea how long she was asleep. She rubs at her face to make the creases go away from where the canvas tote handle has dug into her cheek and watches an unending stream of bodies surge past the car. Oh my god, they were not kidding.

Lonny and Gerri had teased her to be ready for the hordes of knitters as if they were something to be feared like Vikings or Visigoths. Mathilde honestly thought it was a joke, but as they make their way to the entrance of the Duchess Fairgrounds she knows she has never seen anything like this. There are literally thousands of women—maybe there are some men in here somewhere, but all she is seeing are women—wearing hand-knit sweaters, hand-knit shawls, hand-knit hats—many of them wearing all three at once.

With a hastily made plan to meet back up by the button booth in a couple of hours, Lonny and Gerri head off to hit their favorite vendors leaving Mathilde to stand like a stunned rock as a rushing river of bodies draped in every variety of wool pushes past with an urgency usually reserved for Christmas shopping or tent sales.

The smell of kettle corn lures Mathilde to turn and begin walking with the crowd. She grips her purse against her belly, not so much from a fear of thievery but as if it could provide some kind of compass. Before arriving, Mathilde had imagined picking up some yarn for a new project, but now, she is utterly—completely—inundated by the quantities of yarn stuffed into every booth for as far as the eye can see. It is too much. No way to choose. She is out of her depth.

Mathilde lets herself be carried by the surge of chattering bodies as it passes booth after booth of yarn displays. Raw fleece. Carded batts of wool. Knitting needles. Crochet hooks. Hand stitched project bags made from block printed linens. It's endless. It's exhausting.

She wants to stop but doesn't know where to go. Her fists clench and unclench. It's too soon to be out in the world. All these people—so happy and excited. She does not belong here.

Mathilde finds a place to sit on the ground by a cluster of pumpkins. Growing up, Autumn was always her favorite season. It meant back to school, soft sweaters and new books. As an adult, October meant getting out of Dedham to go north for Anjanette's annual art show.

But now, the masses of pumpkins just make her sad. Mathilde wishes she had said no thank you to Lonny. She wishes she were still in bed. This is gonna be a long day and it's going to be embarrassing to meet back up with Lonny and Gerri empty-handed.

Oh, who cares. It's been so long since Mathilde knit anything anyway. Mathilde rubs at her arm. There was that sweater she was knitting in college. She had forgotten all about it until her parents were moving out of 64 Clement and her mother told her she'd found it in some stuff Mathilde had left there. "Just chuck it," Mathilde had said and hung up the phone.

Mathilde was angry with her mother for selling 64 Clement and somehow it felt like this was a way to punish her, but it was Mathilde's stomach that ached remembering how Lonny had helped her choose the lovely gray and cream Lopi yarns. Lonny had encouraged her to knit that complicated sweater—an Icelandic pattern—the hardest thing Mathilde had ever attempted to knit. *You can do it. It's not hard. It's just new.* That's what Lonny always said. But it was hard. Mathilde had been struggling with it and was going to ask Lonny for help when she went home after the semester ended but then, Uncle Wesley died and—

Oh who cares. Mathilde kicks at the dirt. She looks up at the sky and exhales deeply. Better that she didn't have another unfinished project for Mike to tease her about.

A crowd of kids are circling around. This must be a pumpkin carving station. Mathilde stands up and starts walking again; her hips are sore from sitting on the ground.

She comes upon a small break between two vendor booths that looks like a bit of an alley and trundles down it to get free from the crush of bodies, voices and visual overwhelm. At the far end of the lane she comes upon another aisle of booths with nothing but fields behind them.

Tucked into the center spot is a small booth with a quirky sign, *One-Pot Wonders*.

The booth feels like something out of Harry Potter's train station— in plain view—but somehow invisible to the people walking past. Perhaps because it is bordered on one side with a distraction of yarns in neon shades, and on the other, a man loudly hawking spinning wheels.

In the midst of chaos, One-Pot Wonders holds a moment of quiet. A rough-hewn trestle table that might as well have been salvaged from a shipwreck fronts the booth. Bleached and worn smooth, it sits bare. Behind it, a shaker rack with seven pegs display the only goods for sale: seven colors of yarn and not that many skeins in each row.

The stall is clearly plain by choice. A chippy yellow chair sits behind the table. That's it.

There might not be much yarn, but what is here is stunning. Even more fun are the names, a pencil scribble on scraps of cardstock— Malgudi Orange, Rainy Day Yellow, Littleneck Gray, Kumamoto Gold, Sartori Pink—but as extraordinary as each of those are, they are all backdrop to the skeins that hang in the middle of the display, Caledonia Blue.

And what a blue it is—if it even is. The color is unearthly, unworldly. The base mixes seafoam and summer sky with a deep blue of late autumn hydrangea, some strands are almost inky green while woven through are glints of a turquoise as true as the Bermuda sea.

"Lovely, isn't it?" says the woman.

Mathilde looks up. The woman is petite and attired in some kind of Tasha Tudor meets the Marvelous Mrs. Maisel mash-up. She wears a dress over a skirt topped with an apron—or is it a smock—of tiny red flowers. Each piece is a cotton print in a contrasting vintage pattern that somehow all works together. On top she wears a finely knit, obviously handspun, pale sage cashmere cardigan that is so short it's practically a bolero with a great wooden button between her breasts to hold it in place.

The woman could be anywhere between forty and her late sixties. Impossible to tell. Her hair is pinned up with sparkly bobby pins and a tiny, jeweled dragonfly. Her lipstick is a deep pink. There is a teensy swipe of glitter on each eyelid.

"Um," Mathilde agrees, finally. The yarn is unbearably soft and squishy, the exact weight you would want in a favorite sweater. "It's beautiful."

Mathilde turns it in the sunlight. There is something about the yarn. Enchanting, she decides. Kind of like this woman who seems a bit of a fairy sprite herself.

"I was trying for the blue in Mary Cassat's *Woman Bathing*—do you know it?"

Mathilde shakes her head, no. Anjanette would.

"No matter, anyhoo—it is a most wonderful hue." The woman giggles at her wordplay as she pulls at the skein to show Mathilde. "See, it's still in there a little bit."

The woman steps back and half dances behind the table as if they were kids playing store and shopkeeper. "Nothing ever comes out exactly as I imagine, of course. I do it all in one pot and boom—that's it."

The woman keeps talking about the process, the dyes, the plants she uses to make the dyes. Mathilde is not listening closely; she is watching the woman. Mathilde wants to know how a person can be so exuberant and lighthearted on such a hot day, standing by an empty table in the middle of nowhere.

"There's enough of this blue to make a sweater," the woman says.

Mathilde lets that sink in. There's a sweater she remembers, vaguely. Top-down, three skeins, super basic but it would look amazing in this color. She lifts the tag—90 dollars! Mathilde tries not to show shock, but that is a gamechanger. She'll knit a damn hat.

She pays, thanks the woman, and walks off with her one skein of yarn in a brown paper bag feeling like an absolute fool.

Her skin is prickly with heat. She takes off the hoodie she's wearing over a short sleeve t-shirt, but a few minutes later she pulls it back on as the wind is brisk. It's that awful time of season change when she can't get comfortable. Stupid. She should have worn a cardigan, not a hoodie. The crowds seem to be getting thicker, the sun hotter. She feels overwhelmed, overheated, and chilled all at once. Irritated and annoyed—again, she wishes she'd never come. There's a pile of hay bales that seem to be set up as a place to sit. She decides to wait here until it is time to meet up with Lonny and Gerri.

Did you just spend ninety dollars on a single skein of yarn? Lady, you are loco. Mathilde puts her head in her hands. Her palms rub against the terrible haircut. *Is she really walking around in public like this? Why doesn't she do everybody a favor and put the paper bag over her head?* She pulls the skein out of the bag.

Oh my god. It's beautiful. It's luscious. Her back straightens and she takes a deep breath. The yarn is even more dazzling now—utterly gorgeous. Okay, maybe not so crazy. She feels almost lucky. Like she's found a treasure.

Mathilde fingers the soft yarn and thinks again about that sweater— the one she started once Toby began first-grade, but never finished. It has to be the simplest pattern in the universe, the neck is a few rows of seed stitch and the body is stockinette. It only needs three skeins. Fuck it, she stands up. Who cares how much it costs. She hasn't bought anything in ages.

I am going to knit that sweater and finish it she says to herself as she marches back to the One-Pot Wonders booth. She sees a flash of the yellow chair and rushes up to the trestle table.

"Hi," Mathilde calls out to the woman who must be behind the booth. "I was just here and—"

A young woman steps out from behind the curtain. This woman wears blue jeans and a knit cap.

"Yes?" says the younger woman.

"Uh, I was looking for someone else—" says Mathilde. "The yarn dyer?"

"You mean Effie." The young woman smiles. "She's gone. You just missed her."

"Oh." The disappointment jabs Mathilde in the chest. "Oh, okay—may I have two skeins of Caledonia Blue, please?"

"I'm sorry." The girl gestures to the empty peg. "It's all gone."

"But, but I was just here—" Mathilde looks around, a bit desperate in her confusion. There is absolutely no traffic in this booth. People walk right by without so much as a glance.

"I know, it goes fast." The girl reaches up to straighten the few remaining skeins of yellow and gray that are all that's left on the nearly empty shaker rack. Then she reaches into her pocket and produces a business card edged in gold.

"Here, take Effie's card. She might have more back in her studio."

Effie Finisterre. An address in Wales. No cell phone, no email, no website.

"Great," says Mathilde, forcing a smile. "This is a big help.

62 Clement
November 2017

Some people keep a record of their greatest meals. Mathilde's grand-mother did that. There was a small leather bound book that came to her when her grandmother died, a travel journal of Grammy's. Each page a careful record of what they spent each day:—*gas 35 cents, coffee and apple pie 15 cents, crust (too much lard), waitress (a bit curt), pot roast (good—asked for seconds!), carrots (undercooked), restroom (clean).* Her grandmother loved road trips—and apparently—pecan pie, which made frequent appearances in the journal.

Mathilde has never recorded any trips, but in her mind, she holds a roster of her greatest sleeps—those handful of times in her life where the sleep was so deep, so sweet, so utterly transporting that she would want to be able to touch on the feeling again. Lying in bed on the third floor of Lonny's house, she finds that richness.

The door snaps open unceremoniously. It swings wide smacking into the wall and bouncing back. Anjanette stops it with one bare foot. She wears wide legged pajama pants that are obviously a size too large as she has them rolled over at the waist, a cropped t-shirt, and one of Timo's old USPS shirts that is frayed on the bottom hem. Mathilde doubts Anjanette would ever dare wear Timo's shirt in front of Lonny. This must be her secret upstairs wardrobe.

"You, in that goddamned bed." Anjanette holds a watering can and a plastic spray bottle.

Is she here to apologize, wonders Mathilde. Or maybe, she wants me to say I am sorry.

The night before, Anjanette came home to find that Mathilde had washed her laundry and was now folding her clothes neatly into a pile on the kitchen table.

"Are those my jeans?" Anjanette asked. Not pleased.

"I was doing laundry, anyway, thought I'd throw in some of yours."

"Well don't." Anjanette dropped her bags on the bench by the door and kicked off her shoes.

Mathilde finished folding one of Anjanette's long-sleeved t-shirts so that it ended in a perfect flat square.

Anjanette went to the fridge.

"I made some granola this afternoon and there's yogurt—" Mathilde offers.

Anjanette spun around. "Stop being a wife."

"I'm not being a wife."

"Yes, you are." Anjanette grabbed a liter of Sprite from the door of the fridge then bopped the door shut with her hip. She walked around Mathilde, whose hands were frozen atop the stack of warm laundry, to head into the pantry. Anjanette came out with the soda bottle under one arm, a bag of chocolate chips, a box of graham crackers in one hand, a jar of peanut butter in the other and went up to her room.

Mathilde followed a few minutes later leaving the laundry basket outside Anjanette's door before heading up to bed.

The friction with Anjanette has been part of the growing energy between them. She knows this is Anjanette's way of keeping boundaries, but Mathilde needs to feel useful. She needs to feel like there is a point to her. Plus, she wants Anjanette to know how grateful she is for bringing her to Lonny's and letting her stay with them. It has been so healing and good. But as Anjanette's words sank deeper into her chest, the hurt mutated into anger.

Fuck her, thought Mathilde. I was only trying to help. She sat on the edge of the bed fondling the skein of blue yarn that seemed to give her such comfort.

The little card with the woman's address on it fell to the floor.

Effie Finisterre
Brightmore Cottage, 42 Clover
St Dogmaels Wales

In a flash, she has the vision. She will go to the woman's house and get two more skeins. She will knit that sweater. She won't quit or give up. She will finish something all the way through.

And now it's morning. Anjanette is here, but not for apologies. She is waiting for an answer.

"Why do you care?" huffs Mathilde. "You need me for something?"

Anjanette turns to her plants. It is an elaborate routine given the multitude of plants. She doesn't just water them. It's more like a doctor's visit. She asks them questions as she plucks dead leaves. She peers under leaves and makes tut-tutting sounds. Some of the plants get baby talk. The maidenhair fern is treated as if she were a visiting dignitary. Anjanette leaves the room repeatedly to refill the watering can in the bathroom.

Mathilde props the pillow behind her head. She watches as Anjanette takes down the hanging spider plant by the window to inspect it more closely. Her movements are sure, so goddamned contented. Such confidence. Anjanette knows who she is and what she wants from this world.

Before Mike died, there was a small party celebration on the Cape for the wife of one of his friends. Her friends, too, she guesses—though it always felt that they were Mike's friends. The wife had just been promoted to vice president at WGBH. She was two years younger than Mathilde. That was the same week her dentist informed her she was retiring and handed Mathilde a list of suggested replacements. Retiring? Her dentist had kids the same age as Mathilde. She ran half-marathons. She played tennis. She was too young to retire. Twenty-five years, she said with a smile. But what will you do, Mathilde had asked. I'm taking a year to figure that out beginning with a three-week trip to Patagonia, she'd said. Her dentist had a career, had kids and was now starting a whole nother chapter of her life. What had Mathilde done with her life? The thought was crushing.

"You spinning shit?" asks Anjanette, looking at her.

Mathilde pulls her knees up to her chest. "I don't understand how you can even be friends with me. It's like I've been sleepwalking through my whole life. I feel guilty for taking up space."

"No lie about you sleeping," says Anjanette. She turns and places the spider plant back onto its hanger. "But you can quit that taking up space shit." Anjanette pauses. She works a crick out of her neck.

"How about you start seeing it like you're living a fairy tale," says Anjanette. "You been sleeping for a hundred years and now you're waking up—nothing wrong with that." Anjanette mists a plant near the bed then spritzes Mathilde in the face.

"Hey—" says Mathilde.

"I thought you were having lunch with Paul today."

Mathilde's legs jolt out straight. "Today is Monday?"

Cambridge
May 1981

"That's where I live," says Paul.

He reaches across Mathilde to point at a clapboard house painted cherry red that has yellow roses tumbling over a black wrought-iron fence. The bus jolts forward and Paul's arm touches her chest by mistake.

"Sorry," Paul says, putting his hands back on his knees.

"It's fine." Mathilde hadn't been paying attention. She doesn't know what street they are on. The bus driver is clearly trying to avoid traffic on Mass Ave by taking a bunch of smaller streets to get back to school, but Mathilde was thinking about the argument waiting for her when she gets home. This summer is Mathilde's sixteenth birthday and her mom wants to throw a sweet sixteen party. Rosie doesn't understand. Nobody will come.

Mathilde looks back at Paul's house. "It's pretty," she says. "I like the roses. Your mom must be a good gardener."

"It's my dad, actually," says Paul. "He's big into gardening."

"Oh," Mathilde is embarrassed. Why does she always say the wrong thing?

Today's ninth grade field trip to Emerson's house in Concord felt weird. For the first time, Anjanette isn't the one to share Mathilde's bus seat on a school trip. Anjanette has not come back to school.

"I don't think she's coming back," Mathilde says to Paul. Their shoulders jostle as the bus lumbers over potholes. "I bring her her school stuff but—" Mathilde doesn't tell Paul that Anjanette is not doing any of the homework.

Without Anjanette there to be the center of the conversation, Mathilde and Paul have been eating their lunch at the table on the far side of the cafeteria, just the two of them. Paul is Anjanette's friend from art class. He is in all the advanced math and science classes, so Mathilde doesn't have any classes with him, but he is really nice. And it's always easy to talk to him. Especially now when everything feels awful all the time. She doesn't know how to help Anjanette. Her parents tell her it's best not to talk about what happened. Mathilde misses Paul on the days he doesn't come to lunch.

Maybe she should ask him to meet her at Brigham's or to go to a movie. But not like a date.

"What are you doing this summer?" Mathilde asks. That could be an easy way to talk about ice cream and see if he would want to go to Brigham's sometime.

"Oh," says Paul. "We're going to Maine."

"For like, camp?"

Paul shakes his head. His arms are folded across his chest. His dad has a new job up in Maine. They're moving.

"Oh," says Mathilde. Relieved she didn't ask him to go to a movie or anything, but also, kind of feeling something else, too. She had just started to think maybe she and Paul could be friends.

Harvard Square
November 2017

Paul's wife is out of the picture, but Mathilde doesn't ask why. She doesn't want to talk about spouses—dead, gone, missing, or otherwise. She keeps the door to that conversation firmly shut and Paul doesn't seem to mind.

Paul doesn't seem to mind anything. It is nearly one o'clock when she arrives and he looks up with the same open smile as if she were smack on time. When the waitress informs him they are all out of corn chowder, the daily special that he has just told Mathilde was why he chose this cafe, he simply looks over to the menu board and says, "Okay, well you can bring me a tuna sandwich, then."

Mathilde feels doubly bad that she caused him to miss the soup. She orders avocado toast and a cup of tomato soup.

"Oh, you'll like that," says Paul. "It's really good."

Mathilde pulls her lips up into a smile, but inwardly, the panic begins. What a terrible idea this is. Why is she here?

Mathilde unfolds a napkin and smooths it over her lap. How is she going to make it through the hour with Mr. Pleasant when her chest feels like the compressor behind a nail gun—not sure what will shoot out of her mouth but guessing it might be sharp and dangerous.

Every direction she turns her thoughts brings Mathilde pain. She is still processing the fight with Anjanette, but she doesn't want to talk about it with Paul. Mathilde also doesn't want to talk about the discord with her daughter, or the feeling that she has overstayed her welcome, or her dread of November, or the constant anxiety of fascists in the White House, children in cages, the world on fire as it has ever been—probably ever will be—and like she has ever done anything to save it. There is nothing she wants to talk about.

"I ordered us some tea," says Paul as he tips the spout of the ceramic pot and fills her cup neatly before pouring a cup for himself. He sets it down carefully. No rush. A man who doesn't have to be back at the office on a Monday afternoon.

"Are you retired?" asks Mathilde automatically, then immediately wishes that she hadn't. Why was it so easy to be with Paul at Anjanette's art show? Oh that's right—because they didn't talk. He ate pistachios as they moved around the room together, painting to painting. They hadn't had a conversation. They'd been doing the wallflower shuffle.

"Well, I'm no longer with Bose if that's what you mean," he says.

Mathilde doesn't reply. She hadn't meant anything. She didn't even know he worked at Bose. Turns out, Paul has created an online game site for people who love bridge that has a strong following

"Bridge," says Mathilde. "Isn't that for old people? Do they even know how to use the Internet?"

Paul laughs in a way that she knows he has heard the same questions a thousand times and not only is she predictable, she is a big old bore.

"Getting a foursome together for a game can be like herding cats or assembling an infield," explains Paul explains as the waitress sets down their food. "Even when people have a standing arrangement with a group, it's usually not more than once or twice a month. Bridgers are like any enthusiasts, pretty addictive and they want to play as much as they want and whenever they want—two in the morning for the insomniacs—ten a.m. for the bright-eyed and bushy-tailed."

"Two a.m.," says Mathilde. "Who else is up then?"

"Well, see—this is the beauty of it." Paul leans in with excitement. He lays out how his site has over four thousand members from all over the world—the UK, Hong Kong, Australia, Nevada, New York City, Bucks County, Pennsylvania, Menasha, Wisconsin—there is always someone up for a game.

"And you make money doing this?"

"Oh yeah—it's a membership," says Paul. "Ten dollars a month or fifty for the year. Most everyone buys the year pass. For an extra nineteen dollars, you get access to a message board and the classifieds. That turned out to be the biggest winner, and I use that to pay all the taxes."

He is proud of himself. Not in an awful arrogant way, but in a way that Mathilde admires—a quiet confidence. Mathilde does the math quickly in her head. Wow.

"I'm guessing you don't have much overhead?" she says.

"There was the initial investment—got my own server, a high-end database. Have to keep my equipment up, high speed internet—but no, not really. Just my own sweat equity. And since it's all out of my home, I get to deduct that."

"Win. Win. Win," says Mathilde. She watches him drink the last of his tea. "What's the name of your site?"

At this Paul seems embarrassed. Clearly he didn't choose the name.

"I can't change it now, but when I first started out I had no idea it would grow to what it's become so I went along with my daughter's suggestion."

Mathilde waits.

"Jonesingforbridge.com," he says.

"That's not terrible," says Mathilde.

"She said it was like a play on Bridget Jones—" Paul wags his head, still feeling awkward.

"Yeah, no—I got it," says Mathilde. "Your daughter still lives around here?"

"Oh, she moved away," says Paul. "She met a guy in grad school. They're living up in Vancouver. But, with—you know, technology—I see her all the time. You video chat with your kids?"

"Not so much," says Mathilde. "We're more of a texting family."

"Cerebral." He smiles.

Self-absorbed, thinks Mathilde but she gives a little nod to say, yes.

She admires the connection he clearly has cultivated. Maybe fathers have better relationships with their daughters? She thinks of how Timo doted on Anjanette. But what about Mike and Susannah?

"My daughter went to NYU because she wanted to be an actress," volunteers Mathilde. "But now she does any theater work she can get—mostly, she walks people's dogs for cash. Toby, my son, went to Chapel Hill. He lives in Charleston now—he's an interior designer. He's saving to buy a condo."

Paul nods. Why did she tell him all this? He doesn't want to hear about her kids any more than she wants to hear about his.

"Susannah and I don't really have the mother-daughter relationship, thing—you know," says Mathilde. "My son is great. Our steady Eddie, no drama there," she laughs.

Paul nods, listening.

Why is she still talking? It's like a dam has busted and she can't stop. The words just keep flowing out. She tells Paul about the fights. About the misunderstandings. The times she felt so let down. How back in August she had snapped at Susannah in such a violent and hostile way that seconds after she hung up, she had called McClean because she didn't know what was happening to her. She didn't know how to control her emotions. She tells him that this is the first time she has admitted how ashamed she is for doing such a crappy job and getting it so wrong.

"I don't know," says Paul. "From everything I've ever seen, I thought this was the norm for mothers and daughters."

She looks at him. He could not have said anything more perfect, but before she can tell him how comforting it was to hear that, a blast of cold air from the street hits their table as someone exits the cafe.

"I am so done with this weather," Mathilde says, shivering. "I am getting out of here."

Paul does not need her to explain. The first bitter cold day is like a punch in the face, but Paul's surprise at her plan is a mirror to her own. She is doing this? Mathilde says she is and somehow it makes it real.

Mathilde can also see Paul's surprise shift to a disappointment that he tries to mask with a cheery *good for you* smile. Oh god, Mathilde thinks—did he imagine they were going to be friends? Be more than friends? All the more reason to get out. Get out. Now that she had said it out loud the voice in her head is like a megaphone in a gymnasium. Get out.

How fast can she get packed? A passport. Fuck. Where is her passport? The last time she used it was for that trip with Mike and the kids to Quebec City—where the hell did she put it?

"Where're you headed?" asks Paul. "Florida?"

"Wales," she does not want to tell him about the yarn. "I have an errand to run."

"An errand. In Wales." He's funny. He's made her smile, for real.

"Yes. But then somewhere south where it will be warm, like Spain or Portugal."

"So you haven't really got it all planned out yet," says Paul.

"No, I do. Just a few details to dial in."

"What's your Instagram name? I'll follow along."

"Oh, I'm—not. I don't have any—I don't do apps, really. You know, just google maps."

The end of the lunch is all about Paul getting Mathilde onto Instagram and showing her the basics.

"This is how I stay in touch with my kids," he says.

How many kids? Mathilde doesn't ask. She doesn't want to know.

Mathilde heads to the bathroom. Too much tea, she thinks as she comes out of the stall. She catches sight of herself in the mirror. My god, she has got to deal with this hair—it's just not gonna be today. When Mathilde returns to their table, the plates are gone and Paul is out on the sidewalk talking to someone. She stops at the register to pay.

"Oh, your husband took care of it," says the girl. Mathilde is annoyed. Mostly because she wishes he hadn't done that, but also at the cheekiness of this girl to assume they are married. She is about to correct her; he is *not* my husband—but then thinks? Why bother? Who cares?

The wind is unkind. It sends grit into her face and the tissue she had been about to tuck back into her purse flies off into the street. She chases it, stomps it with her foot, then shoves it into the trash can that sits on the sidewalk where Paul is still talking with some old guy.

"Mathilde!" says Paul. "You remember Petey Prescott."

Mathilde hitches her purse up to her left shoulder and leaves her right hand on it, the arm tight across her chest in protection. This old guy cannot possibly be Peter Prescott.

"Once upon a time I would've said, unless you've been doing too many drugs, but at our age, I'll just say, unless you've got the Alzheimer's kicking in." He turns to Paul. "Mathilde sat in front of me for all of homeroom." Petey laughs. The cheeks of his two-day no shave face is grizzled with white. His navy skull cap reveals a mottled forehead that saw a lifetime of too much sun and not enough sunscreen; its pale skin is littered with freckles, age spots and broken capillaries. And, though the cap covers the top of his head, she can tell he is mostly bald. Hair sticks out from his ears. Clearly, no wife around to keep him groomed.

"Ma-TEE-ld Owen," says Petey. "Not Mathilda. Substitute teachers calling it out wrong and you would always correct them."

Again, Mathilde can't be bothered. Who cares. Her arm has not moved from where she grips her bag from sliding off her shoulder.

"It's Mathilde Scott now," says Paul. He fills the silence meant for Mathilde to say something while she turns her head away and tries to remove whatever the hell just flew into her eye.

Mathilde puts the plan together pretty quickly. Direct flight from Logan to Heathrow. Train to Paddington Station. Train to Swansea. Train to Whitland. Cab to Cardigan.

She leaves Wednesday night departing Boston at 9:30 p.m., arriving in London at 9:30 a.m. which will be perfect as another four hours to Wales has her arriving midday. Once she gets the yarn, she can just turn around and go straight back to London.

Mathilde clears out the last of her stuff and gets it all into the bags she came with. She still has to go down to the condo and get her passport and whatnot. All she has here is what she brought to the hospital.

"You're going to Wales." Lonny's words hit Mathilde hard in the belly like a dodgeball. When Lonny says it, it becomes real. Mathilde presses back against the wainscoting of the breakfast nook as if she could melt into the narrow spaces between each strap of wood.

Lonny waits for an answer. Mathilde makes a tentative nod.

"Good," says Lonny. Half of an acorn squash is cupped firmly in the palm of her left hand. With her right hand she scoops the pulp and seeds into the compost bucket that sits next to her on the kitchen counter. Lonny gives the squash one last scraping before setting it face down to join the others on the baking sheet.

Lonny hasn't asked her why she is going. Mathilde is determined not to tell anyone about the yarn. It sounds too unhinged. Crazy. She crosses and uncrosses her legs.

"Why is it good?" asks Mathilde.

"You're asking me?" Lonny turns around to face Mathilde, the wooden spoon sticking straight up in one hand, bits of the orange flesh threatening to drip to the floor. She puts the spoon in the sink and checks the oven temp.

"Maybe it's a bad idea. Too impulsive," says Mathilde, her hands at her temples. She presses the hair against her skull.

"You got somewhere else to be?" asks Lonny.

Mathilde doesn't answer but they both know she has nowhere to be. Worse, she worries that Lonny thinks she has been in this house too long. Overstayed her welcome. Time to move on.

Mathilde begins to list out all the things that might go wrong, why it is probably best that she cancel her reservations.

"Oh good night!" Lonny interrupts her. "Go on and go. Stop feeding worry."

Lonny slides the baking tray into the oven and shuts the door firmly. She turns to look at Anjanette who is coming out of the pantry with a box of vanilla wafers.

"Tell this girl to go on and go," Lonny says to her daughter.

"She trying it," Anjanette says as she walks out of the kitchen without even a glance down at Mathilde who responds by sticking her tongue out. This makes Lonny cackle.

"Squabbling like a couple of seagulls—" Lonny shakes her head. "Thought this house was done with teenagers."

"She started it," Mathilde replies.

In the end, Mathilde begs Anjanette to come with her; she will pay for everything. Anjanette just laughs, steps onto the ribbed mat that automatically opens the grocery store door and enters the shop with Mathilde on her heels like a child who thinks she can get a different answer if she asks enough times. Anjanette shakes a cart away from where they are nested one into the other and wheels it past the fruits and vegetables.

"Who'd take care of my plants?"

"We'll be back within the week," replies Mathilde. "You don't water them more than once a week."

"What about Mojo?"

"I'll pay for a kennel," says Mathilde

"Girl, you are losing your damn mind. You know I don't travel."

Except for the annual family trip each August to Martha's Vineyard—and that one time she went to New York City for the Kara Walker show—Anjanette never ventures far beyond Clement Street. If she can't get there by taking the T or the bus, she doesn't go. Anjanette doesn't have a driver's license or a passport. Mathilde knows this, but still she wheedles.

Anjanette grabs two boxes of oyster crackers and one jumbo packet of double stuff oreos without slowing her pace.

"You haven't even told me what in hell for, you are going all the hell the way across the ocean to some country that might not even be a country." Anjanette pauses and then laughs. "You trying to kidnap me?"

"Wales is a country," says Mathilde. "And you are an artist!! You need to see the world—"

Mathilde is feeling desperate. She cannot imagine making the trip on her own. The night before, she lay in bed and realized (with total humiliation) that she has never traveled on her own before. A trip that is going to require a plane, three trains and two car rides, not to mention a passport, seems like the wrong place to start.

"I'm a local artist," says Anjanette. She reaches into the refrigerator case for a can of whipped cream. "My people are here. Besides, I'm pretty sure Monet didn't get that memo."

"But don't you *want* to see the rest of the world? It's different than here."

"Says the woman who has never traveled."

"I've traveled—"

Anjanette gives Mathilde the fisheye but doesn't bother to prove herself right. Instead she says, "look at Faulkner."

"The guy who made the polio vaccine?"

Anjanette drops a bag of marshmallows into the cart. "Stop playing," says Anjanette. "The Nobel Prize-winning author for literature." She drags out the word literature, emphasizing each 't' the way Lonny would. Anjanette keeps talking as she turns down the cereal aisle.

"He lived his whole life in some small, little Mississippi town." She tosses a box of Rice Krispies into the cart where it lands on the flat pack of corn tortillas. "And you know Clementine Hunter did what she damned well pleased. She made people come to her."

Anjanette's dad Timo talked a lot about Clementine Hunter as a way of encouraging Anjanette's creativity and to make sure she didn't let anybody tell her she couldn't be an artist if she wanted.

"They don't give Nobel prizes for art," counters Mathilde.

"Same difference and besides, I don't paint for prizes. And," Anjanette pulls the cart up to the cashier and begins unloading her groceries onto the conveyor belt, "you have completely missed the point."

SKEIN II

Boston, Logan Airport
November 2017

Mathilde boards the plane and settles into her seat. She adjusts the pillow behind her lower back. This is not so hard. She is doing something new, that's all. This is an adventure. Fifty-two years old. That's not too old for an adventure, is it? This is not a mistake, right? It's fine. She's fine.

Until the woman sitting next to her asks the simple question, "where you headed?"

The panic roars back through the center of her body. Her throat clamps shut. Unable to reply, Mathilde forces a smile and nods yes. Grateful for the window seat, Mathilde turns to watch the night crew in their headphones and orange vests drive carts with shaking cabooses across the tarmac that is lined with endless rows of white lights. She thinks of her son Toby when he was a boy and the brightly colored little trains that hooked together with shiny, flat magnets. He would play with them for hours.

Mathilde feels a jab of guilt. She didn't mean to be rude. She turns back to explain, but the woman next to her is now typing on her phone.

What if Mathilde had answered the question? *I'm going to a place I have never been, where I know no one—except the woman I am going to see who doesn't know I am coming and doesn't even know my name— all so I can purchase two skeins of yarn to knit a sweater that I don't even have a pattern for.*

The woman looks up from her phone. Mathilde smiles and turns back to the window. Yeah, nobody's getting that story. That's crazy town.

Insane. What is she doing?

Mathilde reaches into her bag. She lifts out the soft cloud of blue yarn that she keeps wrapped in a silk scarf and tucks it under the blanket on her lap, as if she were smuggling a cat on board. A gentle warmth stretches across her shoulders and glides down her back. She exhales deeply. Maybe what she's doing *is* crazy. Maybe she's doing it all wrong, but she simply has to jump.

The plane lurches as the pilot releases the brake and begins to pull backward from the gate. Fingers buried in the yarn, Mathilde feels her chest soften and release. A sense of okayness comes over her that she has not felt in more years than she can remember. It feels so good to be carried away. To be held, cupped, in this seat. This blue yarn has cast a spell on her.

Mathilde looks down at the packet of pretzels the flight attendant dropped on her lap. Snack food. Handed out. In case she might be hungry when she just ate an hour ago. As she always does in odd moments, Mathilde can't help but to compare her life to the life of some anonymous person in a similar circumstance.

Mathilde couldn't sleep last night for fear of traveling on this trip alone. At her age. With a cell phone, a wallet full of cash and credit cards and yet, one of her ancestors, maybe more than one, traveled this same ocean in the opposite direction. On a ship. For weeks. Leaving everything and everyone she had ever known for the absolute unknown. Probably not getting up to the deck for sunlight and fresh air very often. How brave of her (Mathilde always assumes it was a female). The average age was twenty, but some of the girls were as young as thirteen. Thirteen. By herself. That's a powerful story. That's a heroic journey. What is missing in Mathilde that she doesn't want to learn more about that girl—devote herself to that? What is wrong with her?

Mathilde presses her cheek against the cold of the window. Aside from making sure her children know Columbus is not a man to celebrate and that Indigenous History is American History, what good did she ever do?

"Mathilde," Professor Gordon says, "Most of the history that's been written about the Irish focuses on the men, but unlike other immigrant groups, the women who immigrated actually outnumbered the men. That's an interesting aspect to explore."

Professor Gordon's office hours are late afternoon on Tuesdays and Thursdays. At first, Mathilde felt shy stopping by both days—as if she would be taking up too much of his time—but since she rarely has to share him with another student, she figures it's okay. Professor Gordon is Onondaga and introduces Mathilde to people she has never read about before: the Naskapi, Micmac, Penobscot, Powhatan, Tuscarora, and Lumbee. She loves learning the differences between each nation and can't believe it was only now, at the age of eighteen, that she understands how what she was taught in school was so twisted.

"Imagine," says Professor Gordon, "taking people from Belgium, Italy, Portugal, Sweden, France, Germany and Scotland and calling them all Moroccans because you were trying to land at Essaouira but got lost and landed in Antwerp instead."

If Professor Gordon carries the helpless rage and wild despair she feels as she faces one atrocity after the next, he keeps it private from her. His manner is gentle, but clinical. There is always a sense of balance; often when she thinks she is going to get sucked under by the horror, Professor Gordon pulls her back by pointing out the silly, the absurd. He makes her laugh. Is this what they mean by gallows humor?

Today Mathilde came by on the pretext of returning a book Professor Gordon lent her. Her real reason for stopping by is that she has finally gotten the courage to propose an idea for an independent study project she hopes he will sponsor. But no. Professor Gordon is shutting her down. Gently, but still, he is clearly wanting her to go in another direction.

"Oh yeah," says Mathilde. She slings her knapsack over one shoulder and holds her puffy jacket across her chest. "I see what you mean."

As she walks back to her dorm room under dark November skies, Mathilde is unaware of how the temperature has dropped. Her chest is hot with fury and confusion.

Once again, she is being pushed away from what she wants. By someone she respects. For good reasons. She is half Irish. It's not like she doesn't understand what Professor Gordon is saying. If she wants to study a population she should focus on the Irish immigrants who poured into this country following the potato famine, her people. She understands, but the tender lump behind her ribs throbs with a piercing ache.

Mathilde passes the brightly lit canteen whose tables are filled to spilling over with students who prefer hanging here than in the dining hall or library. She watches through the large panes of glass. They are laughing—eating the crap food the canteen provides—what are they talking about? They look happy. They're having fun. Why is she so intense? What is wrong with her?

Growing up, Anjanette was always a patient listener. She didn't seem to mind the intensity of Mathilde's interest to learn more about place names like Massachusetts, Natick, Connecticut, Scituate, Sagamore—the list was long. Mathilde kept meticulous notebooks and she would share what she learned with Anjanette as they sat together in Anjanette's room. It wasn't easy to find information so when she did discover a book that had more than the cursory two sentences about the people who were here for millennia before the Pilgrims washed ashore, Mathilde extracted each piece she could, though they often didn't fit together. For

Mathilde, it felt sort of like when you see a broken statue and have to imagine the missing bits.

Anjanette would be drawing or painting or fiddling at the table making something while Mathilde tried to get her friend to be as animated as she was to discover that the Quabbin Reservoir was named for a Nipmuck word and a French word. The sounds Anjanette made as Mathilde chattered excitedly weren't discouraging, exactly, but Mathilde has never met anyone else who shares this deep passion until she is in class with Professor Gordon.

Mathilde jams the door open to her dorm room. She throws her knapsack onto the floor then plants herself, face down on the bed.

Idiot, idiot. She rolls onto her back and pulls the pillow up to her throat. Why doesn't she ever fight back harder? Mathilde wanted to go to college in New Mexico. Her mother convinced her to stay closer to home and attend Boston University. Mathilde can't remember if her father had an opinion about where she went to school, but she remembers him helping her choose history as a major when she filled out the application form.

Her hands feel like two lumps of clay as she remembers that moment when she had to identify a major she wasn't excited about in order to go to a school she wasn't interested in. History seems to be the study of an endless cycle of war and genocide; what she wants are stories about the worlds people lived in, their traditions, their way of life, how they made themselves happy, how they survived being human.

Mathilde sits up. There's only one person she knows who can help her—who understands why she'd be so upset. She wouldn't have to explain and just the thought of talking with him makes her start to breathe easier. She pads down the dorm corridor to the pay phone on the wall and calls Uncle Wesley.

Back in her room she puts on a skirt and sweater because she knows Uncle Wesley will take her to Locke Ober—he always does. As she brushes her hair, she imagines telling Uncle Wesley about the conversation with Professor Gordon and a gush of embarrassment wells up. Last time she and Uncle Wesley talked, everything was feeling so good. Mathilde puts down the brush and stares into the little square mirror.

The day she changed her major to anthropology was such a good day. That was over a year ago now. Her freshman year—barely the first week of October. The sky was blue and the trees were on fire as she walked back to the dorm with the paperwork that named Professor Gordon as her new adviser tight against her chest that was thumping as if she had discovered a hidden doorway. Perhaps there was a place for her in the world.

Wrong again, you big stupid. Mathilde grabs her coat and heads down the hall to wait for Uncle Wesley by the main entrance.

Mathilde blows into her hands to warm them. She watches as students file past on the white cement paths illuminated by street lights. Unspoken dictates have many of the bodies walking by her wearing the same LL Bean jackets, carrying the same canvas knapsacks, wearing the same boots and blue jeans. Mathilde wonders if maybe this is how people feel safe. Do what's expected. Stay out of the abyss of knowing what humans do to each other. It was in one of the books Professor Gordon lent to her that she read what Columbus had written about the Taino, the people that welcomed him, kept him alive, that he then annihilated. "Taino—most lovely, peaceful generous people—they will make good servants."

The short toot of a car horn jolts her back to the cold stone steps. Mathilde jumps up and hurries over to Uncle Wesley's car which hums quietly against the curb.

Professor Gordon does not receive tenure. He leaves at the end of Mathilde's sophomore year and so does Mathilde.

She squishes herself into the back of a yellow VW bug that carries her to a ferry where from the upper deck—wind whipping her face—she watches the island that the Narragansett called Manisses come into view, an island that is called Block Island because of some blockhead sailor named Adrian Block. Whatever, she thinks. The bitterness of her tears mingle with the scent of engine fumes and the sea air. Nothing matters. Who cares.

Her life banks suddenly like a plane making a sharp descent.

Mathilde walks through the Heathrow terminal. She follows the crowd from one concourse to the next. Existential angst surges each time she passes glossy signs that warn of the need to conserve water, save animals from extinction and be alert to the signs of human trafficking. Giant, incessantly repeating videos of runway fashion shows and perfume advertisements feel grotesque. All of it unnerves Mathilde.

She is grateful that it is morning and for the helpful people along the way who direct her to the Paddington Express. Still, she struggles with the currency and exchange rate. It is not until she drops into her seat for the train ride to Cardigan that she finally exhales.

Mathilde doesn't have a bucket list, but if she did, Wales would be nowhere on it. In fact, aside from knowing that it is part of the UK, she really doesn't know anything about this place that her body is hurtling toward. She googled St Dogmaels, a village just beyond Cardigan, and from the photographs she found, it seems idyllic, but maybe that's what all write-ups do.

One bit that caught her interest was that as early as the twelfth century, woolen cloth was exported from Cardigan to Arras in France for use in the weaving of tapestries and she wondered if any of that made it into the Bayeux Tapestries. Bayeux. That was a place she has always wanted to go just to see if the tapestries are as amazing as she has read about. Ironic that she never seriously entertained the idea of going to France because of the language barrier and yet, here she is headed to a country whose words spin her head around.

There is a big river, the Teifi, that cuts through St Dogmaels and from what she can figure out, Effie's cottage might be pretty close to it.

She takes out her phone and prepares an Instagram post. It will be the third one she has posted since leaving Boston. It feels like a way of noting milestones as she completes each section of the journey.

In her first post, she shared a photo of the arrival/departure chart with a close-up on a long row of *on time on time on time*. She told Paul she was really sorry she was late to the lunch and that the real reason was that she has been struggling with depression which she hasn't wanted to talk about. Doesn't like burdening people with her mess. She told him how getting up each morning feels like bringing up a brick from the bottom of the sea which makes her feel so ashamed. She really appreciated what he said about mothers and daughters. In the second post, she took a photo of a postcard in a spinner rack of postcards that featured a bridge. She realized her first post was so self-centered, all about her—so on the bridge photo she merely wrote: hope the games are going well today.

Before she can finish her third post, the woman in the seat across from her comments about how her daughter is always on the phone. Chastened, Mathilde tucks hers away.

"I really never do." says Mathilde. "I have a—a friend, who showed me how to use it, but I'm not any good at it."

The woman is knitting something that looks extremely complicated; Mathilde counts eight different yarn colors in it.

"That's beautiful," says Mathilde.

"Today it is," says the woman and lets out a gust of exasperation. "I've had to tink back twice and I almost threw it out the window yesterday."

"Oh no—" says Mathilde. "Don't even joke. It's really one of the most beautiful shawls I've ever seen. Where do you find a pattern like that?"

The woman looks up surprised. "Oh, I just make it up. I've never been keen on knitting anyone else's patterns."

Mathilde finds that statement fascinating. They drop into conversation about Elizabeth Zimmerman (Mathilde makes a note to get one of her books), the importance of only giving hand knits to people who appreciate them, the merits of knitting in the round vs. flat, and the general disrespect that greets knitters.

"I went to a place a couple weeks ago," says Mathilde. "There were so many people! And they were all crazy about yarn. It was like nothing I had ever seen."

"Rhinebeck?" the woman says, peering up over her bifocals.

"Yes." Mathilde is shocked. "You know it?"

"Oh sure. I've never gone, but that's a big one."

"You don't think it's weird for people to be so obsessed that there's a whole three-day fair?" Mathilde asks, mesmerized by the woman's fingers which never stop moving as she talks.

"Ever known a golfer?" the woman counters.

"Uh, yeah—my husband is—he was, a golfer."

"No one says being obsessed by hitting tiny white balls into a hole while wearing ridiculous pants is crazy. Or kicking a ball up and down a field, over and over without ever getting it into the net, is a waste of time." The woman's fingers move so quickly Mathilde can't follow the stitches, plus she thinks the woman might be knitting left-handed. Hard to tell.

"And what results from their obsession?" the woman asks evenly. Her voice is calm, without the slightest ruffle of argument—like a pond in the early morning where stillness fills the space. "Besides a tub of muddy laundry—nothing. Nothing is made. Whereas our obsession," the woman says.

Mathilde feels a tremor of happiness that the woman has looped her into "our obsession" even though she has told the woman she isn't really a knitter.

"—results in hats, shawls, sweaters, blankets, socks, mittens," the woman continues. "We make things. Beautiful things that last for generations. Well, depending on the care it's given."

"You're Scottish?" Mathilde asks. She hopes it isn't a rude question. As she often does when she wants to know more about the origin of a word that intrigues her, Mathilde had googled "caledonia" and found that it was the name Romans gave to the area now called Scotland. She learned that some believe Caledonia is derived from the tribal name Caledones which meant "having hard feet." She wonders if that means the land was rocky and made their feet tough, or if it means they were stubborn people who couldn't be budged—who fought back.

"Da laek a dat!" the woman says, which Mathilde assumes is a no. "Shetland, born and raised."

It must've been a rude question or, the woman is done talking—or maybe the knitting got more complicated and she has to concentrate because they don't exchange many more words before the woman gets off at Swansea, the halfway point in Mathilde's journey.

Mathilde checks her phone—three hours to get halfway? How did she get this so wrong? She had thought the whole trip was going to take about four hours but now as she thinks about it, maybe that calculation was for driving. She sighs heavily. It might have been a better idea to get a hotel room in London for the night before heading out, but whatever. She is in it now.

Things Mathilde hadn't thought about: it could be raining, she could arrive so late in the day it was dinner time, the street Effie's cottage is on is so narrow the cab has to drop her at the bottom of the hill and she has to walk up with her stupid luggage dragging behind; she would be hungry, cold, wet, and start to cry. It helps that the rain is a sheet of steady mist; no one would be able to tell the cause of her wet face. Not that she has to worry about that. The street is empty.

What was she thinking? Mathilde stops for a moment to catch her breath but also to sob a bit more deeply in humiliation and anger at the situation she is in. The houses are small and neatly tucked back behind a thick stone wall, plastered white, that runs the length of the lane. Mathilde can see the lights on inside. It's gotta be close to dinnertime. She is in a foreign country. She can't just walk up to someone's house at this hour and knock on the door. But she has no option. It's getting dark and she wouldn't know where to begin to get back to the center of the village or find a cab. She keeps shuffling forward.

There it is. *42.* Painted clearly on a plaque next to the green gate that is in the thick wall. Mathilde has reached the end of this fool's errand. The house of Effie Finisterre, that pixie sprite who sold her the yarn all those weeks ago. This is the address the girl at the fair gave her where Mathilde will find two more skeins of Caledonia Blue.

Behind the gate, down a straight walkway that cuts through a small lawn of grass, the front door of the stone cottage is painted in the same dark sage color as the gate. On either side of the door are two large windows and, in a row above the door, are three smaller windows. There are no shutters, but each window is bordered on the bottom with a narrow wooden sill that is also painted the same green.

Mathilde pushes the gate open and thumps her suitcase up to the front door.

"Effie is not here," says the woman who answers. She doesn't seem to be entirely surprised to find a stranger on her doorstep asking for Effie, though. She steps back and opens the door more widely and invites Mathilde inside.

The cottage is not at all what she has imagined. It is old, yes, but the interior is modern and has been fully updated. The sofas and chairs are deep red. A fire burns in the woodstove. All of the interior stone walls have been painted white, only the oak beams above the windows and across the ceiling are unpainted. From the entry, the living room floor stretches out in gleaming wood, while the dining and kitchen areas have enormous squares of gray stone or slate underfoot. Mathilde is aware of the puddle growing around her as she stands dripping.

"Here, luv," the woman says. She helps Mathilde hang her coat and carries her shoes and socks over to the woodstove to help them dry. The woman pulls a pair of knitted footies from a basket and hands them to Mathilde. "Put these on. Your toes must be chilled."

Yes, Mathilde nods. The woman gestures to the chair by the dining table for Mathilde to sit.

"I'm Clara. Effie's sister," she says.

Mathilde tries to see some resemblance between the plain, middle-aged woman sitting in front of her and the playful, whimsically dressed woman she met at the fair. Clara wears her hair in a straight bob to the shoulders. It is the color of charcoal with thin streaks of gray running all through it. There are gold posts in her ears, but she wears no make-up. The only connection Mathilde can make between Clara and her wildly creative sister is that Clara wears somewhat trendy denim overalls over her fair isle pullover.

"Is that Greece?" asks Mathilde. She points to the oversized photo that nearly fills one wall. The image is of a coral pink taverna cobbled together from weathered driftwood with a pergola at the front, a bar on one side and the floor, nothing but sand.

Clara sets down her mug to look at the photo as if she had forgotten it was there.

"Oh no, dear. I don't think so. That's some place in Italy Effie loves to go."

"You've never been?"

"I don't have the same wanderlust that my sister does," Clara says. "I like to keep close to the roost. But you're a traveler coming all this way and now heading on to—did you say, Portugal? Spain?"

Mathilde doesn't want to explain how, really, she isn't a traveler at all. Instead she tells Clara how she met Effie and that her assistant had said she'd have more yarn here at her studio.

"Oh, bad luck," says Clara. "Effie won't be back until Christmas. But here now, it's not as bad as all that—" she says as Mathilde's chin drops.

"I am such an idiot," says Mathilde. "I am so sorry to be disturbing you like this. You must think I'm mental."

"Oh go on—it's not all that."

Mathilde is unconvinced.

"I'll tell you a truth," says Clara. "Effie has always been something of a Pied Piper. As a little girl, she'd bring home kittens and turtles. She made nests in the yard for little birds. My father had to make a pond in the garden for the baby ducklings she rescued. I have learned not to be surprised by who shows up on the doorstep. There once was a woman who came all the way from Sri Lanka in search of some yellow yarn Effie had concocted," says Clara, with a laugh. "Imagine that! You haven't come from as far away as that, now have you, luv?"

"So, there's—" Mathilde feels a bit reassured but wants to make sure she has understood. "There's no more of it to be found, not anywhere."

"Can't be sure of that. Let's ring up Talia," says Clara. "She runs a shop in Palermo and Effie often sends her some of what she makes."

Palermo? Does she mean Italy? Mathilde is concerned. Or, maybe there's a town named Palermo in Wales?

Clara picks up her phone and checks the time. "Oh, it's not that late," she says. "She'll probably still be there." She taps in the number and holds the phone out on speakerphone so Mathilde can listen along.

The woman answers and Clara launches into Italian which leaves Mathilde struggling to follow the conversation. At one point she hears a back and forth of the word "duo" which she thinks means two so that could be good. But, does this mean the yarn is in Italy?

After what was a rather lengthy chat that seemed to veer off into lots of other subjects beside yarn, Clara taps off the connection and puts her phone back on the table face down.

"Well that's settled," she says as she stands up. "They've got the skeins set aside for you. Let's head down to the pub. I'm feeling peckish. You could eat something, yes?"

The rain has stopped. A strong wind is clearing clouds from the sky giving glimpses of stars and a crescent moon. Mathilde follows Clara down the lane in the opposite direction from where she arrived. They have barely walked a minute when Clara steps up to a stone house, larger than her cottage with a sign swinging from an iron hook. *The Hopping Crow.*

"Here we are," says Clara. She holds the door open for Mathilde. Inside is warm and thick with people. Clara wiggles them over to a corner of a table where there is just room enough for both of them to fit. It's as if they are joining a family dinner. Everybody knows everybody. There are rituals and rhythms to all the movements of getting drinks, getting food. No one pays any particular attention to Mathilde. A man comes over and takes their order for two pot pies and a couple of beers. The conversations around them are loud. Clara talks with the women sitting next to them.

Mathilde settles her back against the wall. How incredible is this, she thinks as the man sets the glasses of beer down in front of her and Clara. Never did she imagine she would be dropped into a scene where it's not just that she is the only American, she might be the only person here who isn't local. She sips at her beer, surprised that it's not cold. She observes the conversations, taking note of what people are wearing. She notices how the men seem to be in clusters at the bar while the women sit at tables in groups of two and three. There are little kids and teenagers. It's not at all like a bar scene in Cambridge. Wouldn't Lonny and Anjanette love a place like this?

She wraps her glass of beer in both hands. Mathilde feels a peculiar sensation—an emptiness in her chest—as she wonders what Anjanette and Lonny are doing tonight. Has Anjanette gone out on a date and left Lonny in the house alone? Did Lonny make dinner for them both only to have to put Anjanette's plate in the refrigerator because Anjanette never came down from the studio?

"You alright, then?" Clara asks, taking a moment away from her friends to check in on Mathilde as their dinners are set down in front of them and they begin to eat.

"Yes," says Mathilde as she blows on the spoonful of potatoes and peas to cool it down. "Wonderful."

"Hey mom," Toby says. Her son answers his phone as if calling him out of the blue were a normal thing for Mathilde to do.

"Hi Chicken," Mathilde replies in a low voice in case the walls of the guest room are thin—she doesn't want to disturb Clara whose bedroom is across the hall. "You home from work?"

"Uh, yeah—it's going on eight o'clock," Toby says. "What kind of beast do you think I am?"

"Oh right, of course—wasn't sure. I get the time difference mixed up."

"What time difference?"

When Mathilde explains that she is calling from Wales, that it is after midnight her time, that she just came back from drinking beers in a pub and is now spending the night in the guest room of a person she met only hours earlier, her son takes his phone off speaker phone and stops what he was doing to sit and talk.

Toby asks all the right questions. He makes Mathilde feel like she is on a marvelous well-planned adventure and not just rolling down a hill, randomly bumping into good fortune as she tumbles. She tells him how kind Clara has been and how she insisted Mathilde stay at her place and now the plan is to catch the train back to London in the morning.

"Clara says there is a direct flight from London to Palermo—it's less than three hours—so I think I'll do that. Go to the shop and then, I'm not sure. Maybe head to Spain?"

"Mom," says Toby. "Just to make sure I've got this straight. You are in Wales. And, tomorrow, you are going to Italy—Palermo, for a day. And then, Spain."

"When you say it like that, it sounds like a lot—but it's really more like me going from Boston to Chicago and then to Florida. That's not such a big deal, right?"

Toby doesn't sound convinced. She gets him to update her on Arnie, the rescue puppy that he and his boyfriend have just adopted. She asks about the projects he is working on.

"You sound good—" she says as they wind up the call.

"I am, mom." Toby reassures her. "I'm good."

"Are you good?" Clara asks as she strips down to her bathing suit.

Mathilde is not sure how to answer the question. She is barefoot, wearing a borrowed bathing suit and clutching a towel to her chest. She is one in a group of four women standing at the edge of a river that is moving, fast—quite fast. Clara and her two friends, all three in swimsuits, step steadily through the grasses at the edge of the soft bank and glide into the water like selkies. One of them flips onto her back for a few kicks before slowly, she begins to stroke against the current.

Clara has told Mathilde it will probably be colder than anything she's ever experienced. "But when you get out," said Clara, "you will feel marvelous."

Mathilde could have said no. They would not have been surprised if she had said no. But there was something about the energy between the women as they gathered in the kitchen—still dark out, before tea or coffee—and invited Mathilde to join them. She wanted to be part of their group. She wanted to know why they were so excited by the early morning ritual of a swim in the river.

Now, once again, she questions her decision-making capabilities. What was she thinking? This is not a summer day. The sun has barely begun to lift up over the trees. As she peels down to the borrowed bathing suit, Mathilde hears her mother say as clearly as if she were standing right next to her, *You are going to catch your death!*

I don't care. I want to do this, she insists. She rubs the palms of her hands together vigorously and then up and down the sides of her bare arms as if that could exorcize her mother's voice from her head.

Her first step into the water is scary. The women push through the water to come over and shepherd her in. They take Mathilde by the hands and coax her gently.

The shock as she drops in the water up to her chest is intense. It is a sudden, crushing sensation. It incites a panic of immediate annihilation. She is gasping which brings to mind the moment the baby has crowned and you think you can't do another moment. That panic and breathing through the nose, out the mouth. *I got through that. I got through that* is what Mathilde repeats over and over in her head (she WANTS to go in the river, she WANTS this experience even though it terrifies her). She remembers the birth of Susannah—this is nothing compared to that. This is just walking into a river. The women encourage her, one on each side. They are so respectful of her terror as they talk her through— *"breathe in breathe out"*—*"hyou are doing such a good job,"* they say as they lull her into the river. Sunlight suddenly breaks out from behind a tree to land on the water sending sparkles everywhere.

And then, she is in the middle of the river. She plunges in and comes up with a scream. She fills the air with jubilant, wild squeals. She did it. The women are far more experienced and make no sounds as they melt back into the water. They float and swim as if born to it. Their bodies show the signs of having birthed children and also a deep love of jam and cake, yet in the water, they are weightless, full of grace.

Mathilde is too tense; she can't get to that glorious place. She ducks her head under, rips out one last squeal, then scrambles up the bank through the muddy grasses. She had brought armfuls of warm things with her. She expected she would be freezing, but instead she is electrified. Her body vibrates in a way she can't remember ever feeling before. She keeps her arms still; she doesn't want to lose a single drop of water from her skin. The air feels marvelous. She has never, in all her life, felt more alive.

As she waits for the others to finish their swim, Mathilde pats the towel at her face then wraps it in a turban over her hair. She sits on the extra jacket that she brought.

Bugs in the sunlight—too small to be moths they look like large dust motes but are some kind of creature—move above the water. They float and bob. The insects hover in a group but within it they each do their own erratic movement some spinning in upward spirals—oscillations like in a science class. For them, the air is just like water; it suspends them but also allows their softly darting, random and erratic dance.

Clara taps her shoulder as she and friends towel off and prepare to head back up the hill.

"Not cold, are you?" says Clara.

Mathilde shakes her head, unable to stop grinning. "Not at all."

The selkies' morning ritual ends in the village at the Bara Menyn Bakehouse. They join the line—*the queue*—that leads to the door. Mathilde can smell the bread. When it is their turn to step in, she has that same sensation she did when she got the first glimpse of the inside of Clara's cottage: old but modern. She does feel like she is stepping back in time, but also like she is in a cutting-edge New York City artisanal bakery. The smells, the textures—simplicity's beauty has full reign here.

Mathilde steps outside with a country style loaf in her hands; the bread is still warm. As she follows the group down the cobblestone street, she rips off a piece. The crust is thin and crisp. Inside is soft and chewy and light.

"Good, right?" Clara turns back to look at her.

"I'm dead," says Mathilde, unable to find a better way to express how happy she feels. The group strolls past a giant wooden mermaid that has the most disdainful expression as if she agreed to come out of the water for a photo op but is now so over it. Mathilde laughs at the mermaid's scowl. Everything is funny. She just swam in the Teifi river. There are two more skeins of yarn waiting for her in Italy. She's made some new friends.

"There's your cab," says Clara. She points to the car coming over to where the four women, hair still wet, have been standing by Cardigan Castle eating fresh bread straight out of the oven.

Back in London, Mathilde struggles to keep in touch with the magic of the morning. She smells her wrist, but the scent of the mud and ferns has faded. Might as well take a shower, she decides. That's why she got this hotel room anyway. She figured it was better to get a shower and a night's sleep before she catches a flight tomorrow so that it will be midday, not midnight, when she arrives in Palermo.

When she comes out of the shower, she sees that she missed a call from her daughter. Susannah has also sent a text, *call me when you see this.*

Mathilde pulls on her pajamas and orders room service before settling into the bed—pillows propped up behind her back—to text Susannah back. She has barely hit send when her phone rings.

"You're going to Italy?" Toby must've called her.

"Well, hello to you, too."

"No, seriously Mom," says Susannah. "What the hell is going on with you?"

Normally Susannah's energy and incessant questions trigger Mathilde's need to shut down and push her away, but relaxing on the bed, feeling wrapped in a bubble of her own power, Mathilde simply listens. It's almost a physical punch when she realizes, Susannah isn't mad at her. She is worried about her.

Mathilde opens up and tells Susannah about her trip to Wales. She feels like a teenager recounting a big Friday night when she goes into detail about dinner at the pub, swimming in the river and the young guy named Jack who opened the most amazing French bakery in Cardigan that has people coming from miles around to eat his bread.

"The flight to Palermo is direct and really short," Mathilde reassures her daughter. "I just head there and that's it. No big deal."

Susannah laughs. "Oh my god, mother. No big deal?" She laughs again. "This is huge. I am so proud of you. I can't believe you are doing this. I don't know how it has happened, but I am really, really glad it has happened."

And then, Susannah says something Mathilde cannot possibly have expected.

"You what?" says Mathilde, sitting up to make sure she heard correctly.

"I want to come with," says Susannah. "I'll meet you there. Buy me a ticket to Palermo. I've already checked the flights."

Is this some kind of intervention? Is Susannah worried that she has to find her mother and bring her home like an aged Alzheimer's patient wandering the neighborhood?

"I want to be part of your adventure," says Susannah.

Susannah doesn't mention it, but unspoken between them is that her daughter's birthday is next week. This exorbitant expenditure could be tagged as an early birthday gift, right?

After they hang up, Mathilde receives the text with all the flight info. Susannah's ticket is a staggering sum, triple the cost of Mathilde's. *But isn't that how it goes with kids?* Mathilde finishes the purchase and then picks up the remote to begin channel surfing through British television. There's a knock. Her dinner has arrived. What you would never spend on yourself, she thinks as she pads over to open the door. What you would never allow yourself, you give to them readily when they ask.

Palermo
November 2017

Mathilde nearly staggers as she exits her hotel onto Via Vittorio Eman-
uele. It isn't the medieval stone street that knocks her off balance but
the reams of brochures bulging from her bag, each proclaiming Palermo
as ground zero for UNESCO World Heritage Sites. How has she never
known the wealth of history here? The only thing Mathilde can
remember learning about Palermo is that it holds the undesirable title
of being the most conquered city in the world. She doesn't know if that
is even true but Mathilde feels certain these ancient stone streets have
had no shortage of bloodshed, anguish, and murder and yet, on this
bright blue sky day, in this moment as she looks at all the people
leisurely enjoying their morning coffee *al fresco*, it's as if none of that
ever happened.

Before tucking her map in with the brochures, she checks it once
more, then adjusts her newly purchased sun hat and sallies forth.

Maggazzini Talia is a two-minute walk from Quattro Canti. Mathilde's pace has slowed. She can hardly believing what she is seeing. She is
worlds away from Wales.

The architecture is staggering. The cathedral, the narrow passages
with centuries old tiles covering the walls, the buildings where you look
up to see marble statues tucked under the eaves, the streets lined with
vendors of olives in baskets, peppers, bunches of fresh herbs, drying
pasta and everywhere the smell of pizza.

Talia's place is an upscale home goods shop. It is not large, but if you were looking for the perfect lamp, brass candy bowl, or hostess gift you would find it here. One corner is dedicated to yarn and needles with a few handknit sofa throws mixed in as an example of what you could do with these raw supplies. A woman comes out to assist Mathilde. Turns out, she does not speak any English. Of course she doesn't, you idiot, Mathilde chides herself. *Why would you assume that she would?*

With the help of her Italian-English dictionary, Mathilde gets her question understood by the elegant woman who wears a flouncy floral blouse that stops short of reaching the top of her high-waisted black trousers. The woman reaches under the counter and brings out five skeins of One-Pot Wonder yarns. Four are a watery violet color named *Lux Aster*. One is Caledonia Blue.

Mathilde gasps with pleasure in recognition of her beloved yarn. She grabs it and holds it to her chest. "Yes, yes! This is it!" she says and nods.

"I just need one more," she gestures. Then after consulting her dictionary. "*Ancora uno*," she says. "*Ancora uno.*"

The woman shakes her head no, smiling and sorry. She says some things in Italian. Mathilde keeps looking at her blue skein, squeezing it to make sure it is real. She is so close. But no, after a few minutes going back and forth. She is quite clear that this is the only one.

The woman allows her to use a credit card to purchase it. She then takes the skein out of Mathilde's hands with a laugh—she can feel the possessiveness—and carefully wraps the yarn in tissue before tucking it into a bag that has the store name printed on it. She hands the bag to Mathilde.

"*Grazie.*"

The door opens with a tinkling of bells. The woman lights up with recognition of an old friend, "*Ciao Bella! Tu sei qui! Come stai?*"

Mathilde turns to look. The woman walking in wears spectacular sunglasses. When she sets them up on the top of her head, Mathilde sees that it is, can it be? Effie?

It is Effie. She does not look anything like the kitschy knitter she did at Rhinebeck. Her hair is cut short with spiky bits pulled up like a young

Annie Lennox. A lime green sleeveless cotton tunic is paired with white peg leg pants and wild sparkly silver platform sneakers. A soft cloud of pashmina floats on one arm. Giant orange earrings swing from her ears. Her look is effortless, utterly Italian, chic.

Without missing a beat Effie sees Mathilde and says, "Oh, hello you!"

"You remember me?" Mathilde is stunned.

"Of course darling. You're the sad minx who bought the Caledonia Blue."

"Yes! And I went back to get more, but you were gone so I went to your studio in Wales to get more but you had brought it here and your sister called down and they said they would hold two skeins for me but now I think she is saying there is only this one?"

Effie kisses the woman, Talia, on both cheeks. Mathilde watches as they chatter. The words 'sad minx' loop over and over in her head. Was she a sad minx? Was that just a polite way to say Mathilde is the kind of woman who goes through the world complaining and feeling disappointed? Expecting everyone else to make her happy?

Talia produces tiny espressos from a glass and silver press, Mathilde declines the coffee. Effie drops a cube of sugar into hers and stirs the spoon slowly.

"You're right," says Effie. "It's all gone, but never mind. What about this lovely violet? She has four skeins of it. Won't this do?"

"Argghh," Mathilde says. "Oh, I am such an idiot. You had the three skeins. I only bought the one should have got the others."

Mathilde shakes her head. She finally understands the expression "not sure if she will laugh or cry." She is definitely caught somewhere between those two outbursts. The plane, three trains, the car, going through customs, back to London, the hotel room, the flight to Palermo, another set of customs, catching the right train from the airport to the city center. Finding the hotel. Finding Talia's shop. She pulls at the sides of her head.

Effie settles whatever she had come in for with Talia in beautiful Italian. The two women exchange kisses on both cheeks. Effie tucks her hand under Mathilde's arm so that she is holding her by the elbow.

"Oh, come now! There's only one thing to do to close out a story like that," says Effie. "Sit in the sun and have a brioche con gelato. I know just the place."

Effie spoons her gelato out from the profiterole. Mathilde feels boorish. She didn't ask for a spoon so she eats the whole thing using her fingers, licking up the drips. It is beyond delicious. She could eat ten of these.

In an effort to put Mathilde's experience in perspective, Effie shares some of her travel stories when things didn't go to plan. As she recounts the missed trains, the miscommunications, being lost at midnight in a strange city not knowing the language, the emergency hospital visit due to food poisoning, finding that she had picked up the wrong suitcase and someone else had hers, sleeping in one of the seats on a Ferris wheel because she wouldn't be able to get a ride to town until the next day, Mathilde realizes that Effie doesn't feel like mistakes are ever a problem, or that doing things perfectly is the goal.

"That's how I ever ended up at Valle della Luna!" Effie says, as if getting there was reason enough never to worry about veering off course.

Mathilde looks at her blankly. She doesn't know the place.

"Oh, it's on Sardinia—a marvelous beach," Effie explains. "I met some of the most interesting people on Moon Beach, but it's all over now." She dabs her napkin at each edge of her mouth before crumpling it and tucking it into the empty paper cup.

"These days," Effie says, "when I can, I like to go to a small island you can only get to from Isola delle Femmine." She looks up at Mathilde with the sharp interest of an idea forming. "You should go!" says Effie as the idea takes hold. "Much better than Spain and a lot less expensive, too. It can be a bit challenging to get there, but I'll walk you through it. Oh, this is just the most lovely time of year to head out there."

"Really? Then, would you want to come, too?" says Mathilde.

"If I could," says Effie. She stands and puts on her sunglasses. "I'm catching a flight to Japan tonight."

Who *is* this woman, Mathilde thinks. Japan? She's flying to Japan, tonight?

"Meeting a friend in Sasayama," says Effie. "I mean, Tamba-Sasayama, I should say."

"Well, what incredible good luck that we ran into each other," says Mathilde.

"Hmm," Effie agrees with a coy smile. She tucks her hand into Mathilde's elbow and they walk back to Quattro Canti.

"Is the place you are talking about the one in the photo?" asks Mathilde.

"The photo?" Effie doesn't understand.

"When I was at your house, in the living room there was a big photo of a—"

"Oh!" Effie comes to a full stop, then resumes walking. "Yes—that's the taverna. Be sure to order the fried potatoes. Scrumptious."

"How do I call ahead—make a reservation?" Mathilde isn't even sure she will do this but wants to know just in case.

"Oh no no no," says Effie. "You'll see. It's nothing fancy at all."

As Effie explains what to do, Matilde taps notes into her phone hoping she doesn't miss any important details. Go down to old port, but the ferry only runs every other Thursday and only when the weather is good. Effie scans the sky.

"No worries for you. It looks fine!" she says. "But you have to go this Thursday. There won't be another one for two weeks."

Sometimes the boat doesn't show up until ten or eleven, but be there by eight because sometimes it is early. Be patient, Effie advises. Mathilde also needs to have water and a sun hat since there is no shade on the pier.

"Sometimes the boat driver gets off to have some breakfast, and he will invite you to join him but don't go," says Effie, "because he may not be the driver that takes the ferry back out that morning and another driver will come and take the boat off and you will miss it."

Mathilde stops tapping into her phone. Her stomach is clenched in fear. This sounds like pure chaos. How do you plan around so many variables? Mathilde is not even going to try.

Dedham
Spring 1985

Mike always has a plan. He even plans for Mathilde's objections. On the day he takes her to see the house he has found for them in Dedham, he spends the drive laying out his vision.

"Don't get caught up in what it looks like now," he shouts over the wind from the open window that blows hair across his sunglasses as they drive north on I-95. "It does need a little bit of work but that's all cosmetic. And the big stuff like the foundation and the furnace, I can get the guys to help me with. That's why we can get it at this price." Sweat equity, he repeats as if she didn't understand him the first time.

Mathilde knows from the moment they drive down the street that she doesn't want to get out of the truck. The street is part of a development and all the houses are exactly the same: cheap, fast production houses from the 60s and 70s. When a house is not designed to be charming in the first place, loose siding and rusting gutters doesn't read vintage, but derelict.

"Why don't we just keep looking?" she suggests. The more she looks around, the more panic she feels; there are no trees.

"I've been looking," Mike's voice is tight. "Prices keep going up. This is a great opportunity, You gotta move on something like this."

When Mathilde still doesn't make a move to step out of the truck, he pushes for her to be reasonable. To see the big picture.

"Look, it's just gonna be for a couple years then we'll turn it over," says Mike. "That's how it's done. It's a steppingstone. I've got a plan, you gotta trust me."

Still, Mathilde resists.

"Okay fine," Mike says. "What's your plan, then? Tell me your plan." And of course that is the end of it. She has no plan.

They buy the house—at the top of the market—stretching beyond the last penny of Mike's savings to make it happen and then, boom, the market crashes. Two years after they purchased it, the value of their house is 40 percent less than what they paid for it. It takes twelve years before they are back on their feet but by then, Mike is planning college for the kids. Taking out a second mortgage on the house seems the only way.

Mathilde is not on board.

"That is obscene," she says when Mike shows her the current tuition costs.

"Things cost what they cost," Mike counters.

"They could go to Europe or Canada," says Mathilde. "It's cheaper. And who knows, they might actually get a better education when they can see this country from a new perspective. Anyway, who says they need to go to college—"

"No," Mike cuts her off. "They are going to college. Look what happened to you when you didn't finish."

Oh, that burns. Does he not remember that it was his idea? His idea that they get married and she not finish school? For days after that, she barely says a word to Mike. It is nearly a week before the burning rage subsides because she knows, as much as she wants to put all of that at his feet, she has no one to blame but herself. Everything is her fault.

This is her bed and she has to lie in it.

Palermo
November 2017

Mathilde reaches into her bag and pulls out the skein of Caledonia Blue that Talia wrapped so carefully. She feels ridiculous to be touching yarn on a day as hot as this.

The cafe table is tucked back under a thick awning to protect her from the afternoon sun that is strong and unrelenting. It feels to Mathilde that the sun is actually closer to the earth here than anywhere she has ever been before, as if—were she to step out from under the awning and walk out into the middle of the piazza and lie down, spread-eagle on the ancient pavers—she could quickly be incinerated. No, better still—if a shaman could work a piece of rawhide under her breastbone and then string her up to a pole so that she dangles from her chest, feet inches off the ground, smoke and chanting rising up around her, with witnesses to her endurance ensuring that she would not be incinerated but transformed, into a sun warrior.

Mathilde looks around quickly. She is in public. Could someone notice what weird thoughts she has? No, you stupid cow. Nobody even sees you.

She pushes her sunglasses to the top of her head so she can examine the yarn. The thrill of having scored a second skein—full and rich, every bit as captivating as the first one—is tempered by the dull intonation of disappointment that tolls beneath her success like disapproving church bells. What are you gonna do with two skeins? Better off to have none than only two.

She plucks at the skein gently and slips a finger under one ply to look at it more closely—as if it could provide an answer to the question that is hammering down on her. How did this happen? She is sitting in a foreign country—a part of the world she has read very little about, never really researched, never really thought about visiting—with a hank of wool on her lap when she's not even a knitter, not really, not like the women she saw at Rhinebeck, not like the woman she met on the train to Wales.

She gives the yarn a little shake. *It's your fault, you damn lorelei, you got me here–and where's your other half. I needed two of you.* A shadow drops across the yarn. Mathilde looks up to see the waiter. She nods yes. He takes her empty glass and walks into the cafe. Not sure if this means he is bringing her another limoncello spritzer or not. She doesn't care as long as she has permission to keep sitting here. Maybe she's buzzed? How much alcohol is in that anyway?

She leans back against the hard iron of the cafe chair, her fingers still buried into the wool as if the answer would be found at the end of one of these threads.

Research has taught her one thing for sure: the more you follow a thread, the more it attaches to other threads in an endless web. She knows this and yet, she can't help thinking the past holds all the answers and, like picking at a knot in a necklace with the tip of a pin, if she would just keep at it, in the end, her life and all the lives that came before her would shake out into one long chain and it would all make sense.

But wasn't that exactly what Uncle Wesley warned her against? Hoping to make sense of things—wanting to make sense of things—was a guarantee of misery. Such an odd twist. How unhappiness can grow out from the very opposite intention. Is the problem that she wanted to make her mother happy? Or was it that she tried to make Mike happy the way she always tried to make her mother happy?

She doesn't have all the pieces, but the thread definitely begins in her mother's unhappiness that—from the photographs and stories that Mathilde has collected over the years—began in happiness.

The waiter's shadow crosses the table as he sets down her drink. Mathilde gives a smile of thanks. She takes a sip. It is cold, refreshing. She is definitely buzzed. She gestures to the waiter for a carafe of water. No way she is gonna try to go sightseeing right now.

Nothing to do but wait for Susannah to arrive—her feisty, argumentative, opinionated, thirty-year old unemployed daughter who probably won't bother to pack toothpaste. Susannah will assume the hotel will have some for her or, she can always use her mother's.

Sitting on a wrought iron chair, in an ancient city, surrounded by strangers speaking a language she doesn't understand, one million miles away from all that she has ever known—Mathilde has a moment of absolute clarity. If she is ever going to understand the relationship with her daughter, Mathilde has got to take a hard look at her relationship with Rosie, her mother.

Is this why people travel? To face what they already know but don't want to look at?

But what about Anjanette? She doesn't travel but she faces things, doesn't she? Sure, Lonny and Anjanette fuss at each other a lot and can't help but to annoy each other, but they are super close. It isn't at all like the relationship Mathilde has with Rosie. It's kind of the opposite. Mathilde and Rosie don't argue much at all. They hide behind polite words and never really say what they're thinking. Mathilde takes another sip of her drink. And, they have never been close.

64 Clement
the early years

W eeks after their wedding, Tom begins to grow his hair long and switches from wearing button-down shirts to mock turtlenecks. He and Rosie dance around the living room to their favorite song by the Kinks. They sit on the floor to eat dinner from the low coffee table and talk about how his job at Beacon Press is temporary. He is going to be a writer. They will have lots of kids. And a house by the sea, Rosie always adds. This big old hulk of house Auntie Mae gave them is simply the first step into the big dream of their life that will look nothing like their parents'.

Mathilde knows the stories and has seen the photographs of how things were when her parents first moved into 64 Clement, but all that Mathilde hears now are the constant complaints about the house. *It's so dark*, her mother says. *So drafty. Too many rooms. Too much upkeep.* There is the never-ending battle with mice. And, of course, the house is much too far away from the smell of salt air.

Rosie will do anything to be near the ocean even if it means putting up with Tom's family who always have them come out to Nantucket for a week at the end of June, but then proceed to treat Mathilde and her parents like the poor relations that they are. When Mathilde asks her mother to explain why they are invited in the first place when it is so clear, her grandparents (and aunts and uncles) do not like them, Mrs. Silberman jumps in to answer the question for her.

"They need an audience," says Mrs. Silberman. "If they are just there being rich by themselves, who can they impress?"

Mrs. Silberman is Rosie's best friend. She lives in the nicest house on Clement; it is on the corner and has a wraparound porch. Mathilde's mother met Mrs. Silberman at the YMCA where they both swim laps during the early morning free swim. Mrs. Silberman's kids are grown-up and off at college so she doesn't need to be home at the end of the school day like Rosie does.

Mathilde likes it when Mrs. Silberman is there because that's when she hears her mother laugh. Mathilde pretends to go to her room, but instead, slips down into the dining room so she can listen to her mother and Mrs. Silberman talking in the kitchen. Rosie never pretends there are private things you don't talk about when she is with Mrs. Silberman. Mathilde almost pops a blood vessel in her eyes as she strains to hear Rosie recount, in a very low voice, how things went when she was pregnant with Mathilde—how she can never have any more children.

But sad talk isn't really what they do. Rosie and Mrs. Silberman love to talk about everything that is wrong with the people who live on Clement Street, like the Reillys—*that woman is a disgrace*—her mother says, *she lets those kids run like feral cats*. Or the DeAngelis family who have a blue Madonna in the yard and put up too many lights at Christmas. *I wouldn't mind so much*, Mrs. Silberman says, *if they weren't right next door and blinking! If I wanted to live next to a department store, I'd move to Copley Square*. Her mother agrees, *so cheap*.

Mathilde's father does not like when Mrs. Silberman visits. "I know I've asked you girls not to smoke in the house," he says, sniffing at the air in the kitchen.

"Yes, sweetheart," her mother says. "Yes, I know. I'm sorry. I'll remember next time. Are you ready for dinner?"

And that is that. Until the next time he complains.

Mrs. Silberman is often Rosie's date on Friday nights or sometimes Saturday matinees as they both love going to theater as much as possible. This is a relief for Tom who thinks the stuff his wife wants to see is lowbrow, particularly the musicals which is what Rosie loves most. One Friday night, when Mrs. Silberman is out of town, Rosie takes Mathilde to see *Goodtime Charley* which is in Boston for a trial run before it heads to Broadway.

"You will like it," Rosie says. "It's all about Joan of Arc."

From the spritz of perfume her mother puts on Mathilde's neck before they leave the house, to the way her mother presses in close as they sit on the theater's soft red velvet seats, to the late dinner in a cozy booth eating french fries—going to see *Goodtime Charley* is one of the best times Mathilde has ever had with her mother.

In a flip of how things usually go, it is her mother who keeps checking in on Mathilde. "Are you having fun?" Her mother asks.

"Isn't this wonderful?" Her mother whispers into Mathilde's ear as the audience breaks into applause at the end of a song. Afterward, Rosie takes Mathilde out for dinner and insists she have cake with ice cream for dessert even though it is nearly midnight by the time they finish.

They talk for hours about the story, the songs, the performances, the set. Mathilde loves seeing characters from history be brought to life.

"I could've played Joan, don't you think?" Rosie asks Mathilde. Rosie has been drinking which always makes her silly, but even though she takes a drag of her cigarette and blows the smoke off as if she wants Mathilde to believe she is kidding around, Mathilde sees the part of her mother that wants very, very badly to believe she could be the star of that show.

Mathilde nods. "You would have been even better."

Her mother savors that response in the same way she has eaten each bite of her steak dinner—looking across the table at Mathilde with a deep, close-lipped smile of pleasure.

Mathilde doesn't know if her mother would have been more happy as an actress, but she definitely isn't happy in a big house with no money to decorate it the way Mrs. Silberman's house is decorated.

On the days Mrs. Silberman isn't there, Mathilde comes home from school to find her mother lying on the sofa listening to records.

"How was school?" her mother asks.

"Fine," replies Mathilde.

"That's nice," her mother says to close the conversation.

Mathilde doesn't know which is worse, coming home to find her mother on the sofa asking for Mathilde to bring her another highball—one jigger of whiskey, some ice, fill the rest with ginger ale and a maraschino cherry—while she listens to record albums, or, when Mathilde walks in to find Mrs. Silberman there because that's when Rosie is most critical of Mathilde.

Mathilde is never the way her mother wants her to be, not pretty enough, not chatty enough, not stylish enough.

"You've got to smile more," says her mother as she sets a clean ashtray down in front of Mrs. Silberman. "You've got to practice being charming. Nobody likes a sad girl."

"I'm not sad," Mathilde says.

Her mother sits back in her chair and reaches for a nail file. She strokes the brown strip of sandpaper across one nail in quick, short movements. "Well if you would smile more, then I would know that." Mrs. Silberman watches the exchange and smiles at Mathilde, encouragingly.

You're the one who's sad, Mathilde thinks as she stomps up the stairs to her room, but she never says it out loud because there is no telling what kind of response her mother will make.

Rosie went to Catholic school for twelve years and even though the stories she tells about the nuns are horrible, she doesn't seem to see that she can be harsh, too. Rosie buys all Mathilde's clothes and clearly wants Mathilde to look a certain way. When Mathilde complains Rosie pulls her by the shoulder roughly and makes her look out the window at the Reillys' house.

"Is that what you want? A mother who doesn't take care of her kids?" Rosie's voice is sharp, exasperated. "I only ever got hand-me-downs from my sisters and you get brand new clothes just for you and you are complaining? You are a spoiled brat."

The summer Mathilde turns thirteen, Mrs. Silberman sells her house and moves to a condo in Back Bay. Things around the house seem to fall apart.

Rosie leaves a bag of groceries in the car by mistake that has a half gallon of ice cream in it. Tom cleans up the mess without saying much but when Rosie forgets to pay the electric bill on time, Mathilde's dad paces the kitchen shouting while his wife sits slumped in a chair.

"You're acting like she's moved to California!" says Mathilde's father. "She's three miles away, for chrissakes—not even! Wes is in Boston. That's never changed anything for us. Hell, Wes goes halfway around the world half the time and that doesn't mean we're not friends."

"Being on the same street is different," says Rosie.

After Mrs. Silberman moves away, Rosie has to share all the stories of the Reilly family over the phone. Rosie pulls the phone receiver into the powder room off the front hall so she can talk in private, but Mathilde can hear everything since the phone cord keeps the door cracked open.

There are five boys and one girl in the Reilly family and the front yard is always a mess. When the boys break a couple of spindles in the porch railing playing one of their stupid games, Rosie can't wait to report. "You think he fixed it?" Rosie crows into the phone. "Oh he fixed it, with duct tape."

Mathilde can hear Mrs. Silberman laughing because her mother is laughing so loud the receiver is away from her ear.

It's confusing for Mathilde. She doesn't know if her mother is good or bad because she never knows when Rosie is going to switch from mean to nice.

Across from the Reilly house is a Victorian that has rental apartments. The tenants are mostly graduate students from MIT but sometimes from Harvard especially if they come from another country like India or China. Sometimes the student has his family with him, and Mathilde's mom brings over baskets of cookies at Christmas time.

Rosie loves Christmas. Bing Crosby, Rosemary Clooney, and Jim Reeves play as Rosie presses star-shaped cutters into the dough, sets trays to cool and sprinkles cookies with red or green glitter. It is the only time Rosie loves to cook. She gathers up all of her recipes and makes Swedish ginger cookies in the shape of stars, German Linzer cookies in the shape of wreaths, tiny half-moon Russian tea cakes, sugar cookies shaped and frosted like candy canes, chocolate drops sprinkled with powdered sugar and coconut shortbread squares.

"What am I going to do with all of these?" her mother says as the cookies pile up in the early weeks of December.

Rosie must have taken some cookies over to the renters while Mathilde was in school. Mathilde only hears about it as Rosie recounts what she found to Mathilde's father who is in the den after work as usual. Rosie sets his whiskey on the side table and stands, telling him about her day.

"Oh, Tom. That poor woman. They're living in two rooms. Her husband's gone all day. Off to the library on weekends. I don't think she speaks much English at all. It's gotta be so hard." Rosie is genuinely upset. "They are on the third floor. All of those stairs with a baby and another on the way—and groceries. I don't know how she manages."

"Did she like the cookies?" her father replies without looking up from what he is reading.

Christmas and summer on the Cape are her mother's two favorite times of year; Rosie may have left Hull behind, but her heart is always at the seashore. The only time Mathilde ever sees her mother cut loose is when they arrive at the little shingled house in West Harwichport each summer. The small gray house with its white wicker furniture on a patch of grass by the carport, belongs to someone her father knows. All year, her mother plans for the two weeks each July that they rent that house.

As soon as they pull into the drive, Rosie unbuckles her seat belt and rushes out. The ocean isn't visible from the driveway of crushed seashells, but the roar of the surf and smell of the salt air hits Mathilde strongly as she follows behind her mother.

Rosie's bare legs plunge up and over the soft dune, her skirt buffeted by the wind. With one hand holding her hair back from her face, Mathilde's mother stumbles down through the heavy sand then runs onto the beach. She races straight to the wide waves crashing onto the shore, her arms wide in greeting.

Her mother always cries on the way home to Cambridge.

"Now Rosie, come on.," her father says. "It's not the end of the world. We had a good time. Didn't we?" Tom looks into the rear-view mirror to enlist Mathilde's support.

In 1989, Mathilde's parents sell 64 Clement. The timing can not be better. Unlike Mike and Mathilde who bought at the height of the boom, her parents cash out and make a fortune. Whenever someone asks how they are able to retire early, Rosie croons, "That TIAA CREF was a nest egg!"

But Mathilde knows the truth: their freedom is funded by the sale of the house Auntie Mae gave them. 64 Clement. The house Mathilde loves.

The day her mother calls to tell Mathilde that 64 Clement is sold, Mathilde drops into a ball on the floor.

"How could you sell the house without telling me?" Mathilde shouts.

It is one of the only direct confrontations she has ever had with her mother.

"Why are you so upset?" says her mother. "You have your own house now. You're a married woman. This place is much too big and I've done my time here. We've found a wonderful condo on the Cape. Why aren't you happy for me? We'll be living on the beach. You know this is what I've always dreamed of."

Her parents live on the Cape for five years, but then in 1994, they move down to a condo in a housing complex on Hilton Head, South Carolina. Though the location changes, their lifestyle doesn't. Her mother reads Louise Penny novels, spends hours walking through shopping malls and playing tennis. Her father reads Clive Cussler, Phillip Pullman (he pretends his copies of *Harry Potter* are there for Susannah and Toby), and charts baseball stats.

Once a year, usually in February, Mike and Mathilde make the long drive down with the kids to spend a week with them in South Carolina. Mike loves these vacations. On the way back from the first visit, Mike begins talking about some future day when he and Mathilde will have a condo on a golf course. Mathilde cuts him off at the pass.

"Don't even think about it," says Mathilde. She is tired and frustrated from a holiday that was anything but. She is the one wrangling kids while Mike and her parents lounge by the pool. Outings to miniature golf and pirate's cove make her want to grab an oyster fork in each hand and jab them repeatedly into her skull.

"I don't understand," Mike looks at her as if she is the problem. "You're always wanting to get out of Dedham."

"They're exactly the same," she replies. She can feel her back molars grinding. How does he not get it?

Mathilde takes a moment to look around the room. There is a giant brick oven on one wall. Italian waiters in long white aprons move gracefully between the tables. She is sitting in the middle of a small restaurant in the center of Palermo—how thrilling is this? Although, the restaurant does feel rather touristy which is a disappointment. Mathilde asked the hotel for a recommendation. Too bad she didn't think to ask Effie. No doubt Effie would have directed them to something special. Oh well. Who cares. They're here now.

And, it continues to feel surreal. It doesn't help that Susannah has gone through another one of her 'costume changes,' as Rosie calls them.

The young woman sitting across from Mathilde has modified her appearance to look *au naturel*. The purple dye is gone. Her natural auburn hair, stick straight like her father, is no longer, teased, sprayed, slicked back, or shaped with mousse. It falls in a thick curtain to her shoulder blades. After years of wearing full make-up, her daughter's pale, freckled skin looks practically naked. Susannah wears just a hint of mascara.

Of course, nothing is ever easy with Susannah. Mathilde is already tired of this newest affectation. How long will this one last, Mathilde wonders. Longer than the phase when Susannah refused to eat with a knife and fork and would only use chopsticks?

Mathilde wants to be positive; she tells her daughter how much she likes the change. Her daughter nods in agreement.

"I want to be my authentic self," says Susannah without a hint of irony.

Mathilde reaches for her wine in an effort to fight down a laugh. It is the same gust that would burst up when Susannah, a precocious three-year-old made hilarious pronouncements with absolute seriousness. Mathilde learned to fight the inclination to laugh as that always resulted in her child's tears and outrage at being misunderstood. But now, here she is with her nearly thirty-one-year-old daughter who is still making statements that reduce Mathilde to giggles.

"You're not laughing at me," says Susannah, leaning in to get a closer look in this darkly lit restaurant.

Mathilde sips, coughs, shakes her head, no. "Not laughing." Mathilde coughs again. "This wine is a bit rough on the throat."

Mathilde marvels at how different they are. At thirty-one, Mathilde had been married for eleven years and had a nine-year-old, a four-year-old, and a 30-year mortgage. At thirty-one, Susannah's longest romantic relationship lasted less than a year. She drifts from one living situation to another. Susannah's name isn't even on the lease of the Jersey City apartment she rents with a group of friends who are also in the theater world.

The big news that her daughter shares as they pull hungrily from the plate of antipasti that takes up nearly all of the tiny tabletop that they share: she has received a Creative Capitol Award for 2018 and will be spending six months at the Arkansas Repertory Theater in Little Rock.

"Arkansas!" says Mathilde. She has always wanted to go there.

"Yeah, I had applied to be in Chicago, but they felt my project was better suited for the ART."

"Oh, honey, Arkansas!" says Mathilde, passion rising. "This is—you are so, I'm really—this is really such an achievement. You must be so proud."

Susannah laughs at her mother's excitement. "I'm relieved, for sure—but seriously, what is the big draw about Arkansas? I've never heard you get so excited about some place before. Which is particularly funny given where we are sitting."

There is a long pause and Mathilde can feel something coming. Susannah sips at her wine and gazes at her mother. "I was expecting you to be disappointed that Toby and I won't be home for the holidays. I definitely did not—"

"What do you mean?" Mathilde interrupts. "You said the grant doesn't begin until January. Why won't you be home? And why isn't Toby coming? Why am I only finding out about this now?"

"Calm down," says Susannah. "It's not like we have been planning this for months. It just evolved in the last week or so."

"You're not coming home for Christmas?" says Mathilde.

"I don't want to pay for December rent in New Jersey—so I'm leaving for Little Rock right after I get home from here. The theater has helped me line up a place and they're letting me move in earlier so I can get settled and grounded."

"But, Susannah—you could fly back for Christmas!" says Mathilde. "And I talked with Toby the other day. He didn't mention this. Why isn't he coming?"

"Mom—*Mom*," says Susannah. "Toby's gonna be with Bill and their new puppy. I'm here. Right now. We're together right now. In Italy! That's why I wanted to see you—we'll just squeeze all of—"

"You will be so sad. Christmas in a place you don't know anyone?" says Mathilde. "That sounds awful. I hate the thought of you being all alone like that."

"So don't," says Susannah. The waiter has left the check. Susannah picks it up and hands it to Mathilde. "Let's pay the bill and go for a walk. C'mon."

Mathilde tries to adjust to how awkward yet funny, familiar yet foreign, it feels to be with her daughter. The hotel room, with its rich daffodil-colored blanket, has only the one bed. After all the money she has spent on Susannah's plane tickets, Mathilde wasn't about to splurge on two rooms. This means they are sharing the not quite queen-sized bed and stepping over each other to use the bitty bathroom. The intimacy is overwhelming. Mathilde hasn't gone to sleep and woken up with anyone since Mike died.

Mathilde watches her daughter closely. She notices the details of the clothes Susannah wears, the way Susannah folds her t-shirts, the three different pairs of sneakers her daughter has brought, the nighttime face-cleaning ritual—Mathilde soaks it all in like a gift.

Susannah is confident. She has her own style. She is all grown-up.

Do all parents go through this, wonders Mathilde. You can see the precious infant, the toddler who loved raisins and refused to eat peas, the little girl who would play dress-up for hours, the feral raccoon of a teenager you wanted to hang out the window by her toenails—you see all of this at the very same time you are gazing at an adult who is going to be moving halfway across the country by herself. Does parenting ever stop being so trippy?

Susannah flicks off the bathroom light and bounces onto her side of the bed. Her face is shiny with oil. She pulls the mouthguard from her mouth, drippy with saliva, and sets it on the nightstand.

"Don't you have a case for that? You're not going to put that back in your mouth are you?"

"Jesus—mother," Susannah wiggles to get her body settled under the covers. "You never answered me earlier. What did Rosni say?"

Mathilde pulls her arms in over her chest. She evaded this question about her friend the therapist, but now she is pinned. There are no distractions. The room doesn't have a television.

"You know, the stuff you already know," Mathilde begins. She picks at the blanket. "Um, pretty much normal things. She said my dad was emotionally unavailable and when he tuned in, he gave all his attention to my mom. That my mom was emotionally unstable and gave all her attention to herself. That I had a perfectly normal childhood. Oh, and that I might be having difficulty processing grief. Bougie. Bougie. Bougie."

"Mom," Susannah tone is a bit sharp, corrective. "She did not say that."

"Sweetheart, I think it is inappropriate for us to talk about me like this."

"Why?" Susannah sits up. There is so little physical space between them Mathilde feels cornered.

"I just do."

"But why?"

"Let's talk more tomorrow, okay?" Mathilde's voice is bright, but thin. "I'm tired."

Susannah holds her mother's gaze. Mathilde turns her eyes away. Susannah reaches over for her mouthguard and pops it in.

"Fine," Susannah says, her voice thick with the tongue behind the plastic of the mouthguard. She flips over to one side. Punches the pillow into shape and goes to sleep.

"Two thousand followers on Instagram?" Susannah's voice is loud with surprise. "And 'bat_outta_dedham'? How did you come up with that?"

Mathilde pulls her sleep mask down from where it has been covering her eyes. The sunlight is terribly bright. She has to squint to see Susannah by the window, cellphone in the palm of her hand.

"Mom. How the hell do you have two thousand followers?" Susannah leaps onto the foot of the bed and crawls up toward Mathilde.

"I don't know what you are talking about," says Mathilde. "It's too early to be awake. Can you close the curtains, please. And stop jumping."

"*Buongiorno!*" Susannah gives her mother a kiss on the face, then scooches up to settle back against the headboard pulling her legs into a cross-legged position. She continues to scroll through images.

"It's a beautiful day and we are not wasting it in bed. And, what the hell," she turns the phone to face Mathilde. "You took this?"

Mathilde opens her eyes to see Susannah is holding out the Instagram post with the photo from the train ride back through Wales. The vibration of the swim was with her. And the kindness of Clara. And the fun of the pub. Mathilde pushes up onto one elbow to get a better look at the photograph. It's good.

"Lucky shot," Mathilde says, dropping back onto her side.

"You've been on IG for what, ten days?" Susannah pulls the phone back to continue scrolling as if there were an answer somewhere on how this could possibly have happened. "Plus you are doing it all wrong. You don't write to one person over and over—and who is this guy Paul I'd like to know." She peers more closely, reading another post. "I just—this doesn't make any sense to me."

She looks over to see Mathilde has turned on her side and gone back to sleep. Mathilde feels her daughter's hand on her shoulder shaking her. Mathilde responds with a groan and burrows more deeply into the covers.

"Mother," Susannah says dramatically. "You are getting dressed and we are heading out into the streets to find some coffee. It's going to be fantastic. Look out the window. *Bellissimo! Andiamo!*"

After breakfast at a caffetteria that Mathilde will remember all her life for the toasted almond granita con brioche and the way Susannah gets her laughing. Is she hungover? Is that why she keeps dissolving into hysterical giggles? No, it is Susannah Mathilde thinks as they walk toward the cathedral. Susannah is light and witty and so fucking smart. She's—Mathilde stops hard with the realization that has just hit her like a door in the face. She's vivacious. It's the Irish. It's Rosie.

"You okay?" Susannah asks.

Mathilde nods and they keep walking.

"Wait, no." Mathilde stops. "I want to take your picture." She pulls out her phone and takes a shot of Susannah walking up the cobblestone streets in her neon green canvas sneakers, legs bare, below the thrifted skirt from the '90s—probably something that was made before she was born.

"Now turn around and walk toward me," says Mathilde.

Never one to miss an opportunity to flaunt, Susannah adjusts her aviators and catwalks slowly toward her mother. Her breasts bounce under the tight-fitting t-shirt. Mathilde tucks the phone back in her purse and they continue up toward the cathedral.

"Did you forget to pack a bra?" Mathilde asks her daughter in a low voice.

"Oh my god, mother," Susannah laughs and pulls Mathilde close to her. She tucks her arm though her mother's and squeezes it as they walk. "I tell people about you, but nobody believes me. I wish I had that on video."

Susannah jumps away from Mathilde and turns toward her in the same motion.

"Hey," Susannah says. "Caption the shot you just took of me with that. Say that."

"I'm not doing that—" says Mathilde.

"Yes!" Susannah pulls back in close as they arrive in the piazza in front of the cathedral. "It will be good, I promise."

They have barely begun exploring the history of the cathedral before Susannah is bored and wants to head to the shopping district. Mathilde feels a wave of disappointment roll up and get caught at the bottom of her throat. Disappointed that she is being asked to step away from something that fascinates her and disappointed at the gap between them—Susannah is not interested in the same things as Mathilde.

"You're abandoning Rosalia?" says Mathilde.

"The princess who becomes a saint?" says Susannah. "Yeah, I'm all good. It's an old story. I've heard it a thousand times. Patriarchy. Plagues. It's done. Let it go back to dust already."

"This place is amazing," Mathilde says, ignoring Susannah's summation. "Right where you are standing it was pagan, then the Romans, then Christian, then the Saracens—Susannah!" Mathilde calls her back. "Think about it, then it became Muslim for two centuries—there was a mosque big enough for seven thousand people! You don't find this amazing?"

"No," says Susannah. "I really don't. It's just a testament to why everything is so fucked up in this world. It's a fucking endless game of boys playing King of the Hill."

"Well then," says Mathilde. "You'll like this part where after the Normans came in and slaughtered everybody and turned it back to Catholics again, there was a rebellion against the political corruption and the people set the cathedral on fire."

"Yeah, but—" Susannah shrugs. "It's still here." She peers at one of the informational plaques that has brochures underneath in English. "Oh look—" she says, her voice heavy with sarcasm. "Then the Spanish took over."

Mathilde seizes on even this small contribution. "Look at the dates," she says to Susannah. "That's right around the time de Soto was massacring Quapaw."

Susannah looks at her blankly.

"The Quapaw," Mathilde repeats. "You are going to Arkansas. You might want to know something about it."

Susannah begins walking away. She heads out into the square and turns her head up to the sunshine. Mathilde follows. The square is getting more busy with more people, more tourists. It must be close to noon.

"Do you want to get some lunch?" Mathilde asks.

Susannah shakes her head.

"Do you want to go shopping and we can meet up later?"

Susannah wheels around to face her mother, annoyance popping off her skin in every direction.

"Why do you have to turn everything into a fucking history lesson?" Susannah asks. "Why can't we ever just look at things as they are now? You know? Like, just be in this moment that's here and not digging around in dead stuff that is over." She shakes her head again. "You don't want to talk about anything real. Like what is really going on with you. All you want to do is hide yourself in some stupid fucked up past human bullshit. Like what's that about?"

Mathilde is not prepared for this outburst. She is so confused by the heat rising up in her body and the tears. So many tears begin pouring out of her. From all directions, from the centuries of suffering she had just been tuned into as she stood on the cold stone of the cathedral, from shock and pain at her daughter's anger when just hours ago they were getting along so beautifully. How does this always happen? Why doesn't she ever learn? She thought Susannah had changed.

"Mom, mom—" Susannah is half-carrying her over to where a mass of wrought iron tables and chairs are set out on one side of the square. "Breathe. Breathe."

Susannah settles her mother into a chair, and Mathilde promptly collapses face down onto the table. Her sobbing intensifies which draws glances from people walking past them. Susannah drags a chair close so that she can put her hands onto her mother's back. She rubs her palms in gentle circles as she makes soothing sounds. Her sunglasses fall off and she picks them up and puts them on the table.

Susannah continues to encourage her mother to breathe, taking deep inhales and exhales herself. She strokes her mother's hair, her arms. Her mother lifts her head. The congestion in her nose is making it hard for her to breathe. Susannah digs into her mother's purse and finds some paper napkins.

"Here," she says.

While Susannah is trying on sundresses behind the screen partition set up as a dressing room, Mathilde wanders the aisles of clay figurines. She finds one of a brown dog with a white spot on its head.

"Hey," says Susannah, coming up behind her. "What'd you find?"

"I'm thinking for Toby and Bill." Mathilde holds up the dog and a set of red ceramic espresso cups. "What do you think?"

"Oh, they'll love it." Susannah twirls. "What do you think?"

Mathilde doesn't like the sundress. Susannah's shoulders are covered in freckles and the top is too loose. It's also a kind of flimsy material.

"Nice," she says.

"You don't like it?" says Susannah.

"It's nice—" Mathilde struggles. "Honey, if you like it. That's all that matters."

"I am asking for your opinion."

"Why?"

"Forget it—" Susannah goes back to the dressing room and begins changing. The screen is not particularly effective. It's not hard to see glimpses of her daughter's naked torso as she pulls off the dress and puts her clothes back on.

Mathilde finishes paying for the gifts. Susannah waits for her outside on the street.

"You didn't like the dress?" Mathilde asks.

Susannah shrugs. "I can live without it." She stops to peer into a vitrine filled with sunglasses.

"You want to go in?" Mathilde asks.

Susannah nods. Mathilde follows her into the shop. A middle-aged man with a bald head and full smile booms a greeting to them. Mathilde watches as the man helps Susannah try on sunglasses. She remembers walking around with Susannah in a snuggly on her chest. She would rest her hand on Susannah's head, feeling her breathing against her heart.

"Mom," Susannah calls over. "What do you think?"

"Sensational."

"Really?"

"They're fabulous."

Susannah asks the price. Then sets them back on the counter. She smiles at the man and makes some kind of mumble about needing to think about it and thank you. She holds the door open for her mother.

"You're not getting them?" Mathilde is surprised.

"They're great, but they are also crazy expensive," says Susannah. "I've got these," she puts on her sunglasses. "I'm all good."

Mathilde steps out onto the sidewalk. The sun is hot. She remembers sitting on the bale of hay holding the one skein of blue. The remorse of not buying all three skeins. She pulls Susannah back into the shop.

"*Buongiorno*!" Mathilde says to the man. "Yes—we will take those." She points to the pair Susannah had tried on. The man nods and begins wrapping them up.

"Mom—" says Susannah. "No, seriously. This is ridiculous. I don't need them. You've already spent so money much bringing me here. Thank you, but no."

"Oh yes," says Mathilde as she hands the man her credit card. "Consider it an early birthday present. They were made for you and are exactly what a young rising star director should be wearing. Everyone will want to know where you got them and you can say, 'oh this great little place in Palermo.' You will thank me later."

"I'm thanking you right now," says Susannah giving her mother a huge hug that lifts her a bit off her feet.

The afternoon now rolls out smoothly. The gift of the sunglasses has sated Susannah in some way. She is funny and light again, but Mathilde no longer opens up to the connection so fully. They spend an hour sitting at a cafe. Susannah texts her friends and takes selfies. Mathilde writes a post for IG that she feels might almost be in code to Paul about mothers and daughters. Who else seems to understand it as he did?

It feels a bit icky to Mathilde that she uses gifts to smooth out her relationship with her daughter the way giving biscuits to a dog keeps it loyal, but there it is. She knows her daughter likes her more when she gives her presents. That's just life sometimes.

Palermo
November 2017

Mathilde sits in a hard plastic swivel chair, a maroon and gold nylon smock over her clothes. Susannah stands off to one side watching the hair stylist appraise her mother's situation. This is Susannah's idea. She insisted that Mathilde go to a hair salon, but she didn't have to push hard. Mathilde was ready to finally deal with her hair.

The stylist, however, might not be so ready. As her fingers tentatively separate the pieces of Mathilde's hair, the stylist's eyebrows lift so high they disappear completely behind her dark bangs. Then, with a shake of her head, she claps her hands together twice and smiles with confidence—perhaps bravado—and says, "No worry." Her words are directed more to Susannah than to Mathilde. "We fix."

After the shampoo and cut, Mathilde is spun around to look into the mirror.

"You want to no blow" says the stylist. "Like this." She pulls her fingers through the layers, patting and fluffing the hair until it falls into an approximation of beach waves.

"Mom," breathes Susannah, clearly thrilled. "You look fabulous. Do you like it?"

Mathilde peers into the mirror and preens, just a bit. A feeling of excitement and anticipation wells up within her. Mathilde touches her fingers to the back of her neck. Her hair is shorter than she has ever worn it. Is this why Anjanette changes her hairstyle so often? Is this why Susannah regularly transforms her look so completely? Are they seeking this sensation of looking into the mirror and seeing someone new? Mathilde takes a breath and tamps down the sensation of pleasure. Nothing good can last. Better to be prepared for disappointment.

"Yes," answers Mathilde. "Who knew the solution to my hair was to get it cut in Italy? This shouldn't be hard to keep up. I'll just come back every six weeks."

Susannah makes a face. "How about you just enjoy it right now."

The server waits for their dessert order.

"Tiramisu, grazie," says Mathilde. The server nods.

"Oh Mom," Susannah says, her voice lightly scornful. "Tiramisu? You can get that anywhere." She shakes her hand at the server. "No, no. No tiramisu. Cassata."

The server nods and takes their empty plates away.

"I read it on that app I was telling you about." Susannah says. "Cassata is a regional specialty."

Mathilde is irritated. She wants tiramisu, but she doesn't want to fight with Susannah. Plus, she is resisting the urge to tell Susannah how this regional specialty wouldn't even be part of the culture if it were not for the Arabs who brought the sugar cane, lemons, limes, and almonds with them when they came to this area, but instead her anger boils out awkwardly.

"I'm leaving Palermo first thing in the morning," Mathilde blurts. There's a tumult of feelings. Being with Susannah is too much. She isn't sorry that Susannah came all the way here to join her for a few days— some of it was truly special, but it disrupted the sweet rhythm Mathilde had found. Plus, Mathilde is intrigued. To be able to go to one of Effie's magic places? That feels powerful. Like maybe Mathilde will learn how to be more carefree like Effie. And, Mathilde knows that if she doesn't go to that island with the taverna tomorrow, she never will.

Mathilde sips her coffee.

"You're joking, right?" says Susannah.

Mathilde shakes her head. "Nope. You haven't wanted to do any of the things I want to do. I was happy to have you come join me, but now I want to do what I want to do. And this ferry only runs once a week, so I'll be on it tomorrow."

"Mom!" Susannah is not happy. She sits back in her chair disappointed, angry—the expression so similar to her father's that Mathilde has to dig her fingernails into her palm. She is not going to start crying again in public.

Mathilde sips at her coffee and says with the teensiest bit of a knife jab to the ribs. "You'll be in Arkansas for Christmas. You have your plans and I have mine."

The server sets their dessert in the middle of the table—a lavish cassata.

Susannah watches silently as Mathilde cuts through the elaborate top of the cake. Mathilde finds a way to section out a piece without making too much of a mess. Susannah's arms are crossed over her chest. It does not seem she will be eating any of the dessert.

Mathilde tries a spoonful of the cake.

"It's not bad," says Mathilde. "You know, if you like marzipan."

"Are we going to talk about this?" asks Susannah.

Mathilde puts down the spoon. She's given up on the dessert which is too sweet and layered with things she doesn't like. She takes a moment to think about Susannah's question. The answer comes easily. "Nope."

Leaving Palermo
November 2017

On the early morning bus ride down to Isola delle Femmine, the little port town where she is to find the ferry to the mystical island Effie has told her about, Mathilde writes an Instagram post to Paul. She finds this habit of sharing thoughts and questions, as well as recording all the things happening in her days that seem filled with one experience after another, very soothing. It helps smooth out the heat and confusion of thoughts in her head. And, it helps her to keep track of all the things she has seen and done that she would forget otherwise.

The bus jolts to a stop. An old woman dressed all in black crosses the road with steady steps, like an ant following an invisible straight line. Mathilde watches as the bus pulls past the old woman. She remembers the travel journal that her father gave her as the bus rumbles forward, picking up speed. Yes. She understands the impulse of record-keeping now. Of course, her grandmother's journal would have been far more interesting if she had shared more than the price of gas or how many days it rained. Her grandmother didn't record her thoughts, or how it felt. Did she and her grandfather ever quarrel? Did she only do what he wanted or did she get to choose what they did on parts of the trip? Did her grandmother feel guilty and stressed that she was always getting it wrong or is that an invention for Mathilde's generation?

Did I do the wrong thing, putting myself first? That's what Mathilde writes to Paul. A few days earlier at the cathedral in Palermo, she snapped a close-up of two rocks in the cathedral wall. This was the photo she posted with her question.

Scylla and Charybdis, right? Do I take care of my desires or the desires of my adult daughter? Am I a monster?

Mathilde looks out the window. Mathilde left her daughter in Palermo with cash plus three nights paid in the hotel room. Susannah can now go shopping all day long which is all she wants to do anyway. No doubt, Susanah will meet people, make friends—she always does. Why does Mathilde feel so guilty? It's not like Susannah even tried to meet her halfway.

I don't want to be anyone's mother anymore, thinks Mathilde.

She gasps and looks around as if someone could know she just had such a terrible thought. Mathilde sinks back into her seat. Is it a terrible thought? To want to be free? To just do things the way you want—Anjanette would understand. Mathilde digs in her bag for the two skeins of blue yarn. The power of this yarn to soothe her heart has doubled. It comforts her to have them together, reunited. She holds the skeins close to her chest as she gazes out the window.

The bus ride is short, hardly more than an hour. On her right is the sea. On her left are rocky cliffs. The road winds among low, flat, white commercial buildings. An auto repair shop. A few gritty roadside cafes. Eventually it rolls to a stop and people begin pulling their bags down from the overhead racks and filing out of the bus. Mathilde stands by the side of the bus and watches as the driver tugs her suitcase out from underneath. She is the only one with a large suitcase. Most of the travelers have knapsacks or shoulder bags.

The sight of the ferry landing. Gulls wheeling and squawking in the early morning air—air thick with the smell of the sea—all of it sends Mathilde back to those childhood ferry rides from Woods Hole to Nantucket when she and her parents would go to visit her father's family.

Nantucket
June 1975

Mathilde's mother is tense. Rosie has been up for days packing and repacking—going to the store to buy Mathilde new shorts, new tennis shoes, new underwear. Mathilde's father tells Rosie to stop getting so wound up, *it's just a week, for god's sakes Rosie!* But his words have no effect. The three of them wait in their car for the ferry. Her mother's hair is frozen with hair spray. Her father reads the newspaper.

The summer visit to her grandparents on Nantucket is always the same. The house is the same. Friday night dinner is the same—steamers with melted butter and platters of plain white fish, cod, or haddock, broiled and topped with breadcrumbs. Tennis is in the morning. Then everyone goes to the beach—to their regular spot on the beach—where they spend the middle of the day.

Mathilde's grandmother and aunts bring a picnic lunch for everyone which they eat sitting on blankets. Lemonade from a big plastic thermos that is watery from all the melted ice and gritty with sand that gets in the paper cups. Sandwiches of chicken salad or roast beef, on soft white bread. There is a big tin of potato chips from Pennsylvania and short-bread cookies for dessert.

No one is allowed to go in the water after lunch. "You have to wait an hour after you eat," her grandmother explains. "Or you will drown."

Mathilde sits off to one side of the group watching her cousins make sand castles. Although her back is to the adults, she overhears her aunt's comment and Mathilde knows her aunt is talking about her. *Curls and freckles. Such an unfortunate combination.*

When Mathilde's mother suggests they go into town on Saturday night, everyone just looks at her. The idea of going to a restaurant or walking around town is strange. It is not what they do. Why would you want to leave here, is the unstated response. Her grandmother closes out the suggestion in her kindly way.

"Probably not a good idea to be driving back in the dark," her grandmother says. "The roads can be so tricky at night."

Mathilde watches her mother's body gets small and turn in on itself.

Isola delle Femmine
November 2017

The morning sun pounds down. Sweat streams down from Mathilde's temples. There is no breeze, no shelter. The smell of gasoline and diesel makes the air thick. Each of the two benches are occupied by people who got here earlier than Mathilde. No one greeted Mathilde when she pulled her suitcase, bumping over the uneven slats of the pier, to come and stand with the group. Everyone seems to be absorbed in their own world. One man walks in half circles, fanning himself with a piece of paper.

This group? This grumpy bunch? Mathilde has a sinking vision of them all being at the same hotel together. She looks down at her toes. Painted pink with glittery silver flowers in the center of each big toe. At the hair salon, Susannah insisted they get pedicures.

"You'll thank me," she said.

The pedicure had given Matilde such hope for glamorous, jet-setting energy. She imagined being part of something luxurious, like in a travel magazine. Like the energy Effie had when she sauntered into Talia's shop in Palermo.

Palermo. Why did Mathilde ever leave Palermo? Is she insane? She could be there right now. What was she thinking?

Mathilde looks around a bit desperately. Maybe this isn't the right Thursday? There's no schedule posted anywhere. Mathilde doesn't try to connect with anyone. It's too hot. She doesn't speak Italian.

Abject terror—just like when she was walking through the rain up to Effie's cottage—floods her body and whirlpools in her belly. How could she be so impulsive? There's not even a name or a phone number for this place. Her father's family was right. Stay safe. Don't take chances. Mathilde looks over at all the real ferries that are back at the big landing. What was she thinking? She left that hotel room in Palermo. That very nice hotel room to be going where? There is no app, no travel tips, nothing but her notes, filled with typos, from Effie—a woman Mathilde now believes put some kind of spell on her. But the spell is broken. This bit of old pier that Mathilde stands on—at what feels like the end of the earth—isn't the least bit magical. It is plain. Ordinary. A mistake.

Suddenly, the guy who has been pacing and fanning himself stops to shout and point. A small boat, with the pink and white awning Effie told her to look for, is chugging toward them. When the boat nears, Mathilde can see it is filled to the edge with about eight or ten people.

The driver expertly turns the boat so that it hugs the pier. The boat bobs and rocks. The driver leaps out and swiftly ropes the boat into place. Then he turns and offers a hand to the people who disembark, laughing, full of chatter.

Mathilde's enthusiasm returns as she watches the people getting off the boat. Their energy as a group is filled with an easy exhilaration. This is the energy she feels from Effie, but the group does not resemble Effie in any other way. There are only two older women—the rest are younger and, from what she can hear of their conversations, seem to hail from far-flung places. What bonds them as a group, besides their festive cama-raderie, is that they are all wearing some version of loose cotton clothes in beautiful block prints—kimonos, billowing trousers, halter-tops showing a midriff, t-shirts, and culottes—as if they had all just left a very beachy pajama party.

They disperse quickly up the pier while the driver walks around collecting money from the hot and sweaty group anxious to climb into the boat.

"No, no—" the driver says, discouraging one of them men who has begun to climb in. He says something to the group, pointing up to the cafe across the way. He turns to Mathilde and says in English, "First, breakfast. Coffee, yes?" When he tells the group there is air conditioning in the cafe, there is a collective groan of relief and they move quickly to follow him.

Mathilde pulls out her phone to check her notes. She remembers Effie saying something about this. Instead of joining the group, she moves to sit on one of the empty benches. The sun blazes mercilessly now that she knows there is air conditioning available. She adjusts her hat, sips from her water and watches the group disappear into the café.

Before she puts the phone away, she checks her last Instagram post and sees a huge response. There are many comments on both sides of the issue, lots of heated exchanges. Best of all, in the midst she reads a comment from Susannah.

Oh for god's sakes Mother, I am the thespian of the family. Stop with the drama. All is well. I had an amazing time with you in Palermo. Come visit me in the land of the Quapaw.

Mathilde feels an enormous weight lift off of her. So much relief. She tries to hit like on Susannah's comment but deletes it by mistake. The phone is slick with sweat from her palm. She puts it away. She'll fix that later.

Mathilde perspires, heavily. She could get heat stroke out here. If she joins the rest of the group, she can watch the boat from the café. She stands, pulling the skirt off the back of her thighs where it clings. A young boy in a faded blue and white striped t-shirt ambles down the bleached wood of the pier and makes a graceful leap onto the boat. He starts the engine and begins untying the rope.

"Wait, wait—" says Mathilde. He helps Mathilde with her suitcase and bag. The boy holds Mathilde's arm as she steps onto the boat. Before she can even ask him about the people in the café—the people who, like her, have already purchased their tickets—the boat has chugged away with only the two of them onboard. Mathilde feels an upswell of alarm.

"We have to go back," she says to the boy who doesn't look to be much older than seventeen. She isn't sure he speaks English. "Other people," Mathilde points. "There. In the café."

The boy smiles and nods. He points to the seat cushions under the awning, indicating that she should sit.

Mathilde tries again, more insistent this time. She gestures to the café and tells him there are people there who paid to be on this boat. The boy reaches into the side pocket of his board shorts for a pair of sunglasses and puts them on. The boat cuts through the water at a steady clip. They are deep out to sea. The boy gestures again for her to sit. With the toes of one bare foot he gestures to the cooler by the bench.

Mathilde lets go. She is pretty sure the boy understands and is not going to turn around. Mathilde sinks back against the cushions of the seat, grateful for the awning. A wonderful breeze crosses her face. She takes off her hat to feel the air against her damp head. In the cooler by her feet, Mathilde finds a carafe of water and a container of cold orange slices.

With a section of blood orange crushing cool sweetness into her mouth, Mathilde watches as the cafe, then the pier disappear from view. She tries to process what just happened.. Even if the people in the cafe saw the boat begin to pull away, they would not have been able to catch it. Mathilde feels a surge of excitement and energy. She got it right. Effie prepared her for this possibility and Mathilde followed the directions correctly. Because things have unfolded almost exactly as Effie said they might, Mathilde begins to relax.

Half-reclined on the soft cushions, drinking fresh water and slipping orange slices into her mouth, Mathilde feels like Cleopatra being carried across this expanse of exquisite blue. Is this really happening? Mathilde takes a deep breath. Exhales. She lets a hand loll into the water that foams against the side of the boat. The water is real, moving, alive. Blue sky. Blue water. No other boats, anywhere, but then—far ahead in the distance are big rocks.

As they get closer, Mathilde sees that the boat is going around one side of what now are clearly defined cliffs. After making a long arc out and around the cliffs, the boat drops its speed to a putter and enters a small inlet.

Is this it? Mathilde thought the ferry would be hours long. But no. The water becomes shallow. The boy cuts the motor and jumps in up to his waist. He pulls the ropes and ties the boat to an anchor buoy near the driftwood gangplank. Without a word to Mathilde, the boy clambers back into the boat, dripping water everywhere. He heaves her suitcase onto the gangplank then begins carrying it to the soft sand of the beach. The boy drops her suitcase by a wooden post painted red and white. Then turns and comes back to help Mathilde out of the boat.

Mathilde holds her bag tight by the strap and steps onto the gangplank. She follows the boy to where her suitcase sits in the sand. Set back from the beach in a grove of palm trees and a bounty of pink and white hibiscus is a ramshackle building. Before he heads back to the boat, the boy makes Mathilde understand she is to leave her suitcase at the post and go to the building where maybe she talks to someone about housing?

Mathilde takes off her sandals and holds them in one hand as her feet, with the pretty painted toes, plunge into the soft sand. As she gets closer to the building, she can hear music and the sound of voices coming from the other side which comforts her. People. She is not alone.

She comes around to the front of the shack. Her heart begins to pound. She isn't sure if it is due to the exertion it took to plunge through the thick sand or if she is simply stunned. Does this happen in real life, she wonders. Do you see a photograph and then find yourself standing in it?

The beach shack is the taverna she saw on the wall at Effie's house. Only this is not a photograph. Palm fronds move up and down in the breeze in a sort of soft welcome.

There is music. And people. And the smell of fried potatoes.

Dedham
November 1993

Please God, just two weeks.

Mathilde sends the prayer up to the universe from where she sits on the toilet in the downstairs bathroom with five-month old Toby strapped to her chest. Mathilde flushes the toilet and struggles to stand without waking him. She washes her hands, stares into the mirror then bends her head toward the sink, temples throbbing.

All she wants is a break. A reset. Reboot. Where she can rest rest rest until she is on her feet and able to step back into the storm.

Two weeks of no laundry, no cooking, no cleaning, no putting kids to bed, no getting kids out of bed and dressed, no grocery lists, no waking up in the middle of the night to find an inconsolable child with an ear infection, no stupid playdates when her eyes want to roll back into her head from boredom. Two weeks of nothing. Full stop.

Mathilde takes a deep breath and opens the bathroom door. Never gonna happen.

Today is Saturday. The morning of Susannah's sixth birthday party. There are six other mothers arriving momentarily—all will be wearing lipstick and undereye concealer. The mothers will smile tolerantly as they correct their child's behavior while giving Mathilde appreciative nods and saying complimentary things about the party decor—the table of cupcakes, the basement set up like an indoor theater camp, replete with racks of costumes and a wooden stage that Mike built. (It is always too cold to go outdoors in November so no bouncy castles or pizza in the park for Susannah's parties, Mathilde always has to improvise).

Mathilde walks to the front door and waits. She knows every detail about the day ahead. She has lived it over and over, and over again.

Having an indoor party means pandemonium. All Mathilde can do is let the chaos roll and watch the clock for when it ends. Only then do the minivans—loaded with kids squealing and shouting, poisoned with sugar—begin pulling away from the curb. Mothers wave goodbye, call out thanks. But Mathilde knows better. All they feel is relief that it is over and that it wasn't their turn. No mess for them to clean up.

Mathilde leans her head against the door jamb. Why is this the tradition? What they wouldn't give to have a Saturday free to walk the aisles at Target or read a magazine or take a shower in peace rather than be at another goddamn birthday party, but they all do it. With pasted-on smiles as if this is a game and the winner is the last one to crack.

Why don't any of them ever say—*this is stupid—the kid doesn't need this—here's an invitation for you—my kid's having a birthday—my husband and I are taking her to a play and an overnight in the city to celebrate. I invite you to go take a hot bubble bath. I give you permission to go get a pedicure or better yet, go back to bed with a bag of potato chips.* Why aren't those the brightly colored note cards they send out?

Toby squirms; he is awake. Mathilde calls for Mike to come and take the baby.

Mathilde has been up since five—after dropping into bed around midnight, exhausted from cleaning the house and setting up for the party—to make sure she is showered and wearing an outfit that isn't the same sweatpants and hoodie she wears the other seven days of the week. For the next three hours, she will be handing out cupcakes, watching the little germ buckets sneeze and cough, knowing that she isn't going to get so much as two days of rest, let alone the ludicrous idea of two weeks. Mathilde knows exactly what she is going to get.

A white minivan pulls into the drive. Mathilde smiles and waves. She calls to Susannah to come greet her guests.

At the end of the day, Mathilde will have a destroyed living room, a baby that hasn't napped, a kitchen full of overstuffed trash bags, pink icing on the sofa, and a whopping head cold.

The island
Island time

Mathilde rocks in the hammock. The sun rises. Slowly, the sky and water turn pink.

As she rocks, her fingers bobble the hammock's macrame yarns and a memory surfaces. Mathilde had prayed for two weeks. A begging, pleading prayer for escape, rest, relief.

Turns out, she didn't even need two weeks. It's been what—ten days? Mathilde isn't sure. Since she stepped off the fay boat with its pink and white awning, time billows and stretches.

What Mathilde knows, is that she is a new woman.

She does nothing but eat, swim, sleep, and swing mindlessly in her hammock. Who knew? When there is exactly zero required of you, hours are like whole years unto themselves. This is the great discovery.

The memory of that young mother's prayer propels Mathilde up and out of the hammock. She carries her phone over to the edge of the platform and sits, her bare legs hanging down over top of the driftwood ladder. From the front of her outpost—what she calls this platform tent—she takes a photo of nothing but sea, early morning sky and a sliver of sand.

Mathilde posts the photo to her Instagram account. If Mike took two weeks holiday each year, she types to Paul. Why hadn't she? Her husband had every weekend off, and nights. She didn't have any of that.

She finishes typing the Instagram post, hits send and puts the phone back in her bag. Mathilde takes extra precautions to keep it safe from sand and water.

It is getting easier to climb down the ladder and drop from the last rungs into the soft sand. With her flip-flops between two fingers, Mathilde saunters down to the water. She savors each step along the edge of the waves as they rush and suck around her ankles.

Odd to be sending out such hard memories from paradise. Mathilde stretches her arms out wide and spins slowly to let the breeze lift her skirt. Driftwood interrupts her path as she walks along the shimmering water that sweeps full across the horizon. There are no horrible condos with swimming pools. No resorts for the Mephistopheles crowd. The beach belongs to the sea birds and crabs, the waves and the kelp.

Maybe the heavy memories are surfacing because there is such clarity here, thinks Mathilde. The ick rises to be transformed. Maybe it is only with this kind of time and space that she can look back and process what she wasn't able to see before. And, to let it all go.

Somehow, walking the empty beach in this fresh morning air, the memories no longer feel part of her. It's more like they are stretched out behind her, drying in the hot sun where they become fragile like seaweed that will disintegrate into bits and be swallowed by the infinity of sand.

Mathilde spends the first few days exploring the water and coves, only venturing as far as the tiny bodega that sells the odd mix of goods particular to remote locations: tins of tuna stacked next to batteries, beach towels, aspirin, and jars of peanut butter that cost more than caviar. What stupid American asked for *that* to be ordered in? (Mathilde assumes it was an American).

Yazly, the owner of the bodega, asks if she is enjoying herself. Mathilde nods yes and buries into her gelato. She proceeds to eat the ice cream slowly as she walks the beach back to her sleeping unit—the outpost. She doesn't know what else to call it. Not a room, definitely not a cottage. Effie might have mentioned that there aren't any hotels,

B&Bs, or anything remotely resembling a house for visitors.

Mathilde pays Yazly three hundred euros a week for a platform set on four stilts that is reached by scrambling up a ladder of unmatching lengths of driftwood nailed to the front. The slanted roof has some kind of palms or rushing on top, but looking up at it from inside she can see that it has been created from a mosaic of exterior roofing tiles that might have been found on the side of the road. There is a hammock to sleep in, a linen sheet that doubles as a light blanket and great wafts of mosquito netting to roll down each night that create the four walls. A few hooks nailed into one of the crossbeams is how she hangs her clothes, though most of them stay zipped away in her suitcase which is up off the bamboo floor, atop the one piece of furniture in the room: an old crate with the words "china and glass" stamped across it.

There is no sink, mirror, toilet, or shower. For all that, Mathilde must walk down the beach to the communal area where a quartet of outdoor showers are flanked by a wide, somewhat trough-like sink with a single spigot poised above it. The composting toilet is found set back in the palms closer to Yazly's hut. There are two, though neither has any specified gender attached to them.

The door to the toilet on the left, is fully covered by an elaborate painting of a giant urn spilling over with larkspur, delphinium, hollyhocks, and roses; an image you might expect to see on the cover of a magazine about English manor homes, not really in keeping with the swaying palms and aqua water that softly laps the sand. On the right, perhaps a bit cockeyed—hard to tell if it is the painting or the wooden closet itself that is at an angle—another full painting but nothing like the other one. The one on the right is blanketed in squares of color: red, orange, lime green, fuschia, and turquoise. Mogdalini of a parrot. Mathilde believes that each door was done by a different artist. She gets the sense that the odd artifacts she sees around—windchimes made from beach glass hanging from branches along the road, star-shaped assemblages of leaves, petals and coconut straw that appear in random places, the great spiral of rocks that she came across over by the cliffs—

are some kind of parting gift that people leave behind when they depart the island.

She wonders if she will find something that Effie left.

When she asks Yazly if he has a mirror she might use, he laughs as if it is the funniest thing he's heard all day. "Why you be wanting a mirror?" He tilts his head to one side, a bit flirty and says, "You look just fine."

Mathilde has not yet ventured out at night. She isn't worried about getting to the taverna in the evening, it's the thought of coming back in the dark as there are no lights along the road. But she can only swing in the hammock for so long before she needs somewhere to go and—the bigger truth—she is addicted to the fried potatoes. From her outpost, she can hear the taverna music going until it gets light out. So, she reasons, she can always spend the night sitting at the bar until dawn.

There is plenty of light at the taverna when she arrives at night for the first time. Garlands of twinkle lights are looped in all directions; some are wrapped like a sloppy hug around a few of the wooden posts that define the central area as a dance floor. Mixed in with the lights is a cacophony of tinsel, tulle, prayer flags and ropes of shiny beads. A Buddhist Mardi Gras for St. Nicholas. That, or a wedding planner's worst nightmare.

Fried potatoes are only served at breakfast and lunch.

Mathilde sits on her stool, annoyed. Annoyed that she could be annoyed when she is sitting at a tiki bar with no roof—nothing to obstruct a velvet sky glittering with stars—wearing a tank top and jeans not feeling the least bit chilled. The air is gentle—as soft as if someone wanted to make her cry from so much goodness. And yet, there was no shaking it off, Mathilde is annoyed.

It is the music. They have been playing nothing but *her* music. The songs of her generation. This music was new when she and Anjanette were seventeen. Buying albums at Tower Records. Making mixtapes. They would drive around in the car Mathilde borrowed from her mother. The excitement of having a brand-new driver's license coming second to the thrill of the music at full volume as they cruised up and down Memorial Drive singing at the top of their lungs. The music that was played at their parties, their dances.

Mathilde drinks deeply of her margarita that is nothing like those lemonade cocktails in their absurd glasses. This is in a rocks glass, no salt. A perfect mix of tequila, triple sec, Cointreau and fresh lime juice. She sucks it down and gestures to Antonia who is working the bar for a refill.

Don't they have their own music?

The twang of "Rock Lobster" begins to spiral out of the speakers. Rock Lobster. That is it. Mathilde kicks off her flip-flops and marches out to the center of the dancefloor. Maybe it isn't so much of a march as a wobble when she hits the soft sand, but who cares. These kids don't know what to do with this song. They are bouncing slow like it is a reggae number. No. She doesn't care. Doesn't care who sees her. What they think. What they say. She does not care. Plus this isn't even a dance-floor. It's a sand pit.

Mathilde begins dancing the right way. The way you dance to the B-52s. She jiggles, shakes, hops, bounces, rocks, flaps her arms, squawks. And then she realizes, some of the kids are following along. She is the leader. She does airplane arms, they do airplane arms. When the song drops, and she drops to flip onto her back and wave her arms and legs like a beetle, they do the same.

The song ends. It is followed by "Waiting in Vain." Fine, thinks, Mathilde as she heads back to the bar, brushing sand off her ass. Now you can reggae all you want.

Feeling weirdly triumphant, Mathilde does what anyone would in such a moment, she bums a cigarette off Antonia. It is French and much too strong but she keeps her inhales tiny. She orders a Kahlua on ice.

"Wanna hang out at my place?" A man-boy leans into the space next to her, ringlets of black curls brush his bare shoulders. He is asking her to have sex. With him. This twenty-something year-old. Or maybe thirty-seven, possibly forty-two—no way to know. All she knows is this *much* younger man is inviting her to have sex.

Mathilde reaches down to pick up her flip-flops and lets them swing from two fingers. "Yes," she says.

She follows him out, head shaking lightly in amazement. This beautiful man. What on earth is he thinking? But she allows no answer to that. Her New England harpies are voiceless here. All Mathilde can hear is the growing sounds of the surf as they walk down the beach, leaving the music of the taverna behind them.

The island
Island time

After that first night with Luciano, Mathilde imagined she would have to skulk around the island under the cover of darkness, melt away, disappear with no one knowing where she went. But she doesn't. There is no walk of shame. Nobody cares.

She follows the curve of the beach up to the taverna for a late lunch. A man talking on his cell phone passes her as she steps up to the bar. Before she got here, it never occurred to her that there would be wifi on the island, but go figure. A strong reception. Amazing.

"Not so amazing," says Luciano. His mouth makes a shape as if to scoff at the idea that having internet service on a rock in the middle of the Tyrrhenian Sea is a big deal. He pats the empty stool next to him for her to sit and reaches an arm around her. He points to the cloudless blue sky and places a kiss on her neck. "Satellites."

"Pronto per il pranzo?" asks Papi, Yazly's uncle, as he puts a glass of iced tea in front of Mathilde. "Abbiamo un panino di peperoni e cipolle grigliate con hummus o pomodoro e melanzane grigliate su inslata di mais".

"E frittelle di mais," Antonia calls out from the fryer. Antonia is Papi's daughter and often shows up to help her father with the lunch shift.

"E frittelle di mais," says Papi. His smile reveals four missing teeth.

Mathilde looks at Luciano for translation. She has not understood a word except mais, corn.

"Che ne dici di uno di ciascuno?" Luciano says to Mathilde who nods her agreement despite not understanding a word of any of it. It won't matter. Everything is always delicious.

The taverna is medium full as it has been every day since she arrived which she honestly does not know how many weeks that would be. She is pretty sure it is well into February because she decided not to go home for Christmas and that feels like years ago. It's quite possible she will never go home, she thinks, taking a long swig of her iced tea and looking up at Luciano from under her lashes.

"Ciao bella." He kisses her elbow.

Mathilde and Luciano swim, lounge, linger in bed until they get hungry. They have sex before and after lunch. People must see them. Antonia sees them. Nobody cares. It is only when Mathilde goes down to the bungalow that sells bathing suits and sees herself in a mirror that she gasps. She has been looking at Luciano, his beauty, his vibrant health. Looking at herself is a shock. Mathilde's hair is graying, silver, mixed in with the brassy tones of hair color that she didn't bother getting fixed by the stylist in Palermo.

Her face is the face of a fifty-two-year-old woman.

But, something has changed. Maybe it's the tan. Maybe it's her hair tumbling in soft, unkempt layers. The bones of her face seem charged, her cheekbones strong. Her eyes. Are those her eyes? Those are the eyes of a woman having lots and lots of sex. Mathilde smiles at herself in the mirror.

"It's nice, right?" says Daria, the young woman who runs the shop, coming to stand behind her.

Mathilde nods giving a passing glance to the swimsuit which is bright teal with a giant yellow flower wrapping around one side, the petals reaching across her belly and up to her breasts. Oh yes, Mathilde can see it now. Her hips, her shoulders, her neck. She can see why Luciano would want her. The spark in her eyes, the freckles across her nose. Curls and freckles not such an unfortunate combo, here.

As she pays for the suit, counting out the bills before handing them to Daria, Mathilde has a sharp full memory of how her sex life with Mike ended.

They were having sex and he stopped suddenly. "Are you counting?" he asked.

She had been. Not consciously, not with any malicious intent. It was more a habit that had grown out of something she'd done with the kids. Using numbers to get things done. Counting their fingers so they would let her stuff them into mittens. Counting down minutes so they knew they were going to have to get out of the bath and go to bed. She doesn't know when she started doing it for herself, but it became how she tackled tasks that had to get done.

Carrying the laundry basket up from the basement and counting the steps, *five, six, seven*. Loading the dishes she would look at the sink and count up the cups and plates, *eight, nine, ten* and then silverware, *seventeen, nineteen, twenty-four* as they went into the dishwasher. Somehow knowing the amount and breaking it down always helped. And here she had been doing the same with each thrust. Not knowing how many were left to come but perhaps anticipating would it take forty? Ninety? And he must have heard her although she didn't think she had said anything out loud but on more than one occasion, Susannah had accused her of talking out loud so maybe she had that as a habit, too.

That was the end of their sex life. Mike rolled off. Mathilde didn't think anything of it particularly at the time, but now.

Now, she can see they were not even having sex. Whatever they were doing had no relationship to what she and Luciano have been doing these past weeks. She is not in love with Luciano; she does not imagine marrying him someday. His English is only a few hundred words better than her non-existent Italian. Besides, he is far too young and it is to the edge of her discomfort that they are hooked up anyway, almost to the edge of repulsive only it isn't. He sees her as a sexual being and with him, she is a sexual being and none of it—none of it—is the way she believed things were supposed to be. How it was supposed to feel. How she was supposed to feel about him. None of it. All that she believed about sex, about herself and sex, is gone.

Slow. Luciano keeps having to get her to slow down. Just lie in bed and touch each other? Explore each other? What is that? None of the movies Mathilde and Mike watched showed sex that way. Sex was urgent, fast, violent. Clothes were ripped off. There was tumbling and rapid change of positions. Had she really learned all she knew about sex from movies? Had Mike? They never talked about it. It was just how it was done. But no. Not at all.

Luciano searches for a tattoo. He has never known a woman without tattoos before and he is convinced he simply hasn't found hers yet.

"I've also never waxed my girl bits," says Mathilde as he kisses around her ankles, still on the hunt. He is already well aware of this or, it doesn't translate. Her lack of tattoos is what interests him. He asks no questions about where she comes from. It is as if any other details of her life, driver's license, date of birth, marital status, employment history—none of it matters. She is this woman, now. And it is all she needs to be.

There were times when she would be in the circle with Anjanette that she wondered if there was something wrong with her. Someone would be talking at length about sex, orgasms, relaying all sorts of details. She had never had the experiences they described. Mathilde had long given up that she would ever shake and scream like a cat, tremble like she was electrocuted or go into paroxysms of orgasm. She knew she would never go to absurd lengths to orchestrate a chance encounter with her wild lover in the hopes he would take her into the bathroom of the bookstore, the football stadium, the back seat of the car—wherever she has found him, with the fierce, blind desperation to have that experience only he could give her.

But then, Luciano.

He revels in her curly hair and freckles. His hands are large, palms smooth. His touch sure but also, tender. She did what she always did until he presses her hips into stopping their hurried motion. She releases into the grip of his fingers that hold each side of her pelvis and let him move her like a slow ocean, lifting her higher higher so high she thinks she might lose consciousness and she kind of does as the waves peak and crash taking everything out in its fury and her body and voice are no longer hers but some ancient goddess of the sea and she begins to cry in shame and shock and joy and guilt and such a mix she doesn't even know what she is feeling except she never wants it to end, and it doesn't, there are waves and waves following that first crash that have her sobbing and calling out as if in terror of such a good feeling and all the while Luciano holds her strong, comforting her in words of Italian she doesn't understand. Until she is a slick sweaty underwater creature half off the foot of his bed, and he is pulling her up to the pillows so they can fall asleep and she falls asleep with a single prayer on her lips.

Oh dear god. Please god, let me have this again.

Papi sets down two baskets of food in front of them. Each basket has a grilled veggie sandwich tucked in next to some corn fritters. Mathilde reaches up to Luciano and drags her thumb down one side of his face. She loves that he is always clean shaven. Even Mike had gotten on the trend of growing a beard and she hated it. Luciano wears a cologne of fir and sandalwood that makes her loopy. She puts her nose to his neck to breathe it in. He laughs as if it tickles slightly and gestures for her to begin eating. She lifts a corn fritter to her mouth, checking to make sure it won't burn her tongue, then sinks her teeth into it.

For the first time she can ever remember, her inner anthropologist is quiet. She loves to watch Luciano move. She loves to see what makes him smile. She loves to observe him talking to Papi and his friends at the bar, but she absolutely does not want to know his age or whether he has brothers and sisters. She doesn't want to know where he grew up, how he ended up living here or what keeps him here. She only wants this connection they have, no story. With a story, he becomes human and this bubble of magic will shatter. She knows it will end eventually, but until it does, she wants to float along.

After lunch, Mathilde climbs onto the back of Luciano's scooter and they ride over to his place. Other than a few people walking along the side of the road, the route is empty. Just chickens and the occasional rooster. People use scooters if they need to get to the other side of the island, and Mathilde has seen a couple of vehicles that might generously be referred to as small trucks that bring things up from the ferry, but no cars.

She revels in how wild and free the roosters and chickens, mostly chickens, are. It seems they have full range of the island as she has not once seen them contained anywhere. They do not hustle to the side of the road as Luciano approaches them, but continue pecking where they are in the middle of the lane. They barely look up at the sound of the motor knowing the bike will weave around them.

What does it mean to be wild, she thinks lying back on Luciano's bed as he showers under the spigot outside the window. She looks down on her naked body. The women she knew who jumped on the 'going bald' bandwagon as if that were a way to claim their erotic power definitely thought they were being wild. Mathilde never got on board because one, it seemed like a pain in the ass to keep up and two, she knew the trend had its roots in what prostitutes were expected to do, so nothing sexy about that. Plus check in with any Greek myth: hair is power.

Mathilde strokes her mound of fluff feeling extremely proud that amid all the ways she had let herself down, compromised life decisions, put aside her own choices for what others wanted—she had never acquiesced to the trend of little girl pussy. It might have glimmers of white in it now, but it is all hers. One less area of beauty to upkeep, she thinks.

Particularly on an island. Mathilde puts her hands behind her head as she hears Luciano turn off the shower. She listens as he walks around to the door and comes in.

"What are you thinking about," asks Luciano as he towels off, bringing attention to each part of the body being dried.

"You," she answers, enjoying the look on his face that knows she is teasing him, but not entirely sure.

As Luciano pulls on his pants and then his shirt, Mathilde reflects on this gap of understanding. Of course he can't know for certain. They are strangers. They do not know each other, at all.

Clement Street
April 1977

Sunday morning. Mathilde is curled up in the window seat that juts out from the second-floor landing. From here she can see Anjanette's backyard, the side yard and all the way around to the front garden where the brick pathway drops down to the street. The Colson family's departure for church is something Mathilde loves to watch. The consistency and predictability of the weekly ritual always makes her feel snug and cozy.

Anjanette's brothers, Joseph and Ten, are in the backyard dressed for church—trousers, belt, long-sleeved white shirt, and a tie. Joseph is fifteen and Ten is thirteen, but they still act like little boys. Their navy blazers are folded over the railing. They are tossing a ball back and forth. Joseph does something to provoke Ten and they begin tussling. Lonny snaps the back door open. "You gonna tear up those good clothes?"

"No ma'am!" They say in unison and shove at each other to lay off. Joseph gets the last smack across the top of Ten's head.

"That's what I thought," says Lonny as she holds the screen door open. "Get inside. We're leaving now."

Mathilde's parents only ever take her to church for Christmas, Easter, or funerals. Heading to Nantucket once a year, or going down to the beach in Hull to be with her mother's family are the only times Mathilde feels she and her parents do something like this—be a family, together.

The boys are first out the front door. Jackets on. Ten tugs at the collar of his shirt. Joseph pulls at Ten's sleeve—they are still pushing and shoving at each other but wary of their mother coming along behind. The dress-up clothes never seem comfortable on the boys. Unlike Anjanette who revels in her attire. She steps down the front walk as if her carriage is waiting.

Mathilde marvels at Anjanette. They are both eleven years old, but Anjanette has such panache.

Today, Anjanette wears a fascinator which seem like the ultimate in dress-up. Her dress has a fluffy skirt and matching hand-knit cardigan in soft mohair.

Lonny wears a hat and a beautifully tailored silk dress. Her Sunday clothes are never as exuberant as Anjanette's, but mother and daughter both wear brightly colored shoes. Daniel comes out just before Timo, who pulls the front door shut and locks it.

Mathilde always feels that Daniel has a bit of the dreamer about him, probably because there is often a book in his hand. Unlike his brothers who wear whatever their mother tells them to, Daniel is his own man with his own style. Today he wears a dark turtleneck under his blazer. Mathilde has seen Lonny be a bit sharper with Daniel. Maybe because he is the oldest? Maybe because he tends to resist falling into line?

Timo touches Daniel on the shoulder lightly before walking around the front of the car to get into the driver's side. Anjanette's daddy is a big man and suits never seem to fall quite right. Tight in the shoulders, the jacket is too long and barely buttons shut at the waist. His trousers bag at the ankles. The necktie rides high like a choker. It doesn't look to Mathilde that Timo is ever particularly comfortable wearing a suit, but there is no doubt how proud Timo is of his family as he settles into the driver's seat.

The boys sit in back. Anjanette sits between her parents in front. Lonny holds her purse in her lap. Timo backs their green Dodge Coronet down the drive.

"You spying again?" Rosie voice causes Mathilde to jolt back from the window and knock her head on the alcove wall. Her mother stands at the top of the stairs, her bathrobe dangles open revealing the nightgown underneath. Mathilde knows her mother is trying to be funny, but everything about Rosie irritates Mathilde.

"No!" Mathilde answers hotly. Mathilde holds up the copy of *A Distant Mirror: The Calamitous 14th Century* she just borrowed from the library. "I'm reading."

"Don't take that snotty tone with me," her mother says as she walks over to inspect the book. Rosie looks down, baffled. "Is that for school?"

"No," says Mathilde. "It's Sunday. I can read whatever I want."

"Yeah, but why would you *want* to read that?" Rosie finds the title hilarious.

Mathilde doesn't answer. Her mother continues laughing as she heads into the bathroom and closes the door.

Mathilde is still in the window seat when the cars begin pulling up in front of Anjanette's house.

Timo's car is not always the first one back to their house after church. Other people often arrive first. Women come up the front walk carrying bowls topped in tinfoil, platters wrapped in plastic, their dresses an explosion of bright colors, their earrings big, necklaces sparkling. Their hair is elaborately coiffed. Many wear hats. There is lots of lipstick and everyone wears pantyhose. The men head straight to the backyard to shuck off their jackets and ties. Music begins to play.

Soon, the steady stream of people fills the house and spills into the backyard.

Timo started his barbeque yesterday, early Saturday morning. For Mathilde, it feels like having a restaurant next door with the smell of smoke, tomato, and spices wafting up and down the street. Mathilde's father grills steaks and hamburgers, but he just takes the plate of whatever Rosie gives him to grill. Her dad doesn't do more than that. It's nothing like the cooking out back that Timo does.

After she and Anjanette became friends, Mathilde is invited to come over to the Sunday suppers in the backyard. Of course, her mother would never allow her to go every Sunday.

"You're over there too much as it is," Rosie says. "You will make yourself unwelcome."

But today, Mathilde pushes through the hedge holding the cake she baked specially and walks across the backyard looking for Anjanette.

Most everyone has left. The clean glasses are upside down—lined in neat rows across the shelf to dry. Timo shuts down the fire pit; the grills have been scrubbed with brillo pads and are leaning up against the garage door to be put away for the week. It is the end of the day, or that hard to describe time of day that is late afternoon early evening.

Mathilde helps Ten break down the two long tables and store them under the porch. Mathilde scoops potato salad into tupperware and puts the leftover brownies and cookies into the waxed box with the lid and tucks it up on the pantry shelf where she knows it belongs. She looks around for something more to do, but the women have made short work of the clean-up. Mathilde wishes she could linger, sit on the swing with Anjanette who is lying across it on her back, one leg over the chain, staring up at the sky as it rocks her to and fro. Mathilde never wants the party to end, but she doesn't want to be impolite. It's time to go.

"Thank you very much for having me, Mrs. Colson. I'm going to head home now."

Lonny is rinsing the pitcher that held iced tea. "G'night now," she says. Lonny shuts off the faucet and looks up into the window above the sink, its glass panes dark with evening blue. "Mattie—"

"Yes, Mrs. Colson?"

"You can call me Miss Lonny."

Mathilde nods and sails out the back deck. She floats all the way home.

"Did you have a nice time?" her mother asks from where she and her father sit in the living room watching *60 Minutes*.

"Yes," answers Mathilde, feeling very loving toward both of them.

"Sure smelled good from here," her father says.

"It did get a little loud," her mother says.

"It always does," her father says.

"I'm going to my room," Mathilde says.

Settled onto her bed, in her boy pajamas as her mother calls them, Mathilde pulls her knees up to her chest in a hug of delight. She doesn't know if it is because Lonny likes her or, if enough years have gone by or, if Lonny really liked the pineapple upside down cake she brought that day, but it doesn't matter. Mathilde doesn't care what the reason is.

Miss Lonny is what the cousins call her.

Paul looks exactly the same, just a little bit older, but not old. Actually, young. Maybe because he is clean shaven? The guys on Mike's crew that hang out in Mathilde's kitchen on a Friday night all have beards which make them look old and grody, plus most of them probably are a lot older since Paul must be—

Twenty-three. Mathilde realizes with a start. Paul is her age. His navy crewneck sweater is what a college student would wear or, like a guy who just graduated college. Mathilde feels the chasm between now and when she was in college. That was a lifetime ago.

"Got you some." Mike holds out a small clear plastic cup of cider. He is wearing the plaid blazer his grandmother gave him. It's the blazer Mike always wears if they go to something he thinks will be fancy. As if Anjanette's art shows are ever fancy. Especially this one in the same church basement where they used to meet for Girl Scouts.

The cup of cider repels Mathilde. It makes her think of all the doctors visits when she was pregnant and the endless peeing in cups. She shakes her head no thanks.

Susannah squalls and reaches for the cup. She thrashes in Mathilde's arms.

Mathilde hands the baby to Mike. "Can you please take her outside?"

Mathilde watches as Mike carries Susannah like a red-faced screaming football with legs that kick. Legs in white tights and shiny black shoes.

"She didn't get a nap," Mathilde turns to the room in apology. "She's not usually up this late." People shrug and smile with understanding. They return to their conversations. Anjanette is talking animatedly with her mentor, Dr. M.

Mathilde looks over to see Paul who has turned at the sound of the squalling child and seen her for the first time. She waves and begins to walk over to say hello. Paul looks shocked. Because she is married? Because she is a mom?

That's so weird. Why would he care? Why would he look so disappointed? Her mom, Mike, Annie—they all think she made the right decision. Some people marry young.

Lonny got married when she was twenty. There's nothing wrong with it.

Mathilde puts on her best smile. "Hey Paul. How've you been?"

The island
Island time

Mathilde steps out of the sea, twisting and squeezing her hair. The gentle temperature of the air and water is a tranquilizer. Mathilde has no idea if she was in the water for twenty minutes or two hours. All sense of time has melted away. With a fringed turkish towed looped around her neck, Mathilde steps through the sand back to the outpost, wondering. Is it possible to be done with paradise?

After the intoxicating rush she experienced in the Telfi river, swimming here feels like taking a tepid bath. The warmth and salt allow her to float and swim for hours in a way that the river never could, but the effect is more of a lulling to sleep than a waking up. Even first thing in the morning.

But how can she be finding fault? It is heaven.

Each morning, she lifts her body out of the soft linen cocoon of the hammock, pulls on the batik wrapper she bought from Yazly's bodega and walks out into the golden pink light. She eats fruit, eggs, and fried potatoes at the taverna. She swims, naps, showers. If Luciano is not around, she walks up to the small pavilion, set into the dunes where sometimes, sometimes not, a gentle stretch yoga class or chi gong will be happening. It's never consistent. There is no schedule. Sometimes she sits at the pavilion thinking she has missed the class or there won't be one that day and then, while she sits, people begin arriving and the class slowly takes shape around her.

People are friendly. Dancing at night is the way she connects with them as there is both the language barrier with most everyone and, as with Luciano, a real lack of desire to connect beyond small talk. One of the Australians did make an effort to have deeper conversations with Mathilde, but they quickly realized how little they had in common.

Mathilde climbs up to sit on the overhang of the outpost. As she strokes sunscreen onto her arms, Mathilde thinks about Paul. The easy connection she has with him feels even more valuable to her, but it's getting harder to sustain. Mathilde wants to type an Instagram message to him right now, but has run out of things to photograph. How many images of sand and sea has she already posted?

She wants to tell Paul that there are no books here, that she misses sitting in Lonny's kitchen squabbling with Anjanette. Her happiest place in the world is not here, but on Clement Street. She thinks she is ready to come back, but she is wavering.

What if this is all a dream? What if she goes home and finds she hasn't changed—that the insanity of the world can still crush her down into feeling helpless? That she is still someone who gives up when things go wrong? Someone who quits when it feels hard or scary?

Walking down the beach, Mathilde comes across the word 'querencia' that someone has created out of shells and white stones. A beach chair has been installed next to the word as if to offer a moment of reflection. Mathilde assumes that the word and the chair have been set up as one of the gifts people make before they leave the island since a sign went up two days ago announcing the next ferry. Mathilde will be on that next ferry, although she doesn't yet know what she will leave behind as her offering of gratitude. If Anjanette were here, she'd have a million ideas.

I'll think of something, Mathilde says to herself as she settles into the beach chair and gazes out to the expanse of ocean. Right now just breathe this in. Her thoughts return to that wild river swim in Wales.

She felt so alive. And now?

Mathilde squeezes fistfuls of sand and lets the grains dribble back down to the beach. She watches the waves carry the grains back to the sea. Ribbons of gold and pink ripple across the water as the sun drops down to the horizon. The air around her expands wider and wider in a gentle pulsation of quiet. Her wrists drop loosely to her lap. A sensation of merging with the sand, the sea, the sky—fills every cell of her being.

She feels good. Strong. Ready to go home.

SKEIN III

64 Clement Street
March 2018

Mathilde's flight lands in Boston on a Saturday morning just as a Nor'easter begins to get serious. The Uber driver delivers her straight to Clement Street which already has a good four inches of snow on the unplowed street by the time they arrive.

Anjanette opens the front door with a squeal as the snow swirls in wild gusts behind Mathilde.

"Get in here," she says, pulling Mathilde over the threshold and pushing the big wooden door shut, but not before a rush of snowflakes litter the rug around them.

"You're all freckled and sun-kissed!" Anjanette says. She wraps Mathilde in a big hug then steps back—almost landing on Mojo who continues to bark and skitter about—to get a better look into Mathilde's eyes. With Mojo scooped up in her arms, Anjanette makes a sound in the back of her throat as she assesses Mathilde.

"And maybe more than just the sun that's been kissing you." Anjanette pets Mojo's head with slow, firm strokes.

"Get away from this drafty door," Lonny hustles them into the living room. But then, as she and Anjanette settle next to each other on the yellow sofa, Lonny nods in agreement, "You look good."

Lonny wears a plaid skirt and kelly-green turtleneck with gold hoop earrings and an oversized gold necklace with turquoise stones. Anjanette sits cross-legged in beige, paint-spattered cargo pants. She has on a hoodie with the sleeves cut off, over a long-sleeved flannel shirt, and a bright red patterned wrap tied into a knot on the top of her head. As they watch Mathilde open her suitcase and dig out the gifts she has brought back for them, Lonny pokes at Anjanette's pants.

"None of that better be wet," she says.

"I can take them off," replies Anjanette, offering to sit half-naked next to her perfectly dressed mother.

"Oh, you are fresh," says Lonny as she knocks at Anjanette's knee with the back of one hand.

"C'mere baby," Anjanette says to Mojo who is whimpering to be picked up. She lifts him to her chest.

"Not on my sofa," says Lonny.

"He's not on the sofa," clarifies Anjanette. "He's on my lap."

"Here," Mathilde says, in an effort to quell the skirmish. She hands up the packages, each wrapped in that extra lovely way small boutique owners do so well.

Knitting needles, hand-painted ceramic plates, and a cashmere scarf that she purchased in Palermo for Lonny. A packet of paper ephemera that Mathilde discovered in the back of an old bookshop for Anjanette, plus a wooden box that holds eight glass bottles of Zecchi pigments. And, Mathilde couldn't resist: a pair of the block print drawstring pants from the island bodega. The pair she hands to Anjanette are stamped with a pattern of pink flowers and gold vines.

Anjanette and Lonny express appreciation for the gifts. Mathilde sits back on her heels, happy—a kind of delayed Christmas morning. The months she has been away melt as fast as the snowflakes hitting the carpet. It's as if she never left.

Lonny makes cornbread pancakes. They eat them with warm maple syrup and grilled peaches.

"Tell us about your holiday," says Lonny.

With some slight fabrication and a focus on the food she ate on her trip, Mathilde finds a way to recount most of her stories without sharing anything about the failed yarn hunt or getting too deep into what she was doing on the island. Although Anjanette will not be deterred and is able to root out almost every last bit of Mathilde's fling with Luciano.

"Well now—," says Lonny.

"About damn time," says Anjanette. "You should've brought loverboy home with you. What a souvenir that would be."

"I don't think he would transplant well," says Mathilde. She gestures to the windows being pelted with wind and snow. She looks closer. "Whoa—I gotta get going, it's really coming down out there."

"You are not driving in this," says Lonny. She stands and takes her plate to the sink. Lonny turns to look back at them. "I'm guessing your room is exactly as you left it." Lonny's lifted eyebrows are a pointed rebuke of Anjanette's housekeeping. "You know where the laundry is— if you want clean sheets."

And so Mathilde stays. Happy to burrow back into the third-floor bedroom with its profusion of plants and snowy rooftop views.

64 Clement
March 1977

Walking home from school in March is hard work. The slush on the sidewalks is thick and unpredictable. Mathilde slips even in boots—even when she is trying not to slip. Across the street, she sees the mailman trudging in the opposite direction. The heavy blue sack that is slung across one shoulder seems an added challenge in this slippery mess.

They are the only two people on the street. It is lonely, cold, and dark. Anjanette has stayed late at school for an art project so Mathilde must go straight home. She pauses before heading up the front steps of 64 Clement because her father hasn't shoveled them very well. The mailman has parked his white truck with the red white and blue insignia in front of their house. Mathilde peeks at the window. She is curious because she has heard Timo complain about the mail truck.

Timo says it's a misery. A tin can. Not only is it not insulated, the doors have to be constantly opened into the freezing temps. The crappy gear shift box gets stuck easily.

Mathilde steps gingerly up the front steps that are treacherous and icy. She heaves a sigh of relief when she gets to the front door without wiping out. No wonder Timo's sunny nature always turns sour at this time of year.

In spring and summer, Mathilde sees Timo as the bright sun coming down the street at the end of the day. His uniform is long shorts and high socks, a pith helmet, and the great blue sack slung across one shoulder. Somehow, Timo knows people's nicknames and if they don't have one, he gives them one. Everybody loves Timo. But winter is different.

Mathilde and Anjanette look up from where they are playing in the den off the kitchen. The stomp of heavy rubber boots coming up the back steps means Timo is home. Anjanette's daddy sighs loudly as he takes off his coat, muffler and hat. He drapes his wet socks by the wood-stove and stands there warming his hands, his bare feet.

"Where's that baby girl?" he shouts.

At his call, Anjanette jumps up and runs in to give him a kiss. She insists he put on his slippers while she makes a plate of cinnamon toast for him. Mathilde watches it all unfold through the narrow doorway of the den, as if she were watching a play or a movie.

Lonny gets home in the dark. She hangs her coat and sees Mathilde's boots in the back hall. "Those girls still studying?"

"Too much to ask that people shovel their damn walk?" Timo growls in return. Lonny stands behind him and squeezes her hands up and down his shoulders.

"Oh, you big old bear," Lonny gives him a good smack on the back and begins making dinner. She has to be tired, too, but she doesn't say that to Timo. Mathilde only ever overhears Lonny talk about what goes on at the college with Gerri. It sounds like the hardest part of Lonny's job are the other people she works with, although she clearly respects President Horner.

"Tell me what you're gonna do when you get that pension," Lonny says as she pulls out the skillet and sets it on the stove. Timo plays along.

He talks about the little place they are gonna have on Cane River. They'll spend the winters there and he'll have a boat to do some fishing. Nothing fancy.

"Good," says Lonny. "I'm not keeping house."

"No need," says Timo. He's gonna bring home catfish for dinner and cook it outside on the grill. Timo and Lonny are gonna for long walks together down the lane.

"And me," Anjanette calls out from the den.

Mathilde looks at Anjanette, but doesn't say anything. Doesn't Anajnette know she'll be all grown-up by then?

"Your homework finished?" answers Lonny.

"Just about," says Anjanette.

"Watch your tone," Lonny says to Anjanette.

"Think of all the time you will have to read your books," Timo continues.

What would it be like, Mathilde wonders, if her father said sweet things like this instead of always making fun of what her mother likes.

"Better build me a nice bookcase then," says Lonny.

"A bookcase and a porch swing, for two."

"Three," Anjanette shouts.

"Um hmm," Lonny steps out into the hall and calls for the boys to come show her their homework.

Mathilde pulls on her coat, scarf, and boots—says her good-byes—and walks across the dark yard to her house where her mother is waiting in the kitchen.

Rosie is angry. Angry that her father isn't home yet. Angry that she started dinner too early and now the chicken is dry. Angry, that Mathilde has come home late, again.

"Don't make them have to ask you to leave," she scolds Mathilde. "Where are your manners? You know you need to be home before dinnertime."

Mathilde looks out her mother's kitchen window. Through the hedge are little glimmers of light coming from Lonny's kitchen.

"Are you listening to me," Rosie says. "You spend too much time over there. Why don't you ever have Anjanette over here?"

"Okay, mom. I will." Mathilde heads up to her room. But she won't.

Anjanette doesn't like coming over to her house. And Mathilde understands why.

They meet at Riverbend Park. Paul looks at her boots but says nothing. Mathilde is wearing a pair of Anjanette's boots which are much too big, but that is not the reason Mathilde is struggling to walk in them. Anjanette's boots are shiny silver city booties with pink metallic laces—they provide no traction on the icy path. Mathilde grips Paul's forearm to keep from wiping out.

Paul wears rugged, fawn-colored Timberland boots and a bright turquoise parka. Mathilde likes that he wears a knit cap. When she sees people walking around in freezing temperatures with no hat on, she immediately assumes they are idiots.

"I am an extremely judgmental person," she says to Paul. She likes how she can say whatever is on her mind. Even with Anjanette, sometimes she feels a little bit on eggshells because Anjanette loves to challenge Mathilde which causes Mathilde to shut down. But with Paul, there is no edge, no fear. And, because of the months she wrote little notes to him on Instagram, she feels like they have been in one long conversation since last October.

"But I don't wanna be," she says.

"I have an opinion about that," says Paul.

"Okay," says Mathilde. "Hit me."

"If you could be less self-critical, it would be a lot easier for everyone around you."

"You know what would be easier for me? Tell me some awful things about yourself. At least three," says Mathilde. "That would really help."

"Like we could have a 'who's a worse human being contest?'"

"Yeah, something like that but, you know I would totally crush you, so I wouldn't hold out any hope of winning—" says Mathilde.

Paul finds this very funny.

They haven't been walking for very long, but already her feet are wet and cold. She does not tell Paul this. He is looking up. The sky is in its post-storm beauty. Loads of sunshine. The intensity of blue softened by long swathes of cirrus, lacy and white.

Somehow, with the river rushing on her left and traffic streaming down Memorial Drive on their right, Mathilde allows her words to tumble forth. Maybe because they are walking next to each other and not facing one another, it is easy to spill about her confusion, shame, guilt, frustration. Maybe because Paul makes exactly zero effort to offer advice or to complement her recounting of inner conflict with similar experiences of his own, as they walk, she begins to answer her own questions.

"This is probably why Catholics love confession so much," she says.

"Aren't you Catholic?" he replies.

"Only half," she says. "My dad was Episcopalian, but we never went to church except, you know, Christmas or Easter, but even that we stopped doing when I was in high school."

"Episcopalian. Episcopalian," Paul repeats. "Sounds like another branch of vegetarianism."

"Hardly," Mathilde laughs. "All I remember eating at my grandparents was roast beef and lamb. I don't think vegetables were ever more than a garnish."

"But did you ever go to confession?" asks Paul. They step to the edge of the path to let two guys on mountain bikes ride by, their tires spitting thin arcs of slush as they pass.

"Yeah, but—" she gives Paul a side glance. "I never admitted to anything. I think I just made stuff up."

He laughs.

She follows his lead as they turn right and begin walking up JFK Street. He stops in front of a shoe store. He opens the door for her and she steps in, not sure why he suddenly wants to buy shoes.

"You need your own boots," says Paul.

"You're not coming in?"

"I'll be over there." He points to Grendels, a pub that has been there for as long as she can remember.

She enters the shoe store and goes straight to the window to watch him cross the street.

"Let me know if I can help you find something," the salesgirl calls out to her.

"Yeah," says Mathilde, her eyes still on Paul. "I need some boots."

Mathilde has to roll her wet socks down to get them off. Each foot feels like a block of ice in her hands. When the salesgirl brings her a pair of boots that are lined with a thick layer of fleece, she almost moans as she slips her foot in. They are warm and fit perfectly.

Can it be that simple, Mathilde wonders as she stands at the counter in her new boots. She feels stronger, more capable, more relaxed now that her feet are warm and dry. Seriously? It can't be that easy. She stretches and wiggles her toes to feel the soft fleece against her skin. These boots don't even require socks. The salesgirl hands back her credit card then puts Anjanette's soggy silver booties into the box her new boots came in and drops them into a bag with handles.

"Here you go," she says, sliding the bag across the counter to Mathilde.

With her coat off and her hat stuffed into the shopping bag at her feet, Mathilde can tell Paul notices her tan, her hair, her *je ne sais quoi*, and is weighing the pros and cons of making a comment on her improved appearance—but in the end, he says nothing.

She realizes she wants him to find her attractive. What is going on?

What has happened that she is feeling all this warmth being with Paul? Is it because he's known her since junior high school? He has seen her at her absolute most awkward. There is such a deep freedom in being with him because she doesn't have to pretend to be anything more than what she is. He wouldn't be fooled. And yet, she barely knows him.

Paul asks Mathilde about her trip but there isn't much to tell. He has seen all the photos she posted on Instagram. Her notes were always directed to him. How awkward, she realizes now. Of course, she never posted about Luciano or the wild nights at the taverna.

"The thing about being there—on the island." Mathilde is tentative. This isn't easy to express. "There were no books, no tv, you know. Nothing like that. Really nothing and not a whole lot to do." Mathilde begins to blush as she remembers long afternoons at Luciano's place. She hurries her words. "It's really beautiful there. Like crazy beautiful. But, it doesn't change much. After awhile, it felt like there was just so much space—in my head. Like everything quieted down."

Paul is listening. The tables around them are empty. A sensation of intimacy floods Mathilde. She can't believe she is sitting so close to him— that she is telling him these things. When she was a little girl and her mother would try to get her to share stories for Uncle Wesley the shyness would engulf her like it is now. But talking one on one with Uncle Wesley was always good. He made Mathilde feel understood.

"My Uncle Wesley used to tell me this thing—" Mathilde twists and untwists her napkin. "He'd say I need to stop trying to figure things out. And—" Mathilde drops the napkin and settles her hands back in her lap. The tension that has built up around this sensation of closeness is released with a big sigh. Mathilde smiles at Paul.

"On the island. There was this spaciousness," Mathilde says. "Things got so quiet. It's like my mind stopped. I started feeling okay. Like this really deep sense of okayness. If that's a thing—"

"I think it's a thing," says Paul.

"But now it's like—" Mathilde looks into her mug as she swirls the dregs of coffee around and around. "How do I keep from getting all in my head again, you know?"

Paul nods. "I get it."

"You know what's weird," she says. "It's like I know you, but I don't know you."

"Is there anyone you feel like you truly know?"

Mathilde looks at Paul with interest. "What a great question."

They talk about their kids. Wouldn't they know everything about their kids? But, actually, no. They can only see them through a certain lens—just the way they see their parents. She wants to ask him about his wife, but she doesn't. Instead she asks him about his closest friends—doesn't he know them truly?

Paul seems to have all the time in the world. They have each had coffee and a refill, split a bagel, and now the server is back asking them if they want to order lunch.

"Sure," says Mathilde. The longer she is here, the longer she can put off going back to Lonny's which means loading her suitcase into the car and driving south to the condo in Dedham.

"I could eat something," Paul agrees. They order supreme nachos to split and soup for Paul.

"I'm glad you're finally getting that bowl of corn chowder," Mathilde says as she smooths her twisted napkin across her lap. She looks up to see Paul giving her a strange look.

"What?" says Mathilde. "Don't you remember? I was so late to lunch the other time that the chowder was all gone."

"I remember," says Paul. "Just a little surprised that you do." He taps his toe against her boot.

"Feeling better?"

Mathilde shakes her head smiling. "It's ridiculous."

"What is?" asks Paul.

"Me. How I can be a mewling wretch when it's an absolutely beautiful day and there is not one thing wrong with my life that isn't my own damn fault and the minute my feet get warm, all is forgotten. All my problems melt away."

"Did you actually say, mewling?" says Paul.

"I did. Mewling."

"Mewler?" says Paul like the teacher checking attendance for Ferris Bueller. "Mewler?"

Mathilde laughs. "You know, that would make a good headstone: wife, mother, mewler."

Paul laughs. "You forgot, legendary anthropologist."

"Oh yes," says Mathilde. "Legendary." She can feel he is close to asking her more about her failed career so she swiftly switches subjects.

"Can you believe Anjanette has never lived anywhere but 62 Clement Street?"

"I did not know that," says Paul. He does not seem particularly interested by this fact.

"Oh yeah, straight from the hospital," says Mathilde, leaning back in her chair to give the server more space as he sets the platter of nachos down into the middle of the table.

Over the years, she has heard enough pieces of the story to be able to share it in one long narrative. Some of it is deeply private that she only knows from overhearing conversations between Lonny and Gerri, details she has never talked about it with anyone except Anjanette, but she knows Lonny has always liked Paul and feels he can be trusted. Besides, Paul is always teasing her about her 'hero worship' of Lonny—Mathilde wants him to know why she idolizes Lonny.

Lonny is the youngest of three daughters. Her father owned a successful printing shop with two locations in Baltimore and one in Annapolis. Her mother taught high school math. When she was eighteen, Lonny ran away from home and came North to stay with cousins because she was pregnant. She found work, had the baby, met Timo, and married him in 1962 when baby Daniel was nearly a year-old.

Her parents tried repeatedly to get the couple to move down to Baltimore so Timo could join the family business and Lonny would be back in the fold. Timo was working the night shift at the post office, and Lonny had a sideline hustle as a bookkeeper for a few small businesses.

Neither job was going to ever do more than keep them staying one step ahead of their bills. But, then, the year Tender was born—Joseph had been born the year before—her parents gave up that she was ever going to return to Baltimore so they purchased the house on Clement Street for the prodigal daughter and her family.

When Mathilde once asked Anjanette why they never moved back to Baltimore, she simply said, "My grandparents don't like Daddy," which Mathilde thought was crazytalk since everybody loved Timo. It was only when Mathilde got older that she could understand how Timo wasn't the man that Lonny's family expected for her. Timo was a Louisiana boy who never finished high school.

Lonny was able to stand up to her parents and carve her own path. She went back to school when Anjanette began first grade and got a BA from Northeastern in economics and then went on to complete an MS while working full time in the bursar's office at Radcliffe. She built a career at Radcliffe, first the bursar and then the Director of Finance and Accounting, all while raising four kids.

"I mean," says Mathilde. "I just don't know how she did it. It's just— she's amazing."

Mathilde doesn't tell Paul anything more even though she knows Lonny might have gone even further in her career. Lonny was due for a big promotion when Timo died, but—that April, everything changed. Daniel quit Princeton which caused some kind of huge blow out with Lonny—Mathilde never knew exactly what happened.

All she knows is Timo died. Daniel took off. Anjanette refused to go back to high school. There were no more backyard barbeques for a long, long time.

Mathilde lets the silence grow between them so Paul will have to say something.

"Interesting," says Paul.

"That's it?" Mathilde says.

Paul stretches an elbow behind his back, cracks his neck. He folds his arms across his chest and leans back in his chair to look at Mathilde square in the eye.

"Yeah, I find it interesting that you know everybody's story except your own."

"I don't have a story," she says. "My mom always said I was duller than dishwater."

Paul looks pained. "What an awful thing to say. I'm so sorry."

Mathilde waves him off. "Oh, please. She's right. I've never done anything heroic like Lonny or interesting like Anjanette." Mathilde signals the server to bring the check. She looks out the window.

"It's getting dark," says Mathilde. "We should go."

62 Clement
March 2018

Mathilde sits in her car, parked on Clement Street with the engine still running. Why did she tell Paul all those things? Why did she talk so much? She had no right to tell Paul anything about Lonny's story. He didn't even ask. She volunteered all of that. Mathilde feels exhausted and over-exposed. And wrong.

God, she is just a wrong wrong wrong human being.

It hasn't even been three days since she got back from the island and all the magic seems to have melted away into slush. She hasn't changed. Nothing will ever change.

Mathilde shuts off the engine and leans her forehead against the steering wheel.

On that last visit to her grandmother before she died—her father's mother—Mathilde watched the ease with which her grandmother took out her dentures. How her mouth caved in on itself. What must that be like?

Mathilde imagines unlocking her jaw and then the upper part of her face. What a relief to have them off, soaking somewhere. And then her head—pulling herself apart, section by section, like legos—until her entire body was dismantled in chunks of puzzle pieces, dropped into a fizzy, bath until she was ready to reassemble herself again.

Low voices and the sound of footsteps walking by push her to sit up. Mathilde watches as the couple continue past the car. Did they see her slumped over? No. Besides. Who cares.

Why would Paul think she has a story? Mathilde has no story. She opens the car door and steps out. Lonny's could be made into a book or a movie. Even her own parents made some unconventional choices early on before they became predictable demographic statistics.

Mathilde gazes up at the two houses—62 and 64—sitting side by side, porch lights on. Mathilde can smell smoke from Lonny's wood-stove. God, she loves that scent. Next door, the porch light is on at the hipster's house, but it doesn't look like anyone's home.

When she gets to the second-floor landing, Mathilde sets the soggy silver boots with pink sparkly laces onto the shoe rack that sits in the hallway outside Anjanette's bedroom and looks around. If Lonny saw this it would break her heart, thinks Mathilde.

The hallway is packed like a poorly organized secondhand shop. This is Anjanette's best attempt to store the junk she brings home. The only reason there is so much in the hallway is that the bedrooms are already loaded with cast-off furniture, discarded lampshades, boxes of Fisher-Price toys from the '70s, glass bottles, stacks of magazines and whatnot. Mathilde hasn't ventured far enough in to really look at what decades of hoarding has accumulated.

Mathilde's legs feel heavy as she climbs the stairs to the third floor. She drops her bag and sits on the bed. With a grunt she pulls off the new lovely boots and drops them onto the floor. One. Two.

Then, Mathilde tips onto her side and pulls the coverlet over her.

Mathilde sits up. How long has she been asleep? She rubs her upper arms and pats at her hair to smooth it out. She looks at the clock. It's too late. And cold.

She'll drive back to Dedham in the morning.

Wrapped in one of Anjanette's big cardigans, she pads through the dark house to where all the lights are on in the den. Lonny is watching *Jeopardy*. Mathilde hasn't missed that much, it's still the first round. The volume is a bit too loud for her ears, but Mathilde says nothing.

Lonny's knitting group hosts an Easter bazaar every year for the church outreach. The blanket needs to be done by next week and Lonny wants to get another two hats done. Lonny asks Mathilde to weave in the ends.

Mathilde reaches into a basket that holds a nearly finished knitted blanket and settles onto the sofa, a sea of celadon in her lap, happy to be asked.

"My knitting group is coming here on Saturday to get everything finished for the Bazaar. All hands on deck." Lonny looks up at Mathilde over her bifocals. "You're coming, alright?"

"Sure." Marthilde nods. Lonny looks back at her show.

"Have you picked a winner?" Mathilde asks.

"Child—you know there's no way to know," says Lonny. "Every now and again some grinning clown gets all the way to the end with a high score and then makes the wrong wager." She shakes her head and makes a scolding sound in the back of her throat.

"Oh, come on, you *live* for that moment," says Mathilde. Lonny busts out a big laugh that stretches into a thin whinny behind closed lips as her shoulders shake. She's delighted to be called out.

They drift into a comfortable, non-conversational space as they watch the show together, Lonny's knitting needles click softly.

As Mathilde's fingers work the strands of yarn, weaving the ends back into the whole so they don't show, she gets the urge to be knitting. Mathilde used to love knitting. Why did she ever stop? Forget that stupid blue yarn. Forget that stupid sweater. Just make something else.

"Miss Lonny?" says Mathilde. "There's still that yarn store on Hampshire Street, right? I think I'm gonna stop there on my way out tomorrow."

In bed, unable to sleep after that epic nap earlier, Mathilde fluffs the pillow and rolls onto one side. That was such a nice night. Watching *Jeopardy* with Lonny. Just sitting and knitting.

Lonny looking over and giving an appreciative nod when Mathilde called out, *what is a shaman?* Which was the correct answer.

A shaman. Professor Gordon taught her that shamans believe there is only one disease and only one way to heal from that disease. Disconnection from self, from the true part, the soul part—whatever that is. Mathilde didn't understand it then and is not too sure she gets it now. But maybe she does.

On the island, she felt it. Sitting with Lonny tonight in the den, knitting—she felt it. Her heart feels warm and glowing but then the critical voice rushes in to squash everything down—*you aren't all that. Who was the idiot that didn't buy the three skeins of yarn in the first place? That was stupid.*

Mathilde sits up sharply. No. She argues back. It doesn't feel like that. She didn't succeed? Fine—she failed, whatever. *A colossal failure—* the critical voice hits back—*if you had simply bought the three skeins on that hot October day you would have spent less than 300 dollars total instead of racking up over six thousand dollars on your credit card and only ending up with two.*

The absurdity of it all hits Mathilde like a Texas linebacker. Instead of feeling badly about the mistake, she bursts into hysterics, burying her face into the pillow so Anjanette doesn't hear her screams of laughter. Mathilde's belly aches as the tears roll. When the convulsions have finally passed, she straightens up. She wipes her nose on the sleeve of her t-shirt then sniffs again at the soft cotton. It smells of coconut oil, a scent that was everywhere on the island.

Mathilde flips onto her back and stares up at the ceiling.

So what if she didn't achieve what she set out to do? She had been really, really scared, but she swam in a river. She traveled to Italy. She found a way to set boundaries with her daughter. She went to a remote island where she slept in a hammock and swam in a turquoise sea. She had so much sex that a day came when she could honestly say she was satiated.

Two skeins of yarn. Three thousand dollars each.

Mathilde rolls back onto her side and punches the pillow into shape. She settles her head and closes her eyes, grinning like a fool. Worth. Every. Fucking. Penny.

The breakfast dishes have been washed and dried. Lonny keeps checking the window. She is waiting for the plows to come through once more to get the roads good and clear before she heads over to meet with the church committee who are making preparations for the Easter bazaar.

Anjanette stumbles in per normal. She is barefoot and wearing dropped crotch yoga pants that are pumpkin orange and cuff tightly at the middle of her calves. On her head is a long, striped stocking cap whose pompom bounces against her waist as she moves around the kitchen. Over a purple and yellow tie-dyed t-shirt, Anjanette wears a pink cargo vest covered in pockets that looks like something a cheerleader might wear on safari. The tips of paintbrushes poke out of her vest pockets along with palette knives and rags. She has earbuds in and is clearly in her own world. It seems the only reason she has left her studio is that it is time to feed the machine. As she sets about pulling food together to take upstairs, she cracks open a bag of chips and eats them by the handful as she assembles her breakfast.

Lonny lifts her glasses from her face and sets them carefully on top of her head; she never pushes her glasses up. She turns to Mathilde and asks, "What are the categories today Alex?"

Mathilde catches the pass. "We've got 'Anjanette's first meal of the day' and 'Signs you might not have slept since Mardi Gras'."

"I'll take Anjanette's first meal of the day for 200, Alex," says Lonny.

"Here is the clue: chocolate chips, peanut butter, oreos, butterscotch sauce, and bananas."

"What are things Anjanette will put in a smoothie?" says Lonny.

"That is correct," says Mathilde.

While the blender grinds, Anjanette puts four slices of bread into the toaster oven to melt cheese on top.

"For 400 please, Alex," says Lonny.

"Oh, it's our daily double," says Mathilde, "You can wager up to 500 dollars."

"Let's make it a true daily double, Alex," says Lonny.

"For 500 dollars, here is the clue: kale, spinach, protein powder, flaxseed."

"What are things Anjanette would never put in a smoothie?" says Lonny.

"That is correct!" says Mathilde.

Anjanette turns to face her mother and Mathilde. She pulls one earbud out of her ear and lets it drop to dangle from its cord. "Y'all need your own tv show. It could be like the Golden Girls. Only, you know, less funny." She reinserts the earbud and exits carrying her breakfast in both arms as if she were a waitress.

"Here we go," says the server at Thai Smile, the restaurant Paul suggested. The server sets a narrow plate between Paul and Mathilde that holds two spring rolls and a small blue bowl filled with peanut sauce.

"Thank you," says Mathilde. She takes a sip of jasmine tea before using her chopsticks to lift one of the spring rolls over to her plate.

"You drove up from Dedham?" says Paul.

"Uh, no." Mathilde dips the spring roll in peanut sauce. "I'm staying at a hotel in Framingham while my condo gets repaired."

His eyebrows lift. She shakes her head at the question he doesn't ask. The moment expands, waiting for an explanation.

"I'm an idiot," she says. "The pipes froze while I was away. It's a mess."

"That happens," says Paul. He uses his fingers to take the remaining spring roll and put it on his plate.

"Not to you," says Mathilde.

Paul drinks from his bottle of Sapporo.

"So I have a pair of new boots." Mathilde twiddles the chopsticks.

"Big improvement," says Paul.

She makes a face at him. "I'm thinking—" God, this is so big. Mathilde sips again at her tea. "I'm thinking—"

"You're thinking—" says Paul.

"I might buy a house." The words come out in a gush. Mathilde rushes to try and explain. "After Mike died, I couldn't get out of that house in Dedham fast enough. I sold it and thought it would be wise to buy something for the interim instead of paying rent, so I bought the condo but I've never even unpacked. It's been a year and everything's still in boxes and—"

"Slow down," says Paul. He puts his hand on top of hers. "Take a breath."

Mathilde nods. He takes his hand back. Mathilde puts her hands in her lap and tries to still them.

"I haven't unpacked because I don't want to live there. Not even for a month. Now that I've been back on Clement Street, I know what I want. That's where I want to be."

"There's a house for sale on Clement Street?" says Paul.

"No—I wish," says Mathilde. "I just mean, somewhere near there. Somewhere in Inman Square so I can walk to see Anjanette and Lonny."

Paul lets out a low whistle. "Pretty pricey."

"Yeah, I know—" Mathilde sighs. She looks up at Paul. "You have a way of making things happen—you created your bridge thing, so I thought I'd ask for maybe some help? I've never done anything so huge like this." Asking Paul for help and sharing the idea of buying a house has her cracked open like an oyster revealing its tender flesh. Mike always handled buying the car and any big purchases.

"I thought you told me you did Real Estate at one point," says Paul.

"Yeah, a hundred years ago." Mathilde shakes her head. "But only for like a day—I hated it and quit after a couple months so yeah, I know some things, but it was one of Mike's friends that found the condo for me and walked me though buying it—I hardly remember what I did. I was so out of it—and last summer—god." Mathilde shakes her head again, this time not wanting to think about last summer. "But now is different. I am feeling better. Good. Not so mopey, you know—and ready to—

"Mopey?" Paul interrupts. He suddenly looks much older than her. Like a professor. Like a dad. "You signed yourself into McLean. It's a bit more serious than mopey."

Heat rushes up Mathilde's neck and flames across her face. The truth is searing. Nobody has spoken to her so bluntly about last summer. Her words spit out fast and hot.

"It wasn't like that. I was fine, really," she says. "Ask Anjanette. I was just hanging out eating ice cream. It was not a big deal."

"Then why were you there?"

"Jesus. What the fuck?" Mathilde had liked that their table was away from the door with a wall behind her, but now she felt cornered. Paul would have to pull back his chair for her to get out. "This is none of your business, anyway. Why are you even bringing this up?"

"I didn't bring it up," says Paul. He sips again at his beer, unperturbed. Her discomfort seems to have no effect on him. "I don't like platitudes around mental health. It's one of my pet peeves."

"Oh, well—good to know," says Mathilde. "Glad you've got some things that annoy you. I was beginning to think you were a bit too perfect. You look like Mr. Rogers in that goddamned sweater, you know." Her words are sharp, intentionally unkind. She feels her stomach clench the moment she has spoken. Paul has been nothing but sweet to her. How can she be such a bitch? Her tongue is thick and heavy in the back of her throat. A tsunami threatens behind her eyeballs.

"Here we are," the server puts down a plate of pad thai with tofu in front of Paul and a plate of drunken noodles in front of Mathilde.

Mathilde stares down at her plate. If she lifts her head, tears will start to fall.

"Anything else, right now?"

Paul answers the server. "We're all good, thanks."

With her eyes on the table, Mathilde can hear how loud the room is with conversation. No one will notice the silence between them. She pokes at her food.

"I'm sorry," says Paul.

Mathilde's head snaps up; she rushes to reply.

"You have nothing to be sorry for." She isn't able to keep the tears from bursting forward. "I'm the one to apologize."

Paul helps her by saying nothing and letting her drink water and breathe until she can speak again. She manages to push the tears back.

"I think you just caught me off guard," says Mathilde, with a cough to clear her throat. "I really haven't talked about what happened. It's just too embarrassing, and I kind of want it all to go away."

Again, Paul says nothing. He is listening to me, thinks Mathilde. She waits to see if he is going to say something. Mike would. Mike would have jumped in with all the things she should be doing. Make a plan. Her mother would. Her mother would be changing the subject. The silence is not terrible. Paul eats his lunch. Mathilde begins to breathe easier.

"Why is it your pet peeve?" she asks, finally.

Paul leans forward on his elbows. His eyes are dark brown. With flecks of green and gold. They are beautiful, she admits to herself with a quick caveat that it means nothing. They are friends.

"Do you really want to talk about this now?" He pushes the hair back from where it has tumbled across his brow. The question is rhetorical. She shakes her head, no. He sits back.

The busboy clears their plates. Paul picks up the thread from the beginning of their conversation.

"It sounds to me that you know exactly what you want,' says Paul. "Which makes the job of a realtor much easier. You tell them your budget. Lay out your top three to five big wants and then, start looking at houses." He looks at Mathilde quizzically as if he isn't sure why she is coming to him. "Doesn't Anjanette know someone? She must with all the women in her circle."

"Yeah," says Mathilde. She rubs at the sides of her head. "I will. For sure. I haven't yet cause I don't want to jinx it in case it doesn't work out and then I'll be so disappointed if I can't find something and then have to buy in Arlington or Waterman—not that they're not fine, but—"

"It's not what your heart wants," says Paul.

The tears surge back, not hot. These tears are light, happy. Mathilde feels like a little kid. She couldn't love Paul more. He gets it. He understands what it means to want something with your heart.

"I just," says Mathilde. "I just don't want to get it wrong. I feel like I always get things wrong."

"When I was starting out," Paul pauses. He can see that Mathilde knows nothing about his professional life. "I was an electrical engineer," he explains.

"Oh," says Mathilde. She nods, happy to be the one listening, but Paul doesn't give her as much time to sit in her bubble. He does not ramble on as she does. His words are more compact. There seems to be more space around them.

"There was a guy who was really helpful to me. He was older. He retired soon after I started working there, but this one time, it was late late on a Friday night, and I was still in there. He came by. He could see I was kind of snarled and frustrated. We sort of chatted for a bit and then, before he left, he said something that really connected with me and, it kept on being helpful for me."

"I'm guessing it wasn't a platitude." Mathilde tries to laugh. It was meant to be a joke, but God, that sounded poisonous. The kind of quip Rosie would make. Why did she do that?

Paul pauses.

Mathilde leans forward. "Tell me what he said."

"He said, unexpected outcomes can sometimes be more important than the goal itself."

Mathilde sits back. She gazes directly into Paul's eyes. "That's really good."

He nods.

"That's really comforting," Mathilde says.

He nods again. They sit without saying anything more.

Mathilde rolls the idea back and forth across her mind. If she had gotten to Wales as she planned, and two skeins had been there—she would have turned around and gone back to London and then home. She wouldn't have swum in the river. She wouldn't have experienced Palermo. She wouldn't have had the most exquisite holiday experience of her life. She wouldn't have realized how the happiest place in the world wasn't on some beautiful beachy island, but on Clement Street with Lonny and Anjanette.

If she had come straight back, she would have moved down to the condo, spent Christmas alone. It was a gift that she arrived late. It was a gift that the yarn was not there. A gift that she ran into Effie a second time. All of it. Little treasures she didn't even appreciate in the moment. She can see all of that is true and yet, boom. Here she is, her old self. Her old stuckness. Making sharp comments to Paul. Toads and snakes still jumping out of her mouth. The gifts were wasted on her. She hasn't turned anything into gold.

The waitress puts down the check with an obligatory "no hurry." Mathilde slams her hand onto it. The force of her action causes the dishes to rattle. Paul looks at her in surprise.

"Mine," she says, shifting quickly into a gentler demeanor. No possibility of argument.

"I know a place you might want to check out," says Paul. "There's a real estate office near the library and one of the agents comes in pretty often. A real estate agent who reads books—that could be a fit for you, right?"

They exit the restaurant. Mathilde gestures to her car that is parked in the opposite direction from his. She digs into her purse for her keys. "You live in Carlisle. Why are you hanging out at a library in Cambridge?"

"I work there Tuesdays, Thursdays, and every other Saturday," says Paul.

"Why?" She didn't mean for it to come out so snotty, but she is genuinely surprised. He obviously doesn't need the money and what does a library even pay?

"Are you always so cheerful?" His sarcasm surprises her.

"I'm about average, you know, for a New Englander," she tugs her hat down over her ears. "You, however, are way too cheerful for a New Englander."

"I'm not a New Englander," says Paul.

Mathilde is stung into silence by the sharpness of his words. He doesn't look back and drives off without a wave.

So many women! The circle is buzzing tonight. Anjanette brings in a second low table because the coffee table is overloaded with all the food and offerings. Every seat is taken. Nearly half the group sits on the floor. Mathilde counts twenty-seven people including herself and Anjanette. It feels different with so many women in the room. Is it that it feels crowded? Or powerful? Maybe because it is the end of winter, everybody is stir crazy. There's definitely a mood going on, that's for sure.

Camille, one of the women Anjanette knows from the dog park, is talking about how discombobulated she is feeling since she began menopause. Brain fog, mood swings—ability to incinerate her colleagues with a superhuman gaze of irritation.

Laughter bubbles. It's a laughter of recognition. Mathilde stops to wonder. Is that part of what's been going on for the past two years? Has it been more than grief and life changes? That would explain a lot. Maybe if she'd shown up for more circles in the year after Mike died, this would have become apparent sooner.

The conversation is heating up and not only from the wild stories of hot flashes happening at the worst possible times but because, now that menopause is on the table, the older women in the group have a lot to say. Particularly, how annoyed they are that nobody told them what it would be like. Mathilde remembers trying to ask her mother how the experience of menopause went for her, but Rosie shrugged off the question. "Oh," her mom said. "I don't really remember. I'm sure it was fine."

A ripple of surprise rolls through the group when Mathilde clears her.throat and says, "I have something." This is a change.

"Most of you know my husband died—Mike." Mathilde's voice feels loud in her ears. Maybe because the room is so quiet. "Some of you knew him. It'll be two years this May—next month. And, I know it's almost two years, but it doesn't feel like it. I don't feel like I even understand what time is anymore—"

Mathilde pauses. Does she sound crazy? Do people think she's being weird? She looks up from the floor and slowly takes in the room. No. People are listening. Her eyes fill with tears. Her nose gets runny. She swabs at her nose and keeps talking while the tears run down her cheeks.

"Maybe you know—I mean, you probably do. I got, I went, I—things got really dark and confusing for me last summer and I realized I needed to do something but I didn't know what. And," Mathilde pushes on even though the tears are gaining momentum. "I just—okay. So, there's two things I want to say. First, I want you all to know how amazing Anjanette has been. Amazing. I am the luckiest." Mathilde looks directly at Anjanette. "I'm so grateful. So grateful. You have no idea how much—"

"Ssss-TAHHH-p." Anjanette puts her arm out toward Mathilde, palm flat. She makes a kiss with her lips and curves her fingers together to make a heart that she puts to her chest for Mathilde.

Mathilde laughs into her tears. She has to pause to catch her breath and pull herself together. It takes a few minutes. She hears a few gentle voices encouraging her from around the room. *Take your time. We're here.* The kindness and the way the circle is holding her with such gentleness causes Mathilde to sob harder. Someone hands her a box of tissues.

"Okay," says Mathilde, pushing back on the flood of tears. "I think I'm good. Okay, so—second thing. I'm looking to buy a house near here. If anyone knows a good real estate person, or someone selling—let me know, please."

As questions come in about what she is looking for, Mathilde clarifies. No, not a one bedroom condo. A house—with room for her idea. Her wild plan she has told no one about and here she is saying it out loud to the whole room. Nobody laughs. The women listen. They wait. Mathilde's throat goes dry. Her voice sounds a bit thin at first, but then as she explains her vision, her chest relaxes and her voice clears. "I think there's gotta be someone else like me who needs some time to themself. Time to rest. Recalibrate. And not everybody has an incredible friend to put them up for weeks at a time—" Mathilde smiles at Anjanette who is nodding and looking pleased. Not because Mathilde is loving on her, but because Mathilde is finally talking in the circle.

Mathilde describes how the house will be set up like a kind of sanctuary where women can get rest, take a break, find support. Remember who they are. Come for a few hours, a day, a couple of weeks. When she finishes giving an outline of the idea, Mathilde sits back. The response is immediate.

"Great idea."

"Love it."

"Sign me up." Laughter.

"Get in line." More laughter

Simone, a woman Mathilde has only met a few times, signals to her.

"Gimme your phone," Simone taps her number into Mathilde's phone and then hands it back. "Call me. My cousin is great. She has a license for MA, RI, NH and CT. She will find your spot."

"Thank you," says Mathilde. "But—yeah, I don't want to go that far afield. I'm really kind of looking for near here."

"Ha," Chanda calls out from across the room. "Good luck with that." Chanda is one of Anjanette's ex-girlfriends—one of the ones that thinks they might get back together someday. "You'll never find anything in Cambridge. Places here sell before they ever hit the market. Try going further west."

Mathilde nods automatically and feels the threads of the familiar knot start to try and form in her throat. She stops nodding. "No." Mathilde's voice claps out like thunder. "Not the suburbs. That's not it. I wanna be close—"

Anjanette stands. She is ready to redirect the conversation to someone else. "She can't be too far away from me or she'll shrivel up and die."

"Exactly," Mathilde pretends to be annoyed, but inside she is delighted. This is Anjanette's way of telling her she likes the plan.

"Anybody else got something?" asks Anjanette as she bends over the table and stacks three peanut butter cups into her palm, one at a time.

The living room speakers have been cranked loud. Alicia Keys sings *this girl is on fire* as Mathilde carries a stack of platters back to the kitchen. Mathilde glances toward Lonny's closed door then up at the clock. Oh god, she's gotta go. Mathilde hates driving at night and she doesn't like the idea of it being after midnight when she gets to the parking lot of the hotel.

"Hey." Anjanette stands next to Mathilde, between her and the dishwasher.

"Um, can you move?" says Mathilde, a glass in each hand.

"What are you doing?" Anjanette is a bit high, but not looking happy.

"Loading the dishwasher?"

"I mean, what are you doing staying in a motel?"

Mathilde nudges Anjanette with her elbow and sets the glasses into the top rack. She reaches back into the sink for more. "It's a hotel, thank you. And—"

"My scene's too much mess for your OCD?" says Anjanette.

Mathilde stops. Anjanette is upset with her? When she got back to the condo, Mathilde found that while she was away, the pipes had frozen and burst. It was a holy mess and Mathilde can't stay there until all the repairs are done, but she didn't want to tell Anjanette in case she'd feel obliged to have Mathilde come back and stay with her again. The whole situation makes Mathilde feel so stupid and out of control, but she never imagined Anjanette would misunderstand.

"Oh my god, no." She puts her hands on Anjanette's shoulders.

Anjanette shakes her off. "Your hands are wet."

"That is not it at all. Are you crazy? You know I love staying here," says Mathilde. "I just didn't want to be a bother. You guys have already put up with me so much. I just thought it would be better—"

"Girl," Anjanette crosses her arms and sits back on one leg. "Why you being all Miss Manners and shit? Get your things and go back upstairs."

"I'm sorry," says Mathilde. "It's just—those goddamn pipes—why do I keep making a mess? I feel like I make one step forward and then ten steps back. It's just awkward."

"I'll tell you what's awkward," says Anjanette. "You not telling me shit. Do not do that again."

Mathilde quickly dries her hands on a dishtowel and goes in for a big hug. She buries her face into Anjanette's neck. "Thank you. And, god, you smell good."

"How long until you can get back into your place?"

"Not sure. It's a friend of Mike's that I called. He's gonna do his best. He said maybe end of next week, but I'm guessing it will be more like two weeks."

Anjanette releases Mathilde from the hug. "Good. Time enough for you to make me a couple of baked zitis—one tomorrow, and one for the freezer so it's there when I want it and you really are gone." She turns and gives hugs to a couple of women who have been standing by waiting to say goodnight to Anjanette.

Mathilde laughs. "You just want me here to cook for you."

Anjanette gives Mathilde a look before heading back to the living room. "Well yeah, Boo. Try to keep up."

Dedham
June 1994

Mathilde's twenty-ninth year has been a grind. There should be a party to celebrate her and Mike for making it through, but you can't say that kind of thing out loud. People will think she is a monster. Instead, Mathilde wants people to think she is amazing, with a beautiful new baby boy, a beautiful little girl, a beautiful home and a perfect cake on a vintage cakestand in the middle of a table loaded with flowers and party favors. But, just like the past year that felt utterly out of control, the party quickly slides into disaster.

Moments after the first guests begin arriving, Toby has an explosive poop that goes all the way up his back. The precious outfit that Mathilde has bought specially for the day is ruined. Mike steps in and grabs the baby, "I'll change him," he says, which is a momentary relief. Mathilde can laugh and shrug, as if no big deal and also enjoy the envious glance from one of the mothers who does not have such a hands-on partner. The other mothers barely notice since they are trying to keep their toddlers from pulling at the corners of the tablecloth or grabbing books off the shelf.

Mike's hero status is quickly revoked when he comes back with Toby dressed in a pair of clean but stained gray leggings and a baseball t-shirt that doesn't quite cover the baby's belly.

"That's too small," Mathilde hisses at Mike, angry that he doesn't know enough to put the baby into a cute outfit. She takes Toby from Mike and excuses herself to go back down the hall and change the baby for the third time that morning which causes Toby to begin squalling.

When she comes back into the living room, it is noisy and chaotic due to the focus on the kids. Everyone has arrived and Mathilde sees Anjanette sitting by the fireplace eating the malt balls that Susannah is feeding to her.

Mathilde is consumed with moving the party along and it's only as she comes out of the kitchen with an ice cream scoop in one hand that Mathilde catches sight of her friend through the window. Anjanette is standing at the end of the driveway, obviously waiting for a cab.

Mathilde rushes out the mudroom door and jogs up to her. It is a chilly day, threatening rain.

"What are you doing?" Mathilde asks. "You're leaving?" Mathilde holds up the scoop.

"We haven't had cake and ice cream, yet."

Anjanette gives her a look. In a flash, Mathilde sees what an undertaking it has been for Anjanette to get to the house. She had to take the bus to get the Red Line to pick up the Franklin Line at South Station and then a cab from Endicott. Mathilde wasn't at the door to welcome her in, to introduce her to the other guests. But seriously? Can't Anjanette see that leaving her party before it has even begun is a total slap in the face?

"Why did you even invite me here?" Anjanette is angry, hurt.

"What are you talking about?" Mathilde does not understand what is happening. Why are they standing in the middle of the driveway fighting? Mathilde's blouse is thin and the metal of the ice cream scoop is cold in her hands.

"If one more person asks me how old my kids are, Imma cut someone," says Anjanette.

Mathilde feels everything inside of her begin to crumble. Is there no way to make everyone happy? She goes on the defensive. "So this is about you? You can't be here for me?"

The cab pulls up and gives a short toot. Mathilde and Anjanette stand for a moment staring at each other. The wind blows Mathilde's hair across her face.

"This isn't you," says Anjanette, gesturing to the house where they can hear the muffled sound of screaming toddlers. "I don't know who this is, but it's not you."

"I thought you were my best friend," says Mathilde, her voice hoarse with hurt and anger.

"I thought I was your best friend," says Anjanette. She gets in the cab. Mathilde watches as it drives away.

Clement Street
April 1981

It's a shock to find Anjanette's father sitting at the kitchen table when they get home from school. Timo's shoulders are hunched. He supports his head with his left hand. Timo's right arm is dropped against his body, right hand in his lap.

Anjanette and Mathilde hang their coats and take off their boots, quietly. Ninth grade hasn't been great for Anjanette who only likes the art room so Mathilde was gonna help her with the social studies assignment that's due tomorrow, but this feels serious. More serious than homework.

Timo sees Anjanette coming in for a cuddle and wards her off without looking up from the table. His voice is a mean growl. "Don't touch me."

"Okay, Daddy," says Anjanette, not okay at all. "I can make you some cinnamon toast?"

Timo grunts a no, eyes closed.

The girls tiptoe into the den. They sit on the edge of the sofa. Mathilde reaches over and takes Anjanette's hand.

Anjanette leans close and whispers in Mathilde's ear. "He ate too much Easter candy."

Just like Anjanette, Timo loves candy, cookies, and pie. The two of them make a game of hiding from Lonny just how much sugar they've eaten. But this feels different. Timo didn't go to work today? Mathilde saw a lump on his neck.

Anjanette and Mathilde sit, not sure what to do, not wanting to make any noise that might disturb him. Timo shouts a loud curse, slams the wood table, then moans.

Mathilde leans close and whispers in Anjanette's ear, "Does he need to see a doctor?"

Anjanette shakes her head and keeps her voice low so there is no possibility Timo can hear her. "No, he won't go. It's a dentist. And he won't go. Momma tried."

Why not? Mathilde mouths the words silently.

"Daddy hates the dentist. When he was our age, he went to the dentist—" Another loud moan from the kitchen jolts the girls. Anjanette mouths the last words. He's scared.

It doesn't seem possible to Mathilde that Timo could be scared of anything, least of all a dentist. He has a big scar on one side of his neck. She never knew where it came from, but it made him look tough.

Once, years ago, as Anjanette and Mathilde followed Timo up the stairs out of the woodshop and into the kitchen, Anjanette said, "Mathilde wants to know how you got your scar."

Mathilde froze, horrified—she knew better than to ask personal questions. She felt betrayed by Anjanette and exposed, but Timo didn't seem to mind. He saw how ashamed Mathilde was for being curious and responded to her directly, his eyes bright with mischief.

"That's alright, that's alright." He put a finger on the short, wide scar that started about an inch below his ear. He gave it a couple of strokes.

"Well, story is, I got hooked. That woman right there—" he pointed at Lonny who was lifting a casserole out of the oven. "Hooked me like a catfish. Slapped me on the deck."

"I'll slap you alright," said Lonny. Anjanette grinned, she knew this story and loved to watch the two of them back and forth.

"Course she kept me alive and didn't throw me back in—"

"Yet," said Lonny. So much love between them it shimmered in the late summer light falling through the window. "You think I wouldn't throw you back in?"

"I'm too big for you to throw me anywhere. Besides," he came over to put his face into her neck. "I'm a good catch."

She set the pan down on top of the stove and pushed him away with a laugh. "Anjanette get your brothers." She looked at Mathilde, "You staying for supper, honey?"

Mathilde wanted to say yes with her whole body, but she shook her head.

"No, thank you, Mrs. Colson," she said. "I need to get home."

The screen door snapped shut behind her like a smack on the butt for saying something that wasn't even the least bit true. She pushed through the hedge and walked up the steps to her house where her mother was flipping through the pages of a magazine.

Rosie looked up.

"It's about time you were home. One of these days they are gonna change the locks to keep you out. Go upstairs and tell your father to start the charcoal—I have steaks for him to put on the grill."

Mathilde sits up suddenly in bed. The sound of an ambulance wailing is right outside the house. She rushes out of her room and sees windows filled with red lights flashing. Her mother and father are already halfway down the stairs. It has to be after midnight. The three of them step out onto the front porch.

Her father is in his leather slippers, tying his bathrobe shut over his pajamas. Mathilde's mother is in a sleeveless nightie, barefoot. Porch lights pop on as people come out to see what is happening. Everyone is in their pajamas.

The front door of the Colson house punches opens. Timo is on a stretcher. Medics maneuver the stretcher down the brick walkway to the street. They set Timo into the back of the ambulance. Doors shut. The siren screams as the ambulance shoots up the street and rips around the corner without pausing at the stop sign.

Mathilde's father hurries across the lawn—his robe flapping at his bare ankles. Rosie puts her arms around Mathilde and pulls her in tight. They watch as Tom helps Lonny get into the passenger side of Timo's car and then slides behind the driver's wheel. Anjanette sits with her brothers in the back.

"What is he doing?" says Mathilde. She can't makes sense of anything. Is she dreaming? Her father is driving Timo's car? What is happening?

"He's taking them to the hospital," says Rosie. She presses her cheek against Mathilde's temple. "She must be in shock. She shouldn't be driving."

"But he's in his pajamas," says Mathilde.

"That doesn't matter," says her mother as she guides Mathilde back into the house.

"The infection had gone untreated for too long." Mathilde's father is still in in his pajamas. He sits limply at the kitchen table. Mathilde and her mother have been waiting and waiting for him to come home and now he is finally here. Gray. Unkempt. Her father looks like every bit of blood has drained out of him. He removes his glasses and wipes at his eyes. "It went into his heart. Septic shock."

"Oh my god," says Mathilde's mother. She scrapes her chair over to press in next to him. "Oh Tom. Oh god. He's too young. He's our age. Oh god. Oh dear god. Oh that poor woman—four children." Rosie looks up to where Mathilde stands by the sink.

"Darling," Rosie says to Mathilde. "Come here. Come sit with us."

Mathilde shakes her head. She stares numbly at the sight of her parents looking up at her with so much pain in their eyes. Her mother holds out an arm, beckoning. Mathilde backs away slowly to the door, then spins and runs up the stairs. She stops at the bookcase by the window seat that holds the Encyclopedia Britannica.

Mathilde shuts her bedroom door and sits on the floor with volume S.

Septic shock is a possible consequence of bacteremia, which is also called sepsis. Bacterial toxins, and the immune system's response to them, can cause a dramatic drop in blood pressure and may result in under-perfusion to various organs. Septic shock can lead to multiple organ failure, including respiratory failure, and may cause rapid death.

Mathilde gazes down at the funeral program. She always thought Anjanette's father's name was spelled TEEMO but, no. It was Timo, short for Timothé. Timothé Joseph Colson.

Every pew in the church is packed full. People stand two rows deep along the aisles. Mathilde stands between her parents. She watches as Lonny's sisters walk on either side of Lonny, holding her by the arms, down the center aisle to sit in the front pew. Anjanette and the boys are already in the row. Anjanette's face is swollen, her shoulders shake as she sobs. Joseph and Ten are also crying—their heads are down, chins deep into their chest. Daniel is nineteen, a sophomore at Princeton. He sits unmoving, looking straight ahead, perhaps he is trying to be a man and show no emotion, but he cannot not stop the tears that course down his cheeks.

During one of the songs, Lonny drops to her knees and begins to moan. Not like any other moaning Mathilde has ever heard. The sounds Lonny make are aching, and cavernous. Moans cries, screams, groans, low and deep and loud and cracking, anger and sorrow. If ever there is a sound for alone, that is it. All the while she wails, bodies rock and continue singing which creates a strong, steady river that holds Lonny, carries her cries and gives her the space to put it all out there.

No one stops singing until Lonny's cries become great heaving sobs. She stays on her knees while someone goes up to the front and begins sharing remembrances. Lonny's sisters kneel beside her—they press in close from either side.

Clement Street
April 2018

The backyard on this April morning is soggy. The beams of the split rail fence are gray and sagging. Timo's fire pit in the far corner is plastered with wet leaves.

"Miss Lonny?" Mathilde says. Lonny turns from the window where she has been standing since Mathilde came into the kitchen.

"Paul has built this online community. They play bridge—I have two free memberships. He gave one to me and one for Anjanette—you could use hers. She's never going to play."

Lonny walks over, arms crossed over her stomach, palms cupping each elbow.

"Bridge is all about numbers, right?" says Mathilde, trying to appeal to her love of math.

"I know Bridge," says Lonny.

Mathilde sets their laptops on the table. She walks Lonny through creating a username and password and has a flashback to Paul setting her up on Instagram last October. She takes a breath. That feels like a million lifetimes ago now.

"No, no—" says Mathilde gently. "You don't want to use anything like your real name. It should be something you like or something about you that is unique, but you want to keep it anonymous."

After a few failed attempts—gardnerlady (taken), greenthumb (taken) lovesmath (taken)—

"Taken!" snaps Lonny. "Why are they all taken?"

"It's actually a good sign—looks like there are a lot of gardeners in the group."

They tried "goodshoes" and it worked.

"Goodshoes," said Lonny with a sniff. "I don't think I like that."

"I think it's fun," says Mathilde ready to move on. "Plus, you really do have good shoes."

They both log in and choose each other as partners so Lonny can get oriented. She takes to the format quickly, and Mathilde settles back to enjoy watching her play and connect with their opponents who are in Phoenix, AZ, and Wilmington, DE.

It is the first time Mathilde can remember being in a position to offer something to Lonny and it feels marvelous. Mathilde has loads of memories sitting in this kitchen where Lonny taught her so many things.

Most everything Lonny taught her was simple, but the results were perfect; her egg salad was a masterpiece. Before Lonny, Mathilde only ever knew egg salad meant you boiled eggs. Sometimes they come out with dark rings, sometimes they were rubbery, sometimes they were too soft with a bit of mucous in the center where the white didn't quite cook. However they turned out, you put them in a bowl, chopped them up, plopped in some mayo, and stirred.

This had no relation to what Lonny made. Eggs timed to perfection; soft, cooked through, tender, never rubbery, not a ring in sight—thanks to a dash of vinegar and salt in the water. Let them fully cool. Using a super sharp knife, you carefully cut them in half. Gently loosen the cooked yolk into a small bowl. Slice the whites into ribbons and set aside. Mash the bowl of yolks into a paste. Add Dijon mustard, a splash of Worcestershire, cayenne, salt, black pepper, and mayo. Mix that all together into a light fluffy golden mush and that is what you gently fold into the sliced egg whites.

"I'm hungry." Anjanette is not happy with Lonny's new hobby since it means dinner didn't get started, again. She sits on the counter, picking through a can of mixed nuts, eating only the cashews and macadamia as she waits for Lonny to finish her bridge game.

"Stop breathing down my neck," says Lonny. "I need to concentrate."

"You can't feel my breath," says Anjanette. "I'm halfway across the room."

Mathilde puts down her knitting. Last week, she'd found some pretty ecru yarn at the shop on Hampshire Street and the young girl working there had helped her choose an easy shawl pattern.

"Why don't I order in a pizza?" says Mathilde. Anjanette looks at her in surprise. Lonny who is bent toward her laptop sits up straight for a moment to acknowledge the question. She gives a wave of her hand that says, fine, whatever, buzz off, then leans back toward the screen.

"You like pizza," says Mathilde, as she walks over to Anjanette. She keeps her voice lowered so as not to disturb Lonny.

"I don't mind," says Anjanette. "It's just—I can't remember the last time we ordered in."

"We'll let's do it," says Mathilde, taking charge. "Tell me your toppings and I'll call it in."

"Look at you," says Anjanette.

"Hey," says Mathilde. "I'm a woman who gets shit done."

"I'm taking notes," says Anjanette.

"Who made this?" says Lonny, as she investigates the slice of pizza on her plate.

"I got it from the place on Tremont—Boccia Brothers," says Mathilde. "It's good, right?"

"This tomato sauce—" says Lonny through a mouthful as she reaches down for her napkin. "It's delicious. Let's do this again tomorrow night. No cooking, no clean-up."

"Just so you can have more time to play that game?" says Anjanette.

"Now why are you on me?" says Lonny.

Mathilde tries to head off a skirmish. "Did you know tomatoes are not Italian?"

"What's that?" says Anjanette.

"There was always flatbread. In Italy, in Greece—all over," says Mathilde. "And it was always considered a dish for poor people."

"Ha. Not anymore. Twenty-two dollars for a pizza *before* delivery." Lonny makes a negative sound in the back of her throat as she reaches for another slice.

"Not everybody eats gourmet pizza, Momma," says Anjanette.

"I didn't ask for gourmet," says Lonny.

Mathilde interrupts again. "But tomatoes came from here. They are not native to Europe. In fact, at first people in Europe thought they were poisonous. It wasn't until the 1800s that we started to have what we know as pizza. So really," says Mathilde picking up the bottle of Montepulciano and topping off Lonny's glass before adding to her own. "Pizza isn't only Italian, it's really half Indigenous American."

Anjanette sits back in her chair gazing at Mathilde. She drinks down her wine and holds out her glass. Mathilde fills it halfway.

"You learned all this playing Jeopardy?" asks Anjanette.

Fuck you, almost pops off Mathilde's lips in response, but sitting at the table with Lonny, Mathilde catches herself and smiles instead. "Some of us know how to read."

"Oh my eyes are too big for my stomach," says Lonny. She pushes her plate away that has a slice still on it. "I'll have that for lunch tomorrow."

"If I haven't eaten it for breakfast," says Anjanette.

"Eat my pizza and I will lock you out of this house," says Lonny.

"I'm putting on some tea." Lonny watches Anjanette poking around in the pantry. "What all are you up to in there?"

Anjanette comes out with the cookie tin and a box of cheese straws. "You still eating?" Lonny asks.

Anjanette doesn't answer. She sets the tin and crackers onto the tray she uses to carry food up to her studio.

"Somebody's got company coming," says Mathilde.

"Maybe," says Anjanette. She sashays into the den with her glass of wine.

It isn't often that Anjanette joins them in the den after dinner. There is a bit of back and forth between Lonny and Anjanette over what to watch with both of them trying to get Mathilde to offer the deciding vote.

Mathilde lets them work it out. She sits in the chair by the side table because the light of the lamp helps as she counts stitches. Tonight, Lonny is not knitting, but crocheting a summer baby blanket for Gerri's granddaughter. Anjanette sprawls on the sofa next to her mother, her arms linked behind her head, Mojo nestled into her side, his head on her belly.

Anjanette looks over at what Mathilde is doing.

"Stop looking at me," says Mathilde.

"I'm not looking at you. But if you want, I can tell you what you're doing wrong."

Mathilde was nearly fourteen when Lonny taught her to knit. By then Anjanette had mastered both knitting and crochet. Anjanette began creating her own patterns and would mix knitting with crochet to create little creatures with funny heads. But soon it wasn't challenging enough for her and she moved on. Anjanette had very little patience with how hard it was for Mathilde to get the hang of it.

"Look," Anjanette would point. "See that 'v'? That is a knit stitch. And this," she would say as she flipped the swatch over, "is a purl stitch." Mathilde would nod, but she did not see at all what Anjanette thought was so obvious.

Mojo begins to growl. It is Teddy, Lonny's cat at the door.

"You be nice," Anjanette says to Mojo, stroking his head.

Teddy winds his way along the wall then jumps up and lands on Mathilde's lap which knocks the ball of yarn to the floor.

Mojo begins to yip.

"Hush," Anjanette says to Mojo a bit forcefully. "He's not bothering you."

"Well he is bothering me," says Lonny. "I don't want all these animals in here. Put that cat back in the kitchen where he belongs." Lonny has never been sentimental about her cats. They have one purpose: keep mice out of the house.

"He's fine," says Mathilde, picking up the yarn and helping the cat to get adjusted. "I don't mind." Teddy is a lovely kitty—a silver tabby with soft green eyes and a great head. The cat begins to purr as Mathilde makes long strokes down his back.

"Let her be," says Anjanette. "Mattie never had any pets—or siblings."

"Yeah, my dad is allergic to cats and my mom didn't want a dog—she did want more kids, though," says Mathilde. "But I guess it was lucky she even had one. There were complications. She could never have another one after me."

"You never told me this." says Anjanette.

"Yeah well—" says Mathilde. "Not something I ever think about much."

"Was it the Thalidomide thing?" Anjanette asks. "That happened to a lot of women."

"No," Mathilde shakes her head. "I don't think so. My mom was born after all that, I think? Not sure. I honestly don't know. It's not something she would ever discuss with me."

The doorbell rings. Mojo leaps down barking. He skitters as fast as he can to the front door. Curled next to Mathilde, the cat does not even open its eyes at the ruckus.

Anjanette stands up and sets the remote next to Lonny before going into the kitchen.

Mathilde watches as Anjanette picks up the tray of goodies she has set out and carries it into the front hall. There are sounds of the front door opening, closing—some murmured greetings before Anjanette and her date head up the stairs.

Lonny picks up the remote and looks over at Mathilde. "One more?" Mathilde nods.

A windstorm pounds the house. Metal chimes on a neighbor's porch chatter like a xylophone being hammered by a group of exuberant kindergartners. Mathilde sits up in bed wincing as branches ache and scrape across the roof. Windows rattle with each gust, loose in their sockets. Mathilde checks her phone: two a.m. Mathilde thought the end of April meant they were through the worst of the heavy winds, but no, they are back and last well into the morning.

"Could you sleep through that?" asks Lonny as she comes in to find Mathilde already in the kitchen.

"Did you?" Mathilde responds.

"Oh, I love it," says Lonny. "As long as there are no power outages or trees landing on the roof. A good seasonal clean-up. Mother Nature sweeping out the guff."

And it seems true. Lonny is clearly energized from the storm even though a glance into the back yard shows the work ahead: sticks and branches everywhere, plastic planters knocked from their perch, the lid of someone's trash can tumbled up against the fence.

"The wind is gonna dry up all that mud," says Lonny as she sets her coffee cup a careful distance away from her laptop. She puts on her glasses and logs into her bridge profile.

"Do you need me to turn down the music?" asks Mathilde.

Lonny shakes her head no. "Doesn't bother me in the slightest. Sure smells good, what you got cooking." Those are her last words before she drops into a game.

Mathilde has a playlist of island tracks—songs that Antonia would play at the Taverna. Mathilde had never heard any of them before and kept asking Antonia who they were listening to so finally, Antonia just created a playlist that Mathilde could download to her phone, which is now linked to the Bose that Lonny uses to listen to podcasts.

With the music playing and Lonny happily occupied, Mathilde sinks into the pleasure of cooking. Mashing garlic, slicing red peppers—adding onions and olive oil—the kitchen does smell good and the music from those long dance nights has her swaying about, lost in the no-thinking land of sound and scent.

Mathilde had forgotten how much she loves to cook. The actual act of playing with the elements—seeing what you have, moving from one idea to the next, letting it take shape without any preconceived notion of what she is making. It has been so long since she cooked like this. Making meals for a family crushed the joy right out of it for Mathilde. That was rote. A constant frustration of trying to please everyone and no time or energy for creativity. It was a drill: get them fed, clean it up, do it again.

Anjanette stands in the doorway. "What are you listening to?"

Mathilde points to the phone.

Anjanette picks it up and reads aloud, "*Nguva Ye Kufara?* Chiwoniso? Who's that? I've never heard this—where did *you* get it?" As if the idea that Mathilde could have music that Anjanette liked but never heard of seemed beyond the scope of possibility.

"On the island," says Mathilde, pushing Anjanette away from the counter. "You're in my way."

"This is banging," says Anjanette beginning to dance. Mathilde had already been moving around to the music but now begins dancing with Anjanette as she continues to check the quinoa now and again.

"Where's your friend?" asks Mathilde. "Or was that just a booty call?"

"Just because you haven't met her doesn't make it a booty call," says Anjanette.

"Oh right," says Mathilde. "So it's serious."

"It is," says Anjanette. "I was coming in here to see if you wanted to be my maid of honor."

Mathilde gives Anjanette the finger.

"Is that a no?" asks Anjanette.

The music is good. Even Lonny gets up from the table, takes off her shoes, and begins dancing in her stocking feet. The three of them move about the kitchen.

"What about your game?" Mathilde says to Lonny.

"I'm dummy," she replies. "I have time for a song."

62 Clement Street
May 2018

Mathilde comes down from the third floor slowly. The flat of her palm and tips of her fingers drag along the banister as she navigates the narrow twist of stairs. Could she be going through some kind of delayed adolescence? Being around Paul has her feeling like she is fifteen again and now—now she is going to ask Anjanette to walk her through something a woman her age should have done how many years ago?

Mathilde pauses at the door to Anjanette's studio. Is she really gonna do this? She knocks, which sets Mojo to barking, then turns the knob and pushes the door open.

"Hey-ay," Mathilde calls in.

"Hey-ay," Anjanette answers back without looking up from where she is washing brushes in the utility sink.

"Need your help with something," says Mathilde. She picks up Mojo and strokes his head as she approaches Anjanette. The studio is immaculate. Floor swept. A fresh canvas on the easel. Table surfaces are covered in marks and drips from years of use, but they have been wiped clean, not a scrap of paper or tube of paint is lying about. She must be about to begin something big, thinks Mathilde.

Anjanette turns off the faucet and shakes the fistful of brushes into the sink. She is listening.

"I want to buy a vibrator," Mathilde announces. She can say it in a normal voice because Lonny is downstairs, but still, her voice is a bit lowered.

Anjanette straightens her back. "Well, now," she says, flicking the wet brushes at Mathilde in benediction before wrapping them in a cloth towel and pressing the excess water from them. "Let's hope The Candy Shop is open."

Mathilde holds Mojo to her chest as she follows Anjanette down the stairs and into the kitchen.

"I'm gonna call first to see if they're open," says Anjanette. "I'm not putting on outside clothes and getting all the way there to find out they are closed." She takes Mojo from Mathilde. "Why don't you make me one of those egg and bread things?"

Anjanette sets Mojo on the floor so she can page through her book of phone numbers that lives in the drawer under the telephone. The book is thick with scraps of loose paper, notes, and business cards that spill onto the shelf; it could take her all morning to find the number.

"You know," says Mathilde, as she pulls the cast iron skillet off the rack where it hangs above the stove and walks over to the fridge for eggs. "If you had an iPhone, you could just go to their website."

"Couldn't be me," says Anjanette with the phone receiver tucked between her ear and shoulder as she roots around in the bread drawer to pull out a plastic bag with two slightly squashed hamburger buns. "Make it with these," she says, tossing the buns to Mathilde.

Anjanette sits down and settles Mojo into her lap waiting for someone to answer.

"Hey—hello? Candy?" Anjanette says into the phone. "Hey girl—you open?" She listens. "Oh, uh-huh."

Anjanette looks up at Mathilde. "Yeah, yeah—she's still here. She's looking to get a place of her own, though—you know, someday." Mathilde makes a face at Anjanette.

Anjanette goes over to the fridge and lifts out a bottle of orange soda. "How you doing?" she asks Candy, while holding the receiver between her ear and shoulder so she can twist off the top. Anjanette takes a long swallow, then sits back down at the table. Mojo whines; Anjanette lifts the dog into her lap.

"Yeah?" Anjanette drops into the conversation. Candy has clearly had some kind of a rough go as Anjanette is nodding and every once in a while giving out a big sigh, "Oh, girl, that is hard. That is hard."

Mathilde puts the plate of eggs grilled with hamburger buns in front of Anjanette and goes back to the stove to wipe out the fry pan with a dry paper towel. Anjanette snaps her finger to get Mathilde's attention then gestures that she needs a fork. Mathilde brings over a fork, knife, and napkin and sets them down ending with a pose as if she were a waitress asking if there's anything else. Anjanette ignores her. She is deep in the phone conversation.

Mathilde is only playing at being annoyed. She loves getting to cook for Anjanette. The house hunt is depressing and frustrating on so many levels, but the silver lining for Mathilde is that Lonny has asked her to stay because *it can be days without seeing that one up there.*

"Girl, I hear you," Anjanette says. "I don't, but my friend has a friend into computers—I can ask her to see if he can help."

She means Paul. Mathilde stands in front of Anjanette and shakes her head no. Anjanette ignores her. She finishes the conversation then hands the receiver up to Mathilde who walks it over to set it back on its base.

"So, they're not open, but she's gonna come open up for us." Anjanette says with a big stretch and yawn. She drinks down the last of her soda. "You wanna walk or drive?"

"What was all that about needing help from Paul with a computer?"

"I wasn't talking about you or your boyfriend," says Anjanette, poking Mathilde in the ribs as she passes by on her way to the pantry. She tosses the empty bottle into the green recycling bin. "Melissa has a guy that runs that computer place in Kendall Square, The Right Click."

"Oh," says Mathilde, wishing she had kept her mouth shut. "And he is not my boyfriend."

Anjanette turns back and gives Mathilde one of her looks.

"What?" says Mathilde.

"Bitch," says Anjanette. "You think that man has been coming to my shows all these years to see my art?

Mathilde feels her cheeks get hot as Anjanette's meaning sinks in. She shakes her head and begins to reply but Anjanette waves her off.

"No-no," says Anjanette. "Rhetorical." She turns and heads back down the hall. "I shoulda left you in that damn hospital. You need your head examined."

They decide to walk to The Candy Shop. Mathilde sees their reflection in the panes of glass as they pass a closed storefront. Anjanette looks like a cool chick from Berlin; Mathilde looks like she got lost in an LL Bean outlet.

Anjanette wears a white denim jacket with neon pink Japanese anime stitched onto the back, black joggers with metallic down the sides, and a pair of platform sneakers with giant soles that make Mathilde think of construction truck wheels. Mathilde looks down at her new boots. It never occurred to her to think about whether or not they were stylish, she was so glad they were comfortable. Just like the navy pullover she's wearing—someone gave it to Toby years ago and he wouldn't even try it on.

They cross Mass Ave and head down to Central Square.

Mathilde has always been envious of Anjanette but never more so than when Susannah and Toby were little and she felt buried alive by responsibilities; Mathilde watched Anjanette come and go as she pleased, never beholden to anyone or anything, saying 'no' with zero guilt. From the outside, it always looked like she had it so easy.

But now that Mathilde has been living upstairs from her, she sees that is an illusion. Anjanette *is* beholden. She *is* married. She *does* have a bunch of mouths to feed that never seem to shut up and the moment she gets one passel fed, a new baby's at the door. And, she never gets a day off. The reason Anjanette can't be bothered about food is that, for her, it's a distraction. Her one committed relationship is to her art.

Mathilde thought she knew the reason why Anjanette's romantic relationships always end after a few long months or a short year: Anjanette is immature, unable to make a commitment. When the relationship progresses to the point where her girlfriend expects they will move in together, Anjanette doesn't offer ambiguous resistance, she straight-up says, *that's never gonna happen*. And, by then, the girlfriend will have come to see that being allowed into the sanctum of her studio for a visit now and again is as much as she is gonna get; it is the end of the line— she will always come second to Anjanette's one true love.

The lights are still off at The Candy Shop. Anjanette and Mathilde walk over to sit on a bench and wait. Mathilde presses her shoulder against Anjanette's. She feels she is seeing her crazy amazing friend for the first time. Everything she believed about Anjanette has been flipped on its head. She only appears flighty, unpredictable, or inconsistent because Mathilde's needs, or anyone else's, never get top priority. Even when she spends long full days lounging on the orange velvet sofa or haunting junk shops, her every day is a devotion. There is an unbreakable structure and routine underneath the wild, flowy river of her. It's like she is a nun or a monk—*a nunk*, thinks Mathilde. Though not celibate. Obviously.

Anjanette pulls back to look at Mathilde. She does not understand why Mathilde seems to be giggling to herself.

Mathilde turns to face Anjanette. "Here's what's funny. I used to think you and Lonny were so different, but you are more like her than I ever realized."

"You think?" Anjanette does not agree.

"I do. You are both super-focused with so much drive and always making things, super detail oriented. It's just what you focus on is different, so it looks different. That's all."

Anjanette's eyebrows lift, her chin lowers. "Is that what you are sitting there thinking about? Girl, I thought you were getting all jiggy with it thinking about spending the afternoon with the new toy you about to get."

"Don't be gross." Mathilde slides away to put some space between them. "No—whenever I'm out with you, I feel like I'm with a movie star. Does it ever bother you that you're not famous?"

"Famous?" Anjanette spits the word out.

"Okay, not famous, but, you know—popular. You work so hard. Don't you wish more people saw your stuff?"

"Maybe," says Anjanette without any heaviness. "Maybe—just not every day. Not most days. Most days I don't think about shit like that at all."

They watch as a car pulls up to park. Anjanette stands. "That's Candy."

"If reincarnation is real—" says Mathilde, coming in to stand next to Anjanette as they wait for Candy to walk over, "then brilliant people like DaVinci keep coming into the world and tearing it up with easy success because they are genius. They get better and smarter every time. When I think like that I feel like a worm. Like I don't know anything about how to make a life and be successful. How many more lifetimes do I have to go through before I get it right?"

"If reincarnation is real," replies Anjanette, "how do you know DaVinci hasn't cleared all the levels we've got here and is on some other planet playing some other game?"

Mathilde sits in the car observing teenagers mill about. Is that what she looked like at their age? Her fortieth birthday is around the corner. Mathilde wonders if she looks as old as that sounds.

Oh, come on—Mathilde groans when the clock shows she has been sitting here over half an hour. She puts her forehead to the steering wheel. Susannah's play rehearsal was supposed to end twenty minutes ago. Mathilde hears doors banging open. Shouts and laughter. She lifts her head to watch the kids pouring out. End of the school year and Mathilde can see the rituals of pre-prom hookups happening. Susannah has announced she will not have a date, but is going to prom with a group of her goth friends. Mike doesn't understand.

"Where does she get this?" Mike asks Mathilde. The implication is clear. Weirdness must come from Mathilde's side of the family. "It's just a stage. She's a teenager." Mathilde isn't bothered by Susannah's unconventional ways. In fact, secretly, Mathilde likes how Susannah has no problem going into a rage or expressing her feelings. It gives Mathilde real satisfaction that Susannah will not be controlled by Mike.

"I was a teenager," says Mike. "I had a date for prom."

Gina Imondi was Mike's high school girlfriend. After high school, they were engaged to be married, twice—but it never happened. From what Mathilde gathered when she first met Mike, it wasn't that Annie refused to allow it—more that she kept putting obstacles in the way.

"She was one of those career girls," Mike's grandmother said to

Mathilde as a way of explaining why the high school sweethearts didn't end up together, but Mathilde always knew it had more to do with Annie not liking the fact that Gina was Italian, not Irish.

Gina went to Bentley University, a business school, and was super successful. There were feature articles about her in *The Boston Globe* that Mathilde read. Gina had a huge career, yes—but she also had an equally successful husband, three kids, a big house in Brookline and a golden retriever. Clearly, Gina had a plan.

And that was always Mike's philosophy for life: have a plan.

Mathilde wonders if Mike regretted not marrying Gina—Gina the Italian girl, is the way his grandmother always referred to her.

Mathilde checks the clock and groans again. Come on. Still no sign of Susannah. Mathilde wants to be home in time to make sure Toby eats dinner before tennis practice. And of course Mike will be hungry, pacing around the kitchen if Mathilde gets home late.

She rests her head back and closes her eyes. Mathilde is tired. There has been so much tension in the house lately. Two months ago, Susannah created an advent calendar counting down the days to high school graduation. The calendar is mounted in the kitchen so that she can make a great show of sharing the day's message before leaving for school. Mathilde and Mike try to shake it off as if this is just normal teenage behavior, but in each other's eyes the unspoken question always hovers: does she hate us?

Susannah has always been a challenging kid, but now that she's a teenager, it's like she has morphed into a wild animal. Mike and Susannah seem to be in an endless battle. Again and again Mathilde hears them fight. It has to be a shock for Mike to not get along with his own kid. He is the guy with the jokes at the cocktail party. The neighbor who helps you build your kid's sandbox. The dad with the cooler of beers to share with other bored-out-of-their-mind-parents at intermission of the school play. He is grounded. Gets things done. One big point of contention between Mike and Susannah that causes so much disruption was that if he starts something, he finishes it. His personal code.

Mathilde presses on her eyelids and remembers the battle last weekend when Susannah had to get a school project finished.

"What's the plan here?" Mike stepped into the family room to survey the situation. Susannah had paper cutouts, tinsel, feather boas, giant poster boards, string, rope, markers, scissors strewn around the room. A hot glue gun sat dripping onto a paper plate on the coffee table.

"You are doing it the hard way," Mike wanted to help. "Do it in smaller pieces—it's easier like that."

"Drop dead, Dad," Susannah replied, getting more frustrated.

"Here," Mike reached over to pick up the stapler. "Let me show you."

"NO!" Susannah flared at his interference. "I don't want to do it in smaller pieces." She bared her teeth. "Let me do it my own way."

Mike stormed out, got in his truck and drove off. Mathilde understood. He was afraid of dropping the violence of his father onto his baby girl.

A sharp rap at the window makes Mathilde jump. Susannah is at the car with arms full and two friends who are clearly planning on getting a ride. Mathilde unlocks the door and the teenagers pile in.

Dedham
April 1999

Now that Mike's grandmother Annie has died, they no longer have to go to Pawtucket for Easter. However, Mike still insists on setting up all the same brouhaha of baskets, bunnies, and egg hunts for Susannah and Toby in the backyard. It's Mike who has invited Mathilde's parents to join them. Mathilde finds it ironic that once upon a time, her parents were strenuous in their resistance to Mike and now? He's the one they love most.

All weekend, Mike is the one Rosie sits with to have her cocktail, listening to his stories—borderline flirting. And, Mathilde's dad clearly respects Mike. Not only because his son-in-law has grown a successful business, but because Mike is handy—Tom is useless at repairing anything. Now that Mike is the central focus of her parents' attention, it feels to Mathilde that the only time her mother notices her is to make a criticism.

The kids are running wild from all the candy and Mathilde is beginning to lose her patience with Rosie who has been making a series of digs over the course of the weekend. *That color isn't the best on you, have you thought about having your colors done? It could help you choose the right clothes. Stop biting your nails, you are too old to be doing that. Ham is nice, but really, a leg of lamb is not that much more work—you know how your father loves mint jelly.*

When an actual screaming fight breaks out between Susannah and Toby—Susannah bit off the head of Toby's chocolate bunny—Rosie stands dramatically. "I can't put up with all this."

As if Mathilde has deliberately coached her children to torture their grandmother. It's the last straw and Mathilde snaps. "Good thing you only had one kid then."

The arrow goes straight to the heel. Mathilde is Luke Skywalker sending the bullet down into the precise spot that blows up the death star.

Rosie is crushed. She turns to Tom. Time to leave.

Rosie is in the front seat. Tom tries to make the goodbyes fine, as if everything is fine, but when Mike—holding one kid in each arm—leans over to say bye bye to grandma, Mathilde's dad grabs the moment with Mathilde.

"What possessed you to say something like that?" Tom is stunned. "How could you be so cruel?"

Mathilde feels doubly humiliated to have her father mad at her, too. "You didn't hear the things she's been saying to me?"

"She is your mother." Tom walks over to the driver's side door and climbs in.

Standing on her toes—she is not as tall as Anjanette—Mathilde reaches up to bring the spider plant down. She moves the spout of the watering can in a slow circle to make sure the plant gets an even drink of water. Mathilde walks around the room spritzing leaves as she has seen Anjanette do each week. How has she been living here all this time and never seen how precious each of these plants are? So tender. So fragile. So perfect. The shape of their little leaves, the deep jewel green, the pale-yellow green, the exquisite pink blossoms on the begonia. So much beauty.

"Hello." Mathilde whispers to the maidenhair. Anjanette always talks to them. "You are lovely. I hope I haven't given you too much water."

She makes her way down the stairs as quietly as she can and steps into Anjanette's studio to return the pitcher and spray bottle to where they are kept by the sink. Anjanette's bare feet stick out from the edge of the orange velvet sofa. Holding her breath and willing the floors not to creak, Mathilde tiptoes to the blanket on the floor and lifts it up. She carefully inches the blanket over Anjanette's sleeping body. Mojo stirs and looks up at Mathilde but does not make a sound.

The ping of someone joining the zoom call Mathilde has set up echoes down the stairwell. Mathilde hurries up the steps and closes the door behind her. She settles in front of the screen—her background a mass of green plants.

It's Toby. He is outside on what looks like a condo community patio. Toby is freshly showered, his wet hair slicked back.

"You look like you're doing okay," says Toby, sipping at a smoothie.

"How about you, Chicken?" asks Mathilde. "Is that Arnie? Hold him up to the screen for me. Oh my god, he's gotten so big."

"He's a rascal," says Toby, setting the dog back on the ground. "He chewed Bill's favorite flip-flops and destroyed the dog bed."

"Well, that's what puppies do," says Mathilde. "It'll stop in a couple of months."

Toby's work is good. Bill is good. Charleston life suits them both, though Toby finds the heat a bit much.

"I hope you are wearing sunscreen," says Mathilde.

"Yes, Mother," says Toby. "Calm yourself."

"So Chicken, it's May—" Mathilde isn't sure how to do this. "I just want to know if you are okay? Do you want to talk about anything? Do you think you want to—I don't know, do some kind of get-together, you know a gathering to celebrate Daddy?"

"Uh, that could be good," says Toby. "I mean it's kind of late notice for this month. Bill and I are booked right through the first week of June, but—if you want, July?"

"Sure, honey," Mathilde says. "If that works for you and Bill. Susannah's calling in a few so I will run that by her, too."

"Oh shit—Arnie!" Toby jumps up. Mathilde can hear wild barking. "Sorry Mom. Gotta go."

Mathilde sits facing herself on the screen as she waits for Susannah to call in. She should have realized Toby would not want to do anything spontaneous. He is so much like Mike. Always a plan, a schedule, a strategy. And yet, also different than his father.

Most kids have a 'come to jesus' moment with their families at some point in their adolescence where all pet nicknames are to be sent to the galactic sun for eternal destruction, but Toby has never asked them to stop calling him Chicken.

It was Mike who began calling Toby 'chicken legs' when eleven-year old Toby walked into the kitchen in his white tennis shorts, white polo shirt and white sneakers sprouting skinny white legs that were longer than his body had yet to accommodate. But Toby didn't take the comment as a jibe—he had spent enough time with his dad on job sites that he understood the nature of guys giving each other nicknames.

Toby declined Mike's efforts to get him to go to Pawtucket Red Sox games together. Mike was a baseball fanatic, Toby not so much. *I prefer tennis*, is what Toby said on repeat until Mike stopped asking.

However, because Toby did enjoy working for his dad during summers in high school, Mike allowed himself to believe that one day Toby would join the company—that they would be a father and son business, but, once again, Toby veered. Interior design was what Toby wanted, not construction. He headed south for college and stayed. Toby liked the beach, the lifestyle of Charleston and being close to his grandparents who lived out on Hilton Head Island.

Mathilde witnessed the definitive answer to nurture vs. nature as she watched Toby with his grandfather; her son had the same, innate refined quality of style as her dad, something neither she or Mike had given him.

Early on, Mike asked Mathilde if she thought Toby was gay.

"There's no way to know at this point," replied Mathilde. "We'll see." Then she kind of did a double-take, looking at Mike. "You're not gonna be weird about it?"

"No," said Mike. "Not weird about it. I just don't want him to get hurt."

"Oh well, you can let go of that—" said Mathilde. "We all get hurt."

"You're not following me," said Mike. "I mean terrible. Look what happened to your Uncle Wesley."

The zoom pings and brings Mathilde back into the room. It is Susannah.

"Hey." Susannah's face is so close to the screen that Mathilde can see the flecks of day-old mascara under her eyes. She wears a loden green knit watch cap pulled low on her forehead.

"You wanted to chat?" Susannah says.

"Yeah," says Mathilde. "Nothing urgent. Just wanted to check in. See how you're doing."

"Um," Susannah looks like she might start to cry. She bites at a fingernail. "You mean cause this weekend is the anniversary of Daddy's death?"

Mathilde nods. "I was talking with Toby—"

"Wait—you talked to Toby, like separately?" Susannah seizes on this. "Why did you do that? Why wouldn't you have us on the same call?"

"Do you have to attack me?" Mathilde is already wishing she had just sent a text.

"I am not attacking you," says Susannah.

"Well it feels like you are—" Mathilde crosses her arms over her chest.

"Well maybe if we could all be on the call together like a family we could talk about Daddy together," says Susannah.

"I was thinking it might be even nicer if we all got together—in person," says Mathilde. "Toby and Bill thought July could be good."

"July! That's random."

"Well, honey—people have jobs and—"

"I don't have a job?"

"Okay I can't do this right now." Mathilde moves to end the call but Susannah jumps in to stop her.

"No mom, wait. I'm sorry. I'm sorry. I'm just—" Susannah pushes her cap up off her brow. "I'm really unhappy here. I don't like Arkansas. I want to come home."

"Come home?" says Mathilde.

"Yeah—if you're staying at Auntie AJ's, can I use the condo?" says Susannah. "Me and my friend Sonia?"

"It's a one-bedroom," says Mathilde, stalling for time. She is not prepared for this request.

"We don't care," says Susannah, her face coming in still closer to fill the screen. "One of us'll sleep on the sofa. It'll be fine."

"So here's the thing," says Mathilde. "I'm trying to buy a house and the condo needs to be able to be shown so—"

"That'll work perfect," says Susannah. "You need someone to let people in and show it and keep it looking good and Sonia is a neat freak just like you."

Mathilde tries to absorb how radically different this call is from what she intended.

"Mom?"

"So you're quitting the residency?"

"I'm not quitting—I'm just leaving early."

"Okay," Mathilde needs to get off the call and agreeing is the only way she sees out. "Fine, but this is temporary."

"Understood. Thanks, mom." Susannah sits back from the screen. There's a bit of a smile and the tension between her brows has softened although her face continues to look more pale and fragile than usual. She's clearly still trying to hold back some tears. Sadness? Relief? Mathilde doesn't know. But when they end the call, Susannah still hasn't shed a tear.

Mathilde shuts the laptop and sets it on the floor. She curls onto one side with her knees pulled in to her chest.

"First the wheat is a seed," nine-year-old Susannah's voice sings clear in Mathilde's head. She is reading *Why Wendy Wheatgrass Doesn't Cry* to Mike and Mathilde. Susannah who loves to make everything she learns into a story. It is a picture book she has written about Wendy, the wheatgerm.

"The seed cracks open and up rolls a green head with lovely green leaves to wave at the sun. Hello sun."

Susannah's story has sprung back into Mathilde's mind. A full memory. Vivid and strong. Out of nowhere like Artemis bursting from her father's head.

"That wasn't the last change for Wendy the wheatgerm, but she didn't cry. She grew tall with a crown of golden braids. She would give her crown to feed the village. The women took the crown and trans-formed it into soft brown powder."

Susannah looks up to see if Mathilde and Mike are appreciating the size of the word she has used, *transformed*. Mike beams. Mathilde nods.

Mathilde sits up. What had happened to that book? Is it in the storage unit where she has boxes of things she hasn't even opened? Does Susannah have it? Why hasn't she treasured this? What kind of a mother is she?

"The soft brown powder was flour. Warm yeasty water got poured onto the flour and sprinkled with salt. It took a long time for the flour to become wet dough. The women had to work hard and rub it a lot."

Mike shoots Mathilde a look and they both struggle not to laugh.

Susannah looks up sharply, "What?"

"It's wonderful, sweetie," Mathilde says.

"It's not over," Susannah says crossly, upset by something she can feel between her parents but not understand.

"The dough was oiled before it got laid"—Susannah pauses to turn the page—*"in a pan that got put into a very hot oven."*

Mathilde kicks Mike under the table. A threatening kick. Don't you dare make me laugh.

"The whole village came and gave thanks for the beautiful loaf of bread. And then they went into the fields and did a dance all around Wendy the wheatgerm to let her know how much they loved her. The end."

"Now you can laugh," says Susannah exploding into tears and throwing the book across the table. She runs upstairs. Her door slams shut.

Mathilde's feet dangle off the edge of the bed. She presses her hands against her chest as tears pour down her cheeks. It is such a relief to cry. Maybe that's why the story resurfaced. To help her break through the numbness.

The sobs loosen everything up and out of her chest. This is the fear. That if she begins to cry, she may never stop. Her body bends all the way over so that her fists press under her rib cage which provides a strange sensation of comfort.

Anjanette reaches into the mini-fridge she has under her worktable. She pulls out a can of Sprite. Pours some into a jelly jar that sits on the shelf. She hands the soda to Mathilde who sniffs it, warily—did this have turpentine in it?

"I washed it out," says Anjanette annoyed at being called up on her housekeeping. "You're fine."

"I was remembering that phase when Susannah—" Mathilde drifts off for a moment. "Do you remember those books she did? All on the theme of change? The first one was a caterpillar?'

"Uh-huh—" says Anjanette, laughing. "The bread that got laid."

"Yes!" says Mathilde. "How could I have not held on to them?"

"I might have one," says Anjanette.

"What?"

"Yeah, but only because I'm a hoarder."

"I never called you a hoarder," says Mathilde. "I said you were a pack rat."

"Whatever," says Anjanette.

Anjanette walks out of the studio with Mathilde and Mojo on her heels. They follow her to the bedroom that has three filing cabinets stacked against one wall. Mathilde watches as Anjanette clambers over a loveseat piled with boxes of CDs to reach one of the file cabinets. She goes through a couple of drawers before yanking up a manilla folder.

"Told ya!" she crows.

"That took you no time," says Mathilde, amazed.

"I keep telling you," says Anjanette, walking down the hallway. "I know what all this shit is."

It turns out Anjanette does not have *Why Wendy Wheatgrass Doesn't Cry.* The story she has held on to is *Maize the Cornstalk and her Two Sisters.* Mathilde carries the manila folder back up to the third floor bedroom.

Anjanette has saved this. Auntie Anjanette. Godmother to Susannah.

Mathilde holds folder to her chest as she gazes out the window down to the back yard of the house next door. She sits up so sharply the manila folder slides to the floor. What the hell? She knows what those are.

Those are moving boxes.

Mathilde shifts the posy of daffodils and tulips she just stole from Lonny's front garden (she'll explain to Lonny later) to her other hand so that she can knock again, more forcefully this time.

The porch decking is warm from the sun. Mathilde looks down at her feet, no shoes. She tries to stop breathing so heavily, but her chest is pounding. Not only from rushing down the stairs and gathering everything so quickly and pushing through the hedge, but here she is—standing on her old back porch. She cannot remember the last time she stood here. It is so deeply familiar—like meeting up with a beloved friend—she knows every inch of this porch.

Mathilde did not stop to make a plan, to think things through. She grabbed the flowers, tied them with a bit of twine that she found in the kitchen junk drawer and then pulled an unopened tin of fancy cookies down from a shelf in the pantry. Mathilde can replace them—she knows Anjanette gets them at Cardullos.

Steps approach. A hand pushes at the curtain covering the back door window. Mathilde waves and smiles. She glimpses a woman, blonde hair, before the curtain drops and the door tugs open.

The woman's hair has been professionally lightened; she wears it in a severe page boy to her chin. She waits on the other side of the screen door for Mathilde to explain herself.

"Hi," says Mathilde. She smiles in a way that she hopes does not look like a weird, stalker neighbor. "Hi—I didn't mean to disturb you but I happen to be visiting my friend next door and wanted to come by and say hi. I used to live here. I grew up here. In this house. So I thought I'd come by and say, hi."

"Hi?" The blonde woman does not seem interested in any of this, least of all Mathilde.

Mathilde holds out the bouquet and cookies. "Here," she says. "A little housewarming."

The blonde woman makes a short, cynical laugh. "You got the wrong day for that."

"Oh?" Mathilde gestures to the moving boxes. "You're not moving in?"

"We're moving out." The screendoor snaps open. "You can come in if you want."

Mathilde steps into her childhood kitchen that looks nothing like her childhood kitchen, but her heart immediately roars to life as she sees with delight—this is a divorce kitchen.

Years and years ago, after only a few months of selling real estate, Mathilde quit. She hated real estate, but she had met a woman, Jess, that she really liked a lot who was a terrific real estate agent. Jess began hiring Mathilde to do staging—get a house ready for sale. It wasn't steady work but Mathilde liked it. Jess is the one who coined the phrase "divorce kitchen."

"It's a telltale sign when you see they've put a row of hanging cabinets over an island," Jess explained. "It cuts the kitchen like a knife—really bad feng shui. Quick sale."

Mathilde gazes around. The wall between the dining room and kitchen has been taken out to create a giant, open space. A massive commercial range sits where the old pantry once was. Soapstone counters, a farmhouse sink and rubbed brass fixtures make the whole place look like the cover of a magazine.

"Wow," says Mathilde. She sets the flowers and tin of cookies next to the sink. "You've done so much here. I especially like that." Mathilde points to the row of custom cabinets that hang from the ceiling over the island, cutting the kitchen in two.

Mt. Auburn Cemetery
May 2018

"Honestly? I haven't slept for the past three days." Mathilde feels like she is saying the same words over and over, but if she keeps saying it out loud, maybe it will finally sink in.

The hipsters are moving out. She is buying 64 Clement.

Mathilde stops walking and turns to face Paul. "I need to make some sort of offering to the gods—something epic. Colossal."

Paul gestures toward an empty stone bench by the pond. They've been walking loops around Mt. Auburn Cemetery for nearly an hour and this is the first empty bench they have seen. The trees and flowers are just coming into bloom so people are out in droves to walk the paths.

A young couple walks by pushing a stroller; the baby bleats loudly in a repetitive monotone like an angry seagull. Mathilde smiles and waves at the couple. She wants to kiss the whole world.

"Do you have a closing date?" Paul asks.

"Yes! June twenty-second." Mathilde nearly leaps off the bench. She catches herself. "Sorry—I'm just so over the moon crazy there aren't even any words for—"

"You don't have to apologize," says Paul. "It's definitely not something you hear everyday. And, it's nice to see you so fired up."

"I am fired up. Like I knew the moment I saw those boxes—" Mathilde relives the afternoon again. "As soon as I stepped into the kitchen, I knew. She even told me they wanted to get out fast. They had talked to a real estate agent who said they would need to get all the reno on the second floor finished before they could list it and I told her—I don't care. You don't have to do a thing. I will waive an inspection." Mathilde looks at Paul to see if he appreciates the magic of it all. "The husband never wanted to move here. He's from California and hates the weather. And I guess she came for a job that ended up not working out. All I know is he is moving to San Diego. She's heading back to Brooklyn and the house is mine! Mine. I just—I still can't believe it."

Paul has his legs stretched out long, ankles crossed. Mathilde wants to settle and be equally chill, but she can hardly sit still.

"You think I'm crazy, don't you?" Mathilde answers before Paul has a chance. "I mean, it is crazy. Ridiculously expensive—"

Paul shrugs. "Can you swing it?"

"If I cash out everything, *everything*. And then, I would still need to make one part of it into an Airbnb kind of thing to help me with the mortgage and taxes. You know, the third floor or maybe convert the garage into living space, or both." Mathilde doesn't have a plan. Her lack of sleep has her head a bit toasty fried—is she crazy? Is this all a pipe dream?

"So, you can make it happen." Paul stands. "Ready to keep walking?"

Mathilde tucks her hand into his elbow as they cross the grass and get back on the paved path.

"You haven't told me about this private eye mission we're on," says Paul.

"That makes it sound creepy."

"It is a little creepy," says Paul. "Why don't you just contact the landscaping department and see if they can give you Daniel's contact info?"

"*That* sounds creepy," says Mathilde. "I don't want to invade his privacy. I just want to—"

"Happen to run him to him by total coincidence," Paul finishes the sentence for her.

"Exactly." Mathilde bumps into Paul's side playfully. "Chance encounter."

"And this makes how many times you have been here, *by chance*, this month?"

"Like five—maybe seven." Mathilde stops to gaze at the pond which holds clouds, blue sky, and treetops on its shimmering surface. "Anjanette said she saw him here last September. Cutting the grass. I thought maybe he'd be back now that it's Spring again."

"Do you know why he hasn't been home?" Paul asks.

"I don't know anything, really," says Mathilde. "I could never ask Anjanette. She never said more than that there was some kind of terrible fight between Daniel and Lonny. I know he wasn't happy at school. He was at Princeton, which was Lonny's dream, but I don't know that was what he wanted. Then, when Timo died, it's like everything got worse. Maybe he had a breakdown? I honestly don't know. All I know is that Daniel quit college and went off to live somewhere like Thoreau."

"And never came back," says Paul.

"Yeah."

"Thoreau came back to his mother's house every week to get his laundry done," says Paul.

Mathilde smiles. "Yeah, I've read that, too. Maybe not the best analogy." Suddenly, Mathilde begins to laugh.

"What's so funny?" asks Paul. Mathilde shakes her head, unable to speak. When she catches her breath, she chokes out one sentence before crashing into peals of laughter again.

"Oh my god, I just keep seeing my mother's face when I tell her I'm buying 64 Clement."

62 Clement Street
June 2018

Lonny, Anjanette and Mathilde sit at the kitchen table. On the table is a large, brown grocery bag, a knife and three plates.

"Ready?" Lonny looks at them both. Mathilde nods.

"I was ready yesterday, let's go," says Anjanette.

"Do not rush me," says Lonny as she pulls the bag toward her and carefully unfolds the top, turning the edges down to create a strong hem for the bag that is heavy and full of peaches.

For as long as Mathilde can remember, the first weekend of June means a guy named Pezi Louis drives a truck loaded with fresh peaches up from North Carolina and parks it behind the Ben Franklin Five & Dime on Hampshire Street. But Pezi is an old man now and rides on the passenger side while his grandson drives. And the Ben Franklin is no more. Now they park in the lot behind Lonny's church. Still the peaches are here.

Lonny lifts one out and holds it in both palms. Her nose drops to the edge of the soft fuzz and she inhales deeply. "Oh good night," she says with a smile reserved for her most favorite things.

Anjanette reaches in and grabs one for herself and tosses one to Mathilde who has distributed the plates and knives to each of them. As they carve off slices of the best peaches in the whole world, Mathilde answers their questions for everything she's got planned for next door.

"Toby's coming up the second week of July. He's got all the plans for what needs to be done and reached out to some friends of Mike's who are going to help me." Mathilde sucks the last of the peach flesh and juice from the pit. Her lips and fingers are sticky and she does not care.

"What about the condo?" asks Anjanette.

"The realtor's got an open house happening this weekend—fingers crossed—the market is hot so I hope it goes fast."

"Where's Susannah going?" asks Lonny.

"Well, she doesn't have to go anywhere until it sells so she's got another month at least, but she says she's got some friends in Watertown she's gonna go and stay with. That is, if she finds some work around here, but I don't know there's enough of a theater scene in Boston. I'm guessing she's gonna end up back in New York." Mathilde wipes her fingers on her napkin. "She'll figure it out."

Anjanette reaches for a third peach, but Lonny smacks her hand away. Lonny stands and folds the bag closed.

"These are for the weekend." Lonny carries the bag into the pantry. She calls back over her shoulder to Anjanette. "And I'll know if any have gone missing."

This weekend, Lonny's sisters and their family are coming up to stay for the week. Anjanette's brothers and their families will be coming over, too. Mathilde needs to be elsewhere.

"If Susannah and her friend are still at the condo," Anjanette asks, "where're you gonna be?"

Mathilde sits back, smiling, lips pressed together. "I have a plan."

Mt. Auburn Cemetery
June 2018

Mathilde looks up to see a woman looking at her strangely. The woman shakes her head as if to make sure Mathilde knows that knitting on a hot day in June is wrong, or dumb, or foolish—Mathilde doesn't know exactly what judgment the woman has placed on her—then walks quickly down the path with the stride of someone keeping track of her steps on one of those stupid wrist things.

The path leads around the pond, and from where Mathilde sits on the bottom step of the Mary Baker Eddy Memorial, she can look over at the bench where she and Paul sat together last week.

Wait, Mathilde thinks. Maybe it wasn't the knitting the woman objected to, maybe she thought it was disrespectful to be sitting on the monument? Whatever, Mathilde shrugs. Who cares what other people think.

Because she expected to be here awhile, Mathilde brought a thick seat cushion; there's no way her butt could sit on this hard granite for hours without some kind of support. The cushion fits snugly into the corner of the monument where the bottom step wraps around to create a kind of alcove. With her bare feet in the grass, the cool stone behind her back and shaded by the giant oak, she is comfortable.

It helps to sit here because she's not sure anymore what world she lives in. There is so much stillness here. She doesn't mind the heat. Everything here is alive—the grass, the trees, the air, the dash and scurry of chipmunks. She has lost all sense of time. It feels like the world stopped and centuries passed, as if her life broke off from the familiar patterns and routines and places to spin off wildly into other galaxies, as if she had been reading a novel that transported her to another place and time and then, when she stopped reading, she looked up to find she was back where she started. She remembers Professor Gordon saying, *there are worlds upon worlds.*

Mathilde looks down. This is a good stopping point. She folds the knitting carefully and tucks it into her tote bag. Her butt aches. It is hard to stand up. She begins walking back to where she parked her car. Still no sign of Daniel.

She'll try again another day.

As she winds her way along the path, she appreciates the carefully groomed, sprawling hills of beautiful trees, shrubs, and flower beds. This is an arboretum, not a graveyard—a cemetery. Cemetery, she rolls the word across her mind. From the Greek—*a place to sleep.* The grass is so lush. She loves how the trees are able to grow into their fullest expression with nothing to stop them—no power lines or telephone poles deforming them, no houses or buildings to force the amputation of limbs—the trees have all the space they need. Left to their natural growth, it really shows how unique each one is—she walks past a row of maples; no two are precisely the same.

A band of birders bustles toward her, binoculars bouncing. They crowd the path, so she opts to drop off and make her way through a more heavily wooded area as she continues in the general direction of the parking lot. She sees a narrow way and takes it. Suddenly, out of nowhere, rising out of the green there is a giant stone Sphinx directly in front of her. It stops her cold.

Has this always been here? She checks the date on the inscription, 1872. How has she never seen this before? She starts to read the inscription that is in Latin and English.

"Hey Mattie," a soft voice from behind her causes her to make a strange squawk. She turns to see a man standing about ten feet away. He wears navy sweatpants that are floppy at the ankles and an orange t-shirt emblazoned with the Mt. Auburn Cemetery logo that is loose at the shoulders but tight over his rounded belly. She recognizes him immediately.

Daniel.

He is nearing sixty now and has gotten rather stocky. He was never as tall as his brothers, but he had always had a lithe build. And the sweetest smile.

"Hey Daniel," says Mathilde.

"You recognize me," says Daniel. "Didn't want to scare you."

"I would recognize that smile anywhere."

Daniel makes a small laugh as he walks over.

They stand for an awkward moment.

"What are you doing out here?" Daniel asks. Gentle. Curious.

Mathilde points at the Sphinx as if she could make a story about it when she has only just stumbled upon it and knows nothing about it. She has a hundred thoughts. There is a long pause as she tries to figure out how to respond. She has to be honest. Daniel was always about the truth. He couldn't stand anyone who wasn't gonna tell the truth. In that long pause he registers everything. His mind was always fast and sharp.

He answers for her. "You're here looking for me."

She nods.

A moment. He moves his feet. Looks up at the sky. Pulls his hands up to his ribs.

"Momma? Is it Momma? Is she dead?"

"No—no." Mathilde steps toward him with a rush. "She's fine. They're both fine. Anjanette, too."

She can see his back soften in relief.

Daniel turns and walks over toward the low stone wall where she sees what must be his tools and golf cart. Mathilde follows. Daniel braces himself against the low stone wall.

They sit on the edge of the wall. Under their feet is stuff that must be his, a rucksack, a pile of blankets, some tools in a belt. Their legs dangle, both in sneakers, like kids. Except they are not kids. They are old, middle-aged people.

Mathilde watches the crows. It is getting late.

Daniel reaches down and pulls up his rucksack.

There is a thermos. He hands her a ceramic cup. Just like his mom. Not some cheap ugly mug but a lovely, green, earthenware cup.

"It's tea," he says, as she hesitates to hold the cup under the open mouth of the thermos. She holds her cup steady and he fills it a quarter of the way.

He uses the cap of the thermos to pour himself some tea. They clink cap to cup and sip.

The tea is cold and terribly sweet. "Thank you," Mathilde says. "I am so sorry. I didn't mean to shock you."

"No, it's alright. It's alright then," says Daniel. His soft expression brings Timo into their midst. "I want to know. You good?"

"Yeah—yeah." Mathilde realizes she is not just saying what she knows people want to hear. She is good, really good. She asks Daniel about working at Mt. Auburn. He tells her that he loves being around plants and getting to take care of them. It's a part-time job and only half the year, but he loves it.

"You know what else is great about this job?" He says conspiratorially. "You'll like this part. I have so much time to read and write."

Mathilde nods. "That's perfect. You always were a modern-day Thoreau."

He laughs. His laugh is his own. Mathilde would recognize it anywhere.

"A modern-day Thoreau," He looks at her. "You always had something nice to say."

"Stop. Such a lie," she says. "There's a nest of scorpions under my tongue."

"Nah," Daniel shakes his head. He smiles. "Nah."

Daniel gives his cup a few hard swirls to bring up the sugar that has dropped in the bottom before drinking the last swig.

"You're right." Mathilde takes a deep breath. "I have been coming here hoping to find you. I know it's been a long time, but the world is full of crazy, heartbreaking awful stuff. And, it would be just a wonderful thing if you came and sat on the porch. Miss Lonny—your mom, I know she misses you."

Daniel doesn't say anything.

The sky is getting dark. She doesn't have much time.

"Do you have kids?" Mathilde asks.

He shakes his head. "Naw, nothing like that."

Mathilde watches his eyes as he processes that question. Another world he might have lived, another world flashing by—his brilliance as a Princeton student, shattered under the crush of expectations, the death of Timo, the reality of being a black man in a hateful, racist world or whatever it was that broke him. Mathilde doesn't know. She doesn't ask.

"I was never the family man type, I don't think," says Daniel, finally.

"More of the scholar, poet, monk type—" Mathilde says.

Daniel seems pleased by that. Straightens his back.

"I'll take that," he says.

"I do," says Mathilde. "I have two kids."

"You got kids? You got *two* babies?"

"You don't have to sound so surprised," says Mathilde

"I never thought you'd be the type," says Daniel. "Guess I thought you'd be a librarian or something."

"Yeah, well," says Mathilde. "I have kids. And, lemme tell you, It's not easy. I did a lot of things wrong. I mean I thought I was doing things right, but I really, *really* fucked up. Really missed the mark. The thing is—here's the thing. I was really trying—really trying to get it right."

Daniel is listening.

"For so much of my life I couldn't understand how my mom couldn't be what I needed her to be—and I was so determined to be everything to my kids that she wasn't." She shakes her head. "All it taught me was how wrong I got it about my mom."

Daniel says nothing. A little bark. They look down.

"Who's this?" asks Mathilde.

"Leroy,"

"Bad Bad Leroy Brown?"

"No. No, Le ROI—" says Daniel. "The king, but he keeps it humble."
Daniel reaches down and pulls Leroy to sit in his lap. Leroy is a small,
elderly mutt, maybe nine or ten years old. He is clearly devoted to Daniel.

"He looks pretty regal."

"Oh, he is."

"It's getting dark," says Mathilde. "I gotta go."

"Where you parked?"

Riding through the Mt. Auburn cemetery at twilight, in Daniel's golf
cart, with Leroy sitting in Daniel's lap and the soft summer air all around
them, Mathilde feels like she is in a movie. When they pull up to the
parking lot, Mathilde gives Leroy a pet on the head. Daniel lets her give
him a hug.

Mathilde steps out of the cart. Daniel begins turning the cart around.

"Daniel, will I see you again?"

"We might do," he says.

"If you come to the house, you could see how big your holly tree has
grown. It is huge."

"You take care of yourself, Mattie," says Daniel. He gives a small
wave.

As she watches the golf cart quietly scooter away, she remembers
who he was—the number one son. The one who was going to be a
Senator, be a brilliant professor, someone famous, genius guy, and
instead—here is this kindly man, this gentle groundskeeper.

10 Meadowbird Lane, Carlisle
June 2018

It takes Mathilde almost an hour to reach Carlisle, a small town about twenty miles northwest of Boston. As she exits Route 2 and picks up I-95 north for the short jog before she gets onto Route 4, Mathilde realizes she has never driven out this way before.

How weird to be driving through a town that is brand-new to her when she has lived so close to it her whole life. What did Anjanette say about writers never leaving the town where they grew up because there was always something new to discover? Coming up Paul's drive feels like it did walking up to Effie's house in Wales: awkward, unfamiliar, all of her antennae on full alert.

His house is at the end of a dirt road without another house in sight; it is a lovely, three-quarter cape with a large addition off the back. The front has clapboards painted a pale, robin's egg blue; all three sides and the addition are covered with weather worn shingles. Gardens dominate the yard with perennial beds wrapping across the front and along the sides of the house. In the back, Mathilde can glimpse a network of raised beds for vegetables.

The screen door stretches open with a long creak.

Paul stands in the doorway. "You found it."

"GPS has taken all the mystery out of travel."

Mathilde makes a sweeping gesture with one arm. "This is beautiful." She wants to say more, but it feels like she has just invaded a private space. The quiet is extraordinary. Woodpeckers tap. Chickadees call.

There is a gawky moment before they hug hello.

"Come inside," he says. "I've made some iced tea. Unless you'd rather have seltzer."

"No, tea is great," says Mathilde.

Inside, the age of the cape is apparent: low beamed ceilings, wide plank floors painted red, an enormous brick fireplace whose centuries of sooty patina can't be faked. The fireplace is flanked by plain-faced wood cabinets painted the same soft blue as the exterior.

"What year was this built?" asks Mathilde.

"Where you're standing, 1819," says Paul. "The addition we put on about twenty years ago."

He walks into the kitchen. Mathilde turns toward the wall of books like a bee caught by the scent of a flower; she touches a finger to each spine as she reads the titles.

"Let's go out to the deck," says Paul, a glass of iced tea in each hand.

She looks over at him and points to *The Whole Country Was One Robe*. "This is yours?"

Paul laughs, "Who else would it belong to? Come on." He walks through the kitchen out the back door. She follows him slowly, looking everywhere, taking in all the details of his home which is rich with books, pictures, and handmade objects.

"Thank you," Mathilde says.

"Sure," says Paul, thinking she is referring to the tea he has just handed her.

"No, I mean thank you for inviting me out and letting me stay here," she says. "I'm a goddamned hermit crab."

"Temporarily—" Paul always softens her.

"Temporarily, thank you. Yes, someday soon I'll be the woman formerly known as a hermit crab."

He laughs.

Paul doesn't do small talk which she loves. Once again, Mathilde marvels at how easy it is to be with him. It should feel awkward sitting on his back deck, the sound of crickets full and throbbing in her ears, nothing moving but a soft, small breeze that darts through tall grasses and dances up to flutter some leaves, but her body has begun to relax.

Paul drains the last of his tea and sets down the empty glass. "Make yourself at home," he says.

As he walks up to a wheelbarrow full of mulch with a shovel leaning next to it, he pulls on a baseball cap and gardening gloves. He returns to what he was doing before she arrived.

Mathilde sits. She watches Paul. Her bare feet revel in the warm grass.

It takes Paul close to an hour to fill and empty the wheelbarrow three more times before he tips it to rest, nose down, handles in the air. He comes over to the edge of the porch a few feet from Mathilde, sets the shovel into the tool shed and pulls off his cap. He uses a bandanna to wipe the sweat off his face and neck.

Mathilde takes his empty glass into the kitchen and comes back with it refilled with cold iced tea.

"Thanks," he says, taking it from her.

He sits in the shade of the overhang, cooling off.

"How do you do it?" asks Mathilde. "How do you keep the balance between creating this beautiful life and the news of the world which has always been horrible but seems to get worse every day?"

Paul shrugs. "Different days," he says. "Different ways."

"I feel like I'm back at the beginning of my life—exactly where I was when I was nineteen, but not any more clear about anything. I just want the world to make sense, it's like I am lost in a labyrinth walking the same track over and over—I am so excited about the house—I really am. Like crazy happy thinking about living there and using it to make a difference, but then I catch the news and the enormity of the suffering. The vastness of the never ending insanity. My puny effort can't possibly make a difference. So then I loop back into a kind of—a kind of—" Mathilde looks over at Paul. "I haven't changed at all, have I?"

"I don't know," says Paul. "Somebody said you can't stand in the same river twice."

"Heraclitus," says Mathilde.

Paul's laugh is a gust of surprise. "I love that about you."

Mathilde feels herself flush. There's no denying the energy between them. She has just spent the last hour watching him move about the garden and the physical attraction is layered onto the intimacy she feels with him. Now he has used the word love, even loosely, it is unnerving.

He realizes it, too and rushes in to cover it up with some words.

"You are one of the only people I've ever met who can hold all these facts in your head," he says. "It's remarkable."

"It's not remarkable," says Mathilde. "I just remember stuff."

"So what is it you remember about being nineteen?" asks Paul.

"Wishing I didn't know how horrible human beings are."

Dinner is light. Paul brings in lettuces and peas from his garden. Mathilde shells the peas as Paul puts on water to boil for some angel hair pasta. She listens as he talks about the different varieties of tomatoes he is starting this summer. Paul has her taste the lemon balm he grows in an herb garden outside the kitchen door.

He sets down the bowls of pasta. They begin to eat.

"My sophomore year in college—" says Mathilde.

"When you were nineteen?" Paul clarifies.

"Yeah." Mathilde nods. "Professor Gordon, my mentor, like the greatest professor ever—did not get tenure—so he left. And every day I had to walk by the faculty lounge that was alway full of blowhards who did have tenure. It was like everywhere I looked, so much was straight-up wrong, so much needed to be corrected, so much needed to be reconciled."

Mathilde pokes at the soft wax at the edge of the candle Paul set at the center of the table.

The memories are flooding back in. How overwhelming it felt when her understanding of history and anthropology collided. There was so much wrong in textbooks, twisted national holidays and fucking Ronald

Reagan undoing all the changes that people had given their lives for. Everywhere she had to see sacred names and places being abused while a bootlegger like Cadillac, whose entire identity was a lie, becomes the emblem of American luxury.

"It was like seeing how truly insane the world is," Mathilde says. "And what could I possibly do to save it? And then my Uncle Wesley died—he was really sick, but nobody told me so I never got to say good-bye or help him or—it just, everything sort of crashed. And I look back now and see like maybe I thought getting married was a way to escape. But—" Mathilde makes a wry smile. "Not the answer, clearly."

Paul uses his beer bottle to point at a framed piece of cross stitch that hangs over the back door. Mathilde has to get up to go close enough to be able to read what it says.

"*Oh lord*," Mathilde reads aloud. "*Save us from the ones who have the answers. Save us from the righteous. Save us from the do-gooders.*"

Mathilde spins around to look at Paul.

"Where did you find that?" she asks him.

"My wife made it," he answers. "It was something my granddad would say so she stitched it up for him as a birthday present. When he died, we got it back."

Mathilde looks back and reads it through again, this time to herself. She comes back over to her chair and sits down with a sigh. She was in the middle of telling him about her breakdown, but now she wants to ask him about his wife, his grandfather, this quote, and she still hasn't asked him why he has Vrooman's book and so many other Indigenous History books on his shelves.

"What is it?" he asks.

"We have way too much to talk about," she says. "There isn't enough time."

Paul laughs. He pushes his empty bowl to the side.

"It's not funny," says Mathilde. "I'm serious. I get so overwhelmed. Too many thoughts. Too many images. Too many directions. Too many people in too much pain. I don't know what I should be doing. I want to be a good person but I'm always—lost. What is wrong with me?"

"Earth," says Paul. "Solar System. Milky Way Galaxy. Local Group. Virgo Supercluster. Observable Universe." He repeats this a few more times.

"Is this some kind of engineering geek mantra?" says Mathilde.

"When I get caught in the time loop, yeah," says Paul. "C'mon." He picks up their beers. Mathilde follows him into a small room that has a couch and television.

"You've never seen *Cosmos*?"

"Carl Sagan?" says Mathilde.

"No," says Paul. "The new one with Neil deGrasse Tyson."

They sit on the couch with his dog Finch between them. Cozy in the dark with the only light coming from the television.

When the show ends, they come out to the wide porch swing whose bottom cushion is a full-size mattress so they can gaze up at the stars.

"Feeling better?" asks Paul.

"Do you sleep out here?" asks Mathilde.

"Sometimes," says Paul.

"Earth," says Mathilde, gazing up at the stars. "Solar System. Milky Way Galaxy. Local Group. Virgo Supercluster. Observable Universe."

"It helps, doesn't it?" says Paul.

In college, when Mathilde was getting overwhelmed, Professor Gordon counseled her, "Look," he said. "These are nations we are talking about. They have complex, layered relationships with the nations around them and we have very, very little information and the material we do have—so much of it is suspect because it comes from the invaders. So, your best bet is to choose one. Choose one nation and learn as much as you can about it and in doing that you will learn about the other nations it touched. You would never try to study the full history of Poland, Switzerland, Portugal, and Belgium all at the same time, right?"

Paul interrupts her reverie. "If you had gone on," he asks. "What did you want to study?"

Mathilde makes a groan like a teenager being asked to answer a question she really doesn't want to answer and rolls onto her side.

"I don't want to talk about it because I'm never going to do it," she says, frustration and self-loathing begins rising and she really, *really* doesn't want to feel that in this moment.

"Who cares if you never do it," says Paul. "Just tell me what your idea was."

"I don't know that it was my idea," says Mathilde. "I'm sure some-body—probably lots of people have done this by now but," she takes a deep inhale and rolls it all out in one breath. "I wanted to do kind of a mash-up of Bastian's study of how elementary ideas define the psychic unity of mankind with Joseph Campbell's universal myth."

"See? That wasn't so hard. And the best part is I have no idea what you are talking about. Yet." Paul reaches out to trace his finger over the top of her hip which is making a big curve as she lies propped on one side. "I will, once you explain it to me."

She touches his upper arm, so strong.

"You're so muscle-y," she says.

"You're changing the subject," says Paul. "Which is fine, but don't think I don't notice."

Mathilde keeps poking at his arm.

"You been lifting weights?"

"Gardening," says Paul.

"Ah, the poor man's CrossFit," says Mathilde.

He laughs. She loves that she can make him laugh.

He pulls the blanket across their bodies. They curl into each other and let the swing rock them. When Paul teases her about Nicky Ajemian, her high school crush she teases him back.

"Well you were in love with Susie Teixiera," says Mathilde.

Paul turns her to look at him. "I was never in love with Susie Teixiera," he says.

"I was never in love with Nicky Ajemian," are the last words Mathilde says before they kiss.

Mathilde spends the morning helping Paul in the garden. As she weeds around the spirea that has been overtaken by some kind of vine, she calls out to Paul, "Do you want me to hack this all back?"

He stands and pushes his hat up off his brow. "Yeah, that's good," he says, "Then just dump it all over there." He points to an area beyond the tool shed where a series of piles lead to a composting station. There is a large lattice he is resurrecting from last summer that will allow cucumbers to grow up the side of one of the beds.

They are keeping their distance from one another. Not a lot of talking.

Lonny would love it here, Mathilde thinks as she takes a pause to fill her arms with the vines and walk them down to the clean-up pile. It is so quiet and everything smells so good. She makes a note to herself that when she leaves, she will cut a bunch of sweet peas and bring them to Lonny. Lonny loves deeply fragrant blossoms.

Her footsteps on the grass are audible. Finch sits up to scratch suddenly and the light jingle of his collar is clear even though he is twenty feet away. The quiet is intense, no sound of cars or roads. Mathilde can feel herself expanding into the spaciousness of the garden that extends out to the woods that surround Paul's property. There is room enough, time enough. She practices the mantra as she swings her now empty arms overhead and walks back up the hill to the spirea: Earth, Solar System. Milky Way Galaxy. Local Group. Virgo Supercluster. Observable Universe.

"Do you have a tattoo?" Mathilde calls across to Paul.

"Why do you ask?" he answers.

"I think I might get a tattoo of the *Cosmos* mantra," says Mathilde. "I want to remember it every day."

Paul shakes his head.

"Are you laughing at me?"

"The idea of you getting a tattoo," he says. "Seriously?"

"I'm thinking about it," says Mathilde, a bit defensive. It shouldn't be that funny.

10 Meadowbird Lane, Carlisle
June 2018

Hello you hermit crab, Mathilde says to her face in the small mirror she has just wiped clean of steam. She wraps a towel over her head and pulls on the clothes Paul has left draped over the wooden door of the outdoor shower. Borrowing clothes from Paul? Like they are teenagers or doing what she never did—going to a guy's apartment for the weekend then waking up and putting on his shirt? It feels delicious, like she is getting to have an experience that she missed out on when she was in her twenties.

She lifts an arm up to sniff the sleeve of the shirt. Definitely a hermit crab. It wouldn't take Franz Boas a blue minute to note how much she prefers living in someone else's shell to her own.

But that's about to change, right? Her very own place is on the horizon. How will she make it special?

Paul has rigged up twinkle lights to run alongside the shingled edge of the shower which makes everything feel even more magical now that it is twilight. Has he done this just for himself? His wife moved out over ten years ago. He said he built the shower after she left, so it isn't for her.

Mathilde rubs her head with the towel before leaving it on a hook to dry, then combs her fingers through her wet hair. She walks across the lawn toward the fire pit where Paul is burning pieces of an old stump. So much beauty. The smell of woodsmoke, the squish of the grass between her toes, the color of the evening sky.

The earth is still warm from the afternoon sun under the soles of her bare feet. Without meaning to, she can't help contrasting her bliss with all she has read about the endless carnage, wars, crushed uprisings everywhere, everywhere—the killing fields of Cambodia, the slaughter in Rwanda, the centuries of slavery and cultural annihilation in this country. Will humans keep creating this same dynamic over and over? Is there ever an end to the churning of the milk by the devas and asuras—or does that go on forever? She has to go back and read that myth again—she can't remember how it ends.

Finch explodes off the porch in pursuit of a squirrel and knocks into Mathilde as he races by.

Mathilde joins Paul and sits on the ground by the fire.

"Careful of ticks," Paul says.

"You got a lot of ticks here?" Mathilde asks.

"It's something to watch out for," says Paul.

"Great," says Mathilde.

As she begins to wake up, eyes still closed, Mathilde feels the familiar tremors. Where is she? The bed is unfamiliar; the sheets feel different. She flutters her eyes open. Surprised. Safe. Comfortable. The pink coverlet is soft; it weighs next to nothing. The sheets smell fresh, like they had been dried outdoors.

Morning light streams across the foot of the bed and for a few sweet moments, she feels only that. Her eyes begin to look about the room trying to make sense of her surroundings. Above the bureau is a painting of four women, each wrapped in a different ceremonial blanket, each on a different rung of the ladder they climb in single file to the roof of an adobe building. *Dance Day Ladder*. This is Silva's room. Paul's middle child. The one who lived at home the longest.

The first night they fell asleep on the porch swing. Last night, she slept in here. Has it only been two days? Time has warped.

On the other side of the wall, the sounds of Paul in the kitchen are easy to hear, but Mathilde isn't ready to go out there yet. She looks around the room. The realization hits her like a clap of thunder. How blind could she be? How did she never see this before? Her chin has dropped, mouth open, tongue slack as she stares.

"I am an idiot," she whispers. "An idiot, idiot, idiot."

That scene in *The Usual Suspects,* at the very end of the movie, when the detective turns to look at the bulletin board and all of a sudden everything comes together with a snap. How had she never seen this before? All these years of knowing Paul and it never even crossed her mind. She had to be in his home—in his daughter's room—to finally see.

Mathilde walks out to stand in the doorway of the kitchen. "You're Wampanoag."

Paul lets the screen door slap shut behind Finch who rushes out to the backyard. "Can you be more specific?"

Mathilde hesitates. Uncertain. She rubs one foot against the ankle of her other foot. She doesn't want to get it wrong. "Mashpee Wampanoag?"

"Good try," says Paul, returns to sit at the table where his laptop is open. "Seaconke Pokanoket Wampanoag."

"People of the First Light," says Mathilde. She walks over and sits heavily onto the stool by the kitchen island. Paul gestures to the pot of coffee as if to say, *help yourself.* Mathilde puts her face in her hands.

Paul looks up. He closes his laptop and leans back in his chair. "You are embarrassed."

"Are you fucking kidding me?" says Mathilde behind her fingers. Embarrassed beyond the point of humiliation. Paul *knows* that she didn't know all these years. The feeling of being the biggest idiot ever, burns. And it didn't have to be this way. He could have told her when they were kids. Why didn't he tell her?

"Well what did you think I was?" he asks.

"I don't know—I never thought about it," she says.

"See now you're hurting my feelings—" Paul is teasing her.

"I don't know, you could be Italian, you could be Portuguese—you could be anything."

"Brown hair, brown eyes—we all look the same?"

"Well, now of course I can see it," says Mathilde. "I can see it now. I think we just don't see things if we aren't looking for them. Why didn't you ever tell me? This feels so weird."

"I don't know," says Paul. "There was a time I might have, but then it became a game for how long it would take until you realized."

"Forty years," says Mathilde. She gets up and goes over to the coffee pot and pours herself a mug of coffee. "Jesus. I'm guessing I'm not gonna make it to the Showcase Showdown."

Paul comes over and wraps his arms around her. He holds her close from behind. Mathilde shakes him off.

"You can't hug me right now. I'm processing."

"Look," says Paul. "You got caught up in a history. The narrative is committed to seeing us suffering and dead. It is weird to be invisible, but I have also made choices to let myself be invisible which was one of the big issues between me and Winnie."

Mathilde looks up.

"My wife," says Paul.

Mathilde nods. She goes back to holding her head in her hands.

Sounds from the garden pour through the screendoor, but neither of them move despite the lure of birds calling. Like a fast-moving hurricane, the storm of energy has suddenly filled every inch of space between them. Neither of them touch their coffees.

Mathilde's first words feel like a step forward in a quiet woods, branches cracking sharply.

"A while ago," Mathilde begins. "Anjanette said she should've left me at McLean because I need my head examined if I thought you were coming to her shows all these years cause you loved her art so much."

Mathilde lifts her chin so that her gaze is now at Paul's shoulder. "So I was thinking maybe you did like me, but now—now I am thinking all these years you knew I didn't see who you were. Maybe you kept showing up thinking one of these days I would open my eyes, stop being so blind. And now I think you, maybe you—were hating me all these years."

"Mattie," says Paul. "That hero professor of yours—"

"Professor Gordon."

"Yeah," Paul continues. "Did you ever go to his house? Meet his family? His friends?"

Mathilde shakes her head. "Of course not. He was my professor."

"Got any friends who are Indigenous? Ever spent time in—"

"No, Paul." Mathilde interrupts. "No. I get it." She steps back to create space between them.

"I'm invisible," says Paul, "because you think I'm dead. Because all you do is read books about the past and make up some story in your head about who you think we are."

Paul reaches out and shakes Mathilde by the shoulder, not gently, not rough.

"You wanna know why Anjanette is right? We had just moved back to Massachusetts and I hated everything especially being the new kid in school. My dad is white, you know."

Mathilde looks up. "I didn't know," she says.

"My mom is Wampanoag and so there was always this back and forth. I was kind of on the fringe when we were with my family on her side and definitely an outsider when I was with my dad's folks—it was confusing. And then one day, there was this school assembly and this pretty, strawberry blond girl with beautiful eyes and these cool-ass black boots like she was some kind of punk rocker got up on stage and began doing a presentation on the Iroquois Confederation. A subject she chose. And she was so into it. I looked around and almost nobody was even listening to her. They were bored—talking to each other. But she couldn't read the room. She didn't seem to realize nobody was listening to her. I don't remember ever being in school and anyone ever talking about Native Americans with so much passion. The girl was highlighting their accomplishments and best qualities. She kept saying everything in the present tense like, 'they are' 'they have'—etc. You don't remember?"

Mathilde goes over to the sink to get a glass of water. She takes a long drink before putting the glass on the counter.

"It's funny listening to you. I have always felt so much confusion and somehow," says Mathilde, "in this moment, I am feeling like I was right to feel confused."

"Yeah. complex things are like that."

"Can we take our coffees outside?" Mathilde asks.

All morning they have been talking history, ancestry. Not in any sequential order, but rambling. Mathilde feels she should share what little she knows of her background before she asks Paul for his stories.

A soft rain begins while they are planting potatoes. Paul sets the chunk of potato with its eyes up and Mathilde follows behind. She piles dirt and mulch over the potato until there is a row of small mounds running the length of the bed.

"My mom's family was the potato famine in Ireland," says Mathilde. "You know that story. So that's them, getting out of there. 1845-50-ish, who knows. They were in straight-up survival mode so there's no real records. I just know eventually some of my ancestors landed in Boston and then made it down to the area around Hull. That's where my mom was born."

As Mathilde talks, she is amazed, yet again, that anyone survived. There was typhus on the ships. They had no skills to make their way in a city. No money, absolutely destitute. And then, there was an epidemic of cholera. The women, if they were lucky, got work scrubbing someone's floors and doing laundry and the men worked in quarries or on the docks.

"I mean, that was part of why my dad's family was so outraged he married my mom," says Mathilde. "His family only ever hired Irish to be their servants. They hated Catholics."

And the Irish hated everybody—the English, the Italians, themselves.

It didn't matter that the Irish and Italians were both Catholic, the two groups of immigrants were in a constant fight for jobs and housing. Mathilde had read how in some Irish parishes, Italians were forced to attend mass in the basement.

Before she was in middle school, Mathilde remembers occasional visits to her mother's family in Hull.

Rosie's family always made a big deal of it when they would come down on a Saturday. If it was summer, Rosie's sisters, Mary Catherine and Colleen, would organize a clambake on Nantasket Beach with lots of corn on the cob and coleslaw, though everyone always seemed more interested in their drinks than the food. Beer accompanied lunch; vodka tonics and SeaBreezes were what people had at cocktail hour—a SeaBreeze, Mathilde learned, was merely a vodka tonic with cranberry and grapefruit juice—before switching to wine coolers with dinner. By the time food was being put out on the picnic table, most of the adults were in the bag.

The women, swimsuit shoulder straps digging into their sunburns, would walk about with a complete lack of self-consciousness about their bellies or the blue varicose veins threading up behind their knees that spread across their freckled thighs. The cousins, aunts, and uncles all had thick South Shore accents—they mocked Rosie for pretending that she had lost hers—and used expressions Mathilde never heard anywhere else.

Mathilde watched her father, a blue heron in a flock of seagulls. After his last swim, he changed out of his swimsuit and put on a pair of chinos with a navy Lacoste. He would sit next to Rosie's dad who had liver cancer and had to be helped down to where he was installed in a plastic beach chair. Her grandfather wasn't talkative and that seemed to be what her dad liked about him. Her mother wore Jackie O sunglasses and avoided her sisters by pretending to look after the little kids.

One night, they were gathered around a bonfire passing stories. Mary Catherine's daughter had started one about a great tree with golden leaves, each person adding more to the fanciful tale. When it came to Mathilde's mother she ended the story in short order. *Then a woodsman came along. Took out his ax and chopped the tree down.* People booed and laughed, but none were surprised. Typical Rosie.

"So you are Irish and English," says Paul. "That's a combo of enemies."

"Yeah, no," says Mathilde. "My dad's family is actually from Flanders, or Belgium. Technically, I think they called themselves Walloons."

Her father's ancestors were Protestant; they fled persecution from the Spanish who were Catholic and landed in the Netherlands. Somehow, her ancestor (ancestors? she doesn't know if there was more than one) got in contact with the West India Company and managed to climb aboard a wooden ship and make it across the Atlantic Ocean. They landed in New Amsterdam around 1624.

"Flanders?" says Paul "So you are French?"

Mathilde blows a raspberry. "Please. That whole area got invaded by the Vikings, the Romans, the Germans, the Spanish, and god knows what. Any European who believes there is such a thing as a clear bloodline is mental."

The sound of the rain around them creates a kind of protective shield. Mathilde sits on her heels and tilts her head back to let the drops land on her face. Usually, when she is reading about all the endless wars and senseless bloodshed she becomes paralyzed with horror, an existential angst consumes her that she can't put into words. But in this moment, somehow, the only feeling she has is of the rain, the smell of the dirt, her knees soaked by the wet ground and Paul, by her side.

She tells Paul one of her secrets: she used to love to drive through a car wash. How comforting it was to be inside with the water drumming all around and the great swathes of soap making it impossible to see out the windshield. Her hands off the wheel; the car gently tugged forward by unseen forces below. Giant brushes swooping down to swish and scrub over her. For one perfect moment, she felt safe, with nowhere to go, nothing to do. Of course, now, they don't let you stay in the car as it goes through.

"Some kind of new laws or regulations," says Mathilde. "I have to get out and wait for it on the other side. Such bullshit."

"Let's go in," Paul replies. "The rain's not going to let up anytime soon."

He pushes the wheelbarrow over to the potting shed and tips it to lean against the wall. As they walk from the potting shed to the kitchen door, Paul puts an arm around her shoulder and pulls her close.

"I'm glad you're here," he says. She melts into his body, presses her check against his anorak that is slick with rain and squeezes him back.

They sit on the porch swing and eat cold noodles with peanut sauce. For once, she is doing the listening as Paul shares parts of him she doesn't know. Paul is still married.

"Legally," he says. This way his wife can continue to be covered under his healthcare and they can file their taxes jointly, which is less expensive than if they both filed singly.

"But you're not together," says Mathilde.

"Nope," says Paul. "She lives out on Aquinnah and has no interest in moving back to the mainland." Mathilde waits for him to share more. Paul gestures out to the grass. "It's too bad it's too early for fireflies—this time of night, the whole meadow will light up. It's something to see."

"It's awfully pretty right now," says Mathilde.

The swing rocks as they take in the truth of her statement.

"You know Lonny is loving your bridge site?" says Mathilde.

"Oh yeah, she is on the boards," says Paul. "She's crushing it."

"You gave her that. You gave me Instagram. You have been such an incredible friend to me and I don't understand it. I've been nothing but blind. It took coming into your home to truly see you." Mathilde shakes her head. "I would hate me if I were you."

"Maybe," says Paul, "but I like your nose. I've always liked your nose. And your neck. I like how long your neck is."

"You need to know I don't care if you are objectifying me."

Paul asks her what her favorite food is. "Your number one," he clarifies.

"Toast," Mathilde answers as Paul takes a napkin and wipes peanut sauce from her lips.

"Seriously?"

"Do not judge me for being honest. Wait, that is exactly what you should judge me for—how I am telling you the truth and not trying to be something glamorous or sophisticated that I am not. Which you already know because you've known me my whole life. Isn't that weird? We've known each other our whole lives?"

"Second favorite," says Paul.

"It used to be pizza," answers Mathilde. "But I don't know if that's true anymore."

"I would ask you for your third, but I am not sure how I'm gonna feel to discover you have no taste buds."

As he kisses her. Mathilde thinks, *this is it. This is how my life as I knew it ends. And something new begins.*

Mathilde never had strong feelings about her birthday. She knew some women liked to make a super big deal out of it and lost their minds if their husband forgot it. And then, she'd known women who thought a birthday was something to belittle, bury, or ignore—but for Mathilde, birthdays were just a more better day. Maybe because the weather was always so lovely in early June and things felt lighter and brighter.

Today is especially wonderful. Eleven days until she closes on the house. Paul and Susannah are here with her at the little birthday lunch Lonny and Anjanette are hosting for her. As she looks around the table, Mathilde doesn't know how she could possibly handle any more happiness than this moment.

Paul pushes his gift across the table to her. Mathilde lifts it up. Clearly a mug. She pulls off the paper to find a used, oversized novelty mug with the words *follow your heart* scripted across a rainbow with some of the sparkle worn off.

Mathilde looks at Paul. "Could this be any cheesier?"

"Mom!" Susannah is horrified that her mother would say something so impolite.

Mathilde is laughing. "He knows I love it."

"Got it at a neighbor's yard sale so basically—saved it from a landfill," Paul says. "I thought you'd appreciate that."

"Oh yes," says Mathilde, admiring the mug. "I look forward to filling my home with landfill saves."

"My turn," says Lonny. "Also a find." She hands Mathilde a small paper bag with the One-Pot Wonders logo stamped on it. "The other day I found this in the bottom of one of my project bags. I had completely forgotten about it. But everything in its perfect time. Now I have a little something for your birthday."

Mathilde looks down at the bag. The One-Pot Wonder stamp has her heart beating fast. She opens it and pulls out a skein of Caledonia Blue.

The table waits for her reaction. Mathilde cannot move. She cannot breathe.

"I picked that up for you when we were at Rhinebeck last year."

Mathilde tries to speak. She cannot move her hands.

"It's fine if you don't like it," says Lonny. "It made me think of you. I thought it was pretty." She makes a sound in the back of her throat. "Pretty pricey! But you were having a hard go of it last fall and I thought you could use a pick-me-up. Make a pair of mittens, or a scarf. But then you went off on your trip and I forgot about it. What do you think? You don't like it?"

"Here you go, mom." Susannah replaces the wet cloth Mathilde holds to her forehead with a fresh one—icy cold.

Mathilde sits back against the chair. "I'm okay," she reassures everyone.

"It's a good thing you almost passed out," says Anjanette. "Or I would have to come over there and smack you up."

Mathilde laughs. "You gonna smack me up."

"You know I will. How did you not tell me that whole story? What have I told you about keeping secrets from me? Why didn't you tell anyone?" Anjanette does not like that she didn't know the truth of why Mathilde went to Wales and Italy.

"Well—" Mathilde looks over at Paul.

"You knew?" Anjanette *really* doesn't like that Paul knew and not her.

"So what are you gonna knit now that you have all three skeins?" asks Lonny. "You gonna do that sweater you wanted?"

Before Mathilde can answer, Susannah jumps in. "Knit something for me."

"Oh hell no," says Anjanette, "I'm ahead of your ass."

Mathilde is seized by the dilemma. First she thinks she should knit something for Lonny, but that would be like returning a gift. Then, she thinks for Paul, but no, she'd need more than three skeins to make a sweater for him. Susannah would never appreciate all the work that goes into a hand knit and Anjanette would inevitably get paint on it which would make Mathilde crazy—no.

"I'm gonna knit something for me," says Mathilde.

Lonny nods. "Good. Let's go sit on the porch. And bring the iced tea."

62 Clement
June 2018

Paul has texted Mathilde. *Wanna meet at Mt. Auburn for a walk?* She writes back, *better not.* She explains that she has connected with Daniel and doesn't want him to feel she is invading his space.

What did Anjanette say? Paul texts. Mathilde begins typing. She hasn't told Anjanette, yet. She is waiting for the right—

The screen door snaps open and Anjanette thumps down the steps to sit next to her.

"Whatcha doing?" Anjanette asks. "Texting with your boyfriend?"

Mathilde flips the phone face down. Her heart is pounding from the sudden interruption but also from the secret.

"You don't have to hide it from me," says Anjanette. "Like I care."

Mathilde stalls for time. "He was just asking me to go for a walk."

"The adventure never ends," says Anjanette. She yawns. "It's so hot. I should move my studio down to the basement for the summer. It's like an oven up there." She shifts to get more comfortable and notices the yellow legal pad Mathilde had been scribbling on before Paul texted. "What's this," says Anjanette picking it up. "Planning your wedding already?"

"Stop," says Mathilde. "He's married and I have zero desire to be married."

"Right—" Anjanette snorts her doubt. She starts reading out from Mathilde's list.

"First year, friendship bracelet," Anjanette reads. "Eighth year, mixed tape—you know nobody makes those anymore. Nineteenth year, caramel corn cake and a day at the Peabody-Essex Museum." Anjanette looks over at Mathilde. "What is this?"

Mathilde grabs it back. "Nothing. Just an idea. I've been thinking friendships last way longer than marriages do and they should have anniversary gifts, too. We are forty-four years friends this summer."

"Girl, what is with you these days," says Anjanette. "I think you need to calm yourself down."

"I need to tell you something." Oh god. Mathilde starts sweating for real. Is Anjanette gonna be furious with her? Mathilde is so scared, but she has to tell her.

Anjanette waits.

"Remember how you told me you saw Daniel at the cemetery?" says Mathilde. Anjanette doesn't answer. She watches Mathilde and waits for her to continue.

"So I went there a couple of times." Mathilde avoids Anjanette's eyes. "You know, just in case, right?" Still no response from Anjanette. "I saw him on Tuesday."

"You saw him?"

"Well, he saw me first. But then, we sat and talked," Mathilde isn't sure how much she should say. "He gave me a ride in his golf cart. He has a dog."

Anjanette says nothing.

"Did you know there is a Sphinx in the cemetery?" asks Mathilde.

"Of course," says Anjanette. "Everybody knows that."

"I didn't know—that's where he saw me," says Mathilde. "By the Sphinx." The silence between them grows. Anjanette is clearly thinking about something. It's not like Anjanette to take so long to say something. This might be it. This might be the end of them. Mathilde may have crossed a line, never to be forgiven. Mathilde's panic is mounting and then Anjanette begins to talk.

"Momma took us down to her uncle's place one time," Anjanette says. "He had a bunch of walnut trees and made up this game to get us to do some work. You had to have two buckets full of water. We'd gather up the walnuts in a basket and then we'd drop them into the first bucket and then take two walnuts and rub them together to get off the soft coating around them. The water was always so cold. My fingers would go numb. A little raw. Second bucket we'd put them into for another cleaning. And then we'd pull those out and scrub them with a brush, they'd be so pretty, wet, and gleaming. Set them out to dry. Joseph and Ten would complain the whole time—all that work for a damn walnut. But me and Daniel were a team. And we won."

Mathilde lets the story sit. She says nothing, afraid to say the wrong thing.

Anjanette turns to Mathilde. "What'd he say?"

"He didn't say much. He has a dog. He works at Mt. Auburn part time and likes it cause he has time to read and do his writing."

"You didn't get his number? Where he lives?"

"It was—" Mathilde falters. "I didn't want to scare him away. I tried to tell him how much you miss him and how good it would be if he came by."

"And what'd he say?"

"He didn't—really—" Mathillde's voice trails off. "You mad at me?"

"Yeah, I might be." Anjanette stands up. "But I'm gonna go out there and talk to him myself." She puts her hand on Mathilde's head. "I came out here cause I'm hungry. What are you making for dinner?"

"Stop being a husband," says Mathilde.

Anjanette grabs a handful of grass that she throws at Mathilde before going back into the house. "Remind me not to get trapped with you at the end of the world," says Anjanette.

"Too late," Mathilde calls after her, picking grass out of her hair and feeling the relief wash over her. They were gonna be okay. "The closing's tomorrow."

64 Clement
July 2018

Mathilde wrestles another box over to where she can sit to unpack it. It is getting hotter and more humid with every passing hour. She thinks again about calling a service to do all this for her, but she has set a goal: she will go through every box that came up from the condo.

She has piles for trash, piles for giveaway, and a smaller pile of stuff filling an armchair that she intends to keep. As she drags the utility knife through the top of the box she holds between her legs, she looks around the room. She has been at it since yesterday, but it feels like all she has done is create a bigger mess than when she started.

Every window in the house is open, but her skin is slick with perspiration, her tank top sticks to her back, and is wet under her breasts. Mathilde knows that she will have to bite the bullet and get central air installed; the heating/cooling is gonna have to be updated if she wants women to be comfortable here all year-round. Plus with global warming—she refuses to call it fucking climate change—who knows what the summers and winters are going to be like going forward?

"It would've been nice if you had invested in HVAC instead of spending whatever ridiculous amount of money you wasted putting this goddamned, ugly as shit wallpaper all over the ceiling that I am gonna have to find a way to remove," Mathilde says to the ghosts of the hipsters as she rips the box open and begins sorting through its contents.

Then quickly she says, "I'm sorry, I'm sorry," to karmically balance the complaint. She doesn't want the powers-that-be to think she isn't grateful. The hipsters could have painted the house in floor-to-ceiling yellow polka dots and she would still be to the bone grateful that it was hers.

She straightens her back and uses the hand towel she had come across in one of the boxes to wipe her face. The heat and the grunt work can do nothing to temper her almost constant sensation of joy. She loves the sound of her voice echoing off the empty walls, she loves watching the light move, she loves scrubbing the kitchen floor and cleaning the refrigerator—again, the hipsters could've left the place in better shape, but she doesn't mind; she loves touching every bit of this house.

Yesterday and this morning she had bopped out of bed, got the coffeemaker started then padded around the house barefoot, touching walls, humming bits of songs, standing in doorways, stepping out into the backyard to look up at the house with the cool earth under her feet. It didn't matter she could see all the things she wanted to change— knowing how much work was ahead of her did not feel burdensome. Moment to moment, she felt like a balloon—as if only the tips of her toes touched the ground.

"It's all cosmetic," she reminds herself as she lifts her mug and sips at the now lukewarm coffee. Mike used that phrase.

"Oh honey," she says to Mike as she looks into the box. It's one of his. He was always so sentimental. There are Father's Day and birthday cards from the kids, a felt Pawtucket Red Sox pennant that must be from when he was a kid, leather-bound planners.

The day Mike took her to see the house in Dedham he couldn't have been more proud. Fixer upper didn't begin to describe it, but Mike was adamant he was going to do all the work. Sweat equity, he kept throwing that phrase around, sweat equity.

"I've seen guys do this," he said. "It'll just take us a couple years to get it fixed up and then we sell it and move to something nicer. Step by step."

All his planning couldn't account for how hard it was to build up his own crew and business in a new town where he didn't know anyone. Projects were slow to be completed because the house had to come second. When the market crashed in 1989, it put even more pressure on his construction company because people canceled house projects that were on the books. Mike was forced to go back to his former boss and work with him on commercial projects down in Rhode Island. Eventually he was able to build back up his own business again, but they never gained the edge. Kids were expensive. Mathilde didn't bring in any kind of steady income.

That's the story she always told herself—they got stuck due to finances. But as she sits here now, brimming with the thrill not only of being back in 64 Clement, but of a feeling she has never experienced before—owning her first home—she can see that Mike always loved the Dedham house. He had bought his own house—a family home with a cul-de-sac where his kids could practice bike riding and he could take them to Brigham's after for ice cream. He had never wanted more than that. He had never wanted to move.

Her phone buzzes. It's Paul.

"Hey," she says. "Can I put you on speaker?" She props the phone so she can talk and keep working.

"Finding treasures?" asks Paul.

"Oh yeah," says Mathilde. "Nothing but gold over here." Having lived without all of this stuff for over a year (since she had never unpacked the boxes when she dumped them at the condo), nearly everything is going to be moved out—trash or donation. There were very few things that she was going to keep.

She told Paul about the collection of Hans Christian Anderson tales she had discovered and how Mathilde's father refused to read *The Little Matchgirl* to her. *Too sad*, he would say. *You don't want such a sad story.*

"And I bet that one was your favorite one," says Paul.

Mathilde laughs. It was. She didn't think it was sad. *Winnie the Pooh* was the story her dad always wanted to read to her, and though Mathilde didn't like it particularly, it was enough to have her father in her room, the warmth of his arm around her, the soft scent of pine cologne she could smell in his shirt, the way his voice was soft and measured, even and sure.

Paul is talking. "What time do you want me to come by tonight?" he asks.

"Whenever," says Mathilde. "I'm here. Not going anywhere." She pulls a manila folder that has a rubber band around its middle from the bottom of the box and opens it as she listens to Paul laying out his plans for the day.

A stack of letters tumbles into her lap.

"Paul," Mathilde interrupts. "I'm sorry. I gotta go. I'll see you tonight?" She hits off the phone and scans quickly through the letters, one by one. They are from Mike to Gina Imondi, the Italian girl. His first love. The girl he was going to marry, twice. Gina has returned Mike's letters with a short note, dated January—the month before he married Mathilde.

Mathilde slides down to sit on the floor, the sofa behind her back. She begins reading the letters.

.

64 Clement
July 2018

The hipsters had planted a ginkgo tree close to the patio. At first Mathilde didn't like it because she thought it was a trendy choice, but later when she'd read up on it and discovered how the ginkgo dates back millions of years—to the time of dinosaurs—and how several ginkgo trees stood near the detonation site of the nuclear bomb dropped on Hiroshima and not only survived the blast, but are fully recovered and still standing she felt very, very grateful that the hipsters had planted a ginkgo in her yard—although, Mathilde sincerely doubts that they planted it for the reasons she treasures it.

Mathilde looks up at it from where she sits at the edge of the patio's bluestone pavers. Each branch of the ginkgo is covered in a sleeve of ruffles, tender yellow green.

Sounds of a squabble between Lonny and Anjanette drift over from next door followed by the quick snap of the screen door that ends what-ever disagreement they were having. Will Mathilde tell them about the letters? Will she tell anyone? What should she do with them? What if her kids read them? No, thinks Mathilde. No. She will have to bury them somewhere. Burning them feels cruel. Let some future homeowner—generations from now—dig them up with no backstory, no knowledge of the people involved. They will think they are sweet, romantic, heartbreaking.

Love letters.

Mathilde picks up a fallen stem of ginkgo and rubs it back and forth between her thumb and forefinger to make it twirl—the shape of its leaves, clean and simple, help her focus. Thoughts and emotions are swirling in a thick cloud of confusion across her forehead. She closes her eyes and imagines sitting at a library carrel with a pen and legal pad to carefully parse it out, break it down, separate each piece into its own column as if that could help her find the truth.

If she had gotten a call that informed her that Mike had fallen off a roof, gotten hit with a swinging beam, or that there had been an accident with a nail gun, Mathilde would not have been shocked. Injuries are common among carpenters. But for him to have come back up the driveway from his morning run—to have collapsed on the back steps as if to stay out of sight and not bother anyone—for her to walk out and find him there, his arms crushed under his body, his back in its shiny blue windbreaker curved like a dolphin, his mouth open.

Mathilde's eyes fly open. Her breath is sharp, short. Is she hyperventilating? She puts her head between her knees and tries to slow the images of that horrible morning. *There had been no warning*, she said every time she was asked. *No warning.*

Now she knows better, the signs were there, she simply didn't recognize them. The night before Mike had been complaining that his neck and arm were bothering him. He'd asked her if they had any Pepto-Bismol in the house—he had indigestion. But those are normal things! How could she know? What could she have done differently?

There were so many layers to the shock following Mike's death. She would spiral from one to the next. Mostly, it didn't make sense. Mike was young, 56. He exercised. So many people survive heart attacks. Why hadn't Mike? Mathilde kept searching for answers. *For a heart attack to quickly lead to death, the damage to the heart needs to be great enough to cause the heart to beat irregularly and eventually stop entirely.*

Mike's heart had given out. Could it be that simple? He always saw the world in a simple way. Through Mike's lens, Mathilde lived with her beautiful parents in a Norman Rockwell painting—something he never had. He was determined to be the father he never had but, oh Susannah tested him on every front—she did not act the part he had imagined. Was it wear and tear on his heart? Mike's super sensitive, super caring heart.

When Sandy Hook happened, Mike sat at the kitchen table and cried for hours. He couldn't understand how nobody was doing anything. How this didn't get people to stop the guns. Mathilde didn't have the heart to tell him what he wouldn't be able to handle. Because they didn't show the bodies. They didn't show images of broken babies shot apart–kindergarten chubby elbows and knees. Vietnam only changed when reporters began showing the bodies. When it is sanitized—when you don't see it—people can keep on keeping on.

And now she sees, there were things Mike hadn't told her. She knew about Gina Imondi, but Mike had told Mathilde that it was all over and she believed him. When Mathilde showed Mike the *Boston Globe* article that featured Gina in a piece about women leaders in the tech industry, he made some bland comment like, 'oh, that's nice' before reminding her that he had invited the guys over to watch the game and could she pick up sandwiches. The article mentioned that Gina and her husband lived with their children in Brookline. She was married, but she had kept her last name.

Mathilde begins twirling the ginkgo stem again. Is Gina happy? Does Gina ever look back and wish she could do things differently? Did anyone reach out to Gina and tell her that Mike died? And if she heard the news, did she go into the bathroom and lock the door so she could wail and cry in a way that his own wife didn't do?

Her foot has fallen asleep. Mathilde tosses the leaf and stands, with a groan. Stumbling slightly as she walks with one foot half-numb, half pins and needles, Mathilde goes back into the house. She limps directly to the record player and carries it into the kitchen because she knows she has an extension cord there. The boxes of record albums are by the basement door. She digs through until she finds the one she is looking for.

The plastic cover of the record player is dusty so she carefully wipes it with a soft linen napkin. As she slides the album out of its worn cardboard sleeve, she catches a whiff of something. Unnamed. A scent of the past that used to be familiar. She places the black plastic on the turntable, lifts the needle, and sets it down without a scratch.

This was a song Mike loved. Sounds of Gordon Lightfoot lightly picking out the melody on a guitar fill the kitchen—and then that voice—

If you could read my mind, love, what a tale my thoughts could tell

Mathilde sits. Her foot is now awake, tingling. She presses one toe over the other.

Somehow, once again, Mike has saved her.

The deepest, most awful secret she could tell no one was how free she felt after he died. She was a monster. Her guilt and shame for not feeling the right way—for not loving him the right way—had been like a concrete block holding her under water. But now, she actually is free.

Mike loved Gina. Mike had always loved Gina. Mathilde wasn't the only one at fault.

Her sobs are full body sobs. Mathilde turns so that she can bend over her knees and cry as she never did in the days after Mike died. She cries the way she always thought was the right way if she was a good person, a full body seizure of sobs. What feels so strangely wild as her body rocks and she makes odd gasping sounds is this is not sorrow, not grief—this is love.

She is crying her heart out with love.

She did love Mike. He had saved her. She was drowning and he got her to shore. He had brought her into a world—maybe not the world she wanted but he had kept her alive and moving forward. And they made two humans together. And they had had fun. Sweet fun. Washing the babies in the bathtub. Drinking wine and giggling in the twinkling lights of the tree as they set up the presents for the kids on Christmas eve. Lying in bed listening for Susannah to come home and then, giving each other a squeeze on the hand that she was home, she was safe, they could relax and go to sleep now.

He was her husband. Her wonderful, wonderful husband. And he died.

Clement Street
August 2018

Anjanette's birthday party is in full swing. It is the annual summer back-yard event before the Colson family heads to Martha's Vineyard as they always do for the last two weeks of August.

Buntings and garlands of brightly colored fabric—mostly in African tribal patterns and colors—adorn the beams of Lonny's back porch. Anjanette took charge of decorating for her birthday and made most of the banners herself. "Keep that cheap party shit away from me," is what she said when Mathilde offered to bring in some decor from one of the big box stores.

Lots of women from the circle are here, plus Anjanette's brothers and their families, and of course the crew from church. Long tables have been set up to hold all the food people carry in. Anjanette's brothers, Joseph and Ten, are manning the brick barbeque which fills the air with the rich smoky smell of tomato and spices.

Up on the porch, a table is dedicated for birthday gifts and the presents are piled high, among them quite a few live plants wrapped with a bow.

Anjanette's actual birthday is tomorrow and that is when Mathilde will present her gift.

"Tickets?" Anjanette reads the small print aloud. "Hilma af Klint:

Paintings for the Future?" Anjanette looks at Mathilde. "The hell? I don't even know how to say this guy's name."

"Her name," says Mathilde. "And you will love her. She's a dead Swedish lady but when she was alive, she had a circle of women who would do seances and then paint. You know what else? She knew the world wasn't ready for her paintings so when she died she said they couldn't be shown for twenty years."

They are sitting at the round wrought-iron table in Mathilde's back yard. A caramel corn cake that Mathilde made that morning sits on a plate at the center, sagging a bit in the heat.

"It's in New York—" says Anjanette.

"But not until after your October show," says Mathilde prepared for every objection. "So we have lots of time for you to freak out before you are ready to go."

"We?" Anjanette plucks off a piece of caramel corn cake and chews it slowly. "You coming with me?"

Yes." Mathilde sees the look of distrust in Anjanette's face. "I'm a world traveler now—"

Anjanette leans back in her chair, shaking both hands in 'stop stop' motion. A gust of laughter convulses her. "You just—I can't—you gotta stop. You gonna kill me with this shit."

Mathilde talks over Anjanette's resistance. "We're gonna take the train and I'm gonna pack us lunches with jars of vanilla pudding for you—and no tuna fish."

"No tuna fish," Anjanette repeats. "I don't know—" Anjanette is not about to commit to this.

"I know," says Mathilde. "That's why we have all this time to get you ready because we are doing this."

"It's my birthday present," says Anjanette. "You can't shanghai me and call it a birthday present."

"You shanghai'd me and said it was for my own damn good." Mathilde is not going to give up. She will win this—maybe not today, but eventually. Mathilde will wear her down. "Anjanette, I have read all about this artist. Seriously—it's gonna be super cool. It's at the Guggenheim and it's the first major solo exhibition they've done for her in the United States. You gotta trust me."

"Don't count on it," says Anjanette.

"I already booked the train tickets," says Mathilde.

Mathilde sets the three skeins of Caledonia Blue into a Nantucket basket that was a gift from her mother and steps back to admire the tableau. The color of the yarn is gorgeous against the creamy plaster wall that has the tiniest bit of yellow in it. Until Mathilde has figured out what she is going to knit with the yarn, she wants to be able to see it every day. The basket is centered on the mantle above the fireplace as a way of honoring the magic that has brought her here.

The quiet hum of Paul's motorcycle rolling up her drive has Mathilde checking the mirror in the front hall and pinching her cheeks to make them pink before stepping out the back door of the kitchen to greet Paul.

She watches as Paul lifts off his helmet. They are both startled by Anjanette who makes an ungraceful appearance through the hedge, catching her foot on some low branches and cursing. Anajnette barely acknowledges Paul. She hurries up to Mathilde with an envelope in her hand.

"I thought you guys had already left." Mathilde takes the envelope from Anjanette.

"We're in the car now." Anjanette is panting. "They're waiting for me. I just remembered I forgot to give this to you—it came to us." The sound of a car horn toots impatiently. Anjanette clambers back through the hedge. "It's from Wales!"

Mathilde looks down at the envelope. The ink is in the same loopy scrawl Mathilde recognizes from the handwritten tags Effie put on her yarn. She looks up to see Paul watching her. He knows there was an "errand" in Wales, but he is not entirely sure there wasn't a romance along the way.

"It's not from a man," says Mathilde. "It's a woman." That doesn't change anything for Paul.

"Nothing romantic," says Mathilde. "It's the woman I bought the yarn from." She puts the letter into her back pocket and gives him a kiss. They head into the house, fingertips tangled.

Inside, Paul hands her a housewarming present—also a small envelope—a packet of seeds.

"Hubbard squash," says Paul. "My grandmother's favorite."

"Those are the big blue ones, right?" says Mathilde. She places the packet of seeds carefully on the shelf. It is a simple gift but it feels sacred to her.

"Yeah," says Paul.

"Thank you." Mathilde wants to say the right thing to let Paul know how much she loves this thoughtfulness—that it means a lot to her—but she knows it is not Paul's way to make a big deal of things. Lucky for her, he has the best sense of humor.

"You can help me plant them," she says and gives him a kiss.

He laughs, but his eyes tell her that she said the perfect thing.

The energy between them is too big. She can't focus on making food, or what she was talking about. There's only one thing going on, and she can't let it sit in silence anymore. She leans her hip into the countertop as if it could keep her upright. She pokes at a pile of crumbs by the toaster. How can she be feeling like she is fifteen years old? How is that possible? Are her words going to be childish?

"Here is my concern," Mathilde says to Paul. She pauses. "You have been such a friend to me. Such a good friend. Even when I was prickly and awful and not deserving. I don't know who that wretch of a woman this past year was—but the fact you could see through all that—" Mathilde takes a deep breath. She is in it now. She is gonna have to get it all out. "And now that we are friends, I feel like I can tell you anything—I feel like I have told you everything—I don't want to risk that with romance that might fizzle out or make us not like each other."

She exhales and looks up at him. Strands of hair have fallen low over his eyebrow. She reaches up to push it back so she can see him clearly.

"You think this is going to fizzle out?" asks Paul.

"No," says Mathilde. She plucks lightly at the button of his shirt that sits below his collarbone.

"So what is it that you are scared of?" His hands are on her bare upper arms.

"How much I don't want it to fizzle out."

He slides his hands across the tops of her shoulders and up her neck to bring her face to his for a kiss. Mathilde drops into the connection, letting go of every thought, aware only of sensation—floating, being carried away—as if this moment here is the very beginning of them.

The sound of Susannah coming through the front door is loud and jarring. They pull apart. A bit stunned by the interruption. Susannah is calling out as she drops her bags.

"Mom—whose bike is in the driveway?" Susannah hollers. She comes to a full stop when she sees the helmet on the countertop.

"Mother, what?" says Susannah. "You bought a motorcycle?"

There is a moment of pause before Susannah sees Paul standing beside the pantry.

"Oh, hey Paul," says Susannah. "Oh. It's your bike."

"You seriously think I would buy a motorcycle?" says Mathilde. "What planet are you on?"

"I don't know," says Susannah. She swings in and sits at the island. She reaches for a banana and cracks one away from the bunch. She begins peeling it, takes a bite, and adds, "You've been doing a lot of crazy shit that I would never expect. It's like you're a different person."

"I didn't know you were coming by." Mathilde says this more to Paul than Susannah.

"Well—get ready for some news. It seems I might possibly, not sure, but—quite possibly—" Susannah eats the banana as if it were the first thing she'd eaten all day. "Are you guys making dinner? Cause I can totally stay and join you for that." She does a little bit of a shoulder shake wiggle in her chair, "We can celebrate cause I think this is happening."

"What is happening?" says Mathilde.

"So—a guy I knew in Arkansas had worked with Diane Paulus," Susannah sees neither her mother nor Paul know who she is talking about. "Diane Paulus—the director of the Cambridge A.R.T.—"

"American Repertory Theater," Paul parses the acronym for Mathilde.

Susannah nods. "And I just had a meeting with her!" Susannah squeals. "And she's gonna call me Monday if I've got the job—which I think I'm getting, I mean the meeting went really well and my friend—the guy from Arkansas—put in a really good word for me, so, you know, fingers crossed." Susannah rolls up the banana peel and looks around for something more to eat. "What are you guys making for dinner?"

"I don't know," says Mathilde, coming over to give Susannah a big hug. "You two can figure that out. I'm so happy for you, baby." Mathilde rocks Susannah back and forth. "This is really exciting. I want to hear all about it—what the job is—I just need to check something for a sec."

Mathilde steps out the back door. "Back in a minute," she says over her shoulder. With Susannah here to distract Paul, she can slip outside to look at the letter that has been burning a hole in her back pocket.

Mathilde walks out to the far edge of the porch and squats then slides her butt down the steps until her feet are on the ground. She rubs her bare feet back and forth in the warm grass. From here, Lonny's house feels close, at eye level, like when the full moon hangs so low it seems possible to reach out and touch it.

She digs the envelope out of her back pocket. Inside is a note card with only a few sentences.

I came up with a new color—Dovaldo Green—thought of you. I won't be at Rhinebeck next month—headed to Cuzco, Peru! Would you like me to send you some?

Mathilde pulls the note to her chest and looks up at the sky. Oh, what did Molly Bloom say over and over—yes—isn't that what her Irish heart said? Isn't that how the story begins? The pace of Mathilde's feet rubbing back and forth on the grass speeds up as she leans forward and the waves of delight crash over her. She squishes the paper to her heart as one word loops.

Yes. Yes. Yes. Yes. Yes.

Acknowledgments

It's true. Artists and writers need solitude—time and space to let their visions take shape uninterrupted, but to keep the faith when discouragement balloons? To do the grind necessary to bring their work to an audience? For that, the writer requires a cadre of champions. I am grateful to the loving hearts who showed up for me in all the ways, small and large. They have no idea of their impact so I will just give some shout-outs here.

Many thanks to Rachele Alpine + Andrea Mowry who asked me for another novel.

Blessings to Terri Dautcher for letting me hole up in her guest room for a month (with my dog, no less) so I could work uninterrupted. And, to Anne-Marie Gallant for the best novel writing playlist, ever.

I am so very grateful to the early readers: Rachele Alpine, Page Sargisson, Jewel Washington, Jared Flood, Andi Pyatt, Kate Albus, Tara Murphy and Camille DeAngelis who each provided me with such wild encouragement and terrific notes.

There is no way this book would be shaped as it is without the editing support of Amber Williams, Talia Moon and Donna Freitas.

Grateful to my friend Gaye Glasspie for the adage, "it's not hard, it's new."

Without the magical Kirsten Stoudt (and her book lovin' cousins) putting a fire under my ass, I do not believe I would have done the work to bring this story off my computer and into your hands. Elizabeth Wade walked alongside me for months on end and even answered my call in the wee hours of a Sunday morning when I needed her mad photo skills. All of the beautiful souls who gather over at SQMlove—who have built such a wondrous community for creative experiments to thrive—and who support me in the best of ways.

A very special shout-out to my number one cheerleader Page Sargisson whose unwavering enthusiasm made me believe in myself, as well as for walking me through design decisions on yet another very early morning Sunday call.

And, Tiffany LaTrice. TIFFANY. LATRICE. How on earth am I lucky enough to know this dazzling megastar—she who can do anything she sets her hand to—let alone, get to call her friend. She makes it all look easy. She makes it all fun.

My heart is busting out in a thousand petals of gratitude—and then some.

Elizabeth Duvivier lives in Providence, Rhode Island with her dog Remy.

Squam Studio, March 2024.
Photo credit: James Feighny